WARRIOR'S MOON

By Jaclyn M. Hawkes

Spirit Dance Books

What readers are saying about Jaclyn's books:

I have just one thing to say about Jaclyn M. Hawkes' book **The Outer Edge of Heaven**! I absolutely love, Love, LOVE it! Okay, really, I actually do have more to say about it. . . I never wanted it to end, and when it did, I wanted more. *Debbie Davis*

I have to say that as a writer, I think Jaclyn M. Hawkes has hit her stride. I enjoyed every moment of this story as I laughed, cried, and even went for my own bag of Oreos and glass of milk. Jaclyn M. Hawkes has found her place in clean, contemporary fiction. I would love to see more stories like this one from her. Cheryl Christensen A Good Day to Read

Wow! I absolutely LOVED this book. I could not put it down, not to do homework, not to sleep, not to clean house, nada! Fantastic book! Tamera Westhoff

This book is a fast read and one that you really won't want to put down. You will fall in love with the characters and not want the story to end. I enjoy Jaclyn's writing and hope to read even more books from her. Sheila Staley

Killer dialogue, and the hero was well worth the wait. It was definitely a fun read. Heather Justesen

A Warrior's Moon

By Jaclyn M. Hawkes

Copyright © November 2013 Jaclyn M. Hawkes

All rights reserved.

Published and distributed by Spirit Dance Books. Spiritdancebooks.com

855-648-5559

Cover design by Roland Ali Pantin

Printed in USA

First Printing November 2013

Library of Congress cataloguing in publication data

ISBN: 0-9851648-4-3

ISBN-13: 978-0-9851648-4-3

Dedication

This book is dedicated to warriors everywhere,

both men and women,

who are willing to leave home and family,

risking all,

to battle for a stronger, more noble homeland.

May we never forget their sacrifice,

nor fail them in apathy.

It is also dedicated to my husband.

He's earned my trust ten thousand times over and

I would follow him into any battle anywhere.

Prologue:

Isabella Kincraig knelt before a patch of mushrooms, reached to gather them and then was still. The forest had suddenly become silent around her and the total absence of sound was a warning in itself. Anxiousness held her as motionless as the deer she sometimes came upon as she gathered her herbs here in this wildest tangle of trees. Completely still, she listened while she tried to sense what was wrong.

Something was in the woods with her. The prickle on the back of her neck made her look around anxiously, but she saw nothing among the thickness of the understory. Worried, she turned to wake her small daughter, Chantaya, who slept on a blanket on the moss while Isabella gathered her herbs, but Isabella was caught roughly from behind before she could reach her.

Knowing instantly who it was, she stilled, worried she'd harm her unborn child if she fought him. When he finally moved his hand from her mouth and turned her toward him, she wanted to slap his smiling face as she hissed quietly, "Let me go! My husband will be furious!"

Young Lord Rosskeene simply smiled unconcernedly again. "He wouldn't dare try to challenge me and it's well you know it. I would see him hang. Then you would be only more available to the admiration of a benevolent landlord like myself." His voice changed to an almost amiable cajoling sound. "If you would only agree to be with me, Isabella, you'd find that I can be quite pleasant. Even your husband would appreciate my generosity. If you'd come work right in the manor house, I'd see to it that you made a much greater wage."

He went to caress her cheek but she turned aside and ground out, "Your father would be ashamed if he knew of your behavior!"

At that, the spoiled young lord's smile froze for an instant, then he reached again to touch her face. He moved his hand down to gently encircle her neck as he threatened silkily, "If my father hears from you, I will kill your husband myself and take pleasure in doing it." He gripped her throat for the merest second and then went on less gently, "Don't try to fight me, Isabella. You know I get what I want. Always."

He leaned to kiss her and she jerked her face sharply away. He only chuckled and put a hand to her burgeoning belly and whispered huskily, "Is this child mine, Bella?"

She couldn't help the trembling that overcame her and she began to pray silently but desperately as she said vehemently, "No!" She jerked his hand away and pushed him. "Leave me alone! I must go! Your cook will be awaiting my herbs."

Without letting go of her, he leaned and placed a kiss on her neck where he'd been toying with it. "Ah, food. Another of life's pleasures, but not nearly so satisfying. You know I'd forego nourishment completely to have you, Bella." He kissed her again. "But, alas, Cook truly will be wondering where you are." He rubbed the back of his hand over the spot he'd just kissed and she couldn't suppress a shudder.

Pushing her roughly away, he said, "Go, Isabella. Deliver your herbs. I'll take my pleasure with you another day."

Chapter One

Lightning flashed and in the sudden illumination, three-year-old Chantaya saw the whites of the cart horse's eyes. Chantaya was frightened as well and hid her face from the furious wind in the folds of her mother's cloak beside her on the seat. As a lone drop of rain found its way into the neck of her own cloak and made her shiver, Chantaya wondered again what they were doing traveling in the middle of a night as dreadful as this.

Her papa scooted closer to them on the other side and when he put his arm round them both, she felt secure in spite of the slashing wind and threatening rain. For a moment, she let that feeling and the rocking motion begin to lull her small, exhausted body into a delicious sleepiness, but then seconds later that moment of security was shattered by the flash and crash of another deafening bolt of lightning and the cart was suddenly jerked violently forward. Chantaya unburied her face and looked out to realize they were racing down the rocky track they'd been following which wound down the dark hillside toward a village. Glimpsing a light behind them, she fought to hold onto her parents as she turned to see that the cart, piled high with all of their belongings, had somehow caught fire.

The threatening rain hit in a sudden deluge as the little wagon picked up speed. Chantaya desperately tried to hold on as her father sawed on the reins beside her and her mother put out a hand to hold her against the seat and began to pray frantically. Chantaya was caught up for a moment in the frightening motion, then the cart hit something in the road and gave a mighty lurch that made Chantaya lose her handhold. An even larger jolt to the side jerked her from her mother's grip and launched her headlong clear over the wheel beside them.

There was a terrifying moment of flight, then she hit cobbles and rocks with an impact that knocked the air out of her before rolling to pile up against the side of the muddy roadway. Her chest screamed with agony and a desperate need to breathe. When she was finally able to draw breath, she began to cry in pain and fear as she rolled to look toward the cart.

It was still careening down the rocky roadway, but even as she watched, the frantic cart horse spooked too close to the edge of the track and a wheel went over. The whole flaming load tumbled off the edge in a horrifying cracking and snapping crash, dragging the frightened horse with it. In the near blackness, all Chantaya could distinguish was that the flames twirled as the cart tumbled over and over. Pieces of fire seemed to drip off the load as parts of their burning belongings came loose and were left behind the tumbling wreckage that finally came to a stop near the bottom of the incline.

The storm still raged, but the relative stillness after the violence of the lightning-struck cart was frighteningly ominous to the now sodden and muddy toddler who lay in the track far above the inert wreckage. In the suffocating darkness broken only by the bits of tenuous flame that even now were melting under the sudden downpour, there was no sign of her dear papa or her mother with her great, tiring belly. Nothing moved except the trees blowing in the storm and the slanting rain.

Far down in the village, a door slammed and Chantaya could see a lantern bobbing in the sea of blackness. Still crying, she put a dripping hand to her cheek to rub at the sting there and painfully climbed to her small feet. Mama and Papa were down there with the cart. She wanted to get down there to them. Even in the freezing cold rain, they would bring her comfort.

She tripped in the dark and stubbornly wiped at the hot tears that irritated her eyes as she picked herself back up to slip and stumble on down the track. Without the protection of her parents, the rain drenched her unimpeded and her teeth chattered painfully, even when she wasn't stumbling. The wind blew her cloak against her body and any warmth it might have provided was sucked away with each buffeting gust.

As she finally neared the silent wreckage, she could barely make out her family's strewn belongings. She trudged around Mama's big washing cauldron and then tripped again on some dark item of clothing that was invisible in the inky storm. She fell headlong and then startled as she realized 'twas her papa's face that was there just in front of her own.

Something was terribly wrong. Papa shouldn't be sleeping out here in the rain and the storm like this. He needed to wake up and help her and Mama in out of the weather. Papa did those kinds of things. He always helped her and Mama. That's what papas do.

She patted Papa's face and spoke to him, although her mouth was so cold that it wasn't working quite right. Papa was so sleepy and didn't respond. She patted him much harder and shouted at him above the wind. Something was terribly wrong. She needed to find Mama. Mama would wake Papa up.

§§§§

Storms didn't usually bother him. In fact, he typically reveled in them, but for some reason, a crack of thunder had woken eight-year-old Peyton Wolfgar and he hadn't been able to go back to sleep in his bed in the loft above his parents. The wind whistling through the eves had always been comforting to him secure here in the cottage, but on this night it seemed to carry a warning. He turned on his side and snuggled deeper into the ticking of his bedding and wadded his pillow under his cheek. That was a wicked storm. 'Twas cold even here near the ceiling and it was only early fall.

After another thunderous crash he sighed and got up, tucked the bedding more snugly round his younger brother and quietly slipped down the ladder. He might as well build up the fire since he was awake anyway. Stirring the coals, he added logs then went to the window and cracked a shutter to look out at the wildness of the tempest. God was in a fury at someone on this eve, that was sure. The trees were rocking crazily in the wind that blew sticks and debris straight sideways.

Lightning flashed yet again and Peyton squinted his eyes in the blindness after the glare. He could have sworn he saw something out there. Surely someone wouldn't be traveling on a night such as this and certainly not down the treachery of the briar canyon, yet he was sure he'd seen something.

He cracked the shutter wider and only had to wait a moment or two. The lightning flared again and this time there was no doubt. Up on the rocky dugway down from the ridge above there was a small, but heavily laden cart drawn by a single horse. Lightning struck again further up the ridge and Peyton shook his head and whispered, "God help the poor beggar that be travelin' up in that on a night like this."

Tugging on the shutter, he was just turning to go when lightning flashed seemingly right on top of the cart. Peyton turned back in surprise when the cart burst into flame and then began to race down the dangerous rocky roadway. That track was perilous in the broad light of a clear summer afternoon. And on fire! The cart horse must have gone crazy! As the rain that had been threatening hit with a vengeance, Peyton threw the shutters wide and shouted for his father, then watched in morbid fascination as the cart plunged unchecked down the slope.

His father sat up and rubbed his eyes, muttering about letting the rain in and had only just stood when he stopped stock still as he too spotted the careening cart through the window illuminated by the lightning. "Great thundering Methuselah! Light the lantern, boy! Quickly! Lord only knows what he's about, but he's in trouble! Quick Mother! Build up the fire and find some blankets. We'd best be . . . "

He broke off speaking as the cart, weirdly lit by the flames that were fanned by its speedy descent, tumbled off the edge of the track and began crashing and rolling to the bottom of the hill. As it finally slowed and stopped, Willem Wolfgar shook his head sadly and whispered, "Lord, help us. Bring the lantern, Peyton. 'Tis not likely, but maybe the poor beggar survived."

They were soaked to the skin long before they made it to the wreckage that was strewn for an impossibly long distance down the hillside. Mud pulled at Peyton's heavy boots and the lantern light barely reached out into the sodden dark in front of them. The sucking mud actually tore a boot from his stockingless foot and he had to pause one footed to reach down and haul it out to pull it back on. He shrugged his hood more forward as he heard his father in front of him say almost reverently, "Please no." Peyton hurried ahead to see his father reach down to pick up a dripping rag doll with a torn dress.

Holding the lantern high, they struggled to see through the storm to discern anything at all in the wind whipped gloom. Slowly, they began to walk back and forth, moving a few feet forward with each pass to search for whomever might have been with the cart on this harrowing night, but they found nothing but what appeared to be household items for several long minutes.

But for the lightning, they would have missed seeing the tiny child huddled beside what at first appeared to be a wad of bedding. As the lightning passed, they were temporarily blinded and then as they came near with the lantern, the youngster was gone. Searching around, they didn't find her again, although they discovered that what they'd thought was bedding, was, in fact, a woman, wadded and thrown, but breathing.

Several more moments of searching revealed a man who hadn't survived the wreck and then, finally, they found the child again, hiding near a bush. They could see the fear in her eyes and Willem said in a kindly of voice, "Go to her, Peyton. An eight year old must be less scary than a whiskery man. Pick her up and tell her it's going to be all right and ask her if there were more children in the cart that we need to search for. I'll go get the wagon to bring her parents."

Willem left at a trot and Peyton watched the little girl for a moment and then knelt down a few feet from her and began to speak softly. At first, she hesitated. She was frightened, but she was also obviously completely chilled through and finally, Peyton simply said, "Come little one. We need to get you home to the fire to warm. Come. I'll carry you inside my cloak. Father will bring your Mama." At the mention of her mother, the little dark haired child finally started to stand and tried to walk toward him. She was so cold she could barely move and he caught her just as she fell.

As they walked back toward his home, he asked, "Was there anyone else in the cart with you other than your Mama and Papa?" She didn't say anything, just shook her little head, making water droplets flip off the tips of her hair and run down Peyton's chest under his nightshirt. "No other children?" He asked her further, but she shook her head again.

He met his parents coming back out with the wagon as he trudged through the rain with the cold little girl and he knew from the look on his mother's face that his father had already told her about the child and the condition of her parents. As they continued on, he wrapped his cloak tighter about her and hugged the child a margin more snugly. This little girl had lost at least her father tonight, and possibly her mother as well, from the shape she appeared to be in. 'Twas a thing to be pitied. The child was a mere slip of a thing. Hardly more than a baby.

Peyton got her in and before the fire and knew he had to get her out of her wet things, but he couldn't seem to get her to let go of him. She was gripping his shirt as if she never meant to turn him loose and had all but buried her little face against his chest. He hailed his little brother Tristan to come and help him. Between the two of them, they managed to undo her little shoes and pull her stockings off and try to hold her feet out to the fire's heat, but she still didn't want to let go of Peyton's shirt. She'd at least moved far enough away from his chest that he could see she had several cuts on one side of her face and a rather large one on the side of her forehead.

Tristan brought a cloth and they tried to wipe the blood that had smeared with the rain and then get the cuts to stop bleeding, but as she was still gripping Peyton dearly, it was nearly impossible.

The door of the cottage flew open and his father came in carrying the mother and took her to his parent's bed. As they laid her out, Peyton could see she was heavy with an unborn child and his heart pitied them even more.

His mother began to work over the child's mother while his father went straight back out to find the man who was the closest the village of Navarre had to a physician and to bring in her father. He didn't say it, but Peyton knew they worried the wolves would be at the body if they didn't bring it immediately. He glanced down at the child who still gripped him convulsively while her teeth chattered and wondered how much she understood about what had happened here. He almost hoped she didn't understand at all.

Wondering how to get her warm, he finally had Tristan pull a rocking chair right over to the fire. He wrapped the child into a blanket, wet clothes and all, and sat in the chair and began to rock and then to sing to her quietly. Maybe if she went to sleep, he could get her to let go long enough to get her dry.

Peyton woke up in the rocking chair in the dim light of the stormy morning with a stiff neck. He continued to hold the little girl. They had finally gotten their wet clothes off, but still, she clung to him even in her sleep. He looked over at the bed where her mother lay and knew that although the mother lived, the physician didn't have much hope she would make it and even less hope that her unborn baby would.

His mother and the physician hovered nearby and from bits and pieces of their whispered conversation, he began to understand that they believed the woman would have the baby this very day, even if she didn't wake up. He didn't understand any of that and was content to cuddle the little girl closer and go back to sleep here in the chair. It had been a long, long night.

'Twas the child wiggling in his arms that next woke him. He yawned and stretched and glanced down at her to see that she was quietly watching him with big, dark eyes. She was a pretty little thing, even bruised and banged up and he gave her a weary smile to encourage her. He was still tired to the bone, but if he had been able to help this poor child, 'twas worth it.

The baby wasn't born that day, but it came the next evening and although the mother had finally awakened, she was truly more dead than alive. The baby was living, but it seemed incredibly sickly and Peyton saw the physician glance at Peyton's mother and shake his head sadly as he handed her the tiny blue infant.

'Twas two days before the little girl he'd rescued said anything and then she told them her name was Chantaya and that she was three. For most of those two days, she had clung to Peyton almost desperately. His mother had tried to encourage him that she would eventually become more confident and so he had been willing to let the child hang on him if it would help her.

Those two long days, both of his parents and the physician as well, struggled to help her mother and her baby sister, but in the night of the second day, the tiny, sickly fair haired baby died as they had feared all along it would. From the worried looks of the others, Peyton knew the mother wasn't far behind it, and he took his role of caring for Chantaya even more seriously while the adults worked. It looked like she was going to be an orphan and all they knew about her was that her parents had come from the home village of their Lord Rosskeene up in the northern part of the kingdom of Monciere. At least his own parents would gladly take the child in and care for her as their own, although with her shiny dark hair and eyes, she would definitely not look like one of their own blonde flesh and blood.

After the death of the baby, Chantaya either clung to Peyton, or to her partly conscious mother, and did little else, seldom even eating. But then on the fifth day, she seemed to somehow come to terms with what had happened to her and her family and she suddenly became a different child. She smiled for the first time since they'd found her and began to chatter and take an interest in the family life that was going on around her. She was markedly partial to Peyton, although she would still snuggle gently into the bed next to her mother. But then at other times she would run and laugh and squeal just like any healthy three year old little girl.

Strangely, life after the cart wreck settled into a routine of sorts. The other villagers had gathered up the goods from the cart wreck and had stored them all behind Peyton's parent's cottage, had hauled off the dead horse and wreckage and had helped to bury Chantaya's father and baby sister. They were wonderful to either come into the Wolfgar cottage and help or to at least bring in meals and help with the choring that was being neglected as the Wolfgars fought to save Chantaya's mother.

Peyton and Tristan still had their own responsibilities and Chantaya tagged along with them as they harvested the garden, cared for the farm animals and cut peat for the fire. She had a wonderful intrepidness about her that made her take everything they did in stride. It actually made her a little indignant when they intimated she was too little to try something or said girls didn't do certain things. 'Twas quite endearing, honestly. She was absolutely sweet and the boys affectionately shortened her name to Chani. They adored her and she worshipped them, especially Peyton.

After she became healthy enough to carry on a conversation, Chantaya's mother hadn't said a great deal except to tell them her name was Isabella Kincraig and to thank them profusely for helping her and her family. She truly wasn't up to much and had only told the Wolfgars that her family had been traveling in the middle of a horribly stormy night, with everything they owned in a little wagon, to protect her and her daughter from the unwanted advances of the younger Lord Rosskeene. The young Lord's heinous reputation was growing and the Wolfgars didn't fault the Kincraigs for their flight, even into the face of the furious storm. 'Twas only a pity that their flight had resulted in such tragedy.

Peyton didn't truly understand what Isabella meant by "unwanted advances", but he understood enough that he wasn't surprised to be told in the village one day that there was a man there looking for a young couple with a dark haired little girl. He brought the news home with worry in his eight year old heart. Then he was even more worried when his mother said to his father that she hoped the villagers had the presence of mind not to tell the stranger about Chantaya and her mother.

The villagers must have been discreet to a certain extent, because it wasn't until nearly a month later that the man showed up at the cottage. Peyton was afraid of the aggressive stranger, but he was proud of his mother when she stood up to him.

The man came into the yard where his mother was boiling her laundry and roughly demanded to speak to Kalder Kincraig. Rose Wolfgar straightened to her full diminutive height of just over five feet. "Kalder Kincraig is long dead these past weeks, but you've my blessing to go straight to Hades, if you've a mind to speak with him. Sir." She added this last word on almost sarcastically and then turned back to her washing and for a moment the harsh stranger seemed so outraged at her answer that Peyton wondered if he was going to do her bodily damage.

Instead, he snapped, "Then I would speak with Isabella Kincraig."

Still a bit defiantly, Rose said, "Isabella Kincraig was nearly killed in the wicked cart wreck that killed her husband and isn't up to visitors. I'm so sorry, m'lord, but you'll have to come back next spring. If she pulls through at all that is. She's near to death herself, she is. What is it you want with her?"

The stranger gave a mean spirited grin that exposed crooked, blackened teeth. "She owes my Lord money, she does. Rent owned on the ground they farmed. Took out with me master's rents, they did."

Rose shook her head. "I don't believe you. Not for a second, I don't. But when she wakes, I'll tell her you were here. I will. Now get on wi' you."

"You tell her that young Lord Rosskeene will have his rents. If not his rents, then something else." He gave her that disgusting smile again. "You tell her. I'll be back."

The man left, and Rose grumbled under her breath, "Wicked young master. 'Tis a shame, that's what it is. Lord help us all and what is the world coming to? Lord Rosskeene has been a good and kind lord, he has, but what's to become of us when that young one takes over?"

When Rose told Isabella about him, Isabella sighed sadly. Tears filled her eyes as she said, "We didn't owe him money, but it truly wasn't money he was after. Even heavy with child, he kept trying to force me to come and work for him in his manor house. Kalder could see what was happening and when Rosskeene kept raising the rents to force me to give in . . . Well, we finally left as secretly as we could to protect me. And eventually Chantaya. She looks so much like me."

She closed her eyes and tears seeped out as Peyton's mother spoke kindly, "Forget that now Isabella. 'Tis over, it is. You're just an uncommon beauty, that's all. These spoiled young lords forget their place, I say. But, there's not a thing this young Lord Rosskeene can do what with you laid up. Forget him and focus on getting your strength and your heart back. There's a little dark haired angel runnin' round here who needs some vinegar to keep up with. You worry about little Chantaya and not some young gentry who takes in too much territory. You're safe here."

Isabella swallowed and nodded as she whispered, "Thank you, Rose. Thank you."

Just then, Chantaya came running in the door with a tiny handful of squashed wildflowers, raced across the room and launched herself onto her mother's bed. Peyton grinned as his mother cautioned Chantaya to be more careful and then Rose smiled and said to Isabella, "See what I mean?"

That night, when Rose told Willem as they lay beside each other, she admitted, "Your Mum would have had a conniption to have seen me talk to the young master's messenger like that. She would have thought it disrespectful and completely provocative. And it probably was, but what's to be done in times like these? Isabella's been through enough and these young bloods are completely run amok. Heaven help us when the young Master takes over completely."

Willem pulled her close. "Yes, heaven help us. But Mum was wrong, Rosy. She didn't want me off doing something as dangerous as becoming a knight, but we both know there are more important things than life. God and kingdom. Honor. Integrity. You were right to stand up for Isabella. We must all stand up against evil if we are ever to have security. Apathy and selfishness are the most dangerous things of all. If good citizens say nothing, then evil will prevail.

"In truth, I still wish I'd gone to be Sir Broughton's page. Even if I'd ended up a knight and killed in battle, it would have been better than watching some of the most powerful men in the kingdom of Monciere become corrupted. If we stand for nothing, our whole region, nay our very kingdom will fall in time. Mum was wrong, but we can continue to help our sons understand better than we did. 'Tis the only way to bring needed change."

Rose gently patted his arm around her and snuggled closer. "I'm sure we'll always regret they insisted you stay and choose a safe path, but to me you will always be Sir Willem. You have the strong heart of a knight."

Chapter 2

Isabella eventually did recover enough that she began to support herself by gathering herbs and plants in the nearby woods. It became apparent very soon that she had a gift for both medicinals and for spices and her goods were in high demand both in the village and by the peddlers and drummers who came through on occasion. She stayed with the Wolfgars through the depth of the winter and then in the early spring, the villagers helped her to build a tiny cottage of her own to move into tucked in the edge of the woods not far from the Wolfgars. 'Twas near the village, yet far enough and concealed enough that they hoped to be able to keep her somewhat hidden in case Lord Rosskeene's henchmen came back.

The day Isabella and Chantaya moved into their own little house, Peyton was so sad he near wanted to cry and felt embarrassed for being such a baby at nine years old. Still, Chantaya had become as dear to him as any little sister. Once they were moved, his mother asked him and Tristan to go by and check on them almost every day. 'Twas a chore Peyton did without ever having to be asked twice. The three of them would go with Isabella into the wood and build castles and forts while she gathered her herbs, then they'd all go back to the Wolfgars and Chantaya would help the boys with their chores there as well.

That summer she got her own cottage near the village, when Chantaya turned four, Isabella began to teach her to read. When Peyton and Tristan found them studying together, they thought 'twas interesting and wanted to learn to read as well. Some considered the ability to read almost freakish and Isabella hesitantly approached the Wolfgar parents to see if they would approve of letting the boys learn. Other than the friar from the village church, she was the only one in the whole village and possibly in much more area than that who could read. 'Twas a rare enough gift that although the Wolfgars were ecstatic, they didn't even dare mention it for fear Isabella would be rumored to be a witch and be exiled or worse, and their sons would miss out on the opportunity to become literate.

The day Peyton brought in an ancient and decrepit book and read to his parents, his father beamed and his mother cried and although it had come with a great loss to Isabella and Chantaya, the Wolfgars were incredibly grateful that the two Kincraigs had come into their lives. Now they just needed to continue to help Isabella keep clear of their ever more abusive younger master whose messengers showed up every few months wondering about her. As the years passed, tensions were high with worry about what would happen to the whole estate when this sometimes vicious young landlord assumed complete control as his father eventually turned his lands over to him.

§§§§

The three youngsters were far out in the woods playing hide and seek behind Isabella's house one day when Chantaya, now nine years old, happened upon a small stone house. Knowing that the boys were looking for her, she dropped down upon a grassy bank behind a bush for concealment and began to study the little cottage. She'd had no idea anyone lived out here. In the years they'd lived in Navarre, she'd never seen anyone come from here.

It seemed to be miles from anywhere, but it didn't look abandoned. The shutters were open, and the small porch was neatly swept and held a bench and a wash basin. There was a horse in the pen to the side.

No one was about and while she waited to be found, Chantaya turned her attention to the horse standing there inside the fence. 'Twas nearly white with flecks that looked flea bitten and appeared to be ancient. Its withers were prominent as were its knobby knees and hips and the bones near its eyes had great sunken spaces between them. Chantaya could clearly count every rib, although it stood at a full manger, munching listlessly.

After several minutes, Peyton and Tristan hadn't found her and she decided she needed to go back and shout Alls Free when suddenly the door of the stone house opened and an old man came out. He looked nearly as ancient as the horse, with what was left of his hair gray and his cheeks like leather, but his stride was still sure and straight as he stepped off the porch and around to the bony horse.

Chantaya watched in fascination as the old man lovingly handed the aging steed a carrot and then proceeded to curry the horse with a wooden brush literally from head to tail. The horse didn't look much better when the old man finished, but it obviously enjoyed every moment of its gentle grooming.

When the man was done, he put a lanky arm over the horse's neck and stood next to it, speaking for several minutes and Chantaya almost forgot the boys were looking for her as she watched the old pair's friendship.

Finally, far off, she heard her mother calling and she carefully got up and slipped back over the hill the way she had come and headed for home. As she neared her own cottage, she decided it might be fun to keep a secret from Peyton and Tristan. And she wouldn't tell her mother. Her mother was always terribly worried someone bad would find them here in the forest, but Chantaya knew instinctively that the old man wasn't someone bad. A bad man would never be that gentle with his old horse.

Chantaya was young, but she had learned well from her mother and could find the herbs in the forest nearly as surely as her mother. Sometimes it was almost a game to Chantaya. She reveled in learning about the different plants and what they did and what they tasted like. 'Twasn't long before she knew even the mushrooms and truffles.

When they got back to the cottage and her mother lay down to rest, Chantaya would do as her mother bid her and cook using the different herbs and spices. Even that was like a wonderful adventure to her. How fun it was to take ordinary looking plants and foods and create delicious smelling and tasting concoctions that would make the boys fairly drool when they stopped in to check on them. She could get those boys to do anything she asked of them with a good savory brown gravy or bit of a sweet. That was another adventure in and of itself; getting what she wanted from the boys. They always let her wander further and have a better time because she cooked for them and adored them so.

Of an evening, her mother would build a small fire in the fireplace, then sit near it and tell stories she made up as she sewed their clothing. Chantaya was growing so quickly she needed a new dress every few months and the foraging for plants was sometimes incredibly hard on their apparel.

Sometimes her mother would talk to her about her Papa and what he was like and what a good man he was. Always, she would speak of when Chantaya was grown and she would find a husband of her own and what kind of man he should be. She spoke of kindness and honor and being hard working and at nights Chantaya would climb into her little loft bed and dream of a far off love who had the heart of a knight and the gentle touch of her father.

'Twasn't long after she'd discovered the old man that one afternoon when Isabella and Chantaya were in the woods with Peyton, and as Isabella was gathering herbs near a small ravine, she fell. Chantaya heard her give a small gasp, but didn't think much of it until she looked around and saw her mother lying motionless at the bottom of the wash.

She was not moving and Chantaya gave a larger gasp of her own and tried not to scream. She flew down the side of the wash and was kneeling at her mother's side as Peyton looked over the edge of the hill above her and then vaulted over to slide down to them. "What happened?"

Chantaya shook her head. "I don't know. One minute she was beside me and then . . . She must have hit a rock with her head. Is she going to be all right?"

Peyton nodded, although he grimaced as he did so. "I think she'll be fine. Have you water in your skin?"

"Yes." Chantaya scrambled back up the slope to fetch it, then slid back down. Peyton took her water skin and trickled a bit onto Isabella's face, but she didn't react to it and Chantaya turned a worried face to Peyton again.

He put a hand on her shoulder and reassured her, "She'll be fine, Chani. Don't worry."

Chantaya inhaled a huge breath at his encouragement. She should have known everything would be fine with Peyton here. They sat next to her mother for several minutes, splashing the water again occasionally and finally, Chantaya said, "She's not going to wake up yet, Pey. You're going to have to carry her home."

He looked at her and rolled his eyes. "I can't carry your mother nigh two miles back home, Chani."

Chantaya looked up at him in puzzlement. "Why ever not?"

"I'm fourteen years old, Chani. I'm big for my age, but don't be silly. I could carry her for a time, but we're a long way from your cottage. We'll have to go get my father. And bring the cart."

"But you're strong. I've seen you splitting the wood and carrying heavy things. And that will take hours to fetch the cart! 'Twill be dark! What about the wolves? I'm sure you're strong enough."

He shook his head with a worried look. "I'm not strong enough. I'm sorry. And I don't know what to do about the wolves. Can you stay here with her? I'll build a fire for you and you can keep it burning to keep animals away until we get back. Or do you want me to stay and you go for Father?"

The thought of either frightened Chantaya terribly. Finally, she had an idea. "I know! We'll go to the stone cottage. He'll help us. I know he will! He's old, but he's still strong. I'm sure he is."

"Who? What stone cottage?"

"Just over the hill. There's a stone cottage with an old man and his old, old horse. He'll help us."

Peyton's eyes narrowed, questioning. "What are you talking about? You've been visiting a man in the woods here?"

"No. I haven't visited him. I've just seen him. A couple of times. He's gentle to his horse. He'll help us, I know it."

"Chani, you shouldn't have been anywhere near a stranger. How did you find him?"

Chantaya only got up to begin trotting into the woods and Peyton immediately jumped up and followed her, grumbling as he jogged, "Chani, stop. We can't leave her. You don't even know this man. You know we're supposed to be wary of strangers. What if he's from Lord Rosskeene's?" Finally, he caught up to her and grabbed her by the shoulder. "Chani, it's going to be dark soon. Where are you going?"

She looked up at him, then turned and pointed. "There." Peyton turned to look and was amazed to see the little house. He turned back to her with a surprised look on his face and she smiled. "I told you. C'mon. He'll help us. Hurry."

No sooner had they explained the situation to the old man than he went outside and saddled the ancient horse. He followed the two of them into the woods, leading the horse behind them. Nothing was said as they traveled the short distance and as they reached her mother, the old man knelt beside her and felt for a heart beat at her neck and then opened the little bag that swung at his waist and took out a small pouch. He opened it and held it under Isabella's nose and in only a moment, she groaned and opened her eyes.

For a moment, she looked frightened, then confused. Finally, she sighed and gingerly held out a hand to Chantaya. "I lost my balance and couldn't catch myself. Are you well?"

Chantaya gave her hand a squeeze and then looked guilty for a minute. Finally, she said, "I spoke to a stranger, Mama. I'm sorry. We didn't know what else to do. He came to help you, though."

She nodded toward the old man. Isabella looked up at him, gave a tired smile and said, "Thank you, friend. Where did they find you?"

"Just there in the wood. Do you think you can ride? Old Wallace isn't much to look at anymore, but he'll get you home safe. Are you up to it if I help you on?"

With a grimace, she nodded. "Certainly. Please forgive me for being such a bother."

The four of them slowly trekked back through the wood and it did indeed get dark before they made it out. They met Willem just before they reached the Kincraig cottage. When they were so late, he knew there must have been a problem and came looking for them.

When he saw the old man, his face showed his surprise and then he stepped forward and extended a hand almost reverently. "Sir Mordecai isn't it? You were once one of the Great Council. I remember you well, even though I was only a child. Where did they find you?"

The old man smiled serenely. "Where old knights go to live out their last days, I suppose. I built a stone cottage in the woods and try to stay out of everyone's way. It's been a good life for Wallace and me." He gave a mellow smile again, but then reminded, "We need to get your neighbor in and see to her. She's taken a nasty bump to her head."

Willem nodded. "Oh, yes. Let's get her to her home." The six of them trooped on and took Isabella inside. They helped her to bed, then Willem laid the fire and lit it while Peyton removed her shoes and Chantaya took the baskets and put them away. By the time the fire was lit, when Willem looked around, the old man was gone and all of them were surprised at his leaving so quietly.

After puttering around the cottage while Chantaya made the dinner, Willem commented on what a fine help Chantaya was to her mother. Then as he had a cup of milk with the three of them before he and Peyton took their leave, he shook his head and said, "He was once one of the greatest knights in all the land. One of the King's First Guards, he was. And known near and far for his bravery and loyalty and fierce defense of the crown. In his day, he was a legend. Who would have ever dreamed he lived deep in our woods?"

§§§§

'Twas only a few days later as they were working on their fort in the woods that Peyton said to Chantaya and Tristan, "Let's go back to the stone cottage. I want to show our gratitude properly. We never even thanked him."

Chantaya agreed instantly, "And he has no family. He said he had come there to live out his last days and he mustn't be so alone. It's not good. I'm sure it's not. We need to visit him."

With a nod Peyton said, "'Tis a pity he never had a wife and family. My father said he devoted the best of his life to preserving our safety and that of the kingdom of Monciere. That's probably why he never got married. Felt he was too old or something by then."

Enthusiastically Chantaya said, "Well, we can be his family. I brought a carrot for his old Wallace horse and I even brought Sir Mordecai some honey cakes. I'll bet he never gets many sweets without a wife to care for him."

Peyton laughed and ruffled her hair. "I'll bet you're right. At least not ones that taste as good as yours, Chani. Come. Let's be heading to Sir Mordecai's then. But, I don't think we should tell our parents. I think your mother would worry and our grandmother would come apart at the seams. Our father's mother hates anything to do with the idea of knights and battle. I don't think our parents would mind, but if we don't mention it, they won't have to answer to her. Let's just go and keep it to ourselves." She skipped up beside him, then took his hand and wrapped her other arm round Tristan's waist as they headed deeper into the woods.

When Sir Mordecai opened the door to their knock, they all three were more than a little bit nervous. He must have been able to see that as he gave them a smile that crinkled the sides of his eyes and made him much less intimidating. Peyton was the one who volunteered the reason for their visit. "We've come to thank you properly, sir. You left so soon the other night that we neglected to do so, but we truly are grateful. Truly. Sir."

Sir Mordecai nodded as Chantaya added happily, "I brought a carrot for Wallace, Sir. And some lovely honey cakes. I made them myself for you. I'm only nine, but I truly can cook. Try them, you'll see."

"Can you now? I believe that you can from the looks of you. They do smell good. And Wallace is a fair hog for carrots, he is. Spoiled rotten for them. Although they still don't make him gain much fat on his ribs. He's old now, poor ancient beggar. And he's aging faster even than his old master. 'Tis sad I'll be to see him go, when it's time. He's been a good campaigner. Brave and true ever."

The four of them headed toward the old horse with Chantaya skipping ahead and Peyton said, "Our father told us you were once one of the greatest knights of the kingdom of Monciere. A legend, he said. He said you were nigh to be the reason the whole kingdom didn't fall when some old Lord Argyle tried to overthrow the king."

Sir Mordecai chuckled and said quietly, "Your father exaggerates. The king had things well in hand, I'm sure. But 'twas good that he had those of us of the council and the soldiers to back him. It's important to stand for what is right and fair."

Peyton nodded. "'Tis exactly what our father says. He was once asked to be a page, you know. His mother near expired just at the thought of it and he finally gave up trying to convince her. Lord Broughton chose someone else instead, but I think Father has always regretted that deeply. He would have made a fine warrior. He's a good man, Father is."

They stopped at the old horse and Chantaya fed him her carrot as Sir Mordecai said, "He seemed a good man. And hard it is to go against a loving mother's wishes when you're but a lad. What did he end up doing? Your father?"

"He's a thatcher. And a fine one. But his heart was always far away with the soldiers. At least that's what Mum always says. She says his mother stole his life's dream from him and that that is a thing to be regretted. Squelching a man's passion she calls it. Mother has always said that, although she loves having him home and safe, she'd rather have him truly happy."

Again Mordecai's eyes crinkled. "She sounds to be a good woman as well. Although, I'd wager your father is happy as a thatcher with fine sons and a loving wife."

"He is. But there are times when they speak of what is happening with Lord Rosskeene and young Master

Rosskeene and of the importance of having honor when one also has authority. I believe they worry about the future in the hands of the spoiled young master. He tries to gain riches by raising the taxes instead of raising the hopes of those on his lands. My parents say he doesn't understand that what gives his tenants the passion to try harder is the hope of a better future. They say Lord Rosskeene would be far wealthier if he only helped his folks succeed, instead of discouraging them. It's those times that my parents reflect on whether Father's personal safety was more important than going to battle for right."

Sir Mordecai looked away toward the horizon for a moment, then said quietly, "We all must do that which we feel is best. That's the truth of it. And who is to say what is correct? But we must be true to ourselves or live with the regrets. And in life there will always be some regrets, no matter which course we choose. Hopefully, we just have to live with the lesser regrets."

The two younger children had gone to pick handfuls of grass for the horse and Peyton looked up into the old man's eyes and nodded thoughtfully, wondering just what the old knight was saying with that far-off look in his eyes. Still, he was right. Even as young as he was, Peyton knew he was right. A man had to stand for his beliefs or there would be huge regrets. He knew 'twas true for his own father.

They didn't stay long. Then they walked back through the woods to their fort again with Chantaya bouncing along beside the boys, happy at how much Sir Mordecai seemed to have enjoyed her honey cakes, and Peyton more thoughtful beside her, wondering if they could go back again and visit with the intriguing old knight. Peyton had a million questions to ask and Sir Mordecai probably had a life's worth of fascinating stories to tell.

§§§§

It had been more than six years since the stormy night of the cart accident had brought the Kincraigs to the village of Navarre, but still, there were occasions when a stranger would drop by the weathered old tavern to casually inquire about what had happened to the Kincraig woman.

Invariably, the word would get back to Isabella and she and Chantaya would leave the little cottage and go stay in a small cave back in the forest for a couple of days until the stranger had been seen to leave town. At first, Chantaya hated staying in the cave, even though her mother had blankets and had brought food enough to keep them comfortable. The cave smelled of bears and they could hear the cry of wolves as they sat by their fire at night. Chantaya was always frightened.

Finally, her mother tried to turn these occasional trips into an adventure and would tell Chantaya stories of a young girl who was brave beyond measure and longed for the chance to travel into the forest to learn of what was outside the realm of her small home life. When she told tales like that, Chantaya soon learned to enjoy the time spent away from the cottage and yearn for adventures like the stories.

'Twas during one of these nights away in the cave that her mother stroked her soft dark hair and spoke to her of how Chantaya was going to be a great beauty someday. Her mother said it almost sadly and Chantaya wondered aloud what was wrong, "Why does that sadden you, Mother? Peyton says I will look just like you and he thinks that will be a wonderful thing. He says you are uncommonly beautiful. Is it not a good thing? To be lovely?"

Her mother sighed again, although she smiled as she touched Chantaya's long, silken curls. "No, darling, it's a very fine thing to be uncommonly beautiful. And you truly are. 'Tis just that I worry as well, Chantaya. Sometimes beauty attracts the attention of those who feel they are more powerful than our society. Sometimes being noticed isn't purely a good thing."

Chantaya looked to her in confusion. "What do you mean, Mother?"

Shaking her head, her mother said, "Nothing sweet one. You are far too young to worry about things like this. Shall we braid your hair up? And pull it out of the way? It will keep it from tangling into the bushes near the stream when we pick the mustard."

"You may pull it back if you wish, Mother, but it won't stay. You know that. As I gather the herbs, it sometimes snags on the branchlets and tendrils pull loose until there are curls dangling all about my face and neck. It happens every time. Peyton laughs and pulls them like they are springs until sometimes I fairly want to whack him. He pure torments me sometimes. Tristan as well, but not near so as Peyton. If he didn't smile and help me every time, I'm sure I would be sore vexed."

Her mother only smiled and said, "All boys are like that I'm afraid, daughter. And the fact that you are uncommonly lovely only makes you more fun to tease, I fear. You'll have to get used to it and learn to ignore it somehow. It's only bound to become worse as time goes on. At least it's all in good spirits. I'm afraid that in time, the young ladies will become jealous and their teasing won't all be fun spirited. Sadly, sometimes we women can be treacherous."

"What do you mean, treacherous, Mother?"

Isabella Kincraig only waved a hand and stood to add another log to their small fire. "It's nothing, child. Simply another one of those things you are far too young to consider. Come have some stew. It looks to be ready now."

"It smells wonderful, Mother." She came to stand beside the fire as well and put a hand on her mother's shoulder where she bent to stir. "I'm so lucky to have such a fine cook for a mum. The boys fair do my bidding for food when they come."

"And you're nigh as fine a cook as I am, even at your tender age, Chan. 'Twill come in handy in your lifetime, it will. Many's the time that sumptuous fare has been a means to a good end. It's not just boys who will learn to barter for a taste. Your father once bargained for a fine new horse if I would provide tarts to the master for the birthday celebration of the dowager aunt. My, but your father was proud of that horse. And he looked near as handsome as a bold knight sitting upon it, he did." Her mother had a far off look upon her face that made Chantaya hesitate to intrude on her mother's pondering.

Finally, Isabella seemed to bring her thoughts back to the present and offered what she had dished. Chantaya accepted the wooden bowl of the stew from her mother and asked, "Do you still miss him?" Her mother nodded wordlessly, and softly Chantaya added, "Shall I pray, Mama?"

Nodding again, her mother bowed her own head as Chantaya said a short grace and then quietly began to eat, wishing there was a way to ease that soul deep loneliness she could see in her mother's eyes and that Chantaya could remember more of her father. The only thing she could truly remember was that he had been so tall and dark and such a very gentle man. 'Twas a pity her memory was so hazy.

§§§§

Peyton finished unloading the reeds he'd delivered to where his father was working on one of the roofs of the village. He lifted several bundles up the ladder onto the roof for him, before climbing back onto the cart to go to the edge of the marsh south of town, to cut another load. As he went to slap the reins onto the cart horse's rump, his father called down from the roof, "That's fair enough to finish this one, Peyton. Go on home and find yourself some mischief. You've been a great help today. Thank you."

Nodding, Peyton turned the gentle horse for home and glanced at the sky. Might be there was time enough to go visit Sir Mordecai. He'd been wanting to get back to see the old knight for days now. At home, he put the horse and cart away and stopped to speak to his mother a moment before walking off into the woods, knowing she assumed he was going to see Chantaya and Isabella. He didn't think she would mind him visiting the renowned knight and he set off through the woods at a brisk walk.

Sir Mordecai was sitting on the bench on his porch mending what looked to be the horse's headstall when Peyton emerged from the depth of the forest. The knight's head was up and watching as Peyton stepped out and Peyton had no doubt the old knight had known he was coming long before he could see him. His hair may have been nearly white, but he was as sharp and alert as a young man.

Peyton wasn't sure what to say to such a man of great legend. He was infinitely glad for the kindly smile the old man gave as he saw him approach and said, "Ah, young Peyton. What brings you so far into the woods of a fine day? Could it be you knew that an old man needed a hand from a strong young man like yourself?"

Returning the smile, Peyton said, "I only hope to someday have a portion of the strength that you have in but one of your limbs, Sir. Are you truly in need of assistance?"

Sir Mordecai nodded. "Aye. Indeed. In need of strength and agility and your youthfulness all around. The wind has torn a portion of the thatching loose from the south corner there and I haven't the skill and balance to repair it. And old Wallace has fair knocked the gatepost awry with his scratching and although I'm the one who built it, I can't both push it upright and hold it to secure it. A brawny youth is just what I'm in need of."

Peyton dropped to the bench beside the elderly man with a comfortable grin. "Well, then pray let me have the honor of serving the legendary Sir Mordecai. 'Twould be an honor, Sir."

The old man's roof truly was in a bad way and Peyton was glad to climb up and repair the thatching just the way he often did beside his father. It didn't take but a few minutes, but he was sure the cottage would be far more water tight for his small efforts.

The gate post was a more lengthy matter and they spent a good hour working side by side before the post was once again square and true and sound. The two of them spoke back and forth for the whole of the time and not only had Peyton been right in assuming the old knight would be fascinating to listen to, but he was only grateful he'd been able to help. Coming back seemed much less of an imposition when he knew he'd been of service this time.

At length, he bid his older friend goodbye and headed back into the depths of the forest, wondering not for the first time, what it would be like to be a knight and go off to battle in defense of your kingdom. To his young heart, once you put aside the lack of home and family, knighthood seemed an uncommonly fascinating occupation. 'Twas no wonder his father seemed to be caught up in another time and place when he spoke of Mordecai. It truly was a pity that he had been kept from his dream of serving. Still, he did have the wife and sons that Mordecai didn't. Peyton thought of growing old alone and had to ponder further which life was truly to be pitied.

On the way back he stopped into the Kincraig's cottage and assured their well being, then continued home. At his house he was glad he'd stopped when his grandmother hugged him as his mother asked after Isabella. It would never have done for his grandmother to find out he had become friends with Mordecai and he was grateful to be able to answer honestly.

That night in his bed in the loft, he dreamed of a knight in full battle dress with an armored steed that breathed steam in the cold like a sleek, warring dragon as they fought in defense of a fair maiden with long, dark silken hair and the face of a woodland fairy.

When he awoke and realized it had been Chantaya in his dream, he was anxious. The thought of his beautiful young neighbor at the hands of some unseen enemy was troubling. Chantaya had been through enough in her short life.

Later that afternoon, he wanted to trounce Chantaya himself when she tried to insist she could help carry bundles of reeds up the tallest ladder to his father, as he repaired the roof of the little village church. 'Twas far too high for her safety, but convincing her of that was a day's work of itself, let alone the thatching. Peyton's father had had to tell her to stay down when she flat out ignored Peyton's insistence. She was so intrepid 'Twas absolutely frustrating sometimes. Not a grain of fear in that silly child's head! And climbing a ladder with her petticoats fair rioting in the breeze! It had been near scandalous. There were days when Peyton had no idea how to deal with that girl in the slightest.

He was still mad at her when the three of them walked back home together, and got even madder still when she laughed at him and his frustration with her. At that, she fair got the giggles. She put her arm round his waist to give him a light hearted hug at his obvious vexation and said, "Oh, come now, Papa Peyton. I lived through climbing the tall ladder quite nicely. No harm done. Stop being such an old crone now and laugh with me. 'Twas an adventure, wasn't it? I've never been up that high even when we climb the old tree by the cliff! Wasn't it marvelous? I could see clear to the cross roads! 'Twas fair refreshing! Was it not?"

Tristan chuckled and Peyton gave her a look of disgust and sighed, "Refreshing? One of these days you're going to kill yourself, Chani, with the antics you attempt. And I'm not going to be the one to pick up the pieces. You'll have to go and admit to your dear mother yourself how you ended your young life, because I haven't the heart to break news like that to her."

Chantaya only laughed again and gave his arm a squeeze. "Oh, yes you will, Peyton Wolfgar. You'll always pick up the pieces for me. It's well I know you. You've been my champion always and nothing will change that. It's in the very soul of you. Being a champion. It's fair branded onto your forehead."

She changed her voice to a deeper pitch to imitate him and cupped her mouth and went on, "I am a knight in shining armor who will rescue small children, grandmothers and damsels of all varieties. If you are ever in need, simply call on Sir Peyton, the gallant! I will never let one down." Peyton fair glared at her and she laughed and added, "Ever!"

They had reached the Kincraig cottage and Isabella opened the door to their voices, took one look at Peyton's grimace and Chantaya's giggles and said, "Gracious Pey, what's she done this time to make you so sober? Or do you have a toothache?"

At that, Chantaya went off in a whole new spate of giggles, hugged him once again and walked up onto the porch. She disappeared inside the house as Peyton sighed, shook his head and said over his shoulder as he turned to go, "Just a pretty, dark, curly headed toothache, Mrs. Kincraig. She's making me old and I'm only but fourteen. I hope you have more success keeping her from any refreshing heights than I did this day. Good luck and good night now." He walked away shaking his head with Tristan still chuckling and even Isabella laughed as she followed Chantaya inside.

Ever it was that way. Chantaya diving into every experience of her life as if it were a grand new enterprise and making the three of them laugh through the whole of it. Peyton ever the steady, responsible one who safe guarded her, and Tristan, the easy going third leg of the stool, who smoothed out any wrinkles that cropped up along the way.

That night in his loft bed, Peyton thought back on Chantaya's foray onto the church roof and had to grin to himself in the dark. Yes, it had been unduly foolish, but she had fairly reveled in her risk taking, standing there on the top of the ladder with the breeze teasing both the hair that had escaped her braid to frame her pretty little face, and her underskirts. What was to be done with that girl?

And yes, she'd been right. Peyton would stand by to protect her with his very life until the day he died. She knew him well.

Jaclyn M. Hawkes

Chapter 3

Trips to visit old Mordecai soon became a high point for Peyton. He became good friends with the old man and tried to soak up the legendary knight's wisdom and ways. There was something innately admirable about the honorable elder and it only made Peyton's fascination with him grow as they interacted.

At first Peyton worked beside him at whatever Mordecai was doing at the time, but it wasn't long before Peyton's obvious fascination with Mordecai's reputation had Mordecai showing Peyton his long unused armor and his weapons, and even showing Peyton some basic sword fighting skills.

It also wasn't long before Peyton's parents figured out he wasn't always at the Kincraig's when he disappeared for hours at a time. However, after an initial discussion to ascertain that Peyton truly felt the old knight was a good and decent influence on their son, they only insisted that Peyton let them know from then on when he was going into the woods to visit and cautioned him to keep his friendship with Mordecai discreet around Willem's mother.

Once Peyton knew that he had his parents' blessing, he allowed Tristan and Chantaya to come with him, although Tristan was truly more interested in staying in the village and playing with the boys there. Usually Chantaya was helping her mother to gather the plants and herbs and mushrooms. That left Mordecai to Peyton more often than not and Peyton relished the time. In a way, he felt like he'd grown past the boyhood pursuits of the village and moved on to something of far greater import.

Mordecai spoke of honor and trust and industry, courage in the face of evil, loyalty, guardianship and virtue. Things that until now had seemed like the monotonous lectures of loving parents, but from Mordecai they became the creeds of greatness. Hearing the ancient knight's philosophies was like opening a huge new book of life for Peyton. Just as his parents had always taught, there were things that needed to be fought for. Things that truly were more important than life itself.

It planted a yearning in Peyton to strive. To go further and reach higher and to become more than he'd ever imagined thus far in his life. 'Twas as if Mordecai's earlier greatness opened Peyton's vision to the possibilities of what humans were truly capable of and stretched his own personal potential. 'Twas positively empowering to him even within the limits of their society of peasants and gentry. Until now, he'd always assumed he was a peasant boy, destined to grow up to be a respectable, hard working peasant father like his own. It had never occurred to him that there might be other paths available to him. With the passing of time and with Mordecai's new perspective, Peyton didn't know what he would be as an adult, he just knew he could no longer settle for mediocrity.

Sometimes Tristan and Chantaya came to Sir Mordecai's with Peyton. She always brought her honey cakes or some good thing to give and true to form, she was always right in the middle of whatever Mordecai and Peyton were doing at the time, even though Tristan was often bored of it all. It never even entered Chantaya's mind that a female shouldn't necessarily know how to wield a sword or shoot a bow. And, although at first Mordecai was skeptical, he too soon succumbed to Chantaya's ability to sweet talk anyone into letting her have her way. 'Twasn't long before she could ride Wallace expertly and Mordecai even made a small bow that just fit her to teach her archery and gave her a miniature wooden sword for her twelfth birthday.

By her thirteenth, she was good enough with them that Tristan didn't even bother trying to compete with her and Peyton himself was hard put to keep her from stabbing him when they sparred. And she had learned to handle even Mordecai's new younger, more spirited horse, Bartok, like she was glued to it.

Age didn't make Chantaya any less capricious. She still lived life with an enthusiasm that was at once, entirely endearing and at times entirely dangerous. One afternoon, she spun while sparring and slipped. She took a hard enough spill into the dirt of Mordecai's yard that she gave herself a bloody nose and Mordecai obviously felt horribly guilty.

Peyton didn't feel guilty. He felt like 'Twas finally time to put his foot down and make her stop playing at being some kind of female Robin Hood, before both of their parents found out and forbade them from seeing Mordecai anymore. As he stood beside her putting pressure on the cloth that he held to her nose, he began to lecture her about acting more like a lady. Thinking that it was going remarkably well, he was rudely awakened when she pulled the bloody cloth from her face so she could laugh up at him.

She pushed him away, stood up and picked up her sword. Peyton began to swear and Mordecai looked from one to the other of them in consternation. He was even more concerned when Peyton listened for a second as she began to wheedle him, then simply picked her up and swung her over his shoulder and headed for home which only made Chantaya laugh again. Peyton simply waved at Mordecai and kept trekking into the woods.

§§§§

The old man eventually sat down on his porch bench and shook his head. Never had he conceived of a student like eighteen year old Peyton Wolfgar. He was quiet and focused and completely competent and Mordecai knew that if given the chance, he had the potential to become more legendary as a knight than even he himself had ever dreamed. Mordecai just wasn't sure what to do about that. And he certainly didn't know what to do about this strikingly beautiful, half girl half woman who could do anything and wrap anyone around her little finger. She was an incredibly good little warrior, yet she looked like a woodland nymph and took absolutely nothing the slightest bit serious.

Mordecai looked out at where the two of them had disappeared into the forest and chuckled. At least Peyton seemed to know how to handle her. Mordecai was surprised that she hadn't gotten angry at Peyton, but she just always seemed to laugh at him. And Mordecai was surprised that Peyton didn't get angry at that, but he, in turn, always simply seemed to take Chantaya in stride. Five years apart, but they were quite a pair, those two.

The old knight stood and stretched and walked down to talk to his old horse, Wallace who stood patiently beside his new one and munched lackadaisically. Mordecai wasn't truly spry enough to be teaching these youngsters like this and yet, he wasn't nearly as decrepit as his dear old horse. Wallace was literally on his last legs and Mordecai knew it. He wouldn't be surprised to wake up and find the old boy had died in his sleep any morning now. Mordecai petted the old campaigner, then sighed and rubbed his own shoulder where it ached from sparring earlier. They neither of them were up to this, but Peyton was too good to not train. That was all there was to it.

Peyton and Chantaya were a good ten minutes into the woods when her nose started to bleed again and it dripped down Peyton's back. She had just been going to let him carry her all the way home like an old grain sack over his shoulder, but the bloody nose changed that.

'Twas kind of fun to get Peyton's dander up. Especially when he resorted to carrying her. He'd become all but brawny as he'd matured and she thought it was great to be hefted over those great shoulders. He was so funny when he thought she needed to behave better, although you'd think he'd realize sooner or later that that old lecture about acting like a lady wasn't going to get him anywhere. Who wanted to act like a lady when you could act like a knight? Peyton should have figured that one out. Now, if there had been some grand, fancy ball gown involved like she had seen one time in the dressmaker's shop, that would be one thing. But, village girls had to be content with good, drab sturdy working dresses and they didn't hold a candle to sword fighting.

Peyton put her down when she mentioned the blood on his back. He looked at her with concern as he pulled another cloth from his pocket and put pressure to her nose again. With his other hand, he wiped at the blood on her face with his sleeve, sighed again and said, "Chani, what's to be done with you? Isabella would be horrified."

She rolled her eyes at him. "Oh, a nose bleed never bothered my mother and well you know it, Papa."

He tried to look stern and said, "I'm not talking about the nosebleed, Chani. I'm talking about the sword fighting. And the archery and the riding astride Bartok. Grand Goshen girl, I daresay you'd wrestle me if I agreed to it. It's pure shameful. You're not six anymore. It truly is time you grew up and acted like a lady. You near look like one, if one doesn't notice you're carrying some gruesome weapon. Isabella would be appalled and don't try to deny it. If you don't straighten up, I'm going to tell her myself and she'll make you stay home and learn to sew or something."

"I already know how to sew and I don't think she'd be as thoroughly appalled as you think. She's the one I got my nature from, you know. Why do you think she knows how to read and ride astride as well? She's not exactly your most demure matron."

"Your mother never acts inappropriately."

"Neither do I." She pushed his hand away and gingerly touched her nose to see if it had stopped. "I think it's all right now."

He leaned toward her and gently began to wipe at her face. "You're covered in blood. Isabella will think I tried to beat you. Sword fighting *is* inappropriate, Chani. And you're done. There will be no more sparring girls. It's over.

It should have been over as soon as you began to . . . uhm . . . As soon as you . . . Now that you're not a little girl anymore."

Chantaya put her hands on her hips. "I am thirteen, Peyton Wolfgar. And I'll do as I please, thank you! You are not my Papa."

"You're almost fourteen. And you look like you're seventeen. So act like it. And your Papa would have said the same thing and you know it. Now come. Let's get you home before your nose starts to spout again." He turned and began to walk and she fell into step with him.

Stubbornly, she said, "Thirteen is thirteen. I don't have to act seventeen until I am seventeen and I might not even then if I don't want to. My nose would be fine without some brute packing me around like a sheave of thatching. Why would looking older preclude my learning to sword fight? 'Tis ridiculous!"

"Preclude? Lovely word. But there's no need to impress me because I can read as well as you, girl. And 'tis not ridiculous. People will commence to talk, Chani. You'll get a reputation as a wild girl and the boys will come round and expect . . . Well, they'll . . . Just trust me on this, Chani. You have to behave."

"Peyton, you and Mordecai are the only two people in the world who know I sword fight. Well, and Tristan. Or can shoot a bow or ride astride or throw a knife or anything else. And it's not like you two are going to give me a reputation or start a rumor that I'm a witch. In public I behave perfectly. Always. More than perfect. My mother insists I wear a hooded cloak nearly every time I go anywhere where there are people. She's near ashamed of me for some reason. So you can't accuse me of misbehaving."

His voice softened. "She's not ashamed, Chani. Just the opposite. She's worried people will notice how beautiful you've become. She's trying to protect you."

"Protect me from what?"

"From . . . Simply from . . . You need to talk to her about this, Chani. It's not truly my place, but I can promise you she's not ashamed. She just wants you to be protected. Not every man is going to be as trustworthy as Tristan and me and Mordecai. Especially some of the spoiled gentry who think they're untouchable. And indeed, in many ways, they are. They're . . . " He hesitated and then said, "Just ask your mother. I'm sure as pretty as she is that she learned as young as you."

She looked up at him and for once wasn't sure what to say. Finally, she said, "You're talking in riddles, Pey. I haven't a notion of what you're saying."

"Good then. I wish that you never need know what I'm trying to say. 'Tis a shame you will have to learn. It's not fair, but then life seldom is. Even at thirteen I'm sure you know that by now."

They reached her cottage and stepped up on the porch. Her mother met them at the door and took one look at Chantaya's face still smeared with some of the blood and she quickly glanced back and forth between the two of them as she said, "Great heavens! What has she been up to this time, Peyton? Chantaya, are you well?"

Chantaya nodded as Peyton turned back and said, "She'll tell you, I imagine, Mrs. Kincraig. It's always something with her, but then you already know that. Good evening."

§§§§

Chantaya glanced at Peyton's retreating back and sighed as she went into the cottage door. She went across to the water basin and dipped a cloth in to begin washing her face as her mother asked, "Chantaya?"

"Yes?"

"What ever is the matter with Peyton? He looked sad as he left here? Are you two fighting?"

"No." Chantaya shook her head.

Isabella hesitated and glanced back at the door and asked, "What then? Surely, he didn't hit you."

"No! Of course not. Peyton would never hit me." Chantaya turned aside to the looking glass and finished washing, then stared at herself for several moments before turning back to her mother and asking with great seriousness, "Mama, is it truly completely inappropriate for me to sword fight?"

Isabella looked at her for a second in surprise and then her forehead creased as she tried to understand and then, inexplicably, she laughed. "Is that what this is about? Is that what happened to your nose?"

Looking sheepish, Chantaya nodded. "Yes. And Peyton has decreed I am no longer to sword fight because I am now a grown up girl." She rolled her eyes. "Blast him! I almost feel like I have to obey him because he's infinitely wise and adores me and is always right. Blast, blast, blast him!"

Isabella laughed again as she put her hand over her mouth and struggled to contain a veritable fountain of laughter. Chantaya frowned and then smiled hesitantly with her as she said, "Blast you too, Mama. You're not supposed to agree with him. I'm only thirteen. He's such an old frump. If he wasn't so blasted handsome and usually right, I'd want to trounce him."

Still laughing, Isabella said, "He is always right. Remember? And you're almost fourteen and look seventeen."

"That's exactly what Peyton said. Blast him."

"Stop cursing. He truly said that? What did he say?"

Chantaya picked up a hair brush, pulled the remnants of her braid out and began to brush out her hair. "He said that now that I'm uhm mmm grown up, I need to act more ladylike or the boys are going to think I'm wild and will expect something. He never would say exactly what. And then he said I look seventeen and had to behave respectably and he said . . . " She paused and then turned toward Isabella and asked, "Mother? Why do you insist I wear my hooded cloak into the village? Are you ashamed of the way I look?"

§§§§

After the long talk with her mother the evening of the sword fighting nose bleed, Chantaya truly did try to begin to get more serious about acting like a young woman instead of a little girl, but she was determined that didn't have to mean she couldn't continue to play with Peyton at all the things she loved. She just made sure her hair was more neatly done and that she'd worn a more flattering dress that made her look more feminine as she did it. She wasn't sure if her reasoning was correct, but Mordecai said she looked lovely and Peyton was positively tongue tied that whole first afternoon, so it worked.

She was careful to behave absolutely above reproach in the village and worked twice as hard at gathering the herbs and mushrooms, which was good because her mother tired so quickly in the woods sometimes. Chantaya was literally blooming and her more mature wardrobe required more money than they'd been making. Moreover, even though she went barefoot a good portion of the time, winter was coming on and she'd have to have new shoes.

She did wear the cloak into the village and the hood hid her magnificent hair while at the same time the cape somewhat hid her figure that was becoming increasingly harder to hide. Still, even with the cloak, her face wasn't hidden and now that she was aware of her mother and Peyton's concern, she did notice that more and more of the village boys and men took the time to speak to her. To Chantaya, the whole issue was a bit perplexing and she wasn't sure whether to be complimented and excited, or be frightened and simply try to stay away from the others who began to pay more attention to her.

In a way, it made more sense to just have Peyton or Tristan transact all of their business in the village, but then the idea of becoming near hermits and never going out seemed wrong somehow. It went directly against Chantaya's outgoing nature to want to stay away from all of their neighbors and friends.

In speaking with her mother, it was finally Isabella who made the final decision not to accept living in fear as she said, "Our Father in Heaven has blessed each with their own talents Chantaya, and He was so generous with you. 'Twould be a shame to bury your sweet, happy nature just because of those few who would harm you. Especially when those who you truly need to be concerned with are seldom here in our village. 'Tisn't the villagers, but the gentry who think they're above behaving. No. Better to just be careful and stay with the boys where you can be yourself and still be safe." So Chantaya typically went into the village with the boys who would see her to the shops she needed to frequent before going to run their own errands.

Not long before Chantaya's fifteenth birthday, she took a gift of a mutton pie to a new mother nearby. That became a turning point in her life. The new mother was the daughter of the couple named Bealle who ran the small tavern in town and the next day the Bealles showed up at the Kincraig's cottage. When Isabella opened the door, she smiled and invited them in, then was surprised when the husband asked her to come and work for them at their tavern. Perplexed, she said, "That is gracious of you, but pray, why do you need another cook? Has business picked up so that you need extra help suddenly?"

The wife shook her head and the husband answered, "Nay, but we've never in our lives tasted any mutton pie the likes of yours. Business would boom were we to have dishes that good to offer. Pray say you'll come and work of a supper time."

Unsure of whether to be glad or sad that her daughter was growing up, Isabella answered, "'Twas not me who baked your pie, friend. 'Twas Chantaya. She's ever a better cook than I these months and more. 'Twould be her you be hoping to hire. She's out in the woods gathering herbs just now, but I'll send her into the village upon her return to visit with you. It will have to be up to her to decide."

When she came in with her basket, Chantaya noticed her mother had been weeping and it struck fear into her heart the likes she hadn't felt in years, until her mother told her about the Bealles. She and her mother discussed the offer at length and finally decided it might be a good idea for Chantaya to try it if it would indeed be only for the dinner hour. It would possibly mean a more steady income during the long winter months when it was much more difficult to gather the fresh herbs and mushrooms in the woods. And after all, the Bealles were friends and neighbors of theirs. Surely Chantaya would be safe under their watchful care. So, Chantaya went in search of one of the boys and they went to town. As simply as that, she began to cook in the Bealle's tavern kitchen.

Jaclyn M. Hawkes

Chapter 4

They had been right. Business picked up considerably when word got round about how gifted the new cook was. Business picked up even more when word got round about how beautiful the new girl at the tavern was. Diners more than doubled and travelers began to come from near and far to eat there.

At first Chantaya was anxious. Ever since her talks with Peyton and her mother she had become wary of males in general and strangers in particular, but it wasn't long before she got used to the attention and learned to just ignore the flirting and comments that were directed toward her as she worked. More talks with her mother and Peyton and even Peyton's father had prepared her for how to parry the innuendos and it was actually quite nice to be able to cook and have so many people enjoy it. 'Twas much more fun to cook for a crowd than for just two. Soon Chantaya found herself looking forward to going in for those few hours at supper.

She'd been there for a few months and was completely comfortable with both her duties and the patrons when, for the first time, she questioned working away from home and her mother. A new young man had come in with some of the locals and he began to pay attention to her. She ignored him or brushed his comments off in jest, just as she always did, but then she could hear some comments that were mildly troubling.

As she served another table, she heard the fellows at the newcomer's table say, "Leave her alone, Hershey. I'm telling you, she's Peyton Wolfgar's girl. Leave her be. He's the size of a mountain."

Chantaya went on back into the kitchen, but she worried at the comments like a dog at a bone as she continued to prepare things. Who were they talking about? It had to be her. There wasn't any other her except Mrs. Bealle and she certainly wasn't Peyton's girl. Was someone out there going to truly bother her? And what was that about her being Peyton's girl, anyway? Chantaya wasn't Peyton's girl. More like a little sister. That's what they must have meant. She wished she *was* Peyton Wolfgar's girl. He was the most handsome, entertaining man she'd ever known.

She wasn't anyone's girl. Not yet. She'd hardly even spoken to anyone unless it was someone at church or here at the tavern. Not that she wouldn't like to be someone's girl. She just hadn't had the chance yet. She'd thought about it. But there wasn't anyone who intrigued her in the slightest. Well, the middle Bertram boy was adorably cute in a puppy kind of way, but he was really the only one. And Chantaya wouldn't have truly wanted to get very close to him, but he was handsome.

She worked about, thinking all of these thoughts and being perplexed about why someone would think she was Peyton's girl. Just because they were the best of friends and spent untold hours together didn't mean they were romantically involved, much as she would have loved it if they could have been.

As she rolled out pastry, the more she thought about it, the more the whole idea troubled her. Certainly, she wanted to settle down someday with that elusive image in her head of the strong and gentle man who would be her true love some day. The one she and her mother had often spoken of, but the village boys just weren't terribly tempting. At least not tempting enough to make her want to stop tromping around and pretending to sword fight with the Wolfgar boys. They were far more fun than the other young men around. Especially Peyton. Peyton kept her laughing every day of her life, it seemed.

She pulled another pot of roasted meat out of the oven. Maybe that was a problem. Maybe she should already be someone's girl. After all, she was fifteen. Some girls were married by fifteen. Not many, but a lot were by sixteen or seventeen. Her own mother had married at sixteen. That wasn't very far away. Still, she didn't feel anywhere near old enough to marry. That was actually kind of repulsive. What with the things married people did that her mother had spoken to her about.

Well, some of it wasn't repulsive. Some of it sounded kind of wonderful. Kissing for instance. Kissing would be nice and she loved affection. Just that casual skin on skin touch that made you feel loved, except that she wouldn't be the slightest bit comfortable with some stranger being that close to her. She actually had an issue with people being too close to her. When people got within a foot or two of her she wanted to reach out and push them back. Except for her mother or the Wolfgars or Mordecai. She loved having them close. Their casual affection was very nice. But anyone else. Not so much.

The whole of the evening as she worked around, she sputtered mentally over the stranger in the dining room and whether she needed to get started on being someone's girl. By the end of the night, she was tired and even a little irritable. Maybe no one wanted her to be their girl. Maybe that was the problem. Maybe that was why she was late in getting this whole romance ball rolling. Oh, well. She angrily scrubbed at the last pot that needed cleaning. What did she care anyway? She was perfectly happy just as she was, being a good daughter and a strange kind of little sister and now a cook. Being someone's girl would come soon enough or not. If all it did was make you grouchy like this, what did she need romance for after all?

She finished the last pot and put it away and wiped down the cook table and then shrugged into her cloak. It had been a long night. All that thinking was exhausting. At least it made her finish cleaning up faster. She was ready nearly a quarter hour before she usually was. She glanced out the tavern kitchen door into the darkness and realized Peyton wouldn't be here yet to walk her home. For a moment she wondered if she should wait for him and then decided against it. She'd stop there and let him know she was early on her way instead.

She pulled her hood up onto her head and stepped out the door and then pulled up short when a strange male voice spoke to her out of the darkness, "I'm told you're called Chantaya. Be that true?"

Looking up, she made out the shape of a man standing near the back wall of the tavern in the dark and she stepped quickly away from him as she answered, "It is. Good even to you, sir."

She ducked her head and hurried, but a strong hand snaked out and caught her arm before she could pass him. "Hold up there, lass. There's no hurry this even. I saw you inside and couldn't stop from coming here tonight to see you. I'm called Hershey. Ian Hershey. From down at the Forks."

Without raising her head, Chantaya said, "Yes, well, 'twas good to meet you, Master Hershey, but I must be going." She went to pull her arm away, wishing she hadn't served his table quite so much brown ale tonight. It tended to

56

make perfectly decent men into rascals at times. She desperately hoped this wasn't one of them.

As she pulled away, he roughly grabbed her arm again and said harshly, "Not so fast, young Chantaya. Did you not just hear me say I couldn't help needing to see you?"

His roughness and tone made her instantly angry and this time she did raise her head, pushed her hood back and said brusquely, "Indeed, I did hear you sir! Did you not hear me say I must be going? Now, I beg of you. Nay, I demand you leave me be this moment and let me be on my way! I must be going! Now!" She'd raised her voice and jerked her arm away, but to no avail. The inebriated man only grabbed her again even more roughly and pushed her back up against the wall. As her back hit, she screamed for all she was worth. There was the possibility Peyton had left his house a few minutes early and would hear her even from a distance or maybe the Bealles would hear her inside their house behind her.

Before she could stop him, this Hershey took her shoulder with one hand and silenced her scream with his other. She bit him and then tried to bring her knee up to kick him but she couldn't do more than nudge him as close as he was. He only grunted and cursed, then moved his hand and brought his face down to kiss her. She closed her eyes tightly and jerked her face to the side, dreading the touch of his mouth with its stench of brown ale. *Oh, why hadn't she waited a few minutes for Peyton?*

That moment before his head descended seemed to last an eternity and then, before his mouth made contact, just as roughly as he had shoved her against the wall, he jerked away. There in the darkness, Chantaya caught a glimpse of Peyton's furious profile just as he stepped back and viciously slugged the man. The stranger crashed back against the wall of the tavern and then slowly sank down it to land in a heap at Chantaya's feet with a barely audible moan.

She nearly tripped over him as she turned and buried herself against Peyton's chest where he caught and held her. He wrapped both of his arms round her so tightly she could hardly breathe and didn't even care because she was safe. 'Twas the most comforting feeling she had ever dreamed she could feel.

The anger that had kept her from completely panicking moments before dissolved into near hysteria as she burst into sobbing against his woolen shirt and fisted handfuls of the cloth at his belly desperately tightly. She was safe. 'Twas going to be all right. Peyton had come. The relief was nearly overwhelming. Peyton had come.

For a moment, she wasn't even thinking, just hanging onto him and letting his deep gentle voice find its way through the fear that had flooded over her at being attacked. As she finally began to gain some control, she let herself be drawn into Peyton's voice and his touch where he gently stroked her back and told her over and over again that she was all right.

On some level, she became aware Peyton was speaking to someone else as well over her head. She heard Mr. Bealle and some of the other village men. Then Peyton was gently pulling her aside, still stroking her and talking to her as she struggled to get control of herself. At length, the tears slowed and she literally had to will herself to loosen her hold on Peyton as she wiped her face against his shirt and finally looked up at him.

For a long moment, he simply looked down at her, searching her eyes and then, wrapped her back into his embrace as he whispered, "Are you all right?"

She nodded against his chest and whispered back, "I am." She struggled for another second to stop her tears again and whispered further, "Thank you. I was afraid, Pey. I was so scared. Thank you."

He rubbed her back one more time and said, "You're welcome, Chani. I just wish I'd been a few moments earlier. I'm sorry."

"I should have waited." She shook her head. "This wasn't your fault. I should have waited. I never dreamed he'd be out here waiting for me."

"He was inside earlier?" She nodded again and he sighed and held her even tighter for a moment and then said, "Come. Let's get you safely home. Shall I carry you?"

"No. I'm well. I'll walk. Just . . . Please. Stay close. You have no notion of how comforting you are right now. Your touch. Your strength. It helps me."

He tucked her securely under his arm with his cloak all the way over her and pulled her snugly against him as he turned and headed toward their homes. "If I get any closer we'll trip. Come, your mother will be worried. She'll be aghast at what happened here tonight."

Chantaya shook her head against him. "No. I'll not tell her. She'll only insist I stop cooking there and it has been good for us. It has helped her to be able to cut back on her own foraging for herbs and that's as it should be. Her body is still so weakened from the cart crash. She tires easily and fair limps home. I should cook. It helps her."

"She'll hear about it anyway, Chani. The Bealles will tell her. Someone will. You need to tell her."

She nodded, knowing he was right. "Then I will. I'll tell her 'twas a small thing and that you came and I was fine."

"You don't lie, Chani. You're the most honest person I know."

"No, I won't lie. That's not a lie. It can't be. This has to be a small thing. I can't let it be a large thing."

Peyton was silent for a moment or two. Finally he pulled her even more snugly against him. "You're right. And you're wonderful. I'm proud of you, Chani. You're a magnificent girl."

Tears rolled down her cheeks again and she hoped he didn't see them in the darkness as she struggled for composure. At length she softly said, "Thank you, Peyton. I appreciate you saying that, but I was ridiculously scared. Too scared then to be magnificent."

"'Tis why you're magnificent. Because you were scared and still stood up to him. And now you're still being strong for your mother. That's what *is* magnificent. You were the same that very first night in the storm. You're the strongest girl I know and I'm incredibly proud of you." At that, he leaned and kissed her head where it lay against his shoulder and she stumbled as he echoed, "Incredibly proud. Always."

When she was able to breathe after the surprise of that kiss, she finally said hesitantly, "I thought I drove you mad a good portion of the time."

She could hear his smile as he said, "That too. But you're still magnificent."

She hugged him more closely. "May I remind you of that the next time you want to swear at me?"

"An excellent idea." They stepped up onto the Kincraig cottage porch and he turned to look into her eyes again without letting go of her. He studied her there in the dark for several long moments and then again asked quietly, "You're all right?"

She nodded wordlessly and he went on, "I'm so sorry, Chani. I'll be far more careful of being there early." She nodded again. "But stay inside until I come in, all right?"

"Yes. Thank you."

"Are you ready to face your mother?"

"I think so."

"Are you ready for me to go then?"

Chantaya hesitated. She wasn't sure what she was about him. Between being so roughly attacked and then having him kiss her hair, she was in a complete emotional tussle. At length, she said. "I . . . I think so. Thank you for coming. Thank you for coming every time. Thank you for always watching over me."

The smile was back in his voice again. "You're welcome, Chani. It's what I do. Remember? 'Tis branded on my forehead." He pulled her close one more time. "Good night, Chantaya Kincraig. Sleep well."

Chantaya slipped inside the door and shot the heavy bolt, then turned into the room. Her mother was fast asleep in the rocking chair beside the fire with her sewing on her lap and Chantaya paused for a moment to take a deep breath and lean back against the door to try to clear her head before advancing into the room.

Tears welled one more time, but all she had to do to swallow them was think back on how Peyton had kissed her hair tonight. It had been absolutely strange that he did it, but then when she thought about it, her tummy did this nervous butterfly thing. He was her dearest friend in all the world and he'd rescued her once again. A big rescue this time. Much bigger than the myriad times he'd hauled her out of one pickle or another, but that kiss. That kiss was so different. They weren't truly kissing friends like that usually, although often lately, she'd wished they were and wondered what it would be like.

His kiss tonight must have just been the situation. Still, she sighed. 'Twas unbelievably thought-provoking. Would he still be her same dear friend tomorrow? And why did she hope so much that he would do it again? It had been incredibly nice. Just the thought of it brought a sweet warmth that was new to her. 'Twas near more troubling than the drunken Hershey.

Gently, she woke her mother and encouraged her to go to bed, then Chantaya banked the fire without ever mentioning the stranger at the tavern. There would be time enough to tell her mother in the morning. There was no sense in troubling her when she was so weary tonight.

Chantaya slept poorly and had weird dreams, but when she fought her way to wakefulness, she had only to remember Peyton's gentle hug and his voice in her ear last night to help her relax and go back to sleep. Just the memory of him holding her so tightly helped her to rest again. Still, she slept late and in the morning felt as if she'd never been to bed.

'Twas Peyton's knock on their door and then him speaking with her mother that finally had her up and dressing to come down the ladder from the loft. He watched her quietly as she descended and she could see the question in his eyes as he glanced at her mother and back. She gave him the merest head shake as they went to the table to join her mother for breakfast. Chantaya saw he was concerned and wanted to ask her how she was, but still decided to put off speaking of the stranger. She wasn't quite up to talking about it yet this morning. If she was honest, she wasn't even up to facing Peyton yet this morning. She still hadn't figured out what to think of him and his tender kiss last night.

She made it through breakfast, then took her egg basket and stepped out the door to go care for the chickens. Peyton followed her. She'd barely made it out the door when he took her hand to pull her to a stop and make her look at him. He studied her at length again before finally asking softly, "How are you?"

She'd thought she was only tired until she heard the concerned tone of his voice. She was embarrassed when tears welled into her eyes again. She wiped at them stubbornly and struggled to swallow the lump in her throat and finally choked, "Well. Thank you."

He stepped across the small space between them and folded her back into his hug and said, "I never thought you'd try to lie to me, Chani." He rubbed her shoulders again like last night. "You're a miserable liar, at any rate. You could never convince a body."

She sniffled and said, "Pray forgive me."

For a few minutes, all he did was hug her silently and then finally, tried to jest again. "By all appearances I'm going to have to be the honorable party to tell your mother what happened. You're too busy dampening my tunic, it would seem." She didn't answer and finally, he asked more seriously, "Do you want me to tell her?"

At length, she took a deep, shuddering breath. "No. I'm well enough. Let me go gather the eggs and try to cover these tears and I'll go tell her. I don't know why I'm being a baby this morning. Just tired, I guess."

He tipped her head up and studied her again as he asked, "Bad dreams?"

She nodded. "But they always ended with this handsome, gallant blonde man saving the moment. So don't worry."

He raised his eyebrows. "I'm glad to hear that, girl, but I'm afraid you still look to be in need of a nap. And he left bruises on your cheek." Peyton gently touched her face and then went on, "Shall I go tell the Bealles you won't be coming tonight?"

"No." She shook her head. "This isn't a big thing, remember? What happened to him? Last night?"

"Some of the men threatened him that if they ever saw him anywhere near you again they'd put him in the stocks for a week or hang him, whichever he preferred. Then they dumped him in the back of a wagon, hauled him back to the

Forks, gave him a whipping and tossed him out. I doubt he'll be back in Navarre for a very long time, if ever."

She let out a big breath. "Oh, good. I hope it's never. Pray, let me gather the eggs. I'll be right back."

He followed her to the little henhouse and waited while she stepped inside and came back out with half a dozen eggs. He walked beside her back into the house where her mother studied them closely as Chantaya washed the eggs and set them aside. Peyton folded his arms and leaned back against the wall near the door and watched her quietly, then bid them goodbye and left. Her mother turned to her expectantly. "All right, daughter, what goes on here this morning?"

Puttering in the kitchen with putting the breakfast things away, Chantaya did her best to be nonchalant as she explained, "There was a stranger who had had a wee bit too much ale last even who thought he wanted to speak with me outside the tavern. He wasn't overly polite. Peyton gave him a mighty slug and then brought me home. Peyton's just worried about me. That's all." She glanced up at her mother and then asked brightly, "What are we to be about today? Shall we go into the woods first thing?"

Coming near, her mother turned her face into the light to look at her and studied her thoughtfully before answering, "Yes, the woods first thing might be good. Do you want to talk about this stranger Peyton slugged?"

Hesitating for a just a moment, Chantaya shook her head with a sigh. "In truth, not yet, Mama. Mostly, I'd just like to go on with this day like it didn't happen at all. Does that offend you?"

Gently, Isabella assured her, "No, not at all. I understand. But, know also that you probably should talk about it sometime. If not to me, then to Peyton or Mordecai or someone else you trust. Some things are better dealt with than not."

Nodding silently, Chantaya finished straightening up, grateful her mother was such a calm, gentle woman and somehow knowing her mother understood far too well just what had gone on last night.

In the woods, they stayed closer to each other than they typically did and Chantaya wasn't surprised when her mother eventually brought their sporadic conversation around to the topic of Peyton, when she said, "Peyton seemed quite concerned this morning. Was he well? He seemed different somehow."

Chantaya thought about that for several moments before answering. He had obviously been concerned. He always was, but he'd never shown up first thing in the morning to see about her like he had today. And until last night, he'd never looked so deeply at her quite like that. Usually, he was a bit exasperated with whatever he was concerned about, but then he was also typically rescuing her from some pickle she'd gotten herself into out of being too intrepid. That wasn't necessarily the case here. However, it hadn't occurred to Chantaya that he might not be all right after what had happened.

Honestly, she'd been more caught up in her own fears and going back over and over that tender kiss, than in noticing whether he was all right. Finally, she answered her mother thoughtfully with a question. "He was different, wasn't he?"

Isabella nodded. "He was." But that was all she said for several more minutes as they continued to pluck at the small mushroom patch they had found, both busy with their own thoughts.

Eventually, Chantaya put aside her small knife and looked up at her mother and said, "A man there last even, eating with the stranger, said I was Peyton's girl, Mother." She sighed, wishing again 'twas true and shook her head in confusion. "Why would he say that? Peyton and I are just friends, are we not? He's almost like my brother, isn't he?"

Isabella smiled gently and kept on about the mushrooms. "You are friends, Chantaya. The best of friends. Better friends than I've nearly ever seen. In truth, I don't know that I've been around any young people who are such friends. The only time I've ever seen the likes of you two has been people who are married. But yours has been an unusual situation. It's no wonder you are so close."

She paused for a moment as she worked, and then went on, "As far as brother and sister, I suppose you're close to that, but he's more patient with you by far than he is with Tristan. He ever has been. When we first came here, I was so hurt and couldn't care for you and he did it almost exclusively. 'Twas most amazing. He was so young and so sweet with you. But, no, I wouldn't say you were Peyton's girl. If you were, I would never let you tromp all over the countryside with him as I do. 'Twould change everything. He never flirts with you, does he?"

Chantaya shook her head. "No. Never. Blast him. I so wish he would. In truth, he lectures me rather than flirts. He has this need to keep me safe and well behaved. And teases me mercilessly until I laugh."

Isabella smiled again. "It makes us all laugh, it does. He truly does adore you. It's ever fun to see. He's a fine young man, is Peyton Wolfgar."

Nodding, Chantaya said, "He is. The best. When I thought about being someone's girl last even I'm ashamed to admit I was quite irritable. I'm not sure what to think about romance. I look forward to it, I do. But, in truth, I couldn't think of one other boy that I'd rather be with than Peyton and Tristan. They're much more fun than the other villagers. Peyton especially. And he's ever so handsome." She sighed and grimaced. "I suppose I'll have to wait until either someone comes here who is more interesting, or until I travel somewhere else sometime. They were quite discouraging actually, my thoughts."

Isabella laughed. "You thought a lot about this, it would seem."

With a sheepish grin, Chantaya nodded. "I did. I feel far too young to bother with it, but then I'm only a year younger than you were when you married. That's a sobering idea, it is. What if I never meet someone who interests me more than Peyton? Shall I die old and alone like Mordecai or must I marry someone I don't particularly like? How horrid! I don't think I could do the things you spoke of with someone I didn't want near me."

Again, Isabella laughed, only this time she hugged Chantaya as she did so. "Oh, daughter. Don't worry so. I married young, 'tis true, but only because I loved your father dearly. You needn't worry this way. One day you'll know, without a doubt, that you've found the love of your life. Then the problem won't be that you don't want him near you, I assure you. Then, the problem will be all of the other things in this life that get in the way of being near him. And, in truth, I wouldn't be the slightest bit surprised if one day you and Peyton wake up to find your friendship has become more than mere brotherly."

Chantaya's eyes widened and Isabella grinned at her. "Maybe not, dearest, but you'll have to either bring in droves of newcomers, or go round the whole world before you'd ever find a finer, handsomer, more entertaining young man. Peyton isn't your typical, mediocre village boy. He's quite amazing. And no one could treat you better. That's the truth of it. He handles your free spirit admirably. Don't you think? Not to mention that he does, indeed, keep you safe. 'Tis no easy task with you."

"No. It isn't. I fear I keep him fair juggling sometimes. Still, he's pure adorable when he's so patient with me."

"Well, you are no mediocre girl either, Chantaya Kincraig. Whoever you end up with would have to go just as far to ever find a treasure girl such as you. You mustn't ever forget that. You have gifts and potential that are far above average as well. You should be so grateful."

Chantaya looked down. "I am, Mother. I am grateful. I don't mean to sound ungrateful. I'm just so very mixed up. Thinking about whether I'm not someone's girl yet. It's fair unnerving." She paused and then admitted, "And last night, when I was so frightened, Peyton kissed my hair, Mama. Near startled me. I don't think he even realized he did it. We were somewhat upset last night. And Peyton was so angry with that man that he knocked him cold with one strike. In looking back, I'm most mortified. I was glad, Mother! Imagine that. I've never been so glad. I should be ashamed."

"Why should you be ashamed that a good man fought for your honor and safety? 'Tis what good men do, daughter. God himself would want it. Honor and virtue and life are truly the most precious of anything on earth. No good man would hesitate to defend them. And why should Peyton not kiss you? He loves you dearly, as you love him. It's no wonder he's troubled today. He would never forgive himself if you were harmed." She smiled again. "He's devoted a good portion of his life already to keeping you safe from harm. I doubt he's going to stop anytime soon."

"No. I doubt that as well. He's already made me vow not to come out of the kitchen until he comes inside to get me from now on." She finally smiled a true smile back at her mother. "I accused him of having watching over me branded on his forehead."

Her mother nodded with satisfaction. "That, young lady, is why your mother trusts him so with her daughter." She leaned and smoothed back the tendril curls that had escaped to caress Chantaya's cheek. "Still, you do need to have met lots of young men so you can know for sure who you love. If you settle down, even with the right man, without getting to know others, you may always wonder if you made the right decision."

§§§§

Peyton came back in the afternoon and he and Chantaya went to see Mordecai. Peyton was strangely quiet on the walk there and even while they visited, and finally, on the way home, Chantaya questioned him, "Peyton, are you truly vexed at me?"

He gave her the grin that had been so markedly missing this day. "What have you done now, girl, that I should be vexed over?"

"Well, nothing more than usual, but you didn't even get after me when I let Bartok gallop before I was fairly in the saddle and you took leaves out of my hair and smoothed it without saying anything. Are you well?"

He chuckled. "Oh, so what you're saying is that something is amiss because I'm not vexed at you. Is that it?"

Somewhat sheepishly, she grinned back at him. "Perhaps it is. You didn't answer me. Are you well?"

The smile left his eyes and she could've sworn he sighed quietly as he said, "I am. Still feeling guilty every time I look at the bruises on your face, but well otherwise. Are you?"

"Well, or guilty?" She looked sideways at him with a small smile.

"I already know you're guilty. You've fair admitted it. Are you well?"

She nodded her head positively. "Yes. Absolutely well."

"Absolutely well enough to go cook for the Bealles tonight? Or should I speak with them?"

"I will cook. In fact, I shall cook something fair tempting just to prove that I am well. Would you like to come have supper at the tavern? That way, you'll have a wonderful meal as well as knowing you've watched over me."

He slung a long arm round her shoulder as they walked. "Indeed, I will do just that. You can't get into too much mischief that way. And I shall look forward to supper."

Chapter 5

Peyton lingered long over a tankard of cider after his meal and stared into the flames of the fire as he waited for Chantaya to finish for the night. For the first time in his life, he was at an impasse. Typically, his life was as simple as putting in an honorable day's labor working with his father, then going on to find something to pass the few hours he had to himself and finally falling into bed tired and starting the next day. Lately, however, there was a problem. And last night, that problem had grown exponentially.

Ever since he'd become close to Mordecai, there had been a knowledge that he needed to do more with his life than become a simple peasant thatcher. He'd known it for a couple of years now as he and Mordecai trained for some future service to someone, somewhere. For a long time with Mordecai, Peyton had assumed he would stay in the village and assist with protecting the village, but yesterday Mordecai had spoken of Peyton becoming a squire, then becoming a knight for the king. There was swelling unrest in the realm and the king had great need for honorable, capable warriors behind him to stay the hands of those who would try to overthrow him and harm his loyal subjects. The ever rumbling young Lord Rosskeene was a clear example of that.

While the suggestion of becoming a squire had instantly thrilled Peyton, his first thought was to look over to where Chantaya was just then grooming Mordecai's striking new piebald horse with the wild splash of white across its shoulder. Would it matter if he could have a chance to leave his peasant station behind and possibly become ultimately far more wealthy and well known than a village thatcher, if he had to walk away from that beautiful girl over there? And what would become of her? She wasn't your ordinary village maid.

She was prettier and smarter and far better educated than most girls. And what of that sweet intrepidness that so appealed to something deep inside Peyton? With another she was more than likely to be tagged as peculiar or worse, hailed as a witch and cast out. People didn't know how to deal well with a free spirit like Chani's sometimes. She would be squelched at best and Peyton hated to even wonder at a worse turn of events.

Always, Peyton had known that someday, in the future, he wished to settle down with a good wife and have a handful of children at his knee. Since he was about eleven, those hoped for children all sported dark, silken curls and Chantaya's smile.

It hadn't truly sunk into his mind until now that knighthood and marriage might not meld together very well. And last night, seeing that man standing over her threatening her. And then Peyton holding her in his arms as he tried to comfort her. It had brought a whole new dimension to his dreams of someday.

In his life, he'd teased her and tormented her and even hauled her around from time to time, but never had he hugged her like that and it had done something to his very marrow. After holding her last night and being so angry over another man's rough treatment of her, Peyton had become painfully aware that his someday wasn't all so far in the future. It couldn't be. First off, he'd die if he had to keep from holding her again after finding just how sweet it had been, and secondly, she was too strikingly pretty. He needed to marry her soon if only for her own safety from other interested men. Most would leave her alone if they knew she had a husband, especially one destined to become a knight.

But she was only fifteen. For that matter, he himself was only nearly twenty, but somehow, that sweet, curly headed three year old he'd plucked out of that violent storm all those years ago had grown into an exquisite woman who had become more than his best friend. She'd grown and entwined her life around his until she was part of his soul. He loved her like he'd never known was possible and had absolutely no idea what to do about it.

There was no way he could walk away from her for a mere chance to become wealthy. And yet in that, he knew that indeed some things, like fighting for the good of the land, were more important than life itself. Possibly even more important than true love, although when he was striding close enough to Chantaya to smell the sweet herbs she gathered, that seemed impossible.

Worst of all, knighthood aside, she thought he was just a big brother. How did he make the leap with her from childhood playmate, to her being the mother of his handful of children? She was so sweet and innocent she probably didn't even understand yet how children came to be. She was hardly more than a child herself, although to look at her, you'd never know that. She'd grown to an incredibly desirable young woman. How under heaven could he even speak with her of what he wished to become to her?

He took another swallow of his now lukewarm cider, pushed the tankard aside, glanced round at the now deserted tavern and cocked his head to listen. She was singing in the kitchen as she cleaned up. A clear, sweet song he'd heard before about a lonesome warrior on a far, lonely battlefield. 'Twas fitting enough that it made him groan inwardly. He stared into the flames for another long minute as he prayed silently for the guidance he suddenly felt in desperate need of. He needed far more wisdom than he knew how to scrape up for this one. He needed God's guidance more than ever in his young life. Too much was at stake here, no matter what he chose to do.

Finishing his prayer, he pushed the bench back, picked up his tankard and took it into the kitchen where he put it into her dish pan of warm, soapy water and commenced to wash it and the other last few dishes that awaited her attention. She looked up from where she was wrapping up the vegetables she hadn't used, broke off her singing and smiled at him in surprise. "Peyton, pray tell, what are you up to? You mustn't come in here and do that. Mrs. Bealle will skin me if she thinks I'm making the patrons wash up."

He smiled a lazy smile and reached for another plate. "Mrs. Bealle knows her streak of prosperity would come to a slashing halt if she skinned her marvelous and pretty cook, Chani. I think you're safe after that fine meal, even with me in the kitchen."

Chantaya laughed, but then she came to him and looked up into his eyes for a long moment before reaching up to lay a gentle hand against his cheek. "What has stolen your smile,

Pey? Last night seems to have troubled you even more than me. Or is it something else? Can the cook know?"

He gave her a sad smile and turned back to her wash basin, wishing he could indeed talk to her about all that was on his mind. She was smart enough she'd probably be able to figure out a solution to it all, had he dared tell her.

That night, after he took her safely home and went back to his parents', they were discussing what was to become of the villagers with Lord Rosskeene constantly raising the rents and harassing his tenants as he was. Peyton climbed the ladder into the little loft that now felt incredibly crowded as large as he'd grown, and sprawled down next to his already sleeping younger brother. Would that he could be as carefree as Tristan still appeared. He obviously wasn't overly concerned with the state of the kingdom or alluring girls, snoring as he was.

§§§§

Chantaya spent another restless night what with memories of being accosted and then wondering why Peyton had pulled away from her so obviously. She wasn't sure if he was vexed with her, or just fatigued from worry and two late nights, but he wasn't his usual happy self and it in turn made her feel inexplicably irritable. She couldn't help but wonder if he was deeply regretting his kissing her head when they were upset. She hoped not.

She'd thought a lot about what her mother had said during their conversation about romance and that last comment about being acquainted with lots of young men had struck a chord with Chantaya, especially after how Peyton's kiss had effected her and now he'd pulled so hard away. Maybe her thoughts about Peyton becoming more than brotherly were exactly opposite of what he was thinking or what he wanted. She had no way of knowing except to know for sure he wasn't happy with something just now.

Deciding that at fifteen, it was certainly time to begin the process of making sure she knew what she preferred in a husband, she finished her morning chores and decided to go into the village and do some studying on just what kind of man she desired to marry. She stopped at the Wolfgars to see if either Peyton or Tristan were around to go with her, but both of them were out helping their father with a thatching job over east, so she pulled the hood of her cloak up and set out on her own. After all, she was already older than her mother was when she'd met her father and they'd met in a village. At a shoemaker's shop, if Chantaya remembered correctly.

She started at the millers and picked up flour, but there were only the miller's sons and she knew from long experience she definitely wasn't interested in ending up one of their wives, not in this lifetime certainly. They were shy and backward and nondescript and she hated the way they wouldn't ever look at her when they said something. She couldn't sit across a breakfast table from that for life, that was a sure notion.

Moving on to the smithy, she dropped off the kettle that needed repairing and paused only a moment to admire the brawny shoulders of the apprentice there before she noticed the trouble the young man had with a skin condition on his face. No doubt, the constant heat and perspiration from the fires made his skin worse, but nevertheless, she didn't think he was the one for her. Not when Peyton and Tristan were both incredibly handsome and had superior shoulder muscles anyway. She wondered if she should tell the smithy's apprentice about making a balm of bitterroot to smooth on his face of a night. 'Twould certainly help with those lesions if she could figure out a way to bring the subject up.

Shaking her head at the thought, she turned next to the cobbler two shops down. She had no notion if there were any young men here, because she so seldom purchased shoes, but her mother's needed repairing and Chantaya had to have a new pair for winter anyway.

Stepping into the door, she looked up and into a beady pair of eyes and was at once wishing she had Peyton with her. The cobbler had to have been twenty five years her senior, but that didn't stop him from looking her up and down and then grinning up at her almost leeringly. She quickly left the shoes to be repaired, then stepped back out of the little shop where she paused on the stoop to roll her eyes and take a deep breath. Heavens! Growing old alone like Mordecai was looking better by the moment. This was the least enjoyable morning she'd had in months.

She shifted the heavy bag of flour to her other arm and flexed the elbow that had begun to tire. She was only going on to the market. This inventorying of potential husbands was dreadful and made her shoulders ache. She should have picked up the flour last.

Stepping inside, she selected a packet of needles, a spool of darning thread and some lamp oil before glancing around the store in a half hearted attempt to take stock of any young males, then rolled her eyes and even crossed them. *Land of Liverpool!* The clerk was easily as wide as he was tall and he smiled up at her with thick lips that bulged under a sparse collection of stringy, intermittent, apricot colored whiskers. He pushed off of a low stool to stand, set aside the pastry he was eating, wiped his hand on his trousers and asked if he could be of assistance.

Oh, gracious! She'd forgotten the Larimer's son. He never even attempted to speak to her when Peyton or Tristan was with her. She wanted to put a hand to her forehead just at the thought of marriage to this rotund young . . . She wasn't even sure what to call him. Fellow maybe? He seemed nine years old, but then he had those odious whiskers. What had she been thinking to come in here on a husband scouting excursion. *Oh, Chantaya! Spinsterhood it is for you!* Utter loneliness would be better than this.

Quickly, she paid for her purchases and nearly leaped out the door and headed for home. This was more than enough getting to know the available men. She'd stay unmarried for the next several decades at least after this morning.

She met Peyton coming down the cobbled street and she finally took a deep breath. My, but he was the most refreshing sight she'd seen in ages. Tall and fit, bold and handsome. Oh! And distressed about something. She finally took in his grimace and wondered what had upset him as he strode up to her.

He carefully took her bag of flour and glanced her up and down as if checking to see if she was well and whole, then asked, "What are you doing, Chani? I've been near all over the village looking for you."

"I've simply been making my needed purchases and errands. Pray, whatever is wrong, Peyton?"

People were watching the two of them and she turned and headed back down the way toward their homes as his grimace deepened, and he asked, "I was just concerned. You've been making purchases from every possible merchant in town? The blacksmith, Chani? You don't even own a horse. And alone? What's gotten into you? I thought you hated this kind of venture."

She sighed and rolled her shoulders. "Don't I indeed. It's been dreadful."

"What has? Has someone offended you? Tell me who and I'll speak with them."

"No, no, no, Peyton. I'm well. It's just . . . " She hesitated and then admitted to him, "My mother and I were just conversing the other day of how I should begin to be acquainted with different boys . . . Well, men, so that I might . . . Well, so that when I got married, eventually, in time, of course, I'd not ever wonder if I'd chosen correctly. I was just fretting about that and decided that since I needed these errands done anyway. . . And well . . . "

Peyton stopped dead still in the middle of the cobblestone street and turned to stare at her with wide eyes. She finished lamely, "And, yes, well . . . Well, after this morning, I think I'll simply become a spinster. Like Mordecai. Well, not that Mordecai is a spinster, but . . . Marriage is just now seeming to be a life sentence of punishment. What? Why are you staring at me so, Pey? What?"

"Married! To the Shockleys? Or Quigley Larimer? Chantaya!"

He was fairly shouting even though it wasn't much louder than a whisper. She rolled her eyes one more time and turned to continue walking down the street. He once again fell into step beside her as they headed out of the village proper and she said, "I know, Peyton. Why do you think I declared I'm to be a spinster? 'Twas a thoroughly discouraging experience, I can tell you. I can't even conceive of truly facing any of them across my porridge of a morning. Oh, can you imagine? Ugh!"

Still quietly, but very heatedly, he said, "No! I cannot imagine! Why under heaven would you conceive of such a thing? And you're fifteen. Why are you all of an instant concerned with marriage?"

"Oh, stop shouting. You're being an old ogre."

"I'm not shouting in the least. Answer the question."

"I'll not let you bully me, Peyton Wolfgar. Fifteen is young. I know that. But I have to commence somewhere. My mother was married at sixteen. I'm concerned that . . . "

"Well, your mother married far too young! You're but a child. And you can't go around considering marrying the likes of Quigley! That's revolting!"

At that, she turned on him, ready to do battle, then reconsidered, and began to walk again as she said, "Please, Peyton. You'll make me heave my entire breakfast onto the cobbles. Please. Don't use the M word in the same conversation as the Q word. 'Twould make me nauseous."

Leaning close, he fairly spat, "That's not the half of it, Chantaya Kincraig! Have you stopped to consider what a marriage entails? Have you?"

She sighed. "In truth, I've tried not to. It frightens the dickens out of me. Would you please stop snapping at me, Peyton? I beseech you. I'm quite frustrated as it is. I don't deserve this. I did nothing wrong. Do you suppose I wanted to go about this morning taking stock of all of the misfits? It simply had to be done. Please, 'twas dreadful enough as it was without you haranguing me. I don't understand why this morning has made you so distressed."

He stopped again and stood, this time on the wooded path headed toward their homes. At length, he simply asked,

"Why?" He left the bag of flour balanced on his shoulder and put out both of his large, calloused hands. "Why? Why today? Pray. Help me understand why you would do something like this?"

His tone had softened and for some reason that prompted the tears that had been threatening all morning to well into her eyes. She looked aside and tried to blink them away in embarrassment. She wasn't usually a crier, but she'd felt this way for two days now. He reached into his pocket and took out a handkerchief, handed it to her, and said gently, "I'm sorry. Please forgive me. But I must know. Just tell me, Chani. It's me, Peyton. We're friends. Remember? Why are you worrying about marriage suddenly?"

She shook her head and swiped sadly at her tears. "I have to, Peyton. Don't you see? I'm only fifteen, but I am fifteen. And not a single other male in this village intrigues me. Not a one of them interests me enough to make me want to stop fooling with a sword and the neighbor boys and worry about how my hair looks. Doesn't that seem like a problem to you? I'm supposed to get married to someone, sometime. And like it! Do you know what married couples do, Peyton? I don't know about you, but those things concern me! And it might not be that far off. My mother truly was less than a year older than I am right this very moment. What am I going to do?" The last sentence came out sounding as troubled as she felt and it brought on a whole new spate of tears she hurried to mop.

He was silent for so long without moving or doing anything that she finally looked up, worried, but all he was doing was standing there with his face changing from surprise to confusion to concern, to something that she wasn't even sure what it was, but suspected he was trying not to laugh at her and it made her mad. At least that was better than heartbroken. In disgust, she turned and began to stride up the pathway to her cottage, but he caught her arm and stopped her.

She spun back on him. "What? I haven't the time to stand here and endure you laughing at me, Peyton. Let me go and see to things."

"No. Wait. Don't be angry. I'm not laughing at you. I swear it. Well, I mean I am smiling at you. But only because you're adorable. I'm not belittling you. You're right. Marriage is a big thing. Huge. And truly, some of those things married people do are uhm, uh, concerning. Well, in truth, it's more that I can hardly wait for those things, but I would guess I shouldn't admit that, huh? Sorry." She rolled her eyes and looked up at the sky. He quit smiling and loosened his hold on her arm and said, "What I'm trying to say, Chani, is that . . . "

He hesitated and she looked back at him and he finally said, "I don't have an idea what I'm trying to say, Chani, except that . . . I think your hair is beautiful, just the way it is."

She quit pulling at her arm and looked up at him in confusion. "What?"

"Your hair. I think your hair is magnificent. Especially when it all comes loose and hangs down your back like it does."

"Peyton, this isn't about my hair. Haven't you been listening to me?"

"Yes, Chani, I have. But for the life of me, I don't understand why all of a moment of a Tuesday morning you need to go inspect all of the local drivel for marriage. And what's so wrong with the neighbor boys? You've never taken issue with us before. I thought you liked me. Is there suddenly a problem?"

She stomped her bare foot. "Oh, Peyton, don't you give me that! You know as well as I do that I near worship you. But, what does that have to do with marriage? Or my hair, for that matter?"

"Pray, you tell me, girl. You're the one who's of a sudden desperately in need of matrimony. Where did this come from anyway?"

She was all ready to snap back at him and then instead, let out a long breath and her shoulders slumped as she said, "The other night. At the tavern. They tried to tell that man to stay away from me. That I was Peyton Wolfgar's girl. And that you would protect me from him. He didn't listen, but that's not the point. The point is. I'm not your girl. I'm more your little sister who gets on your nerves sixty three times a day, who you're good to put up with and watch over. I'm nobody's girl. And even that's not the point. The point is, there isn't anyone round here whose girl I'd care to be.

"Other than you and Tristan, or maybe Tommy Bertram, but he's simply like a charming puppy, other than you two, I don't even care that I'm nobody's girl, 'cause they're all morons and dimwits. But that's not good. What if I turn out like Ingrande Fergson? She's getting to where she can scarce get round by herself, but there's no one to watch over her. And folks think she's pure strange living all alone all these years with only that ugly cat. That cat's gonna die and then where will she be? I don't want to be like that." She paused and looked down, and added sadly, "But I don't want to have to marry a dimwit."

She stopped and took a deep breath and looked up at him wishing the tears would just stop already and was thoroughly taken aback when he set her flour sack down, came close and wrapped both arms round her and started to laugh. A soft, warm, deep chuckle that she could hear right through his chest that rested under her ear as he held her. She didn't know whether to be thoroughly offended or just bask in his hug and trust the knowledge that he would never laugh at her mean spiritedly.

While she was still wondering how to feel, he pulled her even closer and said, "Chani, Chani, Chani. What's a body to do about you?"

She sniffled and shook her head against his chest. "I don't know. Even I don't know what to do about myself."

He laughed softly again and said, "I don't know either, girl, but I do know that if you go off and wed some squatty, corpulent dimwit just so you don't end up like Ingrande, you'll break my heart into ten million shards and I'll pure waste away until I die with loneliness. They'll bury me up next to your father and your baby sister."

She completely stilled in his arms for a long, long moment and then finally, pulled away from him slightly so she could look up at him in absolute confusion. *What under heaven did he mean by that?* He simply looked down at her with those sweet, brown eyes that she wanted to lose herself in and then finally, totally at a loss as to his meaning, she asked, "What does that mean, Peyton?"

He gave her a smile that seemed almost a little sad and gently smoothed a tear off of her cheek bone with his thumb as he asked, "Do you truly not understand what it means, Chani? You know me better than I know myself."

Shaking her head, she sighed tiredly. "I don't know what I understand just at this moment, Pey. All I know is that this whole growing up notion frightens me immeasurably and the thought of facing all of it without you makes me want to magically turn back time until I'm seven again and you're making mud pastries with me at the pond. Wouldn't it be delightful if we didn't have to grow up and make decisions?"

"No. Because I do want to grow up with you, Chani. Truly, I want to grow old with you. You needn't face anything without me. Why would you? We're best friends. That's what friends do. They stay together. They cover the chinks in each other's armor and watch over each other. Always."

"But what about marriage, Peyton? You must recognize that we can't simply be best friends forever. What would our spouses say? You've seen how distraught Mrs. Darnell becomes when her husband goes drinking and begins to converse with that blonde woman he almost married instead of her. I don't believe there's truly room for a husband and a best friend in a marriage. 'Tis about one too numerous for a couple. It couldn't be harmonious."

His voice softened. "What if the best friend was the husband? Wouldn't that be harmonious?" She was searching his eyes almost desperately, trying to figure out what he was intimating and he seemed to understand that as he went on, "Chani, is there no way you could ever consider marrying me? Someday. Not right now. When you've had a chance to grow up a portion. Certainly, you look grown up. Unbelievably so, but fifteen is quite young. Is there no way we could simply keep on being best friends and someday go beyond that?" He grinned at her and added, "You wouldn't have to marry a dimwit. Or grow old with only an ugly cat."

She hesitated for a minute while she tried to figure out if he was saying the same thing she was hearing and then asked, "But, Peyton, aren't we truly too good of friends to get married? I mean, we know everything about each other. Even the dreadful stuff. And indeed I do get on your nerves sixty three times a day. You can't deny it."

"Chani, who has the strongest marriage we know?"

"Your parents. Why?"

"Well, don't you think they're best friends and know even the yucky stuff?" She nodded. "And you only get on my nerves seven times a day and that's actually two times less than I get on your nerves and it makes for interesting conversation. Don't you think? We still seem to enjoy being with each other enough to do it every single day for hours and hours."

She was thoroughly surprised with where this discussion was going, but finally got brave enough to ask, "But what about the marriage part, Peyton? The only in marriage part. Wouldn't we want to be able to someday do that kind of thing with whoever we marry? Otherwise, we'd never have any children. Don't you ever want children? We don't even kiss each other. We don't even hold hands."

At that, for the first time in this conversation, Peyton looked uncomfortable and Chantaya felt an incredible disappointment settle into her stomach as he actually blushed and then looked skyward for a second before he answered, "About that . . . " He still hesitated and then looked back down at her, gave her a crooked smile and said, "Uh, Chantaya, would you be completely disgusted with me if I said that, uh . . . On second thought, maybe I shouldn't be quite that honest with you. How about if we try this? Perhaps we could simply keep being friends like we always have been and maybe, in time, we'll decide that we want to kiss each other."

She shook her head. "Peyton, if we're going to actually have this conversation at all, shouldn't we be absolutely honest with each other? Always? There's no way I'm going to talk about someday marrying and in the same discussion agree not to always tell each other the truth. That couldn't make for a strong couple."

"For the most part, 'tis true, Chantaya. But there probably comes a point where people who love each other, but aren't actually wed, shouldn't speak concerning some things because it could be dangerously provocative. I'm not sure if you comprehend what I mean. But there's also a point where maybe we shouldn't speak of some things because it might frighten one of us."

"Which one of us?"

"You one of us."

"Why wouldn't it frighten you?"

He gave her that grin again. "Uh, for the reason that . . . Uhm, remember when I said I'm rather looking forward to some of those things in marriage? I suppose I lean toward being a rogue, because I, uh, I imagine those things are going to be wonderful! Sorry. Just being honest."

She could feel her eyes widen and said hastily, "I think you're right. Maybe we shouldn't talk about this. One of us is definitely frightened."

He put a gentle hand to her cheek and touched her softly, then shook his head. "Try not to be, Chani. None of this should frighten us. It should make us happy and excited. We do love each other. This isn't anything more than the natural progression of a lifelong friendship. We know each other. We know we can trust each other, no matter what. We like each other. We have fun with each other. In truth, is there even any other option? Can you truly say you could walk away from me someday without looking back?"

Leaning her cheek into the palm of his hand, she thought about that and then met his eyes and shook her head. Tears welled into her eyes again as she whispered, "Never."

That made him smile as he whispered back, "Me either."

For a long, long moment, they stood there looking into each others eyes in the dappled sunshine of the path and then Peyton slowly lowered his head and gently kissed her once on the mouth, ever so softly. Raising his head, he leaned close again and kissed her once more on the soft spot of her temple and said, "See, it might not be too bad."

Chapter 6

Her mother spoke to her three times before walking over to stand before her and wave her hand back and forth in front of her face. "Chantaya, pray tell me, are you in there?"

Snapping out of her reverie, Chantaya nodded. "Yes, Mother. What? I'm sorry. I'm afraid my mind is elsewhere."

Drily, her mother said, "Yes, I can see that. Where is your mind, may I inquire?"

"Oh, it's uh, I'm just thinking. What did you want?"

"I'm just wondering what happened to the wash basin? 'Twas here earlier. Pray, do you know where it went?"

"No. I haven't an idea. You didn't put it somewhere?"

"Ah, here it is in the cupboard. Why is it in the cupboard? We never put it in the cupboard."

Chantaya didn't answer again because her mind had gone back to the conversation she and Peyton had had earlier that still seemed surreal somehow. Could it truly be that she and he were to someday wed? And would kissing always be as nice as it had been this afternoon? Maybe the things married people did wouldn't be frightening at all. She checked her hair one more time in the looking glass. He would be here any moment to walk her to the tavern. For some reason, that made her unbelievably nervous.

§§§§

Peyton dropped Chantaya off at the kitchen door of the tavern and then turned back around and headed for Sir Mordecai's. He had to ask him some questions and maybe the time walking would help Peyton clear his head. There had to be a way to marry Chantaya and still be able to serve the kingdom.

He found himself near in a daze as he traveled for thinking back on kissing her today. He'd wanted to do that for a shamefully long time and it was every bit as nice as he'd imagined. Isabella would crown him if she knew he'd been thinking that way about her daughter. He wished he'd reached for Chantaya's hand while he was walking her to the tavern, although, that may have frightened the poor girl more than he already had today. He should never have admitted to so looking forward to marital relations, even if she had asked him to be honest.

The whole conversation had gone unbelievably smoother than he'd expected. He'd known that discussion was coming for literally years now, but had no idea it would come to a head this morning because of some stranger from the Forks. Chantaya had been amazingly funny, even for her breaking down and crying because she didn't want to have to marry one of the frumpy locals or grow old with only an ugly cat. He strode along the forest trail with a sense of absolute euphoria that was foolish in light of his questions for Mordecai. Still, she had basically agreed to some day marry him! 'Twas the greatest dream of his whole life and he wanted to jump logs and spin in circles and shout it to the tops of the trees. Chantaya Kincraig would someday be his wife!

Now he just had to figure out what to do about serving the king.

Mordecai was out in the pen with his horses as Peyton strode up and Peyton had the sense he always had that Mordecai had been aware of his approach long before he got there. That alertness was part of the reason he'd become legendary as a knight and Peyton was working on learning it as well. If he was going to do this at all, he was going to do it well.

His old friend turned to him and then smiled and asked, "Peyton, what has you so energetic this day, lad?" Peyton grinned, but didn't admit anything.

They'd been working together for over an hour before Peyton finally asked the question that burned within him, "Sir Mordecai, do any of the knights ever take wives?"

Turning, Mordecai studied him for a long moment before answering, "I wondered if your attitude had something to do with young Chantaya. Yes, the knights sometimes take wives. Often, in fact. In truth, marriage makes them better at it. More focused and steady and driven. There's something about defending the love of one's life that tempers the warrior's heart. That's not to say a maid isn't sometimes a distraction as well, but it certainly makes victory a greater passion."

Peyton heaved a huge sigh of relief, but then wondered aloud, "Then why did you never marry, Sir Mordecai?"

The old man turned back to his ancient horse and Peyton wondered for a minute if he hadn't heard him and then Mordecai said, "Oh, but I did, Peyton." He turned back to

Peyton with a heartbroken smile. "Christiana Ferron. The fairest maiden in all the land. At least, to me she was. She had hair of the purest gold and a heart to match it. I was much older than her, but she loved me dearly anyway."

Peyton waited in silence, knowing the rest of the story would eventually come and that it wouldn't have a happy ending since Mordecai was here in the woods all alone these long years. At length, Mordecai went on sadly, "We'd tried for years to have a child and finally, she was expecting our first. No two people were ever more in love or more thrilled to soon be parents. But it didn't turn out as we'd dreamed. She died giving birth to the most beautiful, perfect wee blonde daughter. A fair replica of her pretty mother."

"And the babe?"

"Sweet Eliana. She was the light of my life, she was, after her mother passed away." He paused and looked away again before saying, "The plague swept through Valais the winter she was four. I did everything a knight knew to do, but I was no match for such a disease. She died in my arms when the crocuses were just breaking through the last of the snow."

Peyton put a big hand on his friend's shoulder. "I'm sorry."

Mordecai only nodded and looked out across the backs of the horses at something Peyton couldn't see. At length, he turned back and said, "Someday, in the next life, I hope to see them again. Some of the old writings teach of families that last beyond this life. I hope and pray they are right. We've always tried to live worthy if it is so. And I have to believe. Otherwise, I would lose sight of the whole point of this existence."

After a few more thoughtful moments, Mordecai turned back to him. "Treasure her, Peyton. She is of infinite worth.

Treasure her. Nothing can make being an honorable man more important or come more easily than a woman of character. She can strengthen you in every part of your life. She will help you rise to your God-given potential. And remember there are no guarantees. Life is short sometimes. Don't take it for granted."

"No. I won't."

"Do you still wish me to speak to the king concerning your becoming a squire? It will mean leaving her for a time to train and leaving her again every time you're called away to battle. The leaving is hard. I'll promise you that. Although, the honor and the pay was some consolation. Not enough. But some."

"Then why did you do it, Mordecai?"

"Because it was the right thing to do."

Peyton nodded solemnly. "Speak to the king. I will speak to Chantaya."

§§§§

Peyton had dropped her off unquestionably happy, so Chantaya was once again at a loss as to why he was now unquestionably troubled as he picked her back up to walk her home. Whatever could have happened in the short four hour interim? The notion that he was having serious second thoughts about her made her feel slightly ill just at the idea.

She looked up into his face as he helped her on with her cloak, but all he did was give her a sad, half smile and then wrap his arm and his own cloak about her shoulders as they ventured out into the dark.

Still a touch self conscious about their earlier conversation, she walked beside him in silence as she worked to muster her courage to ask him if he'd changed his mind. They were clear past his home and almost to hers before she finally ventured there. "What is it, Peyton? Does the thought of someday wedding me make you as troubled as you look? Have you changed your mind then?"

He gave one small humorless laugh and shook his head and then bent it to kiss her hair again much as he had those two nights before. "I will never change my mind about wanting to be the love of your life, Chantaya Kincraig. That has been set in stone for a decade and more now."

At his answer, she stopped and turned to look up at him in the moonlight. "What then, Pey? What is it that keeps stealing your sweet smile? If it is in my power, you shall have it returned to you."

He looked down into her eyes and even in the dark she could see the devotion that shone there. Then, he looked away and said, "Mordecai wishes to request of the king that I become a squire to one of his knights."

For a moment, she considered that and all it entailed and then said, "But I don't understand. You should be thrilled. 'Tis a great and rare honor. 'Tis what you've dreamed of. Why does that trouble you?"

"Because I shall have to leave you for a time to train. I don't know how long. And then I shall be a warrior, Chantaya. A willing one. Our king is a rare and good steward. But warriors sometimes don't come home to their wives. And their children. Sometimes they give their lives. Sometimes they come home horribly scarred and wounded. 'Tis a risk we would both have to accept."

She gave a gentle shake of her head. "Did we not accept that risk years ago, Peyton when first we realized how very extraordinarily talented you were at everything Mordecai began to teach you? Did we not accept that risk when first we came to realize his presence here was no coincidence? Did we not accept that risk when we came to understand that the forces of evil will always be fighting to take away the rights and powers of those who strive to do what is right?"

She reached up and tenderly touched his cheek. "I accepted that risk before I even understood that I will adore you always, Peyton. And I was proud of you. Now, knowing the man you are and the responsibility you are willing to shoulder for God and country, I'm honored to associate with you. Someday becoming the wife who will stay home with your children and pray for you is a greater honor still."

She shook her head again. "This decision is yours to make Peyton Wolfgar, but I will stand behind you in whatever it is you believe you should do. Whether you stay or go."

He looked into her eyes for another long moment and then pulled her close again and rested his chin on top of her head. For several minutes he just held her like that as they both thought through the significance of what could happen. Finally, he said, "It might be truly hard sometimes, Chani."

Struggling to swallow the lump that had risen in her throat at the thought of being without him for a time or even losing him permanently, she nodded. "I know."

After a pause, he asked, "You're sure?"

"I am."

He pulled back so he could look at her again and she raised her tear bright eyes to meet his. Giving her another sad smile, he said, "I love you, Chantaya."

"And I love you, Sir Peyton."

He leaned his chin against her forehead and said softly, "You must. God help us." After another moment of quiet embrace, he took her hand and turned to lead her the rest of the way home. They had journeyed far in the course of one short day.

§§§§

Mordecai left the next day and was gone for three during which Peyton and Chantaya cared for his old horse Wallace and prayed the horse wouldn't breathe his last breath on their watch. They'd slipped from childhood friends into an unusual relationship of hidden, but committed young love remarkably seamlessly. They hadn't even told Tristan, and in public they acted the same as they always did, but with each other, there was no doubt in either of their heads and hearts about the nature of their relationship. Nothing more had been said about when they would marry, but the fact that they eventually would had become sure. It was indescribably comforting to Chantaya to know what her fate would eventually be.

Once, as they were walking home from Mordecai's, Chantaya asked him, "Why did you never speak to me of our future? Before that day I went into the village?"

"Because you're only fifteen. I thought it would be another year before we would speak of such things."

"But you could have at least let me know a portion of the direction of your heart."

He rounded on her where she walked beside him. "I show you a portion of the direction of my heart every day of your life, Chani. Don't you see that?"

She nodded. "I do. But still, a girl could die of wondering without some kind of hint at your thoughts and feelings."

He took her hand and pulled her back to walking down the path. "And a couple could die of loneliness if a girl's mother found out I was more than her childhood friend. I don't doubt that as soon as your mother realizes my intentions, she'll put a stop to our endless freedom together. And I can't blame her. Knowing someday I shall be your husband makes me wish you were older."

"I shall grow older while you are training, Peyton. How long do you think it will be before they shall want you?"

"I've no notion. I desire to go, but still, I hope it's not straight away. I just got to truly dream of our sure future together. I'd like to enjoy that for awhile. How long do you think it will be before you grow older enough?"

She smiled shyly. "You're the one who says I'm not old enough now, Peyton. Perhaps circumstances themselves will dictate what the timeline of our lives becomes. Our Father's hand is in all of this. We'll live on His schedule. Perhaps all of this is why thou art come to the kingdom at such a time as this. Like Esther, in the old stories of the Jews. Perhaps even I have been sent for such a time as this. How long will you be in training before they let you become a knight?"

He shrugged. "I've no notion of that either. I guess that will depend on how well Mordecai has already taught me and how great their need of new men is. I shall do as I am requested and then come back for you as soon as I can."

For a time they walked in silence, both of them caught up in their own thoughts until finally, Chantaya asked, "How far is the king's castle from here, Pey?"

"Three hours ride east. Maybe four. I'm not entirely sure. Why?"

"I just wondered about how far you would be from me."

"I will always be in your heart, Chani. And the same moon will rise and set over me near the castle as will rise and set over you in your cottage. And I'll come when I can. I swear it."

She pulled him to a stop and when he turned to her, she said, "Do. Do come to me when you can, Peyton. Because I probably won't be able to come to you." She looked down while she made sure she could speak without her voice cracking and then faced him again. "I will miss you, Peyton. And I'll always be praying for you."

"And I for you."

§§§§

Two nights later, Peyton showed up more than an hour early to pick her up from cooking in the tavern and he came into the kitchen and started right in helping her to wash the dishes. She could tell something was wrong, but Mrs. Bealle was in and out and she couldn't question what was on his mind until they were walking hand in hand back down the path to their homes. Actually, once they were walking, she didn't ask, knowing he would tell her when he was ready. When he finally did, it knocked her whole world out of kilter.

He pulled her to a stop in the darkest part of the trees between their homes, taking hold of both of her hands and she could almost feel his despair before he even said anything. For a second they just stood silently, hand in hand, while she waited, but then he dropped her hands and hugged her so tightly she nearly couldn't catch her breath. Against her hair, he whispered, "I'm leaving at first light in the morning."

Then she truly couldn't catch her breath. First light! The despair she'd been able to feel from him threatened to freeze her solid in her tracks and she had to actively concentrate on breathing in and then breathing out. Tomorrow. How in the world could she tell him goodbye so soon? And for how long?

Finally, she pulled her thoughts together and realized the last thing he needed right now was for her to go completely to pieces on him at this news. He already had the pressure of packing and going to a strange place to face new experiences. Of leaving family and friends and home. Right now, what he needed from her was to help him forget the sad parts of this and to look forward to the adventure part of it with excitement and hope.

Literally willing her voice to obey her mind, she said, "So soon? Mordecai got back tonight?" He nodded and she went on, "This is quite sudden, Pey, but maybe that's a good thing. It won't give us time to get upset about you going. Do you know where you're to be yet?"

"A knight encampment near the castle in Valais. I'm to be working with Sir Kendall Bosken. Mordecai says he's a powerful knight and an honorable man and that I can learn a great deal from him and advance quickly. Mordecai trained him himself almost twenty years ago."

She pushed her feelings aside, laid both hands on his chest, summoned all the excitement she could find and said, "How excellent for you, Sir Peyton! One trained by Mordecai himself! I think I've heard the men in the tavern speak of this Sir Kendall. He's reputed to be a brilliant soldier. One of the King's First Guard. Surely this will mean you'll be among great men and have many opportunities to help King Dougal. I'm thrilled for you! 'Tis better even than we hoped, is it not?"

"Indeed. Except for leaving you tomorrow. I thought I'd have more time with you."

For a second, her enthusiasm wilted and she nodded. "Yes. I can't even think on it yet, so let's don't. Let's be happy for you. 'Tis such an honor and a rare opportunity! Let's remember that always. What does your grandmother say? Will she be completely disgusted?"

"Strangely, no. She must have finally come to terms with the fact that my father should have gone when he had the chance, because all she did was hug me and cry and tell me she was proud of me."

"Which is exactly as it should be. And just what I'm going to do. And your mother and my mother and probably near forty other girls in the village. I can quite imagine it."

"Don't let's talk about others or leaving. We have such a short time. Let us enjoy it."

"Keep walking as we're enjoying our time. My mother is going to begin worrying if I don't return soon. She's going to miss you nearly as much as your own mother will."

"I've asked Tristan and Father to watch over the two of you in my stead. They'll do all the things for you and your mother I won't be able to for a time."

There were some things Tristan and Willem couldn't do, like fill the gaping hole that had just been ripped in Chantaya's life, but she knew she couldn't say that. Instead, she asked, "What do you need me to do to help you get ready?"

He shook his head. "Not a thing except to be with me. Let us tell your mother you've returned home safely, and that I'm leaving in the morning, and then, would you stay on the porch and talk to me? I know it's late, but I can't leave you yet."

'Twas everything Chantaya could do to paste on the merest semblance of a smile as she came into the cottage, greeted her mother and explained about Peyton's leaving. Her mother must have understood how she was struggling to stay cheerful, because her mother had the same false smile as she exclaimed over his good fortune and abrupt departure, hugged Peyton goodbye and then discreetly went into the other room to go to bed.

Instead of going back out to the porch, they pulled the big bench from near the entry close to the fire and the two of them piled onto it. Peyton leaned back into the corner of it and gathered Chantaya against his chest and they sat staring into the flames and then into each other's eyes, wondering how to even start to say goodbye to each other. It had been almost twelve years that they had been together everyday and even though they both truly felt it was for the best, it still felt overwhelming. It might have been a trifle easier if they'd both known how long it would be before they would see each other again.

They spoke of everyday things at first and then of hopes and dreams and fears and aspirations and all manner of things that young people in love speak of, and although they were both exhausted, neither was willing to call an end to this last chance to be together. When she finally did break down and openly cry about how far away he'd be, Peyton reminded her that they could write to each other and it was a lifeline they both latched onto and clutched to their hearts. It may take weeks to get messages back and forth, but at least they would be able to try to contact one another when they were apart.

'Twas deep in the night before Peyton finally brought up leaving. 'Twas even later still when he sighed and helped her up from the bench in the near darkness before the last coals of the fire. On rising, he pulled her into a close, gentle hug. This was it and they both knew it. There would be a final goodbye at dawn when he and Mordecai rode away, but tonight was their last time of any import.

The hug lasted and lasted and they held on tighter until at length, he gave a low sound that was almost a groan and Chantaya looked up into his tired face and gave him an exhausted, sad smile. Without hesitation, she stood on tip toe and gently kissed him, wiped at the single tear that overflowed her eyes and then reached to kiss him again. This time, as she did, he gathered her to him almost too tightly and kissed her with all the emotion they'd been trying to channel during the whole of this evening. 'Twas a kiss of friendship and devotion and need, and even of fear and desperation and heartache. All of it concentrated in this first true kiss of passion and when he finally pulled away with a soft sigh, neither of them wanted it to end yet.

Another single tear escaped her eyes and he closed his own eyes and ran a hand raggedly through his hair and then took her hand and led her to the cottage door. There, she stood before him with her head bowed and wondered if it would be any easier if he just didn't leave until that last minute at first light, or even if this should be their final goodbye. She didn't think she could actually do this, now that it was right down to it.

He gently lifted her chin with a calloused hand and looked at her as if he was trying to memorize every small detail of her face and then smiled a hint of a smile, kissed her temple just where a tendril of hair caressed it and quietly stepped out the door into the night. She watched him disappear into the dark, looked up at the moon that would indeed rise over both of them, even apart as they'd be and then slowly closed the heavy wooden door, shot the bolt and tried to cry silently as she banked the fire and climbed the loft ladder to bed. She hadn't realized just what this separation was going to feel like. In truth, she may have tried to change his mind if she had. Dropping to her knees, she began to pray through her tears. God was going to have to help her get through this. That was the only way.

§§§§

Appearing through the heavy mist of morning on the charger that breathed plumes of steam out with every breath, Peyton looked like a warrior. Mordecai rode beside him on Bartok and both horses seemed to sense the import of this day and pranced along, heads held high and tails flowing out behind them as they materialized out of the blackness of the forest. Chantaya had been sitting on the porch step, waiting, struggling not to let the emotions of this morning overwhelm her and as the two soldiers approached, she prayed one more time to be able to tell him goodbye without dissolving into tears. He needed this from her. He deserved this from her. Always, she had been able to lean on him. This morning, she would be strong enough that he could lean on her for once.

He pulled up in front of her and dismounted, tossing Mordecai his reins and Isabella opened the door at the sounds of the approaching riders to come out onto the small porch as well. Chantaya stood and Isabella put her arm round Chantaya's waist and gave her a squeeze as Peyton came forward. He leaned to give Isabella a short hug first, and then moved to Chantaya. For a long moment, he simply looked into her eyes and then seemed to swallow her up in his arms.

She focused on how good it felt and storing that away in her memory and not on the fact that he was riding away from her for who knew how long.

She didn't cry, although tears blurred her vision, and she was able to smile up at him when, at length, he finally let her go enough to look back down at her. He tried to smile as well and it helped when he reached and pulled at a rebellious tendril curl that hung at her the side of her face. It sprung back when he released it and Chantaya shook her head and rolled her tear bright eyes. He chuckled and leaned to kiss her temple and said, "I love you, Chani. Goodbye."

To Isabella, he said, "Pray don't let her do anything that might end her life before I return to watch over her again, will you? For I would miss her so."

Isabella smiled through her own tears and answered, "I will do my best, Sir Peyton Wolfgar. And take care for yourself. God bless you son."

He climbed back on his horse. The two men turned to go and Chantaya felt she would explode from the pressure of holding her tears back until just before they entered the woods again, Peyton turned back and gave her one long, last look. When he was finally gone, she let out a deep, sad breath as she turned into her mother's embrace and let the tears come as she whispered, "God bless and keep you, Sir Peyton."

Chapter 7

For a time, Peyton didn't have a chance to miss Chantaya. After the first afternoon of entering the knight encampment, he was nearly overwhelmed with learning both new protocols and new names and faces. He met the king himself the very first day and was quite surprised when the monarch literally wrapped his arms round Sir Mordecai after first accepting his humble bow before him. The fact that King Dougal loved and respected Sir Mordecai couldn't have been more apparent.

The king had then turned back to Peyton who bowed himself as Mordecai had instructed. The king gripped Peyton's hand on standing and looked him in the eye as he said, "I have heard good things about you, young Peyton Wolfgar. Sir Mordecai has great faith in you, and I absolutely trust his judgment. Thank you for your willingness to serve. 'Tis need this kingdom has for honorable men who are willing to defend our freedoms. Welcome to Valais and I look forward to watching you come of age with us. God bless you son."

Peyton only nodded, unsure of what one said to the king and astounded to be so welcomed by one so powerful.

Somehow, he'd expected the king to be more haughty and less personable to a mere peasant boy.

Meeting the king was actually less intimidating than meeting the other knights and squires. Some of them welcomed him with open friendship, but others showed a reserve that ranged from mild coolness toward him to almost hostility, even though all were respectful of Mordecai. It wasn't hard to understand. Some of these young men had been working their way up to where Peyton was for most of their lives and none of them had any idea of the amount of time he had put in under Mordecai's tutelage before coming here. To some of them, he was an interloper who hadn't paid his dues.

He and Mordecai met each other's eyes after a particularly cool introduction and Peyton knew that Mordecai wanted him to simply prove his worthiness and value to them with his actions; something Peyton had known would be necessary long before arriving here in the first place. And true to his nature, Peyton simply stepped into his new role of squire with the same quiet confidence and work ethic he employed in every other aspect of his life. It wasn't in him to shirk or hesitate. It never had been. It never would be.

Meeting Sir Kendall Bosken was actually more of an event for Peyton than even meeting the king had been. Peyton hadn't realized he would be meeting the king when his entourage had shown up in the knight encampment the afternoon of their arrival, but he had been looking forward to meeting Sir Kendall from the moment Mordecai had first spoken of him upon his return from Valais. Sir Kendall was tall and almost slender under his tunic with salt and pepper graying hair and calm blue gray eyes that quietly appraised

Peyton before crinkling at their outer edges as he smiled at him.

He extended a hand and said, "Ah, Peyton Wolfgar. 'Tis good to meet you. Especially as Mordecai assures me he's already knocked some of the rough edges off of you. It'll be pleasing to be able to finish the job instead of starting with a green youngster for a time. The older I get, the more I appreciate tranquility in my life. These truly young bloods have a lack of that at times. Welcome to Valais."

Again, Peyton answered minimally, "Thank you, sir. I am honored to be here. I hope indeed that I'm not wholly rough."

Sir Kendall had simply laughed quietly as he joyfully embraced Mordecai, the man who had trained him in his own youth and answered, "If you have been round Sir Mordecai for long at all, I am sure you can't be too rough. Sir Mordecai is the best of the best. You are unduly blessed to be in association with him, as was I at your age. There is none finer to have at your back or your side." To Mordecai he said, "Are you well, old man? You yet look fit to take us all. Pray tell me you intend to join us again in battle if need be. At the very least, say you'll resume membership in the Great Council. Your judgment is sorely missed there since your leaving."

Mordecai only shook his head and chuckled. "I am an old man, Sir Kendall. My hands are gnarled and my mind addled. 'Tis time for others to keep the reins."

They quit the embrace, but Kendall kept an arm about the older man. "You are no more addled than the youngest of us. If only the others all had your judgment and vision, man. This kingdom would be in better shape. There are those now who would seek for power instead of for justice."

Mordecai nodded. "'Tis why I have brought you Peyton, Sir Kendall. More like him would put things back to rights. He is wise beyond his years and will indeed be at your back. You will thank me before this kingdom is settled once again. Just get him settled into this life with an urgency. There is trouble brewing. I can feel it in my old bones."

They went on to speak of what the kingdom of Monciere was in need of and Peyton listened well to their talk of strategy and political strength. He had no doubts he could hold his own on a battlefield, in spite of his youth. 'Twas the wisdom of handling people and powers he needed to work on. That and figuring out how things worked here in the city and the knight encampment and near the castle. Those were issues he had no knowledge of.

In some things, being ignorant of the knight's ways was a huge hurdle, but in some, it was fortuitous. Mordecai left him on the morning of the fourth day, and on that same day, he was competing at the joust with other squires in training, when he was pitted against another called Laird on a magnificent dappled gray charger. As Peyton rode out to take his place in the arena, he noted there was a strange quiet to the others and for just a moment, he wondered about it, but soon had to focus on the joust before him and his horse so excited for the competition it was half rearing in nervous anticipation.

As the flag was dropped, he spurred his horse forward and blocked from his mind all but the opponent as he hit this Laird's lance and shattered it. He had been trying to unseat the other young man and was slightly disappointed and then had to wonder why the others who were watching weren't cheering for one or the other competitors as they usually did.

The horses circled around and Laird stopped to get another lance. Peyton sat his mount at the far end of the arena and waited again for the flag to drop. As it descended, he leaped his mount forward, and this time was gratified to find he successfully unhorsed Laird who tumbled off the back of the great charger and landed unceremoniously on his backside in the arena dirt. Peyton nodded to himself in satisfaction and then galloped around to catch Laird's loose horse. That was more like it. Laird had been the only other squire Peyton hadn't unseated in the first attempt. The second round wasn't as satisfactory, but at least he'd been unhorsed.

As Peyton led the other horse back to its rider, he was surprised to be confronted by he who handled the flag that started the competition. As Peyton went to ride past him, the man strode into the arena and Peyton pulled up, wondering why this man who had seemed even tempered these last days, was now scowling at Peyton's approach. He glared up at Peyton and all but hissed, "'Tis the prince, you idiot! Hast thou no sense of honor? Let him win, thou fool!"

The flag bearer stalked back to his platform and Peyton furrowed his brow in trying to figure out just what the man had meant and what he was to do now. The prince. Why had no one warned him he was going against the prince? He should have realized it. Laird wasn't that common a name. But, was it not honorable to truly compete? To Peyton, that was exactly backwards. Falsely handicapping himself was what seemed less than honorable. Had he been the prince, he'd have been offended to be considered ineffective without handicapping the others. Yet, apparently, that wasn't the case here.

Peyton turned again to go back up the arena to take the gray horse to the unseated prince. As he approached, he pushed his helmet shield up and Prince Laird did the same. Peyton eyed him for a moment, trying to read his temperament, but upon being still unsure, he said, "Forgive me, Your Highness. I knew not you were the prince. The flag bearer has just now called me a fool for not knowing and letting you win. Forgive me if I've broken protocol. I'm new here and know not all the rules."

The prince only grinned and shook his head. "If 'tis the rule, it shouldn't be. It's thoroughly deflating. Is not the goal to learn to be the best for battle? As one training for victory, I prefer honest competition. And for once, it was refreshing to have someone truly try their best. You're the first ever to not let me win. I feel fair flattered."

He mounted his horse and then reached across to shake Peyton's hand as Peyton grinned back and asked, "Well, Your Highness, you were the only one I couldn't unseat the first try. Tell me, does your backside feel flattered as well, then? And what does a newcomer do in the third attempt? Now that I realize who you are and also what you prefer."

The prince chuckled. "Who do you fear more? The prince or the flag bearer?"

Still grinning, Peyton said, "Even a new comer knows my answer should be you, but in truth, he appears far more irritable."

The prince shook his head. "Fear the prince. I'll handle the flag bearer."

Peyton nodded. "As you wish, Sire. Have you enough padding for your backside?"

The prince laughed right out. "Have you enough for yours? And is your helmet large enough to fit that ego inside?"

Peyton snapped his shield down and spoke muffled, "It seems to fit just fine. Good luck, Your Highness." The prince only laughed again as he snapped his own shield down and turned to gallop up the field.

Even after their conversation, Peyton wondered what he was to do, but then decided that if he were prince, he'd respect true effort. With that thought in mind, he waited for the flag to drop and then charged up the field and knocked the prince smartly off the back of his horse again and then went to collect the loose gray charger. Bringing the horse back around, he wished for the wisdom of Mordecai for a moment as the flag bearer stomped out onto the field. Peyton respectfully walked the horses over to him and humbly bowed his head as the man fair gave him a tongue lashing and then Peyton continued on to where the prince stood in the dirt of the arena.

Again, Peyton pushed up his helmet shield as he approached and the prince did the same, grinned and then dramatically rubbed where he'd landed and began to limp to accept the horse. Peyton laughed at him and then said, "I thought you said you'd handle the flag bearer."

"Yes. But that 'twas before you doubled up your striking force. In truth, I didn't have near enough padding for that blasting."

Peyton grinned. "Pray, forgive me. Next time, I'll let you win."

"Now you're adding insult to bruising. What did he say to you?"

"Only that I'm no longer to be a soldier, but a potato peeler for the rest of my days on earth."

The prince chuckled, shook his head and groaned as he climbed back onto his charger. "Don't worry. I'll see to it you stay on. We definitely need that kind of skill in battle. Who are you and where did you come from?"

Peyton bowed as well as he could from on his own horse. "Peyton Wolfgar, at your service Your Highness."

"And where did you come from young Wolfgar? I've not seen you and limped to tell of it before."

"Of Navarre. I came to train with Sir Kendall at the request of Sir Mordecai."

Nodding, the prince said thoughtfully, "You are he then. The one Sir Mordecai told us about. He said you were good. He was right. Painfully so."

"My deepest apologies, Sire."

"No. Even bruised, I still prefer an honest contest. You're from Lord Rosskeene's lands then? Have you a moment that we might speak?"

"Of course, Your Highness."

"Good. Come then my valiant friend. Let us talk where your flag bearer may see us. Maybe then he'll ease your peeling sentence to leave you at least a few good years to fight for the king."

The two rode out of the arena side by side as Peyton said, "I pray it is so, Sire."

The prince laughed again. "I'm certain you do. But only because you haven't seen the kitchen maids yet. There's a sassy red head there who makes even a prince wish to spend time peeling potatoes. Do you prefer red heads, Peyton?"

"In truth, no Sire. Forgive me."

"Blondes then?"

"I'm sorry to disappoint, Prince Laird, but no, even with all manner of blondes, I will still dislike potato peeling."

"I see. Is it brunettes then? Would that make you want to keep to the kitchen?"

"Only if it was a certain one, Your Highness. Otherwise, I'd much prefer to be here, knocking the royalty from the backs of their steeds. Readying to defend them in battle."

The prince chuckled again and asked, "The brunettes or the royalty?"

"Both Sire. I stand at the ready."

"Yes, I can see that. Has Kendall said how long before he'll ask to have you knighted?"

"I know not."

Rubbing his thigh, the prince pulled his horse up a distance away from the others present and said drily, "I can't imagine 'twill be long if you can do all manner of things the way you joust. Tell me, Wolfgar, is the younger Lord Rosskeene as belligerent as he seems to be?"

"In truth, Sire. I haven't been round him much, but if rumor is to be believed, he is, indeed, quite quarrelsome and cold hearted. Many from the village of Navarre fear that now that his father has turned all his holdings over to his care, they are doomed to abject poverty from steadily rising taxes. They say he will harass them both monetarily and physically into misery. They are often fleeing to others' lands if they can."

The prince was no longer smiling and said, "Yes, we understand that is so. I simply wondered if 'tis as bad as they say. The younger Lord hasn't a notion that he would be far better off financially were he to help his tenants to become more productive and give them hope of betterment, rather than squelching their hope, in effect squelching their willingness to try. May I ask you a favor, Wolfgar?"

"Anything, Your Highness."

"Will you discreetly come to me with any news of Rosskeene from home? The king is concerned about what is going on with young Lord Rosskeene. His father has been a good steward, but he will not live forever. The people there have always been good, hard working, law abiding citizens and Rosskeene's lands are nearly the largest holdings in the whole kingdom of Monciere. 'Twould be a pity to let a whole region dwindle. Don't you agree?" Peyton nodded and unexpectedly, the prince asked, "Can you be trusted, Wolfgar?"

Peyton turned to look him, then pulled his helmet from his head and met the prince's eyes steadily and said simply, "Yes."

The prince looked back at him just as steadily for a moment and then nodded. "Good. My father has need of those who can be trusted. 'Twas good to meet you, Peyton Wolfgar. Though certain parts of my person may not agree with that statement. Keep training. Perhaps soon 'twill be Sir Peyton that I'm calling you. Good day."

§§§§

Peyton still had to peel potatoes to appease the flag bearer, but that was probably a good thing because some of the other knights and squires had begun to dislike him because he was consistently besting them at the various activities they engaged in. The kitchen punishment, and the fact that Peyton did it so humbly, seemed to ease some of that and Peyton settled into his new life with new friends relatively quickly.

Sir Kendall was thrilled with him and let him know he was and, in truth, sometimes they worked more on the logistics of how to travel and camp and work together with a body of soldiers more than they studied the skills of war. The skills of battle, like sword fighting and archery and even wrestling, Peyton seemed to have mastered as well as any of the knights. 'Twas learning to confer and negotiate and fighting together that Peyton didn't have enough experience in.

He'd been in Valais for well over a fortnight when he and some of the other young men left the knight encampment and went into the township to make purchases. There, on the street, they met with an entourage of soldiers accompanying a fine carriage drawn by four glistening white horses. The squires turned aside to get out of the way as the carriage slowly passed them by and Peyton saw a lovely dark haired young woman through the carriage window. She was watching the squires and soldiers and townspeople and her eyes met Peyton's and held as she passed.

His friend Matthew Ansel, squire to Sir Garrett nudged Peyton with an elbow and grinned at him as he nodded toward the carriage that pulled to a stop at a confectioners just ahead. The young woman was handed out of the carriage and walked inside the shop as Matthew said, "Princess Clarissa. She was looking at you. New meat. She's never seen you before."

Peyton shrugged, uncomfortable with even this slight amount of discussion of a young woman he was making such sacrifices to defend. He shook his head and said, "I'm sure she was simply wondering who the comical looking new squire is."

Matthew chuckled. "You? Comical? 'Tis not what I heard the kitchen maids have said about you. 'Tis said you've fair started a riot in the kitchen with your potato peeling. The maids are all fighting over who gets to work near you."

Rolling his eyes with a grin, Peyton said, "It would seem not. The head cook has actually decided I'm not to peel potatoes anymore. Said I've done a proper penance for unseating the prince."

"Nay, 'twasn't because it was enough penance. Surely not. They'll find a new way to punish you, I'm certain. 'Twas simply a matter of not being able to get the young maids to settle in to their tasks. What with the delicious looking new squire mucking up the routine. Cook said the entire kitchen has lost its focus."

"Delicious?" Peyton chuckled. "And how is it, Matthew, that you have an inside understanding of what the kitchen maids think? Could it be that you have had a similar sentence of potato peeling?"

"Ay." Matthew grinned a knowing grin. "Well, I wasn't so foolish as to unhorse the prince, of course, but I did have my own choring to see to. I, however, took much greater advantage of the fact. I didn't ignore the maids as you appear to. Especially that shapely red one, Meg."

Peyton narrowed his eyes as if in confusion as he looked back to his friend. "I don't seem to remember a shapely red Meg."

Matthew shook his head and laughed. "You, my friend, are a liar! 'Tis surprised that I am. I thought you'd go to your grave rather than tell an untruth."

"Ah, better to twist the truth than taint the reputation of a fair maid."

"Admitting she has the shape of a goddess isn't exactly tainting her reputation, Wolfgar. And your reputation precedes you. 'Tis already known fair cross the kingdom that Peyton Wolfgar isn't likely to be taken under the spell of any of the kitchen maids."

"Are you saying I've already a reputation for staying clear of inane dalliances?"

"Indeed."

"That is a good thing, is it not?"

Matthew smiled again. "That all depends on whether you are a love struck kitchen maid, I suppose. You may be pure responsible for several of them pining to their deaths."

Peyton simply shook his head and chuckled again. "Surely not. You'll have to assure them I was only able to ignore them to see that the meals were produced in a timely manner. Tell them it took all of my self control."

"Lying again. And poorly at that."

"I'm that transparent?"

Matthew grinned again. "Have you a girl back home then?" Peyton nodded and Matthew went on, "I do too, but that doesn't stop me from seeing to it that the maids aren't crushed by my ignoring them."

Peyton shrugged once more. "You'll have to comfort all the maids of yourself then friend. I'm fair too busy trying to learn how to be a squire."

"Three lies all of an afternoon, Wolfgar. You're dominating the whole of us without breaking a sweat and it's well you know it, but your humility is endearing. Even to Prince Laird, although why he's not angry with you is a mystery."

"He didn't appear the type who lets anger spoil his fun much."

"No, indeed he is not. And neither is Princess Clarissa, which is a good thing. At least she won't have you beheaded when you don't indulge her in what you term inane dalliances."

This time Peyton grimaced. "With the princess? What are you thinking? Surely you shouldn't even speak such a thing. The dalliance should be what calls for beheading, not the lack of it."

"Yes, but I saw how she just looked at you. King Dougal has done admirably with his children, but she is still a spoiled sixteen year old girl."

Peyton grimaced. "Now you're frightening me. Certainly a princess has better taste than an unsightly peasant from Navarre."

Giving a low chuckle, Matthew shook his head. "Four untruths. Nay five. You've utterly destroyed my hero worship in mere one conversation. Nothing frightens you, Wolfgar. And unsightly was not the word the maids were bandying about. Delicious was much the more accurate. Further, you're no longer a peasant. Must I remind you? But don't worry, you'll earn every privilege, once we go to battle."

Just then, the princess emerged from the candy shop and there was no mistaking her study of Peyton as she was handed back into her carriage. Peyton gave a miniscule shake of his head and said, "'Tis not battle I'm worried about." Matthew gave him a sympathetic grin as Peyton added, "It's figuring out all the other aspects of this life that has me concerned."

That night as Peyton lay awake in his bunk, staring up at the wooden roof of the soldier garrison he was housed in, he thought back on the conversations of his day. Talk of brunettes had left him sore lonely for Chantaya. That loneliness was easily the hardest part of becoming a soldier thus far. The work and even learning social protocols was nothing to learning to live without seeing her pretty face and hearing her precious laughter every day of his life. It was not even three weeks he'd been away from her, yet, it felt like a year.

He'd been writing a letter that was more like a diary of his life. Every evening, before retiring, he'd written some of the things he'd have spoken to her were she close enough to speak to, as she always had been before. To be able to write to her was a relief in some small way. Still, he would have loved to tell her in person of Sir Kendall's revelation today that he was to be knighted within another fortnight. From what he'd overheard, 'twas clearly a record for advancement in the kingdom.

While it was a fantastic honor, just the fact that he couldn't share it with Chantaya dampened the spirit of celebration that Matthew and some of the others here in the garrison were full enjoying.

Peyton wished Sir Kendall had been able to tell him what their future plans for him entailed. Maybe knowing where he would be and for how long would help to stifle this near suffocating homesickness. Only it wasn't home he was missing. Just Chantaya.

He dreamed of her that night. Over and over he would emerge to a half wakeful state filled with restless memories of her. How she smiled when he teased her and how she smelled as he had held her close. The way her slender form fit perfectly against him as he hugged her, and even how she made him laugh at times when she'd put her hands on her hips in indignation. She was the perfect blend of soft, sweet, tender femininity and intrepid strength.

It empowered him, that mix of softness and strength. Sometimes he had to protect her, and sometimes her competence and yet her confidence in him had a way of building him without her even realizing it. She was the strongest woman he knew, though often she still looked to him for guidance and support. It made him feel invincible and that between the two of them, they could succeed at anything. Her faith in him made him so much more confident than he would have been, but just now, the distance between them also made him miss her desperately.

That afternoon, just before supper, Sir Kendall spoke of having to meet with the king and the King's First Guard. As Sir Kendall took his leave, Peyton glanced up at the gathering dusk and made an almost instantaneous decision. He wasn't required until after breakfasting in the morning. He had nearly thirteen hours until then. Almost eight of it would be taken up in traveling, and he wouldn't get much rest, but that was nothing to him if he'd have a chance to see Chantaya. He was going home!

In the encampment kitchen, he would have felt guilty about one of the maids being overjoyed to be helping him put together a packet of bread and meat and apples, except that he was too focused on leaving to pure notice her. His charger had spent part of the day practicing jousting, but he was still energetic enough that Peyton let him gallop for several miles to take the vinegar out of him before settling him into a long, distancing eating trot on the road to Navarre as darkness fell hard. Chantaya would be surprised, but she would probably be as glad to see him as he was to see her. At least he hoped so.

Chapter 8

Pebbles hitting the shutters of the window in her loft deep in the night startled Chantaya awake. For a moment, she wondered what she was hearing and then for a split second she felt fear that turned into joy when another pebble hit and she realized what that little rock meant. Peyton! It had to be Peyton!

She pulled the covers back in one bold sweep and rushed to the window, shoved up the sash, throwing wide the shutters. He was there in the yard, just about to toss another pebble. Unable to contain herself, she squealed, "Peyton!" He put a finger to his lips and shushed her, but she ignored him as she gathered the hem of her nightgown. "Peyton!"

She sat down on the sill and he started to whisper, "Chani, No! Chani… Chani!" This last wasn't whispered, but still, she swung her legs over and pushed off the sill as he lunged to catch her. He tried, but her momentum took them both down and they landed on the damp ground in a veritable tangle.

Their fall didn't even begin to dampen her excitement and she brushed her hair out of her eyes, leaned up and squealed again as she literally lay on him and threw her arms around his neck. "Oh, Peyton. I've missed you!"

He chuckled as he wrapped his own arms around her and said dryly, "I gathered that. I've missed you too, Chani." For a moment, he simply held her tightly and she seemed to want to melt right into him, but then he gently but firmly put his hands at her waist, lifted her off of him and set her aside as he sat up. He stood and then offered her a hand as he said, "The idea behind the pebbles was to let your mother sleep, you little lunatic."

As he pulled her up to stand beside him, she moved right into his arms as she replied, "I'm sure she's yet asleep. How are you? Tell me all of it! I'm pure dying to hear of it!"

He chuckled again and shook his head as he said, "Even if she slept through your squealing my name and jumping out your window, she still must wake to open the door and let you back in. You'll chill near to death. You can't stand out here barefooted, wearing but a nightgown to speak to me. "

"Of course I can! I'll be perfectly all right if you hold me. Your body will keep me warm. And you can boost me back up." She hugged him tighter still. "Oh, I'm so happy to see you! I've missed you!"

He hugged her back for a long, sweet moment, but then he said hesitantly, "Uhm, Chani. Keeping your body warm with mine, with you only in that thin nightgown . . . I, uh . . . I've missed you, too, girl, but . . . Chani, I'm only human. You're too tempting. Come on." He took her hand and began to lead her around to her door.

Hanging back, Chantaya asked, "Pray, what do you mean, Peyton? Don't let's wake her. Tell me everything you've been doing. These last weeks."

"I mean just as I said, Chani. You're far too tempting. Go in and in the least put on a robe. You're freezing, at any rate. It's cold out here. These last weeks I've been missing you. Ridiculously so. Enough that warming you by body heat is pure foolish. Come."

He turned to go up onto the porch with his arm around her, but she paused and looked up at him in confusion. He met her eyes and then glanced down the length of her nightgown before looking back into her eyes. She saw something there she'd never seen before and it made her heart rate jump as he pulled her back into his arms. She watched the molten glow that sparkled at the back of his eyes in wonder as he slowly lowered his head to kiss her the way she'd dreamed of being kissed these past days and weeks. Oh, how she had missed him!

The door opening behind them didn't truly register, but her mother's loud clearing of her throat to get their attention finally did. Peyton raised his head with a low sigh as Isabella asked sleepily, "What under heaven is going on out here, you two?"

Chantaya patted his cheek, took a deep breath and turned from his arms to the door with a sigh of her own. "Oh, this old frump is insisting I have to come inside and put on something more . . . more . . . " She turned back to Peyton. "More what, Peyton?" He only shook his head with the barest hint of a smile. Facing her mother again, Chantaya went on. "He says that I'm too tempting and insists I change."

Isabella raised her eyebrows and pulled her own wrapper tighter against the cold and said drily, "I should think so. Good gracious. How did you even get out here? Dare I ask?"

Chantaya shook her head. "No. You daren't. You don't want to know, truly. And you needn't look so scandalized. I fully intend to marry Peyton when I grow up."

At that, Isabella folded both arms over her chest and said firmly, "What you intend to do in the future has absolutely no bearing on behaving yourself tonight, Chantaya. Until you are actually married, you still need to dress and act more seemly than this. You are well aware of that." Isabella then turned to Peyton. "As are you, Peyton."

Peyton nodded silently and Chantaya spoke again, "Don't be wrought with him, Mother. I was the one to blame. He truly was trying to make me behave properly. This was my doing."

Isabella smiled tiredly and said, "He didn't appear unduly undone about anything when I opened that door, young lady. Welcome home, by the way, Peyton." She stepped across to hug him and then turned to the door. "We've indeed missed you, son. Do come inside before she contracts some dreaded ailment from the cold in such a state of undress."

§§§§

Peyton took the mild reprimanding from Isabella with complete humility, knowing he deserved it and more and that she would still love him as dearly as ever she had. He had come to know that if ever there was a woman of character, Isabella was it and he was grateful. It was ever she had raised Chantaya to be the same and that character strength was an incredible gift. Still, there was now no doubt of his intentions toward Chantaya, as far as Isabella was concerned. The way he felt about Chantaya had been glaringly obvious as he'd kissed her there before realizing Isabella was watching.

Maybe that was a good thing. 'Twould be that Isabella would do what fell within her power to help the two of them make it to happily ever after. He was sure of that, for he'd ever had Isabella's admiration since that first night he'd rescued Chantaya.

Isabella went back into the other room, presumably to return to sleep, and Chantaya climbed her ladder into the loft to don something more appropriate. Peyton stood there inside the door, stretching the tired muscles of his back and grinning once again at the memory of Chantaya coming flying down out of that small window. What a lunatic she was! There had definitely been no question about whether she was excited to see him. That was certain.

Their reunion hadn't been quite what he'd planned, but then how could he ever have planned the feelings holding her in her thin nightgown had evoked? And the scent of her that he'd remembered night and day for these weeks. He flushed again, just thinking about how that scent and the softness of her body had felt as she'd knocked him to the ground and then snuggled up to him. Never had he felt such a warmth and depth of emotion. It had been shocking to recognize the longing that rushed through him. 'Twas almost disconcerting except that it felt so right and so warm and so deeply compelling.

Hearing a sound, he looked to the loft ladder and watched Chantaya as she descended, now fully dressed except for shoes over the stockings she wore on her feet. Her hair hung freely down her back in all of its rebellious, curling glory and his breath caught as she lightly hopped the last foot or so and turned to all but run to him. She was more beautiful even than he remembered.

She swept toward him so enthusiastically she literally hit into him and he laughed as he picked her up to swing her around in his arms before setting her back down and burying his face into the sweetness of her wild curls and the warmth of her neck. She was definitely still his intrepid Chani.

Again, they pulled the bench from near the door to the fire. They built up the fire's warmth and talked the hours away about all that had occurred in both her life and his. They tried to catch up on all that had happened as well as catch up to the emotions that had grown only stronger during their separation. The fact of their commitment to each other was both glorious and frustrating as they spoke of hopes for the future, but yet had no way of knowing what that future held between this night of sweet reunion and someday. The strength of their friendship was the saving grace that bridged that span and gave them enough hope to face separating again.

They put it off, both consciously avoiding the subject of his leaving until, finally, Chantaya sighed and stood, voicing her concern over his lack of rest. He shrugged, but she shook her head and drew him with her to their small kitchen and fed him leftover soup before again taking his hand and leading him to her door. He sensed her inner struggle as she smiled and bade him go, while at the same moment, her eyes were awash in tears and she clutched him like she was drowning. That was so like her to try to smooth his way, in spite of her sadness at his departure.

Placing both hands on her shoulders, he pulled her to him and kissed the soft spot on her temple. The tears trickled over her eyes and she let out a small sob and kept trying to smile as she scrubbed at the tears, looked back up at him and said, "Go, my friend. God will continue to watch over you,

Peyton. He will bring you back to me. I know he will. Enjoy this adventure. Go learn to defend the crown. Then come back to me."

This last was all but a whisper through her tears. Peyton wrapped his arms around her and held on, drawing strength for the other half of his all night ride through the woods that held far more questionable characters than they should have. At length, she pushed him away, stepped back and said briskly, "Go, Peyton. You must leave, or you'll not make it back and Sir Kendall will not know how truly trustworthy you are."

He searched her eyes for a long moment, pulled the letter he'd written her from his pocket and gave it to her, drew her close again, kissed her once, almost desperately, then quickly turned and stepped out the door before giving in to the temptation to stay.

§§§§

Nothing could make Peyton regret his trip home to see Chantaya, but being asked to attend a gathering in the castle courtyard the next evening to demonstrate their latest training made him wish dearly that he'd gotten a little sleep. 'Twas truly difficult to appear properly respectful to the king when he struggled to keep from yawning, and even more difficult to appear interested as Princess Clarissa wended her way down a line of squires to commend them. As she approached, he stood ever straighter, willed himself to be attentive and literally prayed not to yawn in her presence. He'd already gotten reprimanded for insulting the prince, the last thing he wanted to do, was offend the princess.

Indeed, Princess Clarissa appeared far from offended as she smiled up at him and even leaned in a bit as she fairly gushed her praise in the military prowess he'd just demonstrated. He nodded, keeping his face completely stoic and struggling to suppress the yawn that threatened. He noticed the moon rising behind her shoulder and thought back to Chantaya again. That same moon was rising over the village of Navarre as well. He hoped she had been able to sleep in and rest before having to do her days work and that she wasn't as weary in body as he was just then.

When the gathering finally broke up, he said his farewells and headed back to the garrison. He fair collapsed into his bedding even as the others in the garrison were still talking and laughing around him. Turning on his belly, he pulled his pillow over his head and stretched out in exhausted pleasure. It had been a long two days and his body was stiff from the extra hours riding all night, but it had been heaven to see Chantaya. He grinned there under his pillow at the image of her climbing from her window, but then the grin relaxed as he remembered how she had felt in his arms. She had been pure heaven there, and she had looked unbelievably good in that nightgown.

§§§§

Peyton and Sir Kendall got only busier as the time drew closer to when Peyton would be officially knighted. There was much to do in preparation and Peyton was near overwhelmed with all he was to remember. Of an evening, when he finally stabled his charger and headed back to the garrison to obtain a few precious hours of sleep, he would often look up at that evocative moon and wonder how

Chantaya was. Then, in his bed, he would pray for her. The time was fairly racing by because of how busy he was, but yet he missed her unbearably.

§§§§

Chantaya topped the last rise before Mordecai's and knew immediately that something was wrong when she looked down upon his small cottage. He was outside in his horse's pen, which was typically where she found him, but this time, instead of currying the old horse as it stood, Mordecai was kneeling beside the old white horse as it lay on its side in the pen. When Chantaya reached the two of them, she found just what she'd feared. Mordecai's dear old Wallace had finally reached the end of his earthly existence and was unable to stand and didn't appear to be long for this world.

Going straight to Mordecai, she wrapped an arm around his waist and gave him a small squeeze and let the tears come to match those in the eyes of the elderly knight. She didn't know what all these two had been through together, but she knew it was a lot and had formed a bond nigh unbreakable, even by death.

Half the hour later, when Wallace finally breathed his last, Chantaya didn't hesitate to pick up a shovel and help Mordecai begin to dig a hole in which to bury the sweet, old, trusty steed. The old campaigner deserved every bit as much of a burial as any other honored warrior. When it was deep enough, she helped him slide the old horse in and then cover him up again. Together, they prayed and then Mordecai stood by while she fashioned a small cross and buried it at the top of the mound.

When their little service was over, she gave him a sad smile and offered him the covered basket of honey cakes she'd brought. Together they sat on the bench on the porch and looked out over the new grave, eating the sweets. At length, she said quietly, "Peyton is going to be pure sad he wasn't here to assist us."

Mordecai nodded. "Ay, he will."

"He fair loved Wallace." Again, Mordecai nodded, this time without saying anything. The silence stretched out as the two of them again let an occasional tear fall.

At length, Chantaya knew she had to get back to go to the tavern and she stood. Mordecai stood with her and she hugged him round the waist and said, "I love you, Mordecai. I'm sorry you have lost your dear old friend. I must go, but I'll be thinking of you two, and picturing him up in heaven running around like a two year old in a glorious pasture of emerald green, with God sitting on his own porch bench and watching the horses play." Mordecai looked down and gave her a sad smile and she reached to kiss him on the cheek and then turned to head for home. Maybe remembering where Wallace had gone would bring Mordecai some comfort in his cottage all alone tonight.

In her own home that night, she penned a letter to Peyton and told him about the old horse, and then put the letter with the others, wondering when she would be able to get them to Peyton. She missed him like she'd miss the sunshine.

Chapter 9

Chantaya stopped into the market on her way to the tavern with her basket over her arm. When Quigley Larimer's eyes lit up and he heaved himself out of his chair to serve her, for the ten millionth time she missed Peyton. She always missed, Peyton, but especially when one of the local boys began paying her attention. For some reason, even if Tristan was with her, the locals seemed to have a much keener interest in her now that Peyton wasn't always around and 'twas pure tiring. She hated having to courteously slip away from them, and half the time she wasn't even able to conduct her shopping. Tristan stepped into the shop behind her and she look up and met his half hearted grin as he took in the situation, but then she sighed and hurriedly made her purchases.

On the way out of the shop, two of the other local girls came in and inexplicably, their appearance cheered Chantaya. They reminded her of how blessed she was to have Peyton, even if he was away in Valais right now. She, at least, was blessed with a handsome, virile and incredibly competent beloved. These poor other girls . . . What was to become of them?

Later, in the tavern kitchen, Chantaya hummed to herself as she stirred a bowl of dumplings and dropped them into the kettle of simmering soup, then opened the oven to check on the mutton roasting there. Closing the oven, she absently brushed at the tendril of dark hair that had escaped to tickle her cheek and stepped to the back door of the kitchen for a moment of fresh air. The kitchen was stifling tonight.

She cracked the door and peered out hesitantly, still a trifle nervous about coming out here by herself. She thought of Peyton rescuing her that night and glanced up at the moon rising over the hills to the east. 'Twas comforting to know he was somewhere under this same moon tonight. She continued to look up, although her thoughts were far from the pale orb those wisps of cloud blew over and around. What was he doing tonight? Was he safe? Was he happy? It seemed he had matured ages when he'd come home that night.

Mrs. Bealle came into the kitchen and Chantaya stepped back inside and pulled the door closed behind her. She needed to get back to her duties. There would be time enough to think about Peyton once she was safely home and in her little loft bed tonight. That had become her favorite time of day, of late; when she could finally relax and let her weary body rest and her mind go east to Valais and a handsome young squire who defended the crown. She breathed a familiar prayer for his safety and pulled a loaf of crusty bread to the board to slice. That mutton should be just about done by now.

Carrying two plates in each hand, Chantaya took a deep breath, pushed through the kitchen door and approached the table of nobles who had dropped into the tavern. She had learned to ignore the banter of the locals, and didn't typically let even the strangers make her nervous anymore, but there was something about the way one of these noblemen kept staring at her tonight that made her horribly uncomfortable. The moment he'd laid eyes on her he'd looked surprised and she could swear he'd whispered her mother's name.

He was still watching her and the hair on the back of her neck prickled as she set his plate down in front of him. Then a moment later, as she refilled his tankard with ale it was all she could do not to flinch when he reached up to take it from her. He seemed to sense her reaction and it appeared to amuse him, but his smile did anything but calm her.

Going back into the kitchen, she took another deep breath and went back to preparing the next plates, then was incredibly grateful when Mr. Bealle himself offered to deliver the rest of the meals to the patrons that night. They were definitely busy enough for Chantaya to keep occupied just in the kitchen.

Both Tristan and his father showed up to escort her home that night. 'Twas the first time that two of them had come to see her back and even that was disconcerting. Once safely inside the cottage, she shot the heavy bolt on the door and finally, truly felt safe as she visited her mother for a few moments before heading up to her loft to bed. She settled down into her comfortable quilts and stretched out luxuriously, then prayed for Peyton before dropping off to sleep.

They were just headed out the door the next morning with their baskets to go to the woods and harvest herbs when Isabella pulled up so short that Chantaya bumped into her back in the doorway. As Chantaya looked up to see what had happened to make Isabella stop so suddenly, she heard a man's voice say almost silkily, "Hello, Bella."

Her mother's sudden step back and intake of breath made Chantaya feel instinctively protective as she looked over Isabella's shoulder to see who had spoken. It was the nobleman from the night before and his glittering eyes as he watched Isabella's reaction to him made the skin on the back of Chantaya's neck prickle. He fair exuded evil as he stood there on their porch. Without even having to be told, Chantaya understood this man had been the reason they had hidden in the cave from time to time. He was probably the reason they had come here in the first place and ended up having that horrendous cart wreck that had killed her father.

Surprisingly, realizing that her mother was frightened of this man made Chantaya almost switch roles of a sudden and she stepped around her mother and between her and this man and asked, "May I help you with something, m'lord?"

The man was still staring at Isabella and pulled his eyes away to turn to Chantaya with obvious reluctance and then smiled almost sickeningly. "Yes, yes you can actually." He glanced back at Isabella and then went on, "It has come to my attention that the two of you have been living here on my lands for years, it seems, without paying proper rent. I've come to tell your mother she has two days to resolve the rents due or go to debtor's prison. Unless other arrangements can be made, of course."

Chantaya looked from the man to her mother and back and shook her head. "But this land isn't part of your holdings. And a dispute would have to go before the magistrate at any rate. One can't just toss a body into debtor's prison without a hearing."

The man was watching her mother again. He smiled and said in that same, silky, disgusting voice, "Oh, but I'm afraid I can. Can't I Bella?"

Without preamble, Isabella ground out, "What other arrangements, Rosskeene? What is it you want?"

Making a sound of disapproval with his lips, he said, "Such impertinence." His voice lowered even further as he continued, "You know exactly what I want, Isabella. Don't you? I'm afraid I still need that help in the kitchen you refused all those years ago. Good help is so hard to come by still. Either pay, or agree to come and work for me, or it's prison for you, and the girl will be on her own. And you know I have the power to see it done."

Chantaya looked from one to the other and for the first time in her life, she saw hatred in her mother's eyes. Hatred and fear. It made the need to protect her even stronger. Wondering what to do or say, Chantaya was still at a loss when Lord Rosskeene said, "You have but two days, Isabella, before I send someone to get you. And don't try running this time. My men will be watching. I'll be at the tavern in the village both tonight and tomorrow night for supper. Make your decision and let me know. 'Twas good to see you again, Bella. I've been searching for you all these years. I've missed you."

He reached almost lazily to touch Isabella on the face but she jerked away. Lord Rosskeene only chuckled and turned to go back to his horse and said over his shoulder, "Two days, Isabella. Or your daughter is alone." Climbing on his horse, he rode off, but two of the men with him remained behind, standing at the edge of the wood all but leering at the two women. Isabella turned abruptly and went back inside and shot the heavy bolt behind them.

Chantaya still didn't know what to say, but she was even more confused when her mother suddenly went to the wash basin and vomited violently into it. When she was finished, she wiped her mouth almost woodenly and then went to sit at the table, laid her head down upon her folded arms and began to silently cry.

Watching her, Chantaya was horrified. Even though her mother was physically weakened and almost feeble sometimes because of her injuries from the cart wreck, she was never anything but emotionally strong, -all but tough almost, although she was ever gentle and soft spoken. She'd had to be tough to survive being so hurt and raising Chantaya without a husband in her home.

The protective feelings became even stronger and Chantaya went to her mother and gently rubbed her back and said, "Twill be all right, Mother. We'll figure this out. We'll go to the magistrate. Heavens, if that doesn't work, we'll go to the king! He can't get away with this. Not for long anyway. Don't cry. Please don't cry. At the very least, we'll go work in his household together. There's no way you are up to working full time in the kitchen of a manor house and if we're together, we'll be safe enough. Take heart. We'll be fine. The good Lord will watch over us."

Isabella raised her head and looked at Chantaya and then slipped an arm round her waist and hugged her and whispered, "Yes, He will. Forgive me for being weak. We'll be fine." She wiped at her eyes, but Chantaya could see she didn't believe what she was saying and she sat next to her mother and wrapped both arms around her, wondering just what had happened in the past to make her mother so completely discouraged by one short visit from this evil nobleman. Whatever it had been, it had been truly troubling.

Chantaya's first thought was to run to Mordecai's and speak to him of what was about, but with every glance out of the window, she knew they couldn't chance a long walk through the woods safely and there was an anxiousness that made her forego that idea every time it arose. Even when she considered asking Tristan to go speak with Mordecai, she felt it wasn't what she was to do and pushed it aside as well. Maybe 'twas that they weren't to let Lord Rosskeene's men know about Mordecai's living there. She wasn't sure why she was feeling prompted not to speak with him, but she followed the prompting anyway.

In the end, she decided to keep to their typical chores to attempt to comfort her mother, with only an occasional question thrown in to try to find a resolution to this dilemma that her fifteen years of experience couldn't truly grasp. Still, the constant vigilance of the nearby men was thoroughly disconcerting and by the middle of the afternoon, when it was time for Chantaya to go to the tavern to work, they still didn't have a solution.

Tristan had gone to the local magistrate with a letter requesting an inquiry into Lord Rosskeene's overstepping his boundaries, but Tristan had returned only to report that the magistrate couldn't read and had told Isabella to come back in a fortnight for a hearing. The two men were still at the edge of the wood and had indeed set up a camp there and when Tristan and Willem came to take Chantaya to the tavern, they insisted Isabella come and stay with Rose for the duration. The men followed them. Lord Rosskeene's threat to have them guarded hadn't been in vain.

His intention to eat at the tavern was carried through as well and although Mr. Bealle did all the serving in the dining room, when Chantaya went to the back door of the kitchen to discard her dishwater, there was a man outside standing in the dark there too.

Afterward, during the walk from the tavern to the Wolfgar cottage, Willem and Tristan were unusually quiet and when they got to their home, Chantaya wasn't surprised to find that she and her mother were to spend the night there and she was glad. Willem and Tristan were singularly comforting tonight, as were the other neighbors who lived close by.

The family prayer the five of them knelt together to say was the most comforting of all. As they stood afterward to go to their beds, a sweet, warm peace crept into Chantaya's heart that was infinitely calming. Regardless of whatever was to happen here, at least there was no doubt that their Father in Heaven was aware of them and would comfort them and guide them through it. As she settled onto a pallet spread with quilts next to her mother, Chantaya reached for her hand and spoke of the reassuring feelings of peace she was feeling. For the first time since that morning, Isabella seemed to feel that same reassurance.

They spoke long into the night and at length, came to the decision that they would indeed have to go to work for Lord Rosskeene, at least until they could find someone of power to look into the illegalities of his demands. In the meantime, they would do all they could to stay together for safety. If they arrived at Rosskeene Manor and found it wasn't safe enough, then they would do whatever they had to do to flee, even if it meant running in the dark of night again.

In spite of having come to such a drastic solution, the peace remained and mother and daughter were able to go to sleep, knowing it would all work out in some way. In truth, neither one was sure of how, but they were sure that God was over all. And, after the fact, 'twas comforting to know Mordecai was around, but that Lord Rosskeene wasn't aware of it. Mordecai was old, but he was still incredibly competent and even more importantly, he had powerful friends who were honorable.

The next day, Willem took a message to Lord Rosskeene saying they would come until the legalities were settled and then Willem and Tristan helped them pack a minimum of their things into a cart for the trip north to the manor house. As Chantaya carried her small bag out the door for the last time, she paused to look around, questioning if she was ever going to be able to come back to this little house. It was the only home she could remember. She looked up at the sky, wishing for that reassuring moon, and wondering how far Valais was from Lord Rosskeene's manor. Peyton was going to be horrified when he realized what had happened.

The whole trip, Chantaya worried about her mother, who would give her a sad smile and a squeeze, but then wipe at the tears that intermittently slipped from her eyes. 'Twas an exhausting and worry worn journey.

At the manor house, the old cook there seemed to be a reasonable sort and, in fact, kind as she pursed her lips in sympathy when Isabella and Chantaya were brought before her and explained they were to be her new help. She actually remembered Isabella from before and got a look of fair determination on her face and then a small smile as she said, "Well, the master might be pure vexed about it, but I'll not put you to stay in the very house he lives in. He's bad enough, but that son of his is even worse and 'twould be a mistake to put two such beauties as the likes of you right into the stewpot. The masters would torment you and the mistress hate you, I daresay."

She gave them a conspiratorial grin and said, "I can imagine what he's up to, and he won't be happy, but he likes his dinner, he does. It gives us in the kitchen some wiggling room. There's a place for you behind yon stables. It's only a room, and a small one at that, but the head groom, Master Conrad is there throughout the whole long day and night and he's to be trusted, he is. Lonely these last years since losin' his wife, but secure as an old hound. You'll be safer there than wi' the rest of us here, I 'magine."

Pausing, she shook her head. "I fear you still won't be pure safe, but . . . It's the best we can do under the circumstances. I don't mean to frighten ye, but you'd best be knowin'. He's powerful, Lord Rosskeene is. And believes himself fair untouchable. They all do. And, in truth, to a margin they are. 'Tis a pity they couldn't all be such as the old Lord Rosskeene is. He's a decent sort compared to his son and son's family, but he's getting on in his years. Hardly ever leaves his room much now, except to meet with some who he has manage his other lands. Still, those of us what serves 'em will look out for you, we will. We stick together here, the staff does. Like a family. Ye'll simply be more family. Welcome."

She took them to the room near Master Conrad and Chantaya fair breathed a sigh of relief as she met him. He did indeed seem to be able to be trusted and as he was still young enough and nearly as large and strong looking as Peyton, she was encouraged. With the good Lord's help, and with this beefy groom working nearby, perhaps they'd make it through this ugly wrinkle in their lives.

By the end of the first day, the wrinkle felt pure overwhelming. Lord Rosskeene was evil, that much was obvious, but his sixteen year old son, Damian was even more frightening to Chantaya. As her mother had been bringing vegetables from the manor garden and Chantaya had been at a work table in the kitchen, he'd come through looking for a morsel to eat and when he'd seen Chantaya, he thought he'd found it. He had looked at her almost as she imagined an animal would as it looked at its prey. He'd walked clear round her, studying her and Chantaya's heart had begun to pound in fear when he touched her hair where a tendril had come loose from where she'd twisted it up.

Just then, the cook had come in and hefted her rolling pin at him and the young lord had looked sufficiently intimidated that he pulled his hand away and then left the kitchen, but not before turning to look at her one last time with that predatory gleam. That simple incident had fostered a fear in Chantaya's heart that was near overwhelming. To that point, she hadn't realized just how truly vulnerable she could be here at this corrupt lord's manor. She thought back to how Lord Rosskeene's visit to their home had made her mother literally ill and suddenly, this trumped up indenturement felt fraught with peril.

They were in danger here. Real, true, horribly frightening danger. No wonder her mother had reacted so. These men acted like they could do as they pleased with human beings who they considered possessions. It was sickening and probably more so to one who had been so valued through her life. Peyton would have fair destroyed young Rosskeene for looking at her like that had he seen it! She almost began to worry for when Peyton discovered what had happened. He would want to destroy these men and though he was soon to be a knight, it would still be terribly risky for a knight to tangle with a nobleman.

The incident with young Lord Damian Rosskeene was troubling in other ways as well. Though Chantaya was horribly frightened, she was hesitant to say anything to her already exhausted mother that would further trouble her. Her mother was so haggard of this evening that Chantaya vowed not only to protect her from worry, but to try to ease her burdens in any other way she could as well.

To this end, Chantaya took her concerns in prayer to the only other who she knew could help her in this frightening new situation. She prayed long and hard that night for protection and comfort. Then, the next morning, she took it upon herself to seek out Lord Rosskeene. They had to have specificity to this situation, even as fabricated as it was. To allow Lord Rosskeene to simply have an open ended ownership of her and her mother was beyond foolish. Even prior to going before the magistrate, she needed to know exactly what Lord Rosskeene was demanding as repayment for his supposed unpaid rents.

As she sought him out, she worried he would consider her more than presumptuous and become angry, but he seemed to be mildly amused at her audacity to need to know his price. She had been directed to his library where he was waiting to meet with a merchant and when she asked him for the exact amount he was demanding of her mother, he had shaken his head and smiled as if she was a willful child, and said, "So you want my price, do you? Why are you the one to inquire over what your lovely mother owes me?"

'Twas all Chantaya could do to not snap at him over his imperious attitude and disgusting way of speaking of her mother as she replied, "My mother is indeed lovely. Yet she is also the survivor of a horrible cart wreck that left her near dead. She tires quickly and has great pain when she overdoes. She is not in a condition to work long hours in the kitchen and I wish to know what your demands will be of her."

Lord Rosskeene merely waved a hand noncommittally. "She shouldn't have been living on my lands all these years then without paying for the use of my cottage. Yet, if you are willing to work in her stead, I'll try to see to it that your mother is only required on certain occasions when cook is in dire straits. Does that soothe your pretty daughter's conscience?"

Chantaya closed her eyes and counted to three to keep from speaking in a manner unbecoming of a servant. Swallowing hard and struggling not to grit her teeth, she gave a small curtsy and said, "Yes, Sire. Thank you. But for how long?"

"As long as you have been living on my lands without paying rent, of course,"

Chantaya wanted to tear into him, but instead decided to hold her tongue until the magistrate had ruled. There was no point in arguing with this beast of a human.

All the way back through the manor to the kitchen, she worked to remind herself that she was typically quite sunny temperamented and that God would take care of Lord Rosskeene. She needed only to do what she felt God wanted and had to let go of the circumstances beyond her control. At least now, she could report to her mother that she needn't push herself to such exhaustion here.

Surprisingly, the Kincraigs were able to settle into a routine of sorts fairly quickly at Rosskeene Manor, in spite of the fact that for nearly the whole of Chantaya's life they had lived under their own enterprise and they hadn't been under the rule of any nobleman other than the king. It helped that both Chantaya and Isabella were extraordinarily good cooks. They were told that the quality of the food at the manner became markedly more appetizing with their arrival. And just as cook had intimated, excellent food came with wiggling room, which was their salvation when Lord Rosskeene found out they were staying in a room in the stable instead of the main house.

The groom Conrad also helped to make the Kincraigs more comfortable. His soft spoken kindnesses helped immensely, especially when Chantaya left her mother in their room to rest and went to the kitchen on her own with cook there as a sort of buffer. Knowing Conrad would be there to protect her mother and would, in fact, check in on her with ever a sense of gentle concern was hugely comforting to the both of them.

Even when the two of them went into the woods in search of herbs and mushrooms, if possible, he would typically bring one of the young horses he was training and work the animal nearby to them to insure their security. Several times, they saw Lord Rosskeene watching them, but he never approached with Conrad near. In terms of their peace of mind, he became, quite literally, their guardian angel.

Cook had been correct in her estimation that the masters would try to torment them and that the mistress would hate them. It seemed that both of the Kincraigs were constantly on the lookout for the Rosskeene men, and ever vigilante to avoid them. And although they didn't meet Lady Winifred Rosskeene for several days because she had been away visiting, the very moment they met her upon her return, she appeared to fair detest them. She looked both one and then the other up and down with a pure glare on her powdered face. Then she made a most unladylike sound in her throat as she stomped out of the room to demand of her husband at the top of her lungs why he had ever hired new kitchen help without consulting with her first.

Both Isabella and Chantaya had looked askance of cook, but cook had merely grimaced and lowered her voice to say, "Would that she could send you packing and find ye more genteel nobles to work for, but I fear when Lord Rosskeene makes a decision, she can't change it, much as she'd like to, poor lass. But mores the pity, she'll probably stomp round the place for a day or two just to let us all know for sure how pure vexed she is at both him and the two of you." Cook waved a hand. "Try not to let them trouble you. Respectfully, of course. But once their bellies are full of sumptuous fare, they become much more amiable toward us of the kitchen. Food. 'Tis truly the way to the heart, all told."

She walked across the kitchen and pulled at a small transom window over the door into the dining room and then closed another one high in the wall behind the big stove. Turning back to the others, she shrugged and said, "Twill be much quieter with the transoms closed for the next day or so. They do help with the air flow, but truly 'tisn't worth having to listen to her brewing. The transoms are like listening tubes at times, they are. Nothing much private here in this household with them wide open. Closing them will be like a dose of peace here in the kitchen."

That night, securely in bed, Chantaya asked her mother, "Are all noble households such as this, Mother? Somehow, I expected the staff to be more loyal to their lords and lady. 'Tis pure distrust I feel from Cook and the others. And some of the gossip here is quite disturbing. Did you hear the stable boy telling Conrad that Lord Rosskeene seemed to be recruiting his own military? An army of malcontents he called it. Should he be doing that, instead of supporting the king and his forces?"

Isabella yawned before saying, "In truth, I've never known another noble household that instilled such distrust in the staff. But, I've never known another noble who was as irascible and evil as Lord Rosskeene either. Character begets loyalty, daughter. And Rosskeene knows nothing of character. Only those who seek ill gotten gain as he does are in league with him. The staff here are much as we are. Here because of necessity only. Not for the joy of it. These are hard times. They simply labor for the means of life."

After another thoughtful moment, she continued. "Yet, the staff's attitude is a blessing to us. They have protected us these days we've been here. What's more, Rosskeene's plans keep him from bothering us as I dreaded he would. And who, knows? Perhaps it's the Lord's hand that has us imprisoned here. Perhaps, the distrust here and us hearing this talk of military recruitment is part of His plan. Who better to help keep the crown informed of mounting insurrection than a scullery maid who is the secret love of a knight?"

Mention of Peyton made Chantaya desperately homesick of a sudden. How she missed him! He had probably been knighted already and here she was, leagues further away from him than even before. She was lost in thought for a moment and then finally, she heard her mother say sleepily, "I love you, Chantaya. Good night."

Turning on her stomach, Chantaya replied, "I love you too, Mother. Sleep well." Gathering her pillow into her arms, she looked out the small window of their room to see if she could see the moon, but there was only darkness and a sprinkle of stars. To herself, she thought, *And goodnight to you, Sir Peyton, the gallant. Guardian of maidens and champion of virtue. Builder of confidence and encourager of discovery. I love you. I miss you. Sleep well.*

Long into the night, Chantaya thought about Peyton and considered what her mother had said about informing the crown of mounting insurrection. If Lord Rosskeene truly was trying to build up military forces of his own, unaffiliated with those of the king, then he meant to use them against the very knights Peyton had just become a part of. In fact, if there was to be an attempt at overthrowing the crown, Peyton and the other knights would be the first and greatest target.

Just the thought made her both fearful and indignant. How dare a brutal and heartless man of Rosskeene's ilk even consider besting a king as wise and good as Dougal? 'Twas disgusting and frightening and just what an animal like Rosskeene was likely to do.

As she lay there thinking, the moon finally appeared through the small window and she looked back up at its pale glow and somehow felt reassured. Peyton was there, just east somewhere, under this same moon. And he was strong and wise and willing to give even his very life if needed to preserve the astute and kind leadership of King Dougal. In addition, there were many with Peyton, protecting the king and the people. If the citizens like herself aligned themselves with those honorable men, what couldn't be accomplished and protected, with God's help, of course.

She turned back over and closed her eyes. Right would prevail. It would. God would protect those men of character and honor, and the citizens as well. She merely needed to be strong and do whatever small measure she could to support them. It mightn't be much, but she would do what she could.

Jaclyn M. Hawkes

Chapter 10

A drop of blood dripped from inside the cuff of his tunic near his wrist onto the white linen of the table clothe and slowly spread through the fabric, looking like more than the mere drop it had been. He concentrated on keeping his face impassive and discreetly gripped his left forearm to put pressure back on the bandage his new squire Shaun had placed there earlier. It hadn't been that impressive of a cut he'd acquired in the competition earlier. He had no idea why it insisted on continuing to bleed as it had.

He calmly looked to his left to see if the princess had noticed the drop of blood and then slid the base of his pewter goblet over to cover the brilliant red blotch. He'd won the honor of being seated next to the princess for the evening banquet, but now that he was here, he almost wished he hadn't. 'Twas quite disconcerting to have to remember all the protocols, especially when the princess's subtle and sometimes not so subtle innuendos and behavior near made him forget everything but the need to put distance between the two of them.

At that very moment, she put her foot over to touch him under the table and he glanced up at her. She gave him a smile that left little doubt but that she wasn't going to be stopping the seemingly endless attempts to get his attention anytime soon.

It had started that day in the village and had gone from that first lingering look to these much more overt physical encounters that he had absolutely no idea how to counter. What was this girl thinking? He was a knight, not a nobleman, and barely a knight at that! The ceremony had only taken place that very afternoon. If she kept this up, the girl was going to get him beheaded!

He moved his legs to his right, away from the flirtatious princess, let go of his forearm and picked up his fork again, not giving any other outward sign that he'd felt her nudge under the table. This dinner had already lasted for the better part of an hour and they hadn't even brought out the main course yet. He looked down at the poorly seasoned soup that sat before him and wished once again that he could go home to see Chantaya. She made far the better soup and would never have put her foot on him under the table.

Stifling a sigh, he picked up the goblet again in his left hand and then regretted it as another drop of blood stained the table clothe just beside the first.

The princess noticed it this time and looked at him in concern and immediately stood and put a hand on his arm and said, "Sir Peyton! You're bleeding!"

He tried to smile, despite the fact that he wanted to swear and stood as well to be respectful; wishing he'd had a course from Sir Kendall on how to politely thwart a fickle young noble's affections. The princess's pretty brow puckered with a grimace of concern and she moved her hand on his arm to better see the blood that was now seeping through the sleeve of his tunic. Her face paled noticeably at the sight of it and

Peyton began to worry the girl would swoon on him, in addition to being overly flirtatious with him.

Instead of fainting, she looked up at him and said quite imperiously, "This must be attended to at once! Come, Sir Peyton. I will have the physician summoned immediately." Gathering her elegant skirts in her hand, she fairly pushed him ahead of her toward an arched doorway at the side of the great hall to their left and Peyton tried to smile reassuringly at the other guests who were watching him leave with the princess.

She led him along a stone hallway and through a doorway beyond. In a drawing room of some sort she began to unfasten the cuff at his wrist. He glanced around, wishing for some miraculous intervention to help him avoid her attempting one of those inane dalliances he and Matthew had jested about, but alas, there was nothing. She and he were completely alone in some out of the way area of the castle.

With his sleeve unfastened and cuffed up, she began to pull at the bandage that covered his arm, but he stopped her. He didn't need a physician. The wound had already been seen to. It simply needed pressure applied more steadily than he'd been able to as he was preparing for this banquet. She continued to pull at his arm and he said as diplomatically as possible, "It truly is fine, Princess. But a scratch. By tonight it will be forgotten."

She shook her head. "No. It's bleeding terribly. You must sit and relax, Sir Peyton." She indicated a large padded chair. "Sit here and place the arm just so and I'll have a look at it."

He didn't want to sit, yet he didn't want to offend her either and glanced around once again in hopes of some intrusion. She saw his glance and gave him a sultry smile and said, "You needn't worry about someone bothering us. We're quite removed from the others. Only my family comes here and they are all back in the great hall. You may rest assured we won't be interrupted."

That was exactly what he was concerned about. He sat and even elevated his arm, but kept his other hand securely clamped around the wound to both keep pressure and to prevent the princess from removing the bandage. He needed to keep it intact in order to be able to escape as soon as he figured out just how to do that diplomatically.

That plan changed as the princess took his clamped hand in both of hers and began to rub it in a guise that she was trying to make him let go. It worked. He let go of the bandage with alacrity to move his hand clear to the other side of the chair from her. She seemed to think his hesitancy to let her touch him was humorous as she went back to untying the ends of the wrap with a small smile on her face.

For a moment, she picked at the bandage in a silence that made Peyton even more uncomfortable, and then he was horrified to hear her say almost conversationally, "This would be a most opportune moment for you to kiss me. Would it not?"

He quickly looked up into her smiling face and finally decided he needed to handle this situation once and for all, even if it did put him in danger of offending the crown. Shaking his head with an apologetic look, he replied gently, "Highness, I am but a humble soldier. You are princess of the kingdom. One such as I could never even consider such an offense to your position. 'Twould be unthinkable."

She merely tipped her head coyly and continued her tempting, "Ah, but what if you knew I wished it anyway?"

Giving one more slow head shake, he replied calmly, "Princess, I am confident you would never wish to be so intimate with one such as I."

Rolling her eyes, she let go of the bandage she was fiddling with and straightened to look at him, but he only met her gaze evenly. That seemed to frustrate her and she gave the daintiest stomp with her satin slipper and smiled and said, "Sir Peyton, stop being obtuse and kiss me this minute! I demand it! I *am* princess, and I can have whatever I want!"

Still watching her, he simply said, "No, Your Highness. Please forgive me, but I cannot. It's not my place."

She gave a pretty little grimace of surprise. "But I have just given you an order!"

With another apologetic half smile, he said, "Your father trusts me."

"My father will never know!"

He shook his head again. "But I am worthy of your father's trust."

She gave a small sound of outrage and turned to him in full haughty royalty. "You'll do as you've been told, Sir Peyton, or I shall tell my father that you tried to take advantage of me! Would you disobey me at the price of your life?"

Peyton struggled not to roll his own eyes at the incongruity of her accusation as he said in an infinitely gentle voice, "Princess, you don't understand. I would fight to the death in battle to protect you and your virtue. I could certainly do no less here in your own home. Pray forgive me for being disobedient, but I cannot kiss you. 'Twould not be honorable. Tell your father an untruth at the price of my life if you must. I'm sorry."

For a long moment, she stared into his eyes and then turned aside to go back to working over his bandage, as she said almost too quietly to hear, "Drat your honor anyway, Sir Peyton. 'Tis no fun at all."

"No. I suppose not. Pray forgive me."

She fair yanked at the ends of the bandage. "No. I'll not forgive you. You're a beast to me!"

They both looked up at the sudden sound of chuckling to find Prince Laird standing casually against the doorway across the room. He laughed and shook his head and said, "A beast? You call that a beast? You're nothing but a spoiled brat of a princess. You threatened him with his life! That is the lowest, most disreputable thing I've ever heard! And him not even here long enough to know you would never have done it. I think I'm going to tell Father just to see him warm your bloomers for such treachery!"

She tossed her head and turned her back to him and spat, "You wouldn't dare and you know he wouldn't raise a hand to me at any rate. It's rude to spy on people. Your manners are atrocious! And don't you dare speak of my being spanked in front of a visitor!"

"A visitor who you threatened with beheading for a kiss! You ought to be spanked and much worse!"

At this, she turned on her brother. "Well, he obviously preferred death over my sweet berry lips, so pray, leave me alone!"

Peyton had no idea how to deal with the two of them and felt terribly guilty for embarrassing her in front of her brother who bent over laughing and finally said, "Death would definitely be preferable to having to kiss an imperious troll. Sir Peyton was simply demonstrating the proper judgment of a knight."

"Death would also be preferable to having you for a brother! You're pure beastly! Go back to the banquet and leave us be."

Prince Laird laughed again. "I thought you said he was the one being beastly. And it didn't sound to me like he was ever going to break down and kiss you. You might as well give up begging and go back yourself. Perhaps Sir Peyton would prefer to stay here with me and laugh about you."

She glared at Prince Laird, but still appeared to be winding down as she said sadly, "No. He's far too honorable for kissing, or laughing behind one's back either. You'll soon see. He's a complete saint. It's incredibly deflating. I believe I will go back. See to it his wound is properly cared for will you? There truly was a reason I brought him in here."

Peyton felt even guiltier, but her brother didn't seem to as he continued to tease her, saying, "Beyond seduction, you mean?"

She rolled her eyes. "A kiss is hardly seduction. You're making me sound like a trollop. He'll think even less of me. And if I have to go back to that tasteless potage then so do you."

"I didn't leave dragging a victim like you did. No one will think a thing of me slipping out."

"Oh, pray, give it a holiday, Laird."

With that, she turned back toward the door, but Peyton stepped forward to go to a knee in front of her. He was indescribably grateful for Prince Laird's comic relief, but he hadn't truly meant to humiliate the poor, foolish princess. Trying to make some semblance of amends, he said, "Please forgive me my beastliness, Your Highness. In truth, I was trying to tell you that you were far too precious to be so treated—not that I would prefer death to your sweet berry lips. Indeed, I'm pure certain a single kiss from you would be worth dying for. As I am also certain I am unworthy of such an immeasurable honor." He bowed his head as he finished in what he hoped was an indication of respect.

She put a gentle hand onto his head and said surprisingly meekly, "You're sweet, Sir Peyton. You're still a beast, but you're a sweet one. See to your arm and come back and eat your supper, as nondescript as that soup was. I'm sure those paltry bits didn't fill up a man of your stature."

As she swept out the door, she said to Prince Laird, "See to his wound, brother. It truly was bleeding pure over the table out there."

When the two men were alone, Prince Laird began to laugh again and Peyton looked askance of him as he reached to begin rewrapping the wound on his forearm. Unsure of how to treat the young royal in such a circumstance, Peyton was surprised when the prince went right back to the teasing banter when he said, "That was a truly impressive show of ingratiation. I don't believe I've ever seen such a smooth buttering of tender feminine sensibilities. You're either the saint she was speaking of, or a complete rake."

Shaking his head, Peyton said, "I'm no saint. Surely." With a grin, he asked, "Which is worse? A sweet beast or a complete rake?"

"I imagine that would depend on whether there's a disgruntled princess involved. At least you're not to be hanged or beheaded in the morning. Don't worry. Other than being embarrassed for the next twenty two times she sees you, she'll live. In fact, you've probably imbedded yourself permanently into her heart with that sweet bended knee speech. 'Twas too touching. Truly."

Peyton ran a hand through his hair with a sigh. "Would that I had someone to give me direction in all things female." He bent to use his teeth to tie off the bandage ends.

The prince asked, "You had no trolls—I mean sisters, then?"

Peyton had to work not to grin at his description of sisters before he said, "No. Although, there was a neighbor girl so close she seemed one. Especially when she was small."

"Troll or sister?"

At that Peyton did smile. "Sister. Most of the time she managed to be entertaining rather than irritating."

"Did she move away then? When she was no longer small?"

Dark silken curls and the sweet scent of fresh herbs suddenly filled Peyton's head and he could swear he heard the sound of her laughter. He shook his head and gave the prince a mellow half smile. "No. She grew up into a girl far too beautiful to ever be considered a sister."

SSSS

Even though Cook was old enough to be her grandmother, she and Chantaya became fast friends and Cook kindly didn't hesitate to encourage Chantaya and Isabella to add their knowledge of seasonings and herbs to the fare of the manor house. Cook even ventured into the woods on occasion to learn of the origin of the secrets to Chantaya and Isabella's culinary mastery.

As they searched for mushrooms on one sunny afternoon, Chantaya cautioned Cook at length about the dangers of the mushrooms and how certain ones, or even too much of others, could make a body horribly sick and even possibly cause death. She put extra emphasis on how similar the mushrooms could appear and pointed out the distinguishing characteristics to ensure Cook never made the mistake of mixing them up and taking a poisonous variety into the kitchen.

At that, Cook gave her a sassy grin and said, "Much as I'd love to do away with a couple of the nobles round here, rest easy. I'll leave the use of the deadly things to them as knows best. I'll keep to less dangerous ingredients like flour and eggs and such. I'll also do the serving to protect ye. Heaven knows the Rosskeene men have no need to pester an old woman like me."

Conrad continued to watch over the Kincraigs and he became almost a father figure to Chantaya as she worked around the manor kitchen and gardens. Many were the times when Lord Rosskeene or Master Damian came sidling near, they would take one look at Conrad and then decide they had something else that needed doing. It must have been that they valued Conrad's skill with their horses more than they wanted to press themselves upon the Kincraigs.

Conrad's steady, gentle demeanor to both her and her mother earned a large measure of trust from Chantaya and she often spent time with him in the stables brushing the horses and adding to her knowledge of their care when she wasn't needed in the kitchen. He watched how she handled both the sweet gentle old campaigners, as well as the more spirited mounts of the Master and one evening, when one of the young grooms was ill, Conrad approached her as she worked in a stall and asked, "Have you ridden much, Miss Chantaya?"

She looked up at him, wondering how much she dared to admit. They had become surprisingly close, but Chantaya also knew most peasant girls had no knowledge of riding horses and, in fact, it would have been deemed inappropriate at best. Especially the fact that she rode astride instead of sidesaddle the way the noble women rode.

She looked into his warm brown eyes, remembered how he was almost tender with her mother and decided 'twas safe to admit to him her prowess and said with a somewhat sheepish smile, "Much more than I should have, I'm afraid."

The kindly older man nodded. "I suspected as much. Does your mother know?"

Chantaya scrunched her lips to the side and began a nod that ended in a shake and said, "I'm sure she suspects. I didn't truly have her blessing, but then I also know she can ride astride as well as most men, herself. Pray, why do you ask?"

"You ride astride then?" She nodded mutely, wondering if she was about to be given a fatherly lecture about acting like a lady. Instead, he asked, "Would you be willing to help me work a colt or two then? Just while Sven is out sick. 'Tis shorthanded I am, and if the horses don't behave near perfectly for him, they incur the Lord's wrath. It also might be a good thing to keep in practice, it might."

She was considering his request, wondering what the other staff and the Lord and Lady, and even her mother would think when he added, "I have an old coat and could swipe a pair of the younger lad's breeches. Straight from the wash, of course. If we tucked that lovely mane of yours up under a hat, no one would be the wiser that you weren't Sven himself if we didn't venture close to anyone."

Slowly, Chantaya began to smile a wide, happy smile. She would love to be back astride a horse again and dressing up sounded positively adventurous! "You've got yourself a deal, Conrad, and gladly! Is it too late to go this very even?"

He grinned back. "'Tis late, but a bit o dusk might make you even less distinguishable. There's clean breeches on the bench in the tack room and coat and hat on the hooks. Tell your mother you'll be gone a moment and I'll get the steeds. Be off wi' you now. When next I see you, it's a young groom I'll expect to see."

When she returned, only moments later, he looked at her and then shook his head and said, "Even for the hat, young Sven could never have been so beautiful. Here." He took a clean, folded handkerchief out of his pocket and handed it to her. "Pull up your collar and knot this about your neck and chin. And next time, wear the longer coat. No breeches in the world could hide that figure. If Master Damian ever saw you he'd be nigh out of control. I'd have to near trounce him."

She did as she was told, but laughed and said, "I'm going to take that as a compliment. Although, I'd wear a jester's costume if I had to, to be able to ride again."

They rode for nearly an hour, working the two colts they were on side by side through the woods and meadows around the manor, putting them through their paces and brushing them up on stopping and backing. They brought them in at full dark and once back inside the stables, Chantaya slid off of the leggy sorrel she had been riding with a sigh that was part contentment, part fatigue and part sore hind end. It had been weeks since she had ridden and an incredibly long day since she'd gone into the kitchen to begin preparing the manor breakfast this morning. Still, it had been pure wonderful to be back in the saddle.

As she finally lay down in her bed that night, she wished there had been a way to tell Peyton of her adventure of dressing as a boy and working horses. He probably would have given her that fatherly lecture, but he would have also been happy for the pleasure and the freedom she had found out there tonight. Her spirit seemed to need that sense of freedom. It made this indenturement seem far more bearable after all. She wished that magistrate would hurry and get back with them about his decision.

Peyton still didn't know she was no longer in Navarre. She'd been going to write him of their trouble and the move, but every time she considered it, she decided against it, reasoning that she didn't want the Rosskeenes to know she could write or that she had ties to the knights of the castle. The longer they were here at Rosskeene Manor, the more gossip came to them about nefarious activities of the younger two Rosskeene men, and over time, she had begun to gather that information and even write it down in the event there ever became enough threat that she would need to report it. Things weren't right here at the manor. And it hadn't taken long to realize it. Just how not right they were, remained to be seen.

The next day in the kitchen, when Chantaya arrived to start breakfast, Cook was ill and while Chantaya worried for Cook's health, she also worried about how she would protect herself from young Master Damian without Cook and the hefty rolling pin that she threatened him with.

Chantaya made it through breakfast with only Damian's pointed looks and comments to trouble her, and quickly did up the dishes, but then went back out to their living quarters for the short time until the midday meal, rather than get started on it right away as she typically would have done.

Conrad saw her go into their room, and a few minutes later, he stopped by to ask why she had come out. When she admitted about Cook's absence, he and her mother exchanged a glance, and her mother immediately got up and readied herself to accompany Chantaya into the manor to help her.

While Chantaya appreciated the company and the help, now she worried about her mother's safety as well, knowing that if Lord Rosskeene heard of Isabella's appearance in the kitchen, they would need to worry about him as well as young Damian.

Shortly after the meal, her concerns were indeed founded as first Damian sauntered into the kitchen, followed shortly by his father. Chantaya and Isabella stood side by side at one of the work tables and Chantaya wasn't surprised when Isabella reached for the exact rolling pin that Cook used. That rolling pin, coupled with the appearance of the two had Chantaya's breath catching in her throat and the beating of her heart increased even more than it had when the two had come in.

Neither of the Rosskeenes said anything, although Lord Rosskeene was eyeing Isabella disgustingly and young Damian had a positively lecherous grin as Chantaya looked up at him. Just as Chantaya began to wonder how she was going to reach the dishes stacked on a table near them, Conrad came in the door whistling cheerily and said, "The boys said Cook is under t' scuppers and that ye might be needin' a spare hand. Be this true? I've a moment to help ye, if 'tis."

He picked up a stack of the dishes and brought them across to Isabella and then picked up a dish towel and began to tie it about his waist as both women simultaneously let out breaths. With his makeshift apron in place, he reached across to take the rolling pin from Isabella and asked breezily, "What be needin' rolling, Mistress Isabella? I'll give it a go, I will. I'll flatten anything in my path." He smacked the big wooden pin against a meaty palm with a grin and Chantaya almost wanted to smile herself as the two Rosskeenes walked back out of the kitchen.

Chapter 11

Mordecai pulled his horse Bartok, with the wild splash of white across his shoulder, to a stop in the copse of trees to the south of Rosskeene Manor and got off, leaving him ground tied. On foot, he walked to the edge of the wood to peer out into the gloom of the predawn. Willem Wolfgar had said he'd seen them safely here, but that had been nearly a fortnight ago.

When a week had gone by without Chantaya showing up to visit, Mordecai had been saddened. But by the tenth day, Mordecai knew something was wrong. Chantaya hadn't stayed away from his home for that long since he'd moved there when she was nine.

On the eleventh day, he'd gone to the cottage and upon finding it empty, he'd gone on to the Wolfgar's to learn of Chantaya and Isabella's fate, and then felt guilty for waiting so long to find out why she hadn't come to visit. The thought of the two of them at the mercy of the young Lord Rosskeene had made him near sick. It made him want to strap his armor on and go bring them right back home, without waiting to hear from the magistrate, who was known for his lackadaisical work ethic when it came to matters of the law.

Mordecai stood in the wood, watching the manor house, knowing that if they were indeed working in the manor kitchen, they would soon be stirring to begin the household's breakfast. He knew nothing of the configuration of the manor house, but assumed that door just near the garden he could see, would lead to the kitchen. He was hoping to catch a glimpse of someone at least tossing out dishwater before he ventured any nearer to try and ascertain how Chantaya and Isabella were doing.

He hadn't been watching for more than half the hour when, actually, Chantaya herself appeared, but out of the building he had assumed was the stable. She was accompanied by an able enough looking middle aged man who wasn't Rosskeene, and together they walked to the door near the garden, where the man left her and turned back toward the building they had come out of.

Staying concealed on the edge of the trees, Mordecai watched and mid morning, the same man walked back to the kitchen door and returned with Chantaya. Then a few minutes later, both Chantaya and her mother appeared with baskets and walked toward the same woods Mordecai waited in, as the man came out of the stable on a young horse and rode near them.

At first, Mordecai thought the man must have been guarding them to see to it the two of them didn't try to run away, but as the three of them came closer, he wondered at the easy demeanor of the two women. They didn't appear to be anxious whenever the horseman rode near. In fact, the opposite seemed to be true. When the horseman rode wide from them, their glances toward the manor house did look to hold a measure of wariness. Finally, when the horseman stopped to speak to them only a stone's throw from where Mordecai hid, he realized this man, whoever he was, was actually watching over the two of them as they worked and he rode.

Chantaya went back to the kitchen before the noon hour and then again in mid afternoon. Toward evening, after Chantaya had returned from the manor house, the same man came riding out of the stable, this time with another smaller man on another horse beside him and Mordecai was surprised because the boys who had been working in and around the stables for the day had all appeared to go into the manor house before the supper hour. This new rider must have been inside the stable for the whole of the day, because he wasn't one Mordecai had seen earlier.

Mordecai watched the two of them schooling the young horses in the meadows behind the manor and then, finally, he began to smile. Chantaya was up to her old tricks again and more. She may have been forced away against her will to work for a corrupt Lord, but that was his sweet, young friend out there, dressed in boys' clothing, working that spirited horse. Mordecai could tell just by the way she rode. There wasn't another who sat a horse so gracefully that he'd ever known.

After breathing a sigh of relief at finding the two of them were all right and even seemed to have found some security of sorts here at this corrupt man's holdings, he began to work his way closer to where she was schooling her horse. He needed to speak to her, without frightening her, if possible. He needed to know if they were indeed all right and what he could do to help them get home as quickly and safely as they could. For their sakes, and for Peyton's.

§§§§

Chantaya's mount had been going well under saddle for her, so she knew something was amiss in the nearby wood when her horse suddenly began to want to spook every time she rode near the edge of the small copse of trees. Just when she had decided she would turn and ride on the other side of Conrad from the woods, she glanced left to see Mordecai step from beside a tree long enough to let her see him and then step right back out of sight before Conrad saw him.

She subtly lifted a hand, then rode to Conrad and told him she was going to take a short break in the woods. She turned back toward where she'd seen Mordecai and rode her horse full into the woods where the waning sunlight was quite dim and dismounted and tied the horse to a sturdy limb.

As she turned, Mordecai stepped from the trees near her and she gave a small, whispered squeal as she ran to him to wrap her arms round him in a hug. Feeling suddenly ridiculously emotional, she wiped at the moisture in her eyes as she said, "Mordecai! Oh, Mordecai, I have missed you!"

The gray haired man nodded. "'Tis that I've missed your smile, myself, Miss Chantaya. I've come to see what's to be done about bringing you home. Other than the fact you're nigh a boy now, are you well?"

"Yes. As well as can be expected under the circumstances." She gave him a heart broken smile. "I'm so sorry we left without saying goodbye. They were watching us, so we didn't dare come to tell you. And we're not sure what's to be done about coming home. The magistrate has been delayed and now that we're here, we've been hearing so much gossip about how Lord Rosskeene is gathering his own military forces that we have wondered if us being here isn't fortuitous. No one here knows we have any friends close to the knights. They speak as if we aren't even there sometimes and we're hearing the most frightening tidbits. Enough that we are actually grateful to be here if it means we can find a way to warn the soldiers. We felt it best not to write to you or even Peyton, yet. It sounds crazy, but we're truly wondering if Rosskeene is preparing to go against King Dougal."

Mordecai scowled. "I wouldn't put it past him. He's a scoundrel of the lowest sort."

Looking around, Chantaya said, "I've only a moment, before Conrad will miss me, although I believe he is to be trusted. He's become a fair guardian to Mother and me. But I would still like to keep the fact we have knights for friends a secret. The two younger Rosskeene men are horrible and maybe our being here can do some good. Maybe we can find out enough to get the king to take Rosskeene's holdings away and banish him and free his people from his poor treatment. Would he ever do that if he found there were plans to overthrow the crown?"

"That and more. Rosskeene could be hung for treason. But 'tis not your problem. You and your mother aren't safe here and must be protected. Rosskeene has a terrible reputation for abusing his people. Especially the women."

"The magistrate will rule for us soon enough to protect us. But you yourself have said many times there are more important things than personal safety. I've heard you."

Mordecai shook his head. "No Chantaya. Leave it to the knights. Your mother isn't well and you're but a maid. The danger is too great. What's more, Peyton would be horrified. He already will be when I tell him of your leaving."

From the meadow, Conrad called. Chantaya answered him and then turned back to Mordecai. "I must go. There's nothing to be done for the time being, Mordecai. We're stuck here at Rosskeene's mercy just now anyway. I won't do anything foolish, but I won't ignore what I hear either. I've been writing it down so I can remember it correctly. If you get a chance, please tell someone who has the power to do something about it, that Rosskeene has been gathering malcontents for his own purposes. Purposes that are rumored to threaten the king."

He nodded and she wrapped her arms back around his waist. "I love you, Mordecai. Thank you for coming to check on us. We're all right, so far. Pray that we will continue to be. The staff here is good to protect us, and we're careful to stay together and with others if possible. God willing, we'll be home shortly, and maybe in the interim we can be of help to the crown." Conrad called again and Chantaya let go and went back to her horse, saying over her shoulder, "I must go. If you get word to Peyton, please tell him I love him. Tell him I keep his letter with me all of the time, next to my heart. Goodbye."

As she galloped her horse back through the trees toward the meadow, Mordecai watched her go, wondering how in the world he was going to break this news to Peyton and how Peyton would take it when he wasn't in a position to be able to do much about it.

When he got back to Navarre in the depth of the night, he put Bartok away and then went inside to light a fire and warm himself from the coolness of his night ride. He would rest tomorrow and then leave the next morning to go to Peyton in Valais. Peyton would be crushed, but he needed to know what had happened here.

Although it had merely been a routine circuit round the kingdom of Monciere as a reconnaissance trip and a show of military presence, Peyton felt incredibly proud as he rode beside the other fifteen knights and Prince Laird as they left their final scheduled stop before returning to Valais. 'Twas only late morning and as they came through the junction known as the Crossroads, Peyton looked west toward Navarre, remembering that day Chantaya had climbed to the roof of the village church. She'd been able to see clear to here, there high on the roof with her curls and petticoats blowing. She'd been so happy about that little adventure up the tallest ladder.

He pulled his horse in and paused for the slightest second, looking down the road toward his childhood home and sweetheart. How he missed her! She was just there a few miles down that track. Seeing the prince glance back, he swallowed a sigh and kicked his horse to catch back up to the others. It had only been a few weeks, but it felt like forever since he'd seen her.

Surprisingly, the prince halted the entire entourage at the next inn they came to for a round of cider before continuing on their way. Peyton was still thinking of Chantaya as they all dismounted and he paused, fiddling with his horse's girth, wishing for a quiet moment to himself to remember.

The others had gone inside, when the prince himself returned to the horses and coming close to Peyton, said, "I've a request, Sir Peyton, that I'm hoping you won't deny me. "

Peyton smiled at this young nobleman who had become a surprisingly good friend over the last weeks. "Anything in my power, Sire. I will grant it or die trying."

Nodding, Prince Laird returned his smile. "After coming to know you, Sir Peyton, I believe that to be true. Yet, hopefully, this request won't come at the cost of your life. I wish you to return home and bring me any news of what Lord Rosskeene has been up to. You grew up not far from here, did you not?"

Peyton looked west again and replied, "Just there, Sire. But a few miles. I would bring you news of Rosskeene, and gladly."

The prince turned back for the door of the inn, then paused and looked back at Peyton with a grin. "Perhaps you could inquire of your parents as well as the brunette who turned out too lovely to be considered a sister. It just may be she has some knowledge of Rosskeene we can't do without."

"Indeed, it may. Thank you, Sire. I appreciate this request more than you can imagine."

The prince raised his eyebrows. "You could be right. I've yet to meet any girl who could bring the light to my eyes that mere mention of her brings to yours. I only hope someday to find one. Enjoy yourself. Just see to it you're back in Valais by the morrow. The king has need of such as you." With that, the prince walked back into the door of the inn and Peyton retightened the girth he had just loosened and sprang into the saddle. It may be only for the afternoon, but he was going home.

§§§§

He looked into the empty cottage all but sick with disappointment and concern. The leaves and dust that had blown into the door that stood ajar and piled into the corner made Peyton feel like he'd swallowed a luncheon of rocks.

Not only was she not here, but it was obvious she hadn't been here in some time. Glancing back down the road toward his parents' home he'd just ridden right past a few minutes ago, he shook his head, pulled the door tightly closed, turned back to his horse and spurred it for Mordecai's. It was further, but only marginally and he had a hunch Mordecai would know more about why Chantaya and Isabella were gone than anyone.

The old man was sitting on the porch, seemingly waiting for him as he galloped over the hill and Mordecai stood as Peyton slid his charger to a stop before him. He didn't even have to ask. Mordecai just said, "Rosskeene took them. He saw Chantaya at the tavern and knew she had to be Isabella's daughter. They tried, but he gave them little choice. Told Isabella she either went to work for him for supposed back rents she owed on her cottage or he'd throw her into debtor's prison. Chantaya went with her, of course. I didn't know myself until night before last. I went to Rosskeene's yesterday to check on them. They seem to be well. More beautiful than ever. I was going to come tomorrow and tell you. Forgive me for not being up to it today."

Peyton simply shook his head for a time as he tried to take it in. Finally, he asked, "They've been to the magistrate? What did he say?"

"Nothing yet. But then he's known for dragging his feet and trying not to ruffle any nobleman's feathers. But that's not the worst of it. Chantaya has been hearing rumors of Rosskeene intending to overthrow the crown." He shook his own head. "Trouble's brewing. We've known that. What we didn't know was that your wonderful, sweet, beautiful, *stubborn* girl would get caught in the middle of it. They're in danger and it's well they know it, but she has gotten it into her head that she can help you and the king by staying there and gathering information."

Peyton almost roared, "No!" He looked straight up and took a huge breath and said more calmly, "Surely she knows what Rosskeene is capable of? Of his reputation with women? How can she even consider staying there?"

Mordecai answered evenly, "I doubt she truly knows that at all, Sir Peyton. Isabella has made sure to keep her safe all these years, yes. But you know as well as I do Isabella wouldn't have ever told her just what Rosskeene was truly capable of. Isabella would have hoped to let her keep her innocence unless she absolutely had to tell her. We all would. What kind of people would we be if we didn't try to protect Chantaya's sweet spirit?"

Peyton closed his eyes for a moment, hating to face either the scenario that Chantaya had been harmed or that she had lost that sweet, intrepid sense of innocence. At length, he sighed and said, "And knowing Chani, she would still do what she thought was important, like spy for the king, even if she knew 'twas dangerous."

Mordecai added, "If she thought it truly important." He paused for a moment and then continued, "And Peyton, she may be right. As hateful as the idea is."

Peyton's eyes narrowed. "You would risk a young woman's life and much more for information? It's a matter for soldiers, not girls!"

With the wisdom of ages, Mordecai asked, "How many young women's lives and much more would be sacrificed, were Rosskeene to overthrow the kingdom? And what soldier is in a position to overhear what she is? They all think she is an exquisite scullery maid without a brain in her head. You know that's what most believe of one with her extraordinary beauty." He finally smiled. "Even you and I forget how incredibly bright she is when she turns on her charm."

Rolling his eyes, Peyton admitted, "She definitely does know how to get what she wants. I'll give her that. But she can't stay there. Isabella can't either. She's already been through too much. You weren't here, but the baby she lost when first they came to Navarre had white blond hair. And Chantaya's father's hair was as dark as Chantaya's. I didn't realize it at the time, being nine years old, but since then I've realized Isabella and a black haired husband didn't produce a child that fair. Rosskeene had to have been the reason the Kincraigs left in the dead of night in the first place. To protect Isabella."

Mordecai shook his head. "Well, short of stealing them away in the dead of night again, until the magistrate rules in their favor, they are at Rosskeene's mercy. Crossing a nobleman isn't done. Even a scallywag like Rosskeene. Although there is a positively brawny groom who has taken them under his wing. He's fair guarding them from the looks of things."

"If it takes the dark of night, then so be it. They must be safe. At Rosskeene Manor they are not."

Peyton turned to his horse, but Mordecai's chuckle made him turn back. The older man only put a thick letter into Peyton's hands and said, "We men think that just because we've worked to become the strongest, and bravest, and best we get to make the big, ugly, hairy decisions."

Pausing to think about that, Peyton had to give Mordecai a sad, wry smile. As he mounted and turned his horse north, he knew Mordecai was right. He was going to have to convince Chantaya that staying at Rosskeene Manor wasn't an option, because if her mind was made up, all the knights of the kingdom of Monciere wouldn't be changing it, and he truly didn't want to have to take her against her will.

The afternoon was far spent and evening was pulling the sun from the sky when Peyton pulled his charger to a stop in the same wood above the manor that Mordecai's letter had described. Leaving the horse tied, he reread the details of what Mordecai had learned two days earlier as he'd watched from here and then he went back to the edge of the wood to watch for himself. If she did as she had when Mordecai was watching, then she would be leaving that door near the garden and going to the stable to the left with this groom Mordecai had spoken of.

Glancing down, Peyton realized he needed to take off his armor and his knight's tunic. Whether she stayed or not, it truly was prudent that no one here know the Kincraigs had ties to the king's army.

He had no sooner taken off his things, than he saw Chantaya come out the door, but instead of going to the stable, she walked into the nearby garden with a large basket over her arm. The sight of her made him instantly happy, in spite of the concerns that plagued him, and he tossed his tunic on top of his armor and headed for the thickest cover on the wooded hillside that led toward the garden. Mordecai was right. She was more beautiful than ever.

When he got close, he looked around and then decided he was going to surprise her and slipped into the corn that grew along side the garden. 'Twas the only place a body as large as he could hope to stay out of sight.

She was humming as she worked among the plants and he had to laugh silently to himself when she struggled to harvest a huge green squash that had obviously been overlooked on previous days and had gotten so overgrown that she couldn't pluck it even with the knife she carried to cut the thick stems. She eventually gave up cutting and finally just grabbed the giant thing and leaned back. Peyton was surprised she didn't pull the whole vine up.

She'd quit humming and even pushed the sleeves of her dress up, but it was several moments before the stubborn thing gave way. Chantaya ended up flying backwards right into the corn he was hiding in at the moment. Still smiling to the point he worried his laughter would give him away, he decided the monstrous squash had been fate and as she landed against the corn, he reached out and pulled her into the corn patch with him. Who knew, but what a corn patch could be a truly romantic place?

§§§§

When strong arms came around Chantaya unexpectedly from the corn patch, she knew instantly that Master Damian Rosskeene had found yet another place to lie in wait for her. As the panic welled into her veins, she threw an elbow with every bit of strength she had and was just in the process of wondering whether to throw her paring knife so he couldn't use it against her, or turn and try to stab him when she heard Peyton's low, comforting voice in her ear.

Turning so fast that she almost knocked them both down among the stalks, she did indeed drop her knife as she lunged straight into his arms. He'd had his finger to his lips to encourage silence and so this time, instead of squealing his name, she simply lifted her face to his to kiss him. The corn was more than cover from prying eyes and she had missed him desperately.

She'd merely wanted to kiss him hello, but seeing him so suddenly, and then tasting him and being wrapped in his marvelous arms made all kinds of heady emotions rise up in her. She closed her eyes to hide her tears as much as to enjoy the feel of his kiss. My, he felt as if he'd grown both taller and more muscled in the weeks he'd been gone. She wrapped her arms around him even more tightly and stroked the muscles of his back as he literally picked her up in his embrace as he kissed her. It was instant bliss to let herself be lost in the feel of his warm, firm mouth over hers.

At length, he gave an all but inaudible sigh and finally pulled back. For a long moment, he searched her eyes and then bent again, smoothed away the tendril of hair that had escaped from where it was pinned up and softly kissed her neck. For another few moments, he stayed there near the hollow below her ear and then finally moved his mouth up to her ear itself and whispered her name so softly that she felt it more than heard it.

He whispered it twice. Three times, and then brought his mouth back to hers and after another minute whispered again against her lips, "Oh, Chantaya, my love. I have missed you. Oh, how I have missed you." He kissed her again, hungrily, almost desperately and she seemed to feed on it, taking his passion and drinking it in to store up for later when he was gone again and she would miss him like the very air she needed for life.

She could feel the tears welling uncontrollably again and he must have too because after another few minutes, he lifted his head and then gently wiped at her cheek with his thumb and said softly, "Don't cry, Chani. When we're together is the happy time."

Closing her eyes, she nodded and leaned into him as he tenderly kissed both of her eyelids. That only made her even more emotional, and he pulled her head over against his chest and let out a contented breath and she said, "They're happy tears, Peyton. I'm sorry. I'm overcome. I've missed you. So much. I've dreamed of seeing you again. Hoped for it, prayed for it. Even worried about it. What you'd do, when you found me here. I don't want to get you in trouble, but I've so wanted to see you again. See you, touch you, kiss you. Have you hold me." She raised her eyes to his. "I love you, Peyton. More than ever. And I've missed you."

He looked into her eyes as if trying to memorize them and finally asked quietly, "Are you well?" She nodded without any hesitation, but he still searched her eyes as if trying to read that for himself. After another moment, he asked, "And your mother? Is she well? Does he harm her?"

Shaking her head, she said, "Lord Rosskeene has been surprisingly caught up in his plans for insurrection. It has protected us, if not the crown. Mother is well. As well as can be expected. Her smile has become more rare, and she worries. But I try to keep her from worrying as well as I am able. Conrad helps. He's the groom here. He watches over her. Over both of us."

He took her hand. "I spoke to Mordecai. Come and tell me. I need to hear of what is happening with you."

For the first time, she glanced around and seemed to remember where they were and she hesitated. "I need to get these vegetables picked and then get back to the stables. Mother and Conrad will be wondering what's become of me. And Cook. She'll come to see if I've been . . . "

She broke off and glanced up at him and he prodded, "If you've been what?"

Dropping her eyes, she looked down and then bent to look for her knife as she said casually, "She'll just wonder what has happened to me."

Upon finding the knife, she rose and looked up at him and he said, "You're a terrible liar. Why are you not being honest with me? It's me. Peyton. Tell me the truth."

She glanced around again, although they could hardly see through the thickness of the corn, and then she shook her head. "I can't tell you the truth, Peyton. I can't. Not yet. You would be . . . I don't want to get you into trouble."

His eyes narrowed as he struggled to understand what she was saying and how to react to it, but then there was a sound that brought her head up fast. It was the door from the manor, and then there were footsteps coming their way. Leaning close, she whispered, "It's Cook. I need to go. Meet me on the far side of the stable at full dark."

She went to leave, but he caught her arm and pulled her back. When she raised her face to see what he wanted, he pulled her back into his arms and kissed her once more. Fast, but incredibly thoroughly. Then he let her go again and she stepped out of the corn, working to smooth her hair back into its twist and still keep hold of the knife she held, while at the same time, slow her breathing.

She was all the way out of the corn and almost to her basket before she realized she'd forgotten to bring any cobs of corn with her. Or that it wasn't Cook who had approached, but Master Damian Rosskeene.

Feeling that same panic well again, this time she was doubly worried, because Peyton was right there and if Damian tried to accost her again, Peyton would rain all over him and who knew what would become of that? Peyton could end up imprisoned or even hung. But yet, Damian couldn't be allowed to do to her what he'd been trying to do from the very first day he'd seen her. And Peyton would be in the right to defend her safety and virtue.

She moved to the left, trying to keep a row of tomatoes between her and Damian as she calmly asked, "Master Damian, pray, what are you doing out here? Was there something you needed?"

He was watching her with that same frightening, hungry look in his eyes he always watched her with and the skin on the back of her neck began to crawl as he answered smoothly, "Of course, there's something I need. The same thing I've needed since ever first I laid eyes upon you. But then, I think you know that, don't you, fair Chantaya?"

Picking up the basket, she deftly kept another row of the garden between them as he stepped over the tomatoes and she said, "I'm sure I don't know what you mean, sir."

Leaning, she picked up the tomatoes and squash she'd picked before realizing Peyton was there and put them into her basket and then abruptly turned to go back into the kitchen door. Damian turned just as abruptly, jumped over the plants between them, gripped her arm and said, "Oh, but I think you do. You needn't continue to play the fool with me, Chantaya. It will get you nowhere. I'll have what I want, no matter how you enjoy this game of cat and mouse you play. And this even, neither Cook, nor Conrad is here to chaperone us. Tonight I've got you all to myself. So, do stop this little game of yours and enjoy me. Because I'm certainly going to be enjoying you."

He pulled her roughly against him and Chantaya shuddered, both at his touch, and because she knew what was coming.

At least she thought she knew what was coming. To be sure, she had no idea it would come in the form of a gigantic zucchini!

Surprisingly, she didn't cry out when Damian crumpled to the ground in front of her as the result of having just been fairly smashed over the head from behind with the monstrous squash. She did gasp for a moment, but then when she realized upon looking around, that no one had seen anything, including Damian himself, she calmed somewhat before steeling herself to face Peyton again after what he'd just heard. She had no idea what to do in this situation and stupid tears refused to stay out of her eyes as she looked up at him.

He looked down at her with an emotion she didn't recognize, but for some reason, he didn't start right in with the lecture she'd been expecting. Instead, he simply stepped past the shattered pieces of zucchini and the pathetic Damian, pulled Chantaya back into his arms and almost began to rock her against him as she cried. For several minutes he held her to him almost reverently, and then he gently pushed her away and said, "Go quickly back to the kitchen and finish whatever your doing. I'll toss the squash refuse far into the corn. He probably won't remember anything when he comes to. Hurry and then I'll meet you beyond the stables in a few minutes at full dark." She nodded woodenly but didn't move and he nudged her. "Go, Chani. Go now. Quickly, before someone comes."

With one last look, she turned back for the kitchen, honestly worrying Peyton would do something to Damian while he was out cold. And Damian deserved it! He was a beast! Chantaya feared desperately for Peyton's safety, but she also knew without a vestige of a doubt that Peyton couldn't watch and listen to something like that and not take action. Not while there was a breath of life in his body, he couldn't. He simply wasn't made that way, and thank goodness! That had been a close one. For the thousandth time since she and her mother had stepped out their door to find Lord Rosskeene standing there, Chantaya wondered if they were going to survive this.

In the kitchen, she put away the vegetables, told Cook good night as calmly as she could and then hurried out to speak with her mother in private before going to meet Peyton. She trusted Cook and Conrad after these last weeks, but still felt it would be best for everyone involved if none but her mother knew Peyton was here. Especially after what had just happened in the garden with the humongous zucchini. She said a silent prayer as she walked that Damian hadn't been killed by the gigantic thing. That would be the very worst if Peyton would hang because of an overgrown squash.

On further thought, she grinned to herself as she remembered Sir Mordecai drilling it into Peyton's head that anything could be a weapon if you kept your wits about you. Peyton had certainly taken that admonition to heart. He'd fair knocked a man cold with a vegetable! She grinned again to herself, in spite of her still pounding heart. Peyton was definitely her hero, no matter his weapon.

Living where a body had to go past Conrad's lodgings to get to the Kincraigs' had been a definite benefit to Chantaya and Isabella as far as the Rosskeene men were concerned, but getting back out to meet Peyton after telling her mother he was here was a different proposition. They didn't want Conrad to know Peyton had been there in case Damian was more than just knocked cold in the garden. To that end, she was back to sneaking out the window, but this time, with

Isabella's assistance, and the window was all but too little to fit even Chantaya through. 'Twould be that Peyton would indeed have to boost her back into the small opening when the time came.

She had to stand on the chair and then on her mother's hands and it was such a tight squeeze that as they tried to fit her voluminous petticoats through, Chantaya sighed and then laughed and soon the two women were fighting the giggles. Then, on the outside, Chantaya fair plopped off the sill and landed on the grass and twigs below with an unceremonious groan and Isabella peeked her head out to inquire in a whisper, "Are you all right?"

With another groan, Chantaya stood and brushed off her dress as she whispered back, "Fine. Absolutely well. I've just become intimately acquainted with a number of pine cones is all. They make pitiful padding, I can tell you, Mum."

Isabella chuckled quietly again. "I imagine so. Do be careful, daughter. And behave yourself, young lady. 'Tis questionable enough that your own Mum is pushing you out a window in the dark of night to go and meet a man."

"Ah, but of all the men in the whole of the world, Sir Peyton is truly the most honorable. 'Tis certain. You needn't worry."

"If I was worried, I'd not help you out, silly. Give him my love and do hurry. 'Tis far he must travel and tomorrow might be a long day at the manor if Master Damian was damaged by the mythical gourd of battle."

Chantaya giggled again and slipped into the dark. Damaged. She ought to be praying that Master Damian hadn't been truly harmed, but, in truth, having him out of commission, even for a time, would be such a blessed holiday.

She stepped quietly along the wall of the stable and then slipped through the rails of the paddock to move silently among the horses Conrad kept there. One spooked slightly as she appeared out of the darkness but quieted at her touch and she was incredibly grateful they had come to know and trust her in her time here. Speaking softly to them, she could move among them much as Conrad himself would have been able to.

At the far side of the stable, she slipped back through the rails and moved to the deepest shadow under the trees, wondering what had happened in the garden after she had gone back into the kitchen.

Peyton was suddenly there in front of her. He made no more sound than a ghost as he materialized out of the gloom and once again, she moved into his arms. She tried to tell herself it was because of the urgency to be quiet that she needed to be that close to him, but silence had little to do with the fact that it was heaven to be back within his strong arms after so many weeks without him. His gentle hug was the substance of dreams come true.

At length, even though she was the more familiar with the grounds, he took her hand and confidently led her through the moonless darkness into the thickest of the woods some distance from the outbuildings before turning to hold her to him once again. Reveling in both his strength and the incredibly comforting sense of safety his arms brought, she breathed in his scent and felt the tension melt from her bones as he kissed her hair. Goodness, but she had missed him.

Wishing she could simply bask in his arms without having to face the conversation she knew they needed to have, she resolutely looked up at him when he leaned back a measure. Knowing he was going to want her safely away, yet having no means to that end, and now, with the whisperings of insurrection, and believing she needed to stay regardless, made her hesitant to speak.

She would have dearly loved to be safely away and back in Navarre, or nearer him in Valais. He had to know that. And in truth, she sensed he did. Still, she knew in her heart he was going to do all in his power to see her safely away from Rosskeene Manor, even if that meant fleeing. But she also knew that, at the moment, leaving was a near impossibility, what with Peyton gone to serve the king.

Two women alone, one of whom was not physically strong, and with only minimal funds, was a recipe for misery, were they to try to escape Rosskeene's grasp, and both she and Peyton knew it. Moreover, she now firmly believed she needed to stay here. Indeed, felt as if God himself had had a hand in them being here. But how to convey that conviction to Peyton in the face of what they both knew were the Rosskeene men's intentions toward her and her mother? And how strangely incongruent with the basic need to seek protection against men of their ilk.

Looking into Peyton's warm, dark eyes, she knew he too sensed all of this as he returned her gaze with his own troubled one. Finally, he simply asked, "What do you wish of me, Chantaya Kincraig?" He gently touched her face with calloused fingers. "I will resign my knighthood and find a way to take the both of you away. Or I will go personally to the magistrate. I will petition the king himself to secure a settlement. What do you wish me to do for you?"

Chantaya leaned back into his chest and closed her eyes to inhale the very essence of his strength against her cheek as the moon rose over the hills to the east, bathing the woodland around them pale silver. She shook her head against him.

"No… Thank you, Sir Peyton. You would do all of that and more and I know that, but what I want of you, even what you want of me… No, my love, this time and place. This whole situation. 'Tis bigger than what we want. The question we must ask ourselves and each other isn't what we want. Is it?"

She heard him release a long breath before he asked softly, "What then?" After another moment, almost bitterly, he followed with, "Why?"

Wrapping her arms round his waist and holding tight, she said, "Because, there is that in you which is unable to settle for less than your best. You have that in your soul which seeks for greater heights. We both do. Indeed, I would wager you've been one of the great ones since the very beginning of time. Long before we even were born here to this earthly life. It's who you are. To the soul. A guardian. A hero."

She reached to gently kiss him and then continued almost apologetically, "A hero's way isn't an easy way, Peyton. And yours is the character of a hero."

Pulling her tighter to him, he said bitterly, "Hero be damned."

She shook her head again. "No. Heroes get cold and tired and hurt. Lonely. Sometimes they're even killed, but damned? No. 'Tis the one thing the adversary who rules the hearts of the wicked the world over can't do. He can never take away your honor, no matter what other price he extracts."

Peyton was silent for several long moments. Finally, he said, "It's one thing for big, foolish, brute men to play hero, Chantaya. It's wholly another for a sweet, innocent, young woman. There are worse things that can happen than dying."

Nodding, she asked quietly, "How many more young women would be at risk were Rosskeene to become king?"

Through gritted teeth, he said, "Let someone else live in danger for the kingdom, girl."

"You would never even consider turning away from this, were you the one who could aid the crown."

"I am a knight!"

At that, she raised her head to look at him and said, "And I am your mate."

Chapter 12

All the way back to Mordecai's, Peyton thought back over that conversation with Chantaya. She was sweet, and smart, and beautiful, and frustratingly strong. And how he loved her for it! But it troubled him deeply.

The thought of her there at mercy of such men made his stomach clench in fury, but in the end, she had been right about being willing to take risks for the good of the whole kingdom. Still, he hated every bit of it. Hated it with a passion that threatened to burn a hole in his very belly if he let it eat at him.

He let his horse have its head at a fast trot on the moonlit trail as he thought back over the things they had spoken of. For hours they had spoken there in the shadows of the trees, sharing information, and sweet kisses, before he'd helped her back into her small window, feeling as if his heart was slamming shut to leave her there like that. It had been awful leaving her in Navarre to go into training. But that had been nothing to the hell of knowing he was leaving her at such risk at Rosskeene Manor.

Her and Isabella both. It made him feel less than the shadow of an honorable man. What manner of hero was he to ride away from her there? And yet, what manner of man would he have been to go against what he knew the both of them were to do? 'Twas God's will. He knew it was. Still, he hated it. It was going to take every bit of faith he had to trust in God to keep her safe in such a situation.

Deep in the night, as the pale moon settled into the crags of the mountains to the west, he approached Mordecai's cottage to find the old man sitting on his porch waiting for him. Together they turned Peyton's charger in with Mordecai's piebald horse and then walked side by side into the little stone house. Surprisingly, Mordecai knew exactly what had happened. The conversation as Mordecai set out bread and cheese and cider wasn't on simply bringing them home, but on the logistics of how best to aid the two Kincraig women and resolve the rumblings of insurrection.

As Peyton went to settle onto a pallet spread before the fire for a few hours rest, Mordecai's big hand gripped his shoulder. Peyton met his eyes, knowing the old knight understood just what he was up against, as no one else ever could have. Mordecai had the soul and character of a hero as well. It was unbelievably comforting to know Mordecai was there at his back, fighting for the same things he was.

Late the next morning, when Peyton was admitted to see the prince, the teasing grin that lit up the young royal's face upon seeing Peyton faded as he took in Peyton's exhausted countenance and then heard the details that Chantaya had documented and given to him there in the woods of Rosskeene Manor. The prince questioned him at length about the entire situation and then Peyton had to appreciate this honorable man even more than he already did when, instead of exclaiming over the threat to the crown, Prince Laird asked after Chantaya, understanding the risk that she was taking in being willing to stay there at the manor to intercept information.

In a way, Peyton was proud of Chantaya, but in a way, it galled him to have to admit that he'd left her there. He had no way to explain to the prince just why he'd finally given in and ridden away from her, but the prince seemed to be able to grasp what had transpired.

In the end, he too had gripped Peyton's shoulder and said, "Let us pray that the good Lord will assist us, and then let us fight to bring an end to the situation quickly and get her out of there. I thank you for your willingness to seek this information for me. I thank her for hers as well. She must be an extraordinary maid indeed. Come to me anytime in the future that you feel you have information I am in need of. I'm sorry that for once, seeing her didn't bring that light to your eyes. Go ye now to your quarters and rest, for there will soon enough be more need for your reconnaissance. God bless you, Sir Peyton."

§§§§

Chantaya was more tired than usual the morning after Peyton was there, but she was still the first one into the kitchen and set about starting the cook fire, wondering whatever had happened to Damian the night before. She'd glanced toward the garden as Conrad had seen her in, but could see nothing in the dark of the predawn.

Cook came in just several minutes later, looking even more tired than Chantaya and her first comments set Chantaya's mind somewhat at ease. After an exhausted yawn, Cook said, "Strange doin's going on round here in the night. Stranger than usual, I mean. Seems that Master Damian went missing last even and was finally found, out colder than the ice of winter on the stoop near the side door.

The physician's been here near most all night. Damian finally came to in the wee hours, but doesn't seem to have an idea of what happened to him. Says the last thing 'e remembers was coming into the kitchen for a morsel after supper, 'e says."

Cook gave another yawn and grumbled, "It's more than a morsel of food 'e wants when he comes snooping around in this kitchen after a fine meal, I'd wager. Seems for once, he was on the receiving end of the roughness. Still, it's what's to be expected from the company they keep round here lately. I can't abide the type of blokes what idles around here in the shadows. Sometimes the Master 'imself sees them right inside the house 'ere, 'e does. I have to fair choke to death for lack of air for closing all the transoms to block what I'm 'earin'. And now wi' fall coming on, we'll pure freeze for lack of warmth what wi' the transoms shut up tight. What's to become of us all, Miss Chantaya?"

Spreading her own hands toward the cook fire, Chantaya answered, "We'll be fine, we will, Cook. We'll open the transoms and have the heat and air, even if we have to listen to the evil of it all. It's strong enough we are to withstand mere talk." With that, she gave Cook a one armed hug and went to open the two transoms in the room as if to make a point.

Cook only shook her head and said, "In 'ere it's not so bad, but off the butler's pantry, when I'm polishing the sterling, my goodness the things a body 'ears. 'Tis right through the wall from the young Lord's study, it is and you can't imagine the things I 'ear there. 'Tis pure frightening!"

Shaking her head in commiseration, Chantaya soothed, "Then 'twill be me who polishes the silver from now on if that bothers you, love. The skin of the young is much thicker these days. I'll do the silver and you can see to something else when there's mischief about the house."

Chantaya gave her another hug and a smile as she began to start mixing the dough for the breakfast. Cook patted her back in return and said, "You're good and true, you are, Chantaya. Makes an old woman believe there's hope to be had in the future with a new generation as solid as yourself. God bless you my dear. God bless you. We'd best make up a goodly amount what with the physician not appearing to be leaving anytime soon. Hopefully, you'll have some peace here without any treacherous visitors for a time. Seems Master Damian is still addlebrained from whatever 'twas that accosted him in the night."

Glancing down, Chantaya noticed some squash seeds on the stone floor of the kitchen. She subtly pushed them under a low shelf with the toe of her boot. She made a note in her head to inspect the garden in the light of day for incriminating zucchini innards, as she answered, "Whatever indeed. Must have been a pure frightening weapon to have addled a head as hard as Damian's. What do you wish of me to work on for luncheon?"

Master Damian was truly indisposed for a few days from the mythical gourd of battle, but that didn't impede his father's devious dealings, by any means.

Chantaya had hoped when she'd offered to polish silver to be able to gain valuable information from listening through the transom into Lord Rosskeene's study and that's exactly what happened a mere fortnight later. What she learned made her realize that her corrupt employer was planning to move against the crown much sooner than she had believed heretofore.

She could actually hear remarkable well there as she polished and she was horrified to realize that in only two day's time Rosskeene had plans in place for a fair mob of miscreants to rob the King's Treasury right in the city of Valais. Not only would taking the king's gold enable Rosskeene to fund a larger and stronger army of the war loving mercenaries he had been sending for, but it would cripple the king's ability to provide for his own armies and people.

It was only early afternoon that she understood what was being planned there on the other side of the manor's wall, but she had no idea what to do about that information and stewed about it for the remainder of her work day. By the time she returned that evening to their little room off the stable, she had made a decision, but then truly wondered if she could indeed see it to fruition. She needed to get word to Peyton, who was nearer to where the robbery would take place, but she had no idea of the route to Valais. Truth be told, she hardly had any knowledge of the way back to Navarre except that she believed it to be a relatively straight shot back down the road to the south.

She would have to simply get word to Mordecai, but she also needed to do it without letting anyone there at the manor realize that she'd done it. She was going to try to not even tell her mother, knowing she would only be terrified for her daughter's safety during the long night ride through woods and trails that were much more dangerous than they would have been during the light of day.

As she let herself into their tiny home, she was pleased and surprised to see her mother sitting just outside the door with Conrad at a table they'd set up, their heads bent over a small slate. Both of them were so engrossed in what Isabella was showing him that, for a time, neither even realized she was there. She went back out to the stable and hid her saddle outside in the paddock and had to smile to herself. 'Twas so like her mother to want to teach another to read, especially another as good and kind as Conrad. The idea of the two of them finding more than a mere working friendship had crossed Chantaya's mind on more than one occasion. 'Twould be perfect for the two gentle, lonely adults to find companionship in each other.

Chantaya used their lack of attention to gather a small packet of supplies to take with her and then readied what she could and went back out into the stable to make ready there as well. How she would be able to get past Conrad would remain to be seen, but she knew it had to be done.

Later, when her mother had dropped off to sleep, Chantaya pulled out the clothing she had pilfered earlier and began to dress. Remembering what Conrad had said about disguising her figure, and knowing that she had far to go and would have to go fast, she took a length of cheesecloth that she'd brought from the kitchen, and after undressing, she began to wrap the length around her chest, trussing it down as tightly as she could. It would both somewhat hide the fact she was female, as well as protecting her from the constant gait of the horse running for hours.

She wore the long coat, and tied a large handkerchief around her neck and chin, and then pushed her hair up under a hat she tied down to keep in place. With that done, she left her mother a short note, hoping she'd be back long before her mother woke to read it, and then, as silently as possible, she let herself out the door into the stable, praying she wouldn't wake Conrad.

She'd been on the road for more than two hours, alternately trotting and then galloping, before hearing the first indication of someone else approaching. At the first sound of hoof beats, she pulled the horse off the road and into the woods alongside and halted him, once again praying they wouldn't be detected, in spite of the frantic beating of her heart. Chances were, anyone she would meet here in the woods, far from any town or village in the depth of the night, would not be a model citizen. Especially not if they found she was female.

When the group of three riders went off down the road in the direction she had come, she breathed a huge sigh of relief and returned to the road and the distance eating gallop. She knew her horse was getting winded, but this was more vital than saving the horse's wind, or even his life. She needed to get word to Mordecai at all costs.

Twice more, she moved off the road to avoid riders. Once a lone horseman and once a pair of walking horses carrying riders who were singing and carrying on as if they'd spent the hours drinking in the village pub before traveling. Her horse actually nickered at their horses as they passed her by, but thank goodness they were too caught up in their rousing song about ale to notice. As they finally went on their inebriated way, she resumed her journey, not sure whether to be grateful for the waxing moon that had appeared to bath the woods in light, or be frightened by how bright the deserted roadway had become.

After what seemed like a never ending foray through the forbidding night, she ultimately recognized the countryside and turned off into the woods toward Mordecai's cottage. Somehow, just turning off the road, and knowing he was close was incredibly reassuring, even if the forest around her was much darker than the road had been. At least here there weren't likely to be any highwaymen who would attack or harm her.

Mordecai was standing at his door in a robe, but carrying a sword as she approached his home and she was gratified to realize she truly wasn't recognizable as he held the sword up and asked, "Who goes there?"

She sighed and wearily slid from the tired horse's back. "It's me, Sir Mordecai. Chantaya. Chantaya Kincraig. I need you to get word to Peyton of an attack on the King's Treasury. In two nights hence. They're going to storm the east gate with battering rams."

As her feet hit the ground, she all but fell under the horse's belly as her legs buckled with cold and fatigue and Mordecai fair leaped to catch her and help her into his house, exclaiming as he did so, "Miss Chantaya! You've come all the way from Rosskeene Manor by yourself in the dark of night? Were you harmed? Are you well?"

She collapsed onto a chair before the few coals that were left of Mordecai's fire. "I'm well. Weary. And cold. A trifle frightened." She gave him a tired, sheepish smile. "Well, in truth, ridiculously frightened. But I made it. That's all that counts. Could I trouble you for a drink of water? I brought a small water skin, but it's pure hard to drink as you're trotting. And would you be so kind as to get word to Peyton and the others? I have to turn right back around and return or they'll know I've told on them."

Mordecai nodded as he put wood on the fire and brought her water. "I'll get word to them. But not before I see you safely back to your mother. 'Tisn't safe for you to ride through the night like this, but then, 'tis that you know that. And you came anyway." He dropped an arthritic hand to her shoulder and gave it a squeeze. "These are extraordinary times. And you're an extraordinary maid. 'Tis grateful the king will be for loyal subjects such as you, Chantaya Kincraig. You are a worthy match for a valiant knight of the kingdom. Eat a bite now, and quench your thirst and let's get you back safely to your stable and then I'll go to Valais with your information."

While she rested for a moment and ate, she told him the details of what she'd heard and he puttered around his house much the same as she had earlier at her room, packing a bit of this and that. After a moment, he came to her with a small, narrow bladed dagger in a brown leather sheath. He set it on the table next to her and said, "Put it in your boot."

He walked into his other room and returned a few minutes later wearing his breastplate and the portion of his armor that protected his forearms, strapping on his sword as he walked. Moving to his fireplace, he reached to the top of the mantle and came away with a much smaller sword that he brought back to the table to Chantaya.

He stood holding it for a moment, then set it next to her tankard of water and said softly, "'Twas my wife's. She was a gentle soul to the bone, but still, she asked me to teach her the rudiments of fencing. I used to like to think 'twas an excuse to be with me, but . . . I would like you to have it. I pray you will never have need of it, but you might with times as they are. You know how to use it. And it will make the ruse of you being a lad that much more believable. Just promise me you will do everything in your power to avoid battle, rather than engage in it. Otherwise, there's a knight in Valais who will slay me in the morning."

Rising from her chair, Chantaya shook her head. "I can't take your wife's blade, Sir Mordecai. 'Twouldn't be right."

He merely shook his head, put on his cloak and said, "She would wish it. Come. We must ride hard to get you home in time for the Lord's breakfast."

She had no idea how long they'd been traveling when Mordecai pulled up and said, "Come up behind me on Bartok. Your mount is all in, as are you. Ride behind me and lean on me to rest as much as possible. I'll lead your horse."

Nodding, she dismounted and climbed on behind him. Even with the tension of the ride, she was in danger of falling from her horse with fatigue. Twice while she rode behind him, he pulled off the road to conceal them in the woods as other travelers came by and she was amazed at how much less frightening it was to have him there with her.

In the past, she had imagined the life of a soldier to be exciting and it was. Too much so. She was doing what she felt like she had to, but tonight's ride had made it surprisingly clear that she would much prefer to leave all things heroic to the likes of Mordecai and Peyton. She was much happier in a dress and in a home. Far and away happier.

She'd actually fallen asleep and found as she awoke that Mordecai had hold of her arm to keep her from sliding off the horse behind him. They had pulled up in the woods and upon looking around; she realized they were in the trees beyond Lord Rosskeene's stable near where Mordecai had met her those days ago. She hugged him gently and whispered, "Thank you, Sir Mordecai. God bless and keep you."

With that, she slid off Bartok and took the reins of her own horse that was too tired to even whinny at the other horses in the stable. With a last wave at Mordecai, she led the horse back to the paddock, unsaddled it and turned it loose with a grateful sigh. She literally dragged herself and the saddle as silently as possible back into the stable, returned the saddle to its rack and crept past Conrad's room into her own.

She carefully shut the door, listened for a moment to hear her mother's steady, even breathing and then stripped her boy's clothing and weapons and thrust them far under the bed. She took the note she'd written to her mother, wadded it and put it inside her discarded boot and then gratefully sank into the softness of the straw ticking. She may only have an hour until she had to be back in the kitchen, but she was going to enjoy every moment of it.

§§§§

Peyton knew as soon as he saw Mordecai sitting Bartok at the edge of the road beside the encampment that something was wrong. The fatigue fair rolled off of the old knight and his countenance and even the resolute set of his aging shoulders spoke of tension as well, not to mention the fact that he wore the breastplate of his armor under his cloak.

Leaving the others, Peyton rode toward his aging friend and with a flick of his gaze, the both of them headed for the garrison where Peyton lived. As soon as Peyton found why he was here, he was going to send Mordecai in to borrow his own bed. The man looked exhausted.

Once in the privacy of Peyton's room, Mordecai told him of Chantaya's ride and the information she brought. The old knight met his eyes, but neither of them spoke of the danger that weighed on them like the sacks of the king's gold she had ridden to protect. If they did, it would be Peyton's undoing. Instead, he set his own shoulders with a determination to bring a swift and sure finish to the threats of Lord Rosskeene. That was the solution to best protecting her.

Leaving Mordecai to rest, Peyton rode to the castle to speak to the prince. They had only just over a day to handle this particular threat and in order to successfully negate it; they needed to handle it with secrecy.

Prince Laird never asked where the information Mordecai brought came from and Peyton was glad. To have had to voice aloud again to this royal that he was leaving his love in such risky circumstances would have tempted him to take her from Rosskeene Manor, which he knew wasn't what was needed. The delivery of this plot only illustrated that. She truly was in a singular situation to intercept information. 'Twas increasingly valuable for the crown, yet still, how Peyton wished it wasn't an innocent young woman. And certainly not his innocent young woman.

§§§§

When Chantaya went back out to their rooms after clearing away the luncheon, she had been going to simply take a moment to refresh herself and pull her rebellious curls back away from her face, but her mother rose upon her entrance with a concerned look on her face.

She put a gentle hand to Chantaya's cheek and asked, "Are you well, daughter?" Isabella's forehead creased with worry as she mused, "You don't feel overly warm. Yet you don't look so good. Perhaps you should lie down for a time. I'll go and help Cook with the supper this even. I fear you're coming down with something."

Chantaya yawned but smiled at her. "Oh, no. Were I to stay here, you'd dose me with that nasty concoction of yours that threatens to kill a body. I learned long ago 'tis better to die of disease than to be near dead of the cure. I'm fine. Just a trifle weary. I must not have slept well last night."

Isabella laughed, but then said, "Well, then, I will come and help you with the supper. 'Twill make the time fly faster and then we'll go down to bed early."

Nodding, Chantaya said, "Thank you, Mother. I truly would appreciate that. Although, hadn't you better work with Conrad on his letters again this even? 'Twould not be prudent to let the time pass and have him forget his lessons. I'll rest, and you can help him. Or are you overly tired as well?"

"Yes, 'twould be good to keep him going. Like one of the young horses he's starting. And no, I'm not overly tired. Rest now, and I'll wake you when it's time to go back in."

Chantaya sighed and lay on the bed, but said, "Actually, I need to go in a trifle earlier than usual. There's more silver that needs seen to."

Her mother looked at her pointedly and then nodded, knowing exactly what Chantaya was saying and appearing in agreement. There certainly had been an inordinate number of strange and not necessarily respectable seeming visitors this day. Perhaps the transom off the butler's pantry would be of import this afternoon. Although Chantaya dearly hoped not to hear something else that needed to be taken to Peyton. She was truly weary enough this day without that.

Chapter 13

All day, trusted men of the King's First Guard had been unobtrusively trickling into the walled treasury building and the area around it. They'd come in ones and twos and from different directions and unless you were counting, you'd not know that a goodly number of the crown's most valiant soldiers had gathered in and near the King's Treasury. There were also scores of troops held at the ready in areas of the city nearby. Chantaya hadn't been able to ascertain exactly how many men would be in on the attack, but there were many more soldiers waiting at attention than there normally would have been on a sleepy Thursday in early September.

Sir Peyton wasn't at the Treasury on the east side of the wall, but nearer the castle with the prince himself and several others of the King's First Guard. Peyton was by far the youngest of the King's First Guard, but since the evening of his knighthood ceremony when he'd refused to kiss the princess, he'd been consistently included with those guarding the royal family. He'd wondered about that at first, but there had been hints from Sir Kendall and others that somehow he had been found to be worthy of the utmost trust from someone in the royal family. Peyton wasn't sure who it was that had deemed him so worthy, but he was infinitely honored and glad of it, especially at times like tonight when the family needed to be secure at all costs. This was why Peyton had come here to this place at this time.

At dusk, the King's First Guard took the prince, went into the castle proper and closed both the gates and drawbridges in the wall, and in truth, the waiting was thoroughly frustrating. The attack, when it came at just past midnight, was almost anticlimactic from that distance from the Treasury. In reality, it was only about an hour before word came that there had indeed been a vicious attack intended for the king's gold, but because of the intensified guard, the would-be thieves had been easily surprised and over powered and some sixty of them had been captured alive and taken to the dungeons to be questioned by the Chief Captain. It had been an unprecedented success for the king's army and they hoped to be able to get enough information from the prisoners to be able to punish Lord Rosskeene.

This news, although proof enough that there was indeed a plot underway to weaken the crown, was also proof that the information Chantaya had brought was valid. That was both reassuring and incredibly frightening. She was right and had been a huge help to those keeping the kingdom of Monciere secure, but she was also fair in the center of a veritable military tussle. Much as Peyton was grateful that they'd been able to stop the attack, he would much rather have found that it had all been a false alarm and that, in truth, Chantaya was safe and secure in her new employment. Alas, she wasn't secure at all.

§§§§

Lord Rosskeene, far away in the security of his manor, was furious when he heard the news of the failure to steal the king's gold. He slammed the riding crop he was holding against the nearby table and stalked across the room, swearing bitterly as he went. He turned back and lashed out, "Fools could have taken the gold! How were you defeated? There was nigh two hundred of you!"

The shaggy mercenary who had been the only one to make it out and return, who knew Lord Rosskeene was involved, shook his head. "Somehow, they knew we were coming, m'lord. There were soldiers everywhere, I tell you. We hadn't a chance."

Rosskeene shook his own head and closed in on the man to snarl through gritted teeth, *"No one knew. No one knew but me and a handful of others who never left here until last night. I kept them here just for that reason! They couldn't have known! You're all just imbeciles."* He threw the crop this time and spat, "Get out of my house. Go and find me more men who are capable this time!"

The blood of anger darkened the man's face and as he turned to go, he said over his shoulder, "I'll find more men, but you keep your plans hidden. 'Twas they knew we were coming."

When the man was gone, Rosskeene turned to the decanter at the table and, filling a glass, took three long swallows and then dashed the glass and remaining contents to the flagstone floor. *Had they known? Two hundred men should have been enough! How could they have known?*

His wife rushed in at the sound of the shattering glass. She took one look and jumped right into haranguing him and he angrily glared at her and stalked from the room. *What had ever possessed him to marry her?* For the thousandth time, his thoughts turned to Isabella, out there living in his stable.

'Twas time he brought the Kincraig women into the house where he'd have the access he'd intended to have to them. Conrad was the finest horse handler in the land, but there was something about him that kept one from all out challenging him. Not that he was afraid of the man. He, Lord Rosskeene, was Lord of nearly the largest holdings in the whole of the kingdom. He simply had more important things to do than worry about having Isabella, but there were times, like tonight . . . He again heard the high pitched rasp of his wife's voice ranting and swore once more. Once he was king . . . How had the knights known?

§§§§

The second week in September, it rained most of three days, so it was a surprise to Chantaya when, on the first clear evening, as she and Conrad were working the young horses in the meadow, she heard a horse whinny from the nearby wood and looked up to see Mordecai appear momentarily from the trees. Later that night, he left her a wooden cage full of six pigeons that she was to conceal in the rafters of the stable loft. He told her in case of another emergency the likes of the last; she could simply carefully tie a small message to one of the bird's feet and turn it loose. That the bird would fly back to Mordecai's home where they lived in Bartok's shelter. He would watch for the birds' return and pass on the messages without Chantaya having to take such a dangerous journey. They were a wonderfully comforting gift.

As fate would have it, only two days after Mordecai brought the birds, while working the afternoon in the butler's pantry, Chantaya was brought up short when she heard Lord Rosskeene and the man he was with speak of the gathering of the Great Council that was to convene at the castle the next day. Chantaya had known the king had called a meeting of the nobles two days hence that Rosskeene would attend, but she hadn't known the Great Council was to meet a day earlier.

As she polished, she was brought up even more sharply to realize Rosskeene was speaking of an attack on the Great Council while they met. She shook her head. She must have heard wrong. Who would attack the greatest of the knights when all twenty were gathered in one spot? They were the very best and bravest, the mightiest soldiers and the most loyal to the crown. To attack them would be suicide.

She paused in her work. It would either be suicide or brilliant! The knights wouldn't have their battle armor or weapons while meeting in the great hall of the castle. And they probably wouldn't be expecting an attack while they were gathered in the strength of their numbers. But if one was able to successfully slay both the council knights and the entirety of the royal family at the same time, the kingdom would be completely vulnerable to the overthrow of the mightiest nobleman. It would be a thoroughly decisive military victory, were it to succeed.

The thought made her stomach churn and then the next thought, when she realized that Peyton would be among the first line of those guarding the king and Great Council, made her veritably ill. He would be in the most heated of battles.

Waiting to hear the rest of what Rosskeene was planning, she then returned the silver to its proper place and went back through the kitchen and toward the stables, indescribably grateful for Mordecai's delivery of the pigeons. She wondered how long it would take a bird to fly home and then for Mordecai to discover it. The meeting was the very next day. She needed to send the message immediately.

In her room, being quiet so as not to wake her napping mother, she penned the message, folded and rolled it into a tiny scroll, then procured thread with which to secure it to the bird and went back through the gathering gray dusk out into the stable. Conrad was no where to be seen, and she quickly climbed the loft ladder. Kneeling in the hay beside the small wooden cage, she took one of the pigeons from it and then struggled to tie the miniature scroll to the wiggly leg of the frightened creature.

After the third attempt, she finally figured out how to hang on to the thing and tie the message. She let out a sigh of relief and up ended the flustered pigeon only to have the message slip out of the thread she'd secured it with.

In frustration, she carefully untied all she'd done and was just beginning to start all over, when she heard footsteps and whistling in the stable below her. Knowing it would be only moments before someone climbed the loft ladder to begin feeding the horses, she hurriedly returned the bird to the cage.

As she went to set the cage aside, she was horrified to find she hadn't hooked the latch properly and in less than a second, all six of the birds flew out of the opening. In a tight group, they all flew into the rafters above her and settled onto a beam where they proceeded to warble and coo at each other as they paced back and forth just a foot or two above her head. Quickly, she closed the big loft door at the end of the stable to keep them from escaping.

At least they hadn't flown completely away! She tucked the tiny scroll into the pocket of her dress and hurried to descend the ladder. Conrad had a wooden net on the wall near his quarters he used for fishing. Perhaps if she brought it up, she could recapture the birds.

Racing down the alleyway of the stable, she met one of the young grooms who worked with Conrad. Slowing to a more decorous pace, she nodded at the shy young man that she knew admired her and continued on. She had to catch those birds and quickly!

With the net in tow, she once again climbed the ladder, only to realize that the groom was up there and had opened the door she had closed so he could feed the horses in the paddock below. Just as she appeared through the opening in the floor, he tossed a forkful of hay and Chantaya was dismayed as the flying hay spooked five of the birds off the beam. They took flight and this time, they did indeed fly straight out the door of the loft.

'Twas all she could do not to cry out. Only one left!

When the last bird paced a few more steps and then took flight as well and followed the other five out into the freedom of the gray evening sky, she did cry out. They were gone! Gone! And without the neatly rolled little scroll that held the vital message. She closed her eyes for a moment in complete frustration. How had she been so clumsy? What would Mordecai think when he saw the birds but no message? She hoped and prayed he'd at least understand something was amiss and start this way to see what had happened.

The groom made a sound and she opened her eyes to see him looking at her hesitantly. She glanced around and realized he thought she'd followed him up there. Blushing crimson, she hurriedly mumbled something about watching the birds and headed back down the ladder. He probably thought she was a complete dolt or worse. And she was.

She put her hand to her head, sighed again and looked outside one more time at the heavy, leaden clouds that piled on the western horizon, obliterating the sinking of the sun. There was nothing for it. It didn't matter if the sky itself fell. She had to get word of Rosskeene's plans to the castle. She squared her shoulders as she silently uttered a prayer in her mind, *Lord, you've helped with everything else I've needed to do. Please, help me one more time to accomplish this.*

Hours later, deep in the night, as she rode the trail through the woods in the drenching rain, she indeed felt like the sky was falling with the downpour. 'Twas raining buckets. She clenched her teeth against the chattering cold and pulled the hood of her cloak down over her hat and forehead a margin further. At least with this nasty weather, she hadn't encountered anyone on the road on this darkest of miserable, cold nights. She rubbed a rivulet of rain from the tip of her nose and looked around to try and distinguish anything in the near blackness. She had to be getting close, didn't she? She'd been unable to go much faster than a shambling trot because she couldn't see, but she had been riding for what felt like years.

Ten minutes later she realized she'd thought too soon that no one would be about on a night like this as her horse's ears swiveled forward and back several times. Something was out there. Chantaya couldn't see what it was, but the horse sensed it. She pushed the hood of her cape back so she could see better, slowed the horse even further and rode with her hand resting on the hilt of the sword Sir Mordecai had given her.

Bursts of wind drove the rain nearly sideways and the droplets that had gathered on the overhanging trees fell in a torrent with each gust. She blinked to clear her eyes and looked all around as her horse snorted into the blackness and sidestepped nervously. Whatever was there was close. She could feel it in the tautness of the horse's muscles and the tenseness of the back of her neck. Another prayer seemed to spring from her mind almost of its own volition. Instinctively, she knew she needed a higher power to get her through this.

Suddenly, her horse shied violently to the right as a rider lunged out of the trees on the left. Chantaya fought both her fear and her horse's head as she veered around the rider and slapped her heels to the loyal steed under her. He'd been toiling along willingly in this miserable weather and obviously tired, but he put on a burst of speed when she asked him anyway.

Wiping her eyes again, she tried desperately to see what was ahead and failed. 'Twas simply too dark. She steeled herself, half expecting to run into something if the trail turned without her being able to see it. The horse under her seemed to be able to sense where the road went and she let it have its head as she turned to see how close the other rider was behind her.

She could hear hoof beats above the rustle of the storm and with a sinking heart, she realized it wasn't a single rider, but two that followed her. Two riders. How was she ever going to handle two? She leaned forward and shouted encouragement to the horse as she thought about Peyton. In her head, she asked, *What should I do, Peyton? You're wise. Help me be brave enough to get safely through this.*

As willing as her horse was, she knew it was tiring and the riders behind her were nearly upon her. The horse suddenly stumbled beneath her and went to its knees and she knew she was going over its head. Kicking her feet from the stirrups, she tucked her head and rolled, her hand never leaving the hilt of her sword and as she landed with a jar that near drove the breath from her, she came to her feet, drawing the sword as she did so.

The two riders' horses had passed her and they spun them to return. As the first one passed by her, she slashed with her blade across the breadth of his thigh and then turned to the other one who sprang lightly from his horse. While she focused on the man afoot in front of her, she heard the other groan. She had no idea how injured he was and she continued her non-stop prayer, hoping he was at least out of it enough to give her a moment to disarm this one.

The man in front of her circled her warily in the darkness and then said, "'Tis a little man we have here, Morley. Feisty, but slender. 'Tis but a boy, he is. Have you any gold, boy? Give it to me now and perchance, Morley and me will let ye get back on your steed and ride away on this lovely night for travelin'." He gave a sickening laugh that completely belied his words and then lunged toward her with his own blade.

She parried and thrust and grew slightly more hopeful when she saw he was clumsy as he came round to face her again. Chancing a glance at his companion, she looked back just in time to ward off another thrust and cautioned herself not to take either of them lightly.

Countering his moves, their blades rang in the night and the meager light bounced off the dripping steel with an eerie gleam. She circled away from the injured rider and settled into fighting the way Sir Mordecai and Peyton had trained her and focused on using every bit of force she could muster to make up for her much smaller size. This was no carefree spar in the grass of Mordecai's meadow. 'Twas even more than a fight for her life. Her survival and possibly that of the crown depended on her and she thrust and spun with an intensity born of that.

She fought the one, trying always to tell where the other was and then suddenly a shadow moved on the other side. For a sickening moment, she thought there were now three until she saw the face of her own horse materialize out of the misty blackness. She gulped her relief, feinted left, then slashed and finally connected as she cut deeply into the man's shoulder and chest. At that, the slash only seemed to anger him and he came back at her more viciously than ever and she felt the bite of his steel against her own ribs along her side and to her back and drew in a gasping breath.

His blow as well made her bear down more surely. She turned back on him in near desperation and began to drive him backward with a strong series of parries and thrusts. For a long moment, she fought like a fiend and then, finally, he left himself open.

She shuddered as she drove her blade deep into the thief's chest. She felt it penetrate and even felt his body cringe as he knew she'd dealt him a killing blow. She felt her own pang deep in her belly at the realization, but then had to turn from him almost instantly to face the other who had dismounted his horse to challenge her as well.

This man limped markedly from her earlier slash, but he was far the more skilled with a blade and she needed every bit of her training to hold him at bay. They fought there in the dark for several minutes, swinging, countering, thrusting and slashing. Once, she stumbled over the other fallen man who had only the life left in him to grasp at her ankle as she fenced and he nearly caused her demise when he did it. Once more she felt the pain of steel piercing her skin, this time on the point of her shoulder. Again it served to bring her to a more intense focus and she jerked her foot free of the fallen thief's hand in time to counter the limping swordsman.

She was tired. Tired to the soul and cold to the bone and when she again heard hoof beats bearing down upon them from the trail ahead, 'twas nearly more than she could face. With a sense of desperate discouragement, she breathed another silent prayer, "Please God, help me. Please. Don't let these evil men triumph. Nor Rosskeene." She spun and stabbed as hard as she could, but the other man was prepared and countered and she went on silently, "Please. Preserve us a kingdom. Most are righteous. Please help us. Help me."

As the approaching horseman closed in upon them, she thrust one more time, fighting with everything she had, but was once again parried. Frightened beyond belief, she tried desperately to hear Peyton's voice of encouragement in her head and then, miraculously, she heard Mordecai's instead as he leaped from the piebald with the white shoulder and drew his own sword.

With a single, mighty slash, he stilled the wounded man forever and then wrapped an arm round Chantaya's shoulder as she dissolved into tears against him, shuddering to think how close she had just come to failing in her quest. She took a huge, relieved breath. Mordecai would help her warn the crown. It was an immense relief to be able to share that responsibility.

For a moment, he patted her back, and then, when the first thief moaned, Mordecai urged her back to her horse saying, "Come, young Chantaya. There might be others along anytime. Let us get back off the road. Are you well? Were you hurt?"

She caught her horse, leapt into the saddle and followed him into the blackness of the trees, honestly not sure how badly she had been hurt in the swordfight. That she had been cut, she knew, but she'd had no time to even question how deeply.

When they were far into the wood, Mordecai pulled up in the lee of a huge old tree and helped her down. In the dark and the rain, as she told him of the impending attack on the great council and royal family they tried to determine how badly she was hurt. Although, with no light and the storm 'twas impossible to tell. She was wounded, but honestly, she was far more uncomfortable from the cold than the slashes. Mordecai listened gravely as she told of why she'd come and then he paused for a long moment to consider their course of action.

She knew just what he was thinking. She needed to get home, but they had only a matter of hours to get the message back to Valais to the other knights, and she could almost see Mordecai struggling to decide if he had the time to get her home safely and still return to Valais in time. As the old knight wiped at the water that dripped from his white hair, she knew as well that he also had to gauge whether he was physically up to the grueling hours in the saddle in the cold rain. This ride had been incredibly taxing to her and she was young. At least he had an oilskin cloak that shed the water. She hadn't been able to find one in the stable.

Making a sudden decision, she moved once more to her horse and asked Mordecai, "Are you able to make it still to Valais? Is there yet time? How long before morning?"

He nodded, but then added, "There's time enough to go to Valais. It's going to Rosskeene Manor and back to Valais that I question. But we must get you home."

Climbing back aboard her streaming horse, she shook her head. "No. I shall be fine. You must away to Valais. The knights must be warned. That is most important." She could see him vacillating and went on pleadingly, "Sir Mordecai, this has been a difficult night for me. Truly. Please don't let it be for naught. Go to Valais. The kingdom is far the more important. Please. I beg of you."

The old man looked at her for a long, long moment there in the sodden darkness. Finally, he nodded gravely and stepped into his own saddle. Turning back to her, he said, "I'll see you safely past those men." She nodded, unbelievably grateful for his understanding. This ride was going to be hard enough as it was just fighting the weather. More fear was the last thing she needed.

Once they were well past where she had been attacked and the bodies still lay in the road, they pulled up and there was another moment as he struggled once more with leaving her alone. Finally, she leaned across and gave him a one armed hug and said, "I must go. Thank you once again for coming to see about me." He merely dipped his head and then, as they went to turn from each other, she paused once more and pleaded, "Don't tell him. About the sword fight. 'Twould kill him. It couldn't be helped, but he needn't know. Just give him my love." Again, he merely nodded and, at length, turned his horse and trotted away.

Her horse seemed to know they were headed home and it perked up, in spite of the storm and the hours it had traveled. She wished desperately for a bit of that perkiness herself as she shivered violently and the wounds on her ribs and shoulder began to ache with the miles. At least the cold kept the fatigue that made her feel heavy and incredibly clumsy at bay.

There were times when she wondered if she was going to be able to make it. Her hands were so cold she could hardly hold the reins and her feet were numb in the stirrups. Still, the rain beat down, pummeled by the wind, and the fear that rode with her ramped up with every strange sound the gusts carried.

For miles, she kept hearing someone behind her. Over and over she wondered if more highwaymen were coming. Finally, when she got a glimpse in a flash of lightning, she realized the two thieves' horses had followed her horse. 'Twas a great measure of relief to know she wasn't being followed by more murdering thieves. She looked up into the unrelenting storm, wondering if the moon was up there somewhere above it, and if it was raining where Peyton was. She hoped and prayed he was somewhere warm and safe tonight.

By the time she made it to the manor, she was nearly past worrying about Peyton, or highwaymen, or even about whether anyone at the manor would detect her return. By then, her mind had all but ceased to function. At that point, all she cared for was that she didn't fall off her horse and freeze to death in the middle of the road.

When she got there, she rode right into the alleyway of the stable and leaned over the neck of her horse, truly wondering if she could dismount by herself. At length, she concluded she couldn't and was just about to call out to Conrad for help when his room door opened.

At first, he growled, "Who goes there?" When she tried to answer him from her nearly frozen mouth, he realized it was her and rushed to catch her as she literally fell off the exhausted horse. Speechless with surprise, he carried her clear to the room she shared with her mother before he was able to exclaim over her sodden and bloody state.

When her mother opened the door at his knock, wide eyed and not yet awake enough to even realize Chantaya wasn't in their bed, the only thing that kept her from crying out was Conrad's gruff whisper for quiet. They helped her inside and her mother struck the light as Conrad laid her on the bed and instantly began to build a fire in their little fire place while her mother began to peel off the dripping layers of her clothing.

She had to give her mother credit for durability. Finding her daughter half drowned, mostly frozen, wounded, and dressed as a boy didn't shake Isabella's nerves unduly. Even finding that her daughter had spent the entirety of the night riding through the robber wood in the rain carrying military secrets didn't seem to rattle her as Chantaya worried it would.

They listened gravely as she attempted to explain through chattering teeth what she'd been doing. As they took her hat and cloak, the wounds to her ribs and shoulder became more obvious and Isabella inhaled a quick breath as Conrad asked, "What happened here, Chantaya? These are deep cuts."

The two of them stood looking at her in concern and for a single moment, she considered telling her mother an untruth, but she couldn't do it. As Conrad put pressure on her shoulder, she sighed and tried for lightness as she admitted, "I uh, I had a bit of trouble with a sword wielding highwayman." As her mother gasped out loud, the knowledge that she had had to kill one of the men brought tears to Chantaya's eyes and she looked away as she wiped at them.

Conrad put a calming hand upon both of their shoulders, and said mildly, "'Twould seem you triumphed. Here, hold this pressure, Isabella. I'll bring bandages." He went out the door and Chantaya met her mother's eyes, pleading that she not ask any more questions of a night that had already been more than she could bear.

Turning away to bring a damp cloth to clean her up with, her mother looked saddened as Conrad returned with bandages to patch her up from those he used on the horses. When Conrad left at length to care for the thieves' horses as well as hers, and begin his morning chores as the sky slightly lightened in the east, Isabella finally sighed and laid a gentle hand on Chantaya's forehead for a moment before helping her the rest of the way out of her wet things.

Once they were alone, after wiping away the rain and dirt and blood, and then draping a quilt around her, her mother silently stitched at the wounds on her ribs and shoulder as Chantaya did her level best not to do more than gasp in pain at each sweep of the needle. At least the cold that still had her teeth chattering had partially numbed her. When she was through, Isabella wiped at her own tears as she smeared a harsh smelling salve on the stitches and then covered them with clean bandages.

At length, when she was all of a piece again, Chantaya took a deep breath and began to clean up the mess. As she set aside the small sword, Isabella grimaced, and when she pulled the dagger from her boot, Isabella put both hands on her hips and finally said, "All right, young lady. How long have you been doing this and why in the world haven't you told me what you were doing? What if you had died out there tonight?"

Turning back to her mother, as she rummaged for dry, warm clothing to wear in to begin making breakfast, Chantaya tried to smile past her chattering teeth. "I didn't want you to worry, Mum. I only did what I had to do. Nothing more, nothing less. This was only the second time. I swear it." Her mother still looked doubtful and Chantaya added gently, "'Twasn't as if I wanted to go about like I did. And I didn't die. The good Lord sent Mordecai."

Jaclyn M. Hawkes

Chapter 14

Peyton was up early after a strangely restless night, but had yet to leave his room when there came a quiet knock upon his door. He glanced out the tiny window to see it wasn't even light out and went to the door to see who under heaven would be knocking at this hour. When Mordecai stepped inside wearing his armor, soaked to the bone, and obviously drawn with fatigue, Peyton's heart began to pound within his chest as he instantly suspected something was terribly amiss and Chantaya was probably involved somehow.

Peyton went to help Mordecai with his dripping cloak, but the old knight shook his head. "No. I must see to Bartok. There's trouble brewing. I need you to come with me to the castle. Get your things." He gave Peyton a tired smile and added, "And wear your oilskin. It's damp out." The old man's touch of humor helped to ease the worry and Peyton gave him a hesitant smile in return as he realized Mordecai had learned over the years to roll with whatever came his way in just this manner.

Mordecai went to go back out the door, but Peyton stopped him with a hand on his arm. The two looked steadily at each other for several seconds and then Peyton only shook his head and let the older man's arm go. If Mordecai had known for sure that Chantaya was all right, he'd have already mentioned it. Peyton turned back to his room, hurriedly pulled up his bedding and stomped into his boots, muttering a prayer as he did so. What had she gotten herself into this time?

Peyton strode into the stable to assist the older man and when he saw that the horse was lathered and fair exhausted, his concern increased even further and he edged closer to hear what Mordecai had to tell him. As they spoke quietly, Peyton hurriedly saddled his charger and then switched Mordecai's saddle to his squire Shaun's horse. The two of them mounted and headed out into the rain for the ride to the castle.

At the gates the guards there stepped close to peer into their faces, but upon recognizing Peyton, they opened the gate and let them through without question. Mordecai looked up at him for a moment as they hurried through to the servant's entrance of the castle. There, they pounded on the door. When a tired cook opened it, they stepped inside and Peyton quietly said, "We need to see Prince Laird, straight away. Please, go and tell him. We're Sir Peyton and Sir Mordecai."

The still sleepy cook was surprised as she looked up at the two of them standing there in their dripping armor. She started to say something, then looked them up and down and decided against it. Instead, she simply nodded and turned into the interior of the castle. A few moments later, she returned and seemed even more surprised as she said, "He said he'll meet you in the salon. Follow me please."

When the prince walked in mere minutes later, he was fully dressed, in spite of looking as if he'd just been hauled out of bed in the dark by a servant. He met the two's grave looks, shut the heavy door, and asked, "What is it?"

Peyton looked to Mordecai to speak, but the older man gave a miniscule head shake and Peyton started in. The prince listened quietly until he finished, and then only asked, "Same source as the attack on the treasury?"

Both knights nodded and Peyton confirmed, "The same."

Prince Laird gave Peyton a long look as he considered this and then said, "I'll go get my father. Have a seat."

Mordecai looked at the puddle of water the two of them were standing in, but the prince only waved a hand as he walked to the door. "'Twill dry."

The king took longer to appear, but he was fully dressed as well when he accompanied the prince into the room and walked straight across to embrace Mordecai. Stepping back, he looked the sodden old knight up and down and said, "Do they not allow you a moment of peaceful respite from your life of military greatness? You look well, Sir Mordecai. A trifle tired perhaps, but fit as a bull. Thank you for coming to me this wet morning. I want you to know I truly appreciate it." He turned and shook Peyton's hand and added, "And thanks to you as well, Sir Peyton. Let us retire to the breakfast room and acquire a strategy as we eat, shall we?"

§§§§

The streets of Valais didn't appear to be expecting a major military attack that morning, and, in fact, it was only a matter of an hour or two after the attempted coup before the streets were back to their normal daily pace of people going about their own business. The reality was that few of the townspeople even realized the Great Council had had a meeting, let alone that an attempt to overthrow the king had taken place.

True, there had been an inordinate number of strangers moving about, as well as battalions of troops quietly coming and going, but strangers weren't unheard of. And the troops moved about occasionally on military business, and were more unobtrusive this morning than they'd ever been.

As quietly as it all came about, the fact of the matter was that there had indeed been an organized attempt to harm both the Great Council and the crown, and the state of the castle dungeons was another matter entirely. The cold, stone cells were fair to bursting as there were fully hundreds more prisoners being held there this afternoon than there were that morning. There were also cart loads of bodies being taken to burial in the cemetery on the far western edge of the city. They were the remains of those who hadn't survived the short, decidedly one sided battle that had occurred in the castle courtyard at just before noon.

But Lord Rosskeene didn't see the state of the dungeons, or the cemetery either one as he arrived in his carriage at a little after one o'clock that afternoon. He'd come expecting to step into the role of monarch. To courageously and magnanimously step in to comfort and protect a kingdom thrown into chaos by the death of its entire hierarchy, but he couldn't find even a margin of chaos. Instead, he was wondering whether his coup attempt had gone so smoothly as to cause no upheaval at all, or whether it had failed as completely as it appeared to have failed. Or if it hadn't even occurred, which was what the case seemed to be. There was simply no activity in the streets whatsoever to indicate a battle of any kind.

As his carriage drove past the seemingly placid castle, he felt a seething anger arise in him. Nothing! There was nothing going on at all and he glared around at the unassuming peasants in fury. What had happened here this day? He'd sent literally hundreds of men, under the command of fairly competent soldiers. 'Twas impossible that they'd not been victorious in such a surprise attack, so then where were they all? And why wasn't anyone in the street noticing that the king and his heirs and his stronghold of knights had been slain?

Rosskeene cursed viciously and slammed his elegant driving gloves to the seat beside him. What had happened here today? Had anything at all happened here today?

He glanced around one more time and closed his eyes in an attempt to rein in the fury. He had to remain calm. He needed to go on to his meeting with the noblemen tomorrow as if nothing had gone on at all. No one knew he was involved. In truth, only a couple of the most key men had known he was the mastermind of this attack. He'd seen to that, just in case the impossible happened and they hadn't succeeded. Like before, he had made sure to keep his own noble name clear of any wrong doing. It had been a vitally smart idea, apparently.

SSSS

King Dougal nodded for the entrance of his Chief Captain, hoping for a more heartening report that they'd found some willing to witness against Lord Rosskeene. The Chief Captain had been in the dungeon for most of two days, but had yet to bring news of any luck in finding one who would admit to knowing who was behind this second and more vicious attack on the crown.

They knew from Mordecai and Peyton's informant that it was Rosskeene, but Dougal preferred to take the matter before one of the magistrate's so that any proceedings would be considered absolutely above reproach. Dougal was known throughout the land to be fair and generous, and he was. Moreover, he wished to remain known that way. It made governing so much easier and Monciere prospered because of it. Beheading or hanging the wealthiest nobleman was apt to make ripples.

However, thus far, they had only the informant's word to stand against Lord Rosskeene's. If it came down to it, Dougal would do whatever he needed to do, with or without the magistrate's involvement, and he'd soon need to, but he preferred it otherwise. So, the Chief Captain kept interrogating. All were hoping eventually, they would find one who could testify.

§§§§

Two evenings after the attack, Prince Laird asked Peyton to report to him in the castle again. They had met numerous times over the last day and a half and Peyton knew Lord Rosskeene had reported to the noblemen's meeting acting as if all was right in the world. Nothing had been said to him, but the placid tone of the king's family had an undertone of tension that only those most trusted were allowed to glimpse.

Princess Clarissa had been quietest of all. Finally, the Queen herself had suggested a royal masquerade ball to try to promote a sense of well being in the kingdom until the problems with Rosskeene had been settled. Surprisingly, the king had agreed and a date just ten days off had been set. Under the circumstances, Peyton had been convinced they were all lunatics until Mordecai explained to him of the importance of keeping the appearance of peace and prosperity in the land.

When Peyton reported to the prince, the prince's signature grin was back on his face as he rose upon Peyton's entrance to his study. The worry over Chantaya that had plagued Peyton since Mordecai's arrival made it hard to return the smile, and the prince said, "Oh come now, Sir Peyty. Have you been eating pickles for supper? Surely there must be a smile in there somewhere."

Peyton finally grinned and returned, "Forgive me, Prince Lairdy, I must simply be fatigued. I'll do better, I swear it, Sire."

The prince nodded, "Good. See that you do. Your glumness has cast a veritable pall round the entire kingdom. How is Sir Mordecai?"

The smile faded again as Peyton replied, "Quite ill I'm afraid, Your Highness. Unfortunately, his long night in the rain has taken a toll. But he'll be fine, in time. He truly is as a strong old bull."

Shaking his head, the prince's own smile slipped as he said, "'Tis a shame his wife and daughter died. One who has served as he has deserves more in his old age than a cottage and a loyal horse."

Peyton agreed, "Indeed, Sire. But he has more than that. He lost his wife, but my family loves him as our own and Chantaya near worships him. She's every bit the daughter to him and him a father to her. Or a grandfather. At any rate, she fair adores him."

"But she's hours away at Rosskeene's manor, is she not?" Peyton only nodded, the ugly truth painful to say out loud.

The prince sensed his discomfort and assured, "Not for long, Sir Peyton. My father won't take much more of Rosskeene's antics. We'll deal with him and get your girl and her mother out of there. That's what I wanted to see you about. You must find a way to bring her to the ball, if possible. 'Tis why Mother chose a masquerade ball, so your love could come and Rosskeene not be the wiser. He's likely to be there, of course. I also wanted to ask you to go home and see to a few things there. See to it that Mordecai is cared for properly and check on your Chantaya. God willing, she made it home safely the other night. And while Rosskeene is here in Valais for a time, perhaps you and your father and brother could get a sense of how the farmers and other tenants are doing there. No?"

"Of course, Sire." Peyton hesitated, unsure of how to voice his next concern. "About that ball, Sire. Chantaya is the loveliest and fairest of all God's daughters, but she is a peasant, Sire."

The prince nodded. "I understand that, Sir Peyton. That factored into the decision of the masquerade ball as well. You haven't seemed to have come to terms with the blessings of your knighthood. 'Tis the only situation that can gracefully overcome the blasted class system of this world. You see, even though most of the nobles have forgotten how they came to be nobles in the first place, that being that their ancestors were trusted warriors for the kings in days gone by and were given gifts of land, the crown has not forgotten. We still reward those whose service is of great worth to the kingdom, such as the sacrifices of yourself. And your Chantaya. She will only remain a peasant until she is married to a knight. I'm assuming that won't be overly long, with the way you speak of her."

The teasing grin was back on the prince's face and Peyton shook his head and laughed as he said, "I pray not, Sire. Still, we've gone to lengths not to let Rosskeene know she has ties to the soldiers. I may not be able to spirit her away from Rosskeene's household for a ball and still keep our secret. And it's a fair bet she hasn't a gown. Perhaps it's best not to expect her at the ball."

Nodding quietly, the prince said, "Do as you think best." But then he qualified that by grinning again and adding, "But don't be fooled into thinking that a woman who can save a kingdom can't find a ball gown. If I know my sister, the troll, you remember the one?" Peyton smiled and the prince went on, "She's already begun working on that. Strange brain that she has, she probably thinks if she helps with the gown you'll finally kiss her. I wouldn't do it, by the way. She probably tastes like a troll as well. And that can't be toothsome, eh? But please don't tell her I warned you. She can be such a punishment at times when she's put out with me."

He grimaced dramatically before going on. "Take as long as Mordecai and the people in Rosskeene's lands need and then report back to me at the ball, with the girl in your arms, if God wills it."

Peyton had no trouble smiling as he shook the young royal's hand and said, "I will do my best, Sire. And thank you, Prince Laird. I appreciate the chance to see to Mordecai and Chantaya. And the others. God bless, Your Highness."

The prince began to walk Peyton to the door and grinned one more time as they glimpsed Princess Clarissa approaching down the hall. To Peyton he softly said, "You may need God's blessing yourself, Sir Knight. Here comes the troll now. Remember. Don't taste her." The prince made a surreptitious gagging sound and then straightened his face when his sister looked at him suspiciously.

Even the appearance of the princess couldn't stop the grin that spread across Peyton's face as he bowed respectfully before her and said, "Good evening, Your Highness."

She was still looking at the two of them suspiciously when Peyton raised his face and turned to finish walking down the hallway of the castle to leave. The princess fell into step with him and she asked, "What was he saying about me just now? And I know you don't lie, Sir Peyton, so out with it." Peyton could hear the prince burst into laughter as he went back into his study.

Trying to decide what to tell her after her quip about honesty, he was thoughtful for a moment and then said, "He was telling me you could possibly recommend someone to help with a ball gown for a friend of mine." Looking down into her eyes, he could see she suddenly wasn't happy with him and he questioned if he wouldn't have been better off admitting the prince had said she probably tasted like a troll. He sighed, wondering how he could ever learn to deal with the princess more ably. Maybe bringing Chantaya to the ball was a good idea after all. Who knew with female creatures? Certainly not him.

The princess walked with him to the front door of the castle, where she put a hand on his arm as he went to open it. When he looked down at her, she gave him a subtly pouty lip and said, "I was actually hoping you were going to be escorting *me* to the ball, Sir Peyton. Father says I must either be with a prince, one of a select handful of nobles, or one of the knights of the Great Council or one of the King's First Guard. So, it must be you, Sir Peyton. There is simply no one else I could bear to have escort me." She could see his hesitation and added, "You won't have to kiss me. So you needn't worry."

Peyton smiled tiredly and said kindly, "Princess, I'm grateful you would think to honor me, however, I am but a humble knight. I am far from worthy to escort a princess. And I will still be guarding you and your family that night. Forgive me, but I must decline. I'm unfit. Surely there is someone worthy you could bear to have escort you."

"But you just said you needed a ball gown for a friend. So you must be going."

"Yes, I'll be going, God willing I can find her a dress and get her here."

"Then why can't you escort me? I already have a dress and I'm here."

Prince Laird came through and to the door with them, grinning like a jester. Sidling up to them, he said, "What are you doing, Troll? He's tired, can you not see that? Pray, let him go."

She gave him an irritated look and said, "I am trying to influence him to take me to the ball, so that I am not stuck with either an old man or a spoiled, pouty neighboring prince. You know what Father has decreed. It's clearly Sir Peyton's civic duty to rescue me from such a fate. And you are more than welcome to mind your own business!"

Prince Laird shrugged and grinned. "Spoiled and pouty will suit you perfectly. Why not go with a kindred spirit?"

She stomped a dainty foot. "Laird, stop it this moment!"

He came and put a friendly arm about her shoulders. "Oh, all right. I'm sorry you're a spoiled and pouty troll and that I drew attention to that fact. Perhaps I should put it this way. Are you one who believes in marital loyalty?"

She puckered her brow in confusion. "Of course. What do you mean?" She paused, frowning and then turned to Peyton in shock. "You're married? Oh, Sir Peyton, I'm so sorry! Please, forgive me! Why hasn't someone told me you were married?"

Peyton shook his head and grinned, wondering how he always got stuck in the middle of these two. "I'm not married, Princess. That's not what he meant. He simply meant that I wish I was. There's a girl back home I fair worship."

There was an uncomfortable pause and then she finally said, "Oh." She looked at him sadly and at length asked, "Why didn't you just say so? I would have respected that."

Having no idea what to say, Peyton hesitated and the prince chuckled and said, "Maybe it was private, Troll. You may not believe this, but to some, love is precious and treasured."

Surprisingly, the princess seemed positively penitent and softly said, "Yes, I suppose so. And someone who is too honorable to kiss, or lie, is probably one of those types to whom love is sacred." She turned to Peyton and said, "Please forgive me for trying to get you to do what I wanted. I'm sorry. I had no idea you were in love with another." After a moment, she added thoughtfully, "'Tis a pity there aren't more men like you."

The prince leaned and kissed her on top of her head and said, "It truly is a pity, Sissy. Mostly that you didn't find him sooner. Maybe he could have overlooked the fact that you're a troll and he could have fallen madly in love with you. As it is, it's too late. His heart is taken. I know this for a surety because he didn't even look at Meggy Rylander in the garrison kitchen. He's the only man on this continent who hasn't. His love must be true."

At that, the princess was the one who laughed. "Indeed. It must. I've heard mention of this Meg, although I've never heard her called Meggy. And how is it, brother, that you not only call her Meggy, but you know her last name?"

"Oh, simple. Her father is our father's blacksmith. We're close, Milton Rylander and I."

"Oh, I see. Indeed. 'Tis uncanny how close you are to father's smithy." She rolled her eyes and turned back to Peyton. "Laird is correct, Sir Peyton. You do look weary. Go to your rest, and I'll not pester you about the ball again. In fact, I'll see to it that your love has a gown to make you proud. What color are her eyes?"

Peyton hesitated a moment as he wondered how to handle her offer and both she and the prince laughed as the prince said, "They must be most heavenly eyes, to make him moon over them like that. Or is it that you don't remember, Sir Peyton? Surely you haven't made this girl up just to keep the trolls at bay."

Shaking his head one more time, Peyton said, "They're blue. As blue as the velvet sky of evening."

The princess sighed and Prince Laird nodded, "Poetic. I like that in a knight. It instills confidence in their rugged battle skills. And her figure? Dare we ask?"

Peyton flushed and the prince chuckled. "Apparently, we dare not. Just give us this. Is she taller or shorter than the troll here?"

"Taller. Several inches."

"And heavier or more slender?"

Again Peyton hesitated and the prince chuckled and said, "Look at him, Clar. Torn between telling an untruth and offending a princess. He's fair squirming, he is. 'Tis that he thinks you're fat. He's simply too purely polite to say so."

She hit him with her elbow and he made an exaggerated groan as Peyton said, "I'm certain she's not so slender as you, Princess. Rest assured. In fact, she's probably not nearly so in places."

Again the prince grinned and laughed down at his sister and said, "What he means is she has a better figure as well. Isn't that what you mean, Sir Peyton? Very discreetly put, by the way."

Knowing he was burying himself, Peyton straightened and said, "Your figure is, in all ways, incomparable, Princess. Ignore your brother. Respectfully, of course. 'Tis his responsibility to tease you. And alas, I think I should remove myself before Prince Laird here gets myself beheaded. You needn't worry about the dress." He dipped his head respectfully. "Goodnight, Your Highnesses."

He turned to leave, but the princess called him back. As he turned, she said, "We truly will arrange for the dress. The both of us. He'll help me. He's got surprisingly good taste. Goodnight, Sir Peyton."

When Peyton told Mordecai, who was resting on Peyton's bunk at the garrison, what the prince had asked of him, Mordecai immediately swung his legs over the edge of the bed and went into a coughing spell. Concerned for his ill friend, Peyton asked, "What are you up to, Sir Knight?"

Grumbling under his breath, Mordecai said, "I'm getting my trousers on. What do you think? We're going to check on Chantaya. I've near gone out of my mind for wondering if she made it home that night."

Peyton was surprised and asked, "Now? You want to leave this evening?" Peyton shook his head. "You're ill. Go back to bed."

Mordecai only responded by lifting his breastplate into place and saying, "Don't you speak to me thus, you young ingrate. You may be bigger. And stronger. But 'tis that I'm more stubborn. Go get our horses. I'll stop in the kitchen and get a bait of supper and meet you in the courtyard."

For just a moment, Peyton felt he should argue, much as he didn't want to. But then he decided that Mordecai probably truly couldn't rest until he knew for himself that Chantaya was all right, and Peyton felt the same. Plus, taking advantage of the current break in the storm made sense. Moreover, when they got to Rosskeene Manor, they'd need to check on her under the cover of darkness anyway. After considering all of this while Mordecai continued to dress, when the old man looked askance of him, Peyton ultimately smiled and turned for the door. "I'll get the horses."

Jaclyn M. Hawkes

Chapter 15

Chantaya put the last supper dish away and then sniffled as she looked round the kitchen, wondering if it would be acceptable to sweep the next morning, instead of last thing at night as they typically did. She was as tired tonight as she'd been immediately after her rainy night ride a day and a half ago and the cut on her ribs seemed loath to heal. It had scabbed over, but even with her mother's nasty salve, every time she changed the bandage, the scabs ripped off and bled. That made it still ridiculously sore. At least the wound on her shoulder was finally staying clean and dry.

Cook looked at her sympathetically as she lifted a hand to brush across Chantaya's damp forehead and said, "We're going to let the rest of it go, young Chantaya. Your mother took care of most of it earlier and the master's gone anyway. What do we care if Lady Winifred fusses? Get yourself off to bed. 'Tis the best thing for a touch of the weather like ye have. Come. I'll walk with you, in case that young lord gets any ideas into his head."

Gratefully, Chantaya nodded. Bed sounded positively divine just now. Together they walked to the stable and then Cook turned back around to go to her own room when Isabella stood from where she and Conrad had been pouring over a book at the table near their door. Gently, her mother felt Chantaya's head and then shook her own and said, "You're warm, daughter. And your nose is red from running. Go to bed and I'll bring you some heated rocks in a moment."

Again, Chantaya nodded. They would get no argument from her. She was still tired from her ride. As she passed by Conrad, she dropped a friendly hand to his shoulder and asked, "Are the new horses fitting in, then? They seem to be well."

"They're well. And fine pieces of horseflesh. I imagine when the master returns, he'll insist they belong to him since they showed up here that morning. They're as fine as any horse in his stables."

She gave him a tired smile. "I think they're yours. You're the one who found them and took care of them. They must have known what a soft heart you are." She leaned and kissed his cheek gently. "Goodnight, Conrad. Goodnight, Mother." She yawned and noticed it made her throat ache and she added sleepily, "I do love you both."

Once she was inside and had shut the door, Conrad's eyes met Isabella's and they smiled. Chantaya was weary and sick enough to be just a touch out of it this evening.

'Twas late. Her mother was long asleep in the bed beside her when a soft knock came at the door. Chantaya stood tiredly, threw on a warm wrapper and then paused to call out, "Who's there?" Conrad's voice reassured her and she opened the door and then couldn't help the tears that flooded into her eyes as she saw both Peyton and Mordecai standing beside Conrad in the near darkness of the stable.

She instantly stepped out and wrapped one arm around each of them and then felt foolish when all she wanted to do was hold on and cry. The incidents of the past days, and even how weak this cold caused her to feel made her incredibly emotional about the two of them.

For several moments, no one said anything, and then at length, Conrad said, "I'll bring some blankets so you can visit on the bench here without disturbing her mother. And Sir Mordecai, you look to be in about the same shape she's in. Could I interest you in a bunk in my own room then? There be four beds and just m'self livin' in there now. So, there's one for you as well, Sir Peyton. For as long as you can stay with us. No one ever goes in there but me. 'Tis lonely at times, but ever private."

The knights nodded and Mordecai said, "We would be forever in your debt, sir. Lead the way. 'Twas that we needed to know she was safe before we could stop for the night."

"I understand. Especially after what she told us of that even. Follow me." At the door to his room, Conrad showed them where to sleep and then asked, "Do your horses need looking after?"

Mordecai tiredly shook his head. "No. We left them safe in the wood. They'll be fine until morning. But thank you."

Before he turned to go in search of more blankets, Conrad said, "No. Thank you, Sir Mordecai. She wouldn't say much of the other night except that God sent you in the nick of time. And we are grateful, her mother and I. She's become like a daughter to me. To most all of us here. Thank you. The whole kingdom thanks you." He touched Chantaya on her tear wet cheek. "Thank God for you, Sir. For showing up in the nick of time."

Weepier than ever, Chantaya hugged Mordecai one more time and then took Peyton's big hand and led him back to the bench Conrad had indicated. She literally climbed onto his lap to snuggle into his neck. They'd no sooner gotten settled than she began to sniffle and then to cough several times in a row. It made the wound on her ribs ache terribly, but she couldn't put a hand there to hold it with Peyton watching.

He looked down at her in concern anyway and pulled her closer and said, "You sound just as Mordecai. He got your same draught that night. Do you feel as miserable as you sound?"

She shook her head against him and whispered, "I have never felt better, Peyton Wolfgar." She struggled to contain her tears and repeated, "Never better. I've missed you, Pey. I'm trying to be strong. And patient. But sometimes, especially such as tonight, when I'm fair sick and whiny, I miss you desperately. Seeing you there was as . . . " The tears came into her voice again. "And seeing Mordecai, as well. Oh, 'tis that I've wondered if he got through and if you both were safe. I both hoped and feared you were in battle. I've prayed for you over and over. I thank God you're safe. That you're both safe. I love you, Peyton."

He smiled tiredly at her, wiped at her tears and leaned to kiss her gently. "I love you too, Chani. I'm so proud of you. And incredibly frustrated. I'm sorry you're ill because of your ride. What did he mean that Mordecai came just in the nick of time?"

Chantaya stilled, trying to put the images out of her head and wondering what to tell him. She said simply, "'Twas cold, and dark. I was frightened. I wasn't sure how long I could go on. But he came. I've never in my life been so grateful for anything."

He pulled her more securely to him and said, "But it's over now. And God willing, this whole mess will be over and 'tis soon you'll be back at my side. Where I can see you and hold you. Hear you laugh and smell your sweet skin." He paused and kissed her slowly one more time. "Where I can kiss you. And touch you. And know you're real and not part of my dreams born of desire and a warrior's moon. Where I can be certain you are safe and watched over."

She looked up at him in sleepy confusion. "But Peyton, even if I leave Rosskeene Manor. You'll still be in Valais and I in Navarre. How can you touch me? And kiss me?"

Shaking his head, he leaned his cheek against her hair and whispered huskily, "No, my love. The time's past for that. I can't live like this anymore. We can't. Either I must come home, or you must come to Valais. I can't live without you. I miss you, and not knowing if you're safe is the purest hell. My spirit is suffocating without you."

She looked up and into his eyes and all the worry and fear and loneliness in her heart seemed to fade. They were going to get through this. She could see its truth there in the warm liquid fire of his brown eyes. There was a fairytale ending waiting, if they could just endure for a short while longer. They were going to make it. Soon.

Snuggling back into his warm, strong chest, she said, "You are a knight of the kingdom. My knight. You can't leave your duties. As soon as I can, I'll come to you." She yawned, and closed her eyes as she moved even closer to him. "Just as soon as the magistrate rules. I shall come. I love you, Sir Peyton."

§§§§

Occasionally, she coughed in her sleep and would put a hand to her ribcage when she did as if it hurt. She ranged from shivering to sweating with her fever, and at times, there was a strange concern in her countenance that made him worry. Peyton was nearly as tired as she seemed to be, but still, he wasn't willing to let go of her just for the sake of rest. 'Twas heaven to hold her there on the bench in her stable and know of a certainty, for once, that she was safe and whole and at peace.

He dozed between her coughing spells. They seemed to be less frequent and he hoped that just his being there and holding her would strengthen her and help make her well. It certainly strengthened him.

Always, she had been that way for him. From that very first frightful stormy night when her father was killed, helping her had somehow made him stronger and brought a need to take care of her and protect her. Ever it had been so. He leaned and gently kissed her warm temple and closed his eyes again. How he loved this sweet, spirited, young beauty.

Toward morning, the candle on the nearby table guttered low and as the sky outside the doors just began to lighten, he gently lifted her and carefully took her back to her bed and tucked her in beside her still sleeping mother. He would have liked to continue to hold her forever, but he needed to get out of sight before the stable woke to its chores. As he retired to his own bunk in Conrad's room, he wished Chantaya would be able to take a day or two to heal her body from its sickness instead of having to return to her kitchen. So much would change when they married.

§§§§

When she woke, just for a moment, she thought she'd dreamed Peyton had come, and Mordecai. But then she could smell him, and realized she was in bed still wearing her wrapper and knew it hadn't been a dream. He'd been there. Holding her, and kissing her and telling her he couldn't live without her. She sat up, wondering if he was still there somewhere, or if he'd had to go.

As she rose, she was incredibly light headed. Her mother came to her and gently pushed her back down into the bed, and said, "Stay in bed this morning, Chantaya. I've spoken with Cook and she and I will manage without you. The master is still gone and we'll be fine while you rest."

Lying back, she gave her mother a tired smile. "He came. He and Mordecai both came." She closed her eyes and sighed. "He smelled so good, Mum. He still smells the same, even if he is a knight now." She opened her eyes back up and asked, "Is he gone? Did they leave in the night? He was so tired. But he held me instead of sleeping. I hope he's not always that tired. Is he gone?"

Isabella shook her head. "No, daughter. He's still here. Both he and Mordecai are sleeping like the dead in Conrad's room. Mordecai sounds to be as ill as you. Perhaps he'll sleep the day through here. Rest now, and after I've fed the family, I'll bring you some chamomile tea."

Turning over and pushing her hair away from her face, Chantaya said in a tired voice, "Thank you, Mother. Don't go alone, will you? Have Conrad see you over and make sure Cook is at hand. Even with the master gone, Damian is there."

Soothingly, Isabella answered, "I'll be fine. You rest. Conrad will be nearby somewhere."

Still weary, Chantaya asked, "Do you think he loves you, Mum? Conrad?"

Smiling almost tenderly, Isabella nodded. "I do think so, Chantaya. He loves us both. As we love him. He's been a blessing to us here."

Chantaya sighed, "I do love him. He's so good to you. Do you think you could ever marry again, Mother? After losing Papa?"

"Perhaps."

Chantaya nodded and closed her eyes, but then struggled to open them back up and said, "Please ask Peyton not to leave without telling me goodbye, Mother."

§§§§

Isabella brought tea, but Peyton was the only one awake enough to drink any of it. It made him homesick to visit with her as he ate. How long it had been since he'd visited either her or his own mother like this.

Once he had eaten, Isabella made sure the stable was empty and then he stepped across to Chantaya's room to speak to her before slipping away to check with the farmers and tenants as the prince had requested. Chantaya was still sleeping, but on Isabella's urging, he gently woke her and spent a heavenly few minutes sitting beside her, enjoying how pretty she was all tousled and sleepy. She was a beautiful girl, but never so much as just now when she seemed so vulnerable and fragile. 'Twas all he could do to make himself kiss her goodbye and leave her.

After dark that evening, he once again slipped into the dimly lit stable. This time, Chantaya was awake and dressed and looking like she felt much better than she had earlier, although that same sad shadow still hung at the back of her eyes at times. As strange as it felt to visit her in her room, he stayed there with her, with Isabella's blessing, because they wanted no one to see them and didn't want to chance making Chantaya more ill by visiting out in the chill of the autumn evening air.

He held her again, this time in a worn padded chair someone had salvaged when the manor had discarded it. 'Twas incredibly sweet to be there with her for the balance of the evening, talking and planning. Sometimes kissing and sometimes doing absolutely nothing but being together. Chantaya was still ill and not feeling energetic, so it was wonderfully refreshing to know Peyton didn't have to rush back to Valais this time as they let Mordecai recuperate as well under Isabella's care.

When they could tell Isabella was tired and wanted to come in and go to bed, Peyton broached the subject of the masquerade ball, and although Chantaya's eyes lit up, she hesitated for a moment and then said, "I'd love to attend a real royal ball in a lovely gown, Peyton, but there's just no way we could manage it, even if the princess could find me a dress. How could I get the time away from the kitchen? Or get there? And even with something over my face, wouldn't Rosskeene recognize me?"

Peyton listened to all her concerns, but then only smiled and repeated what the prince had said, "Sweet Chantaya, I truly believe that a girl who can save a kingdom can find a way." He stood and pulled her into his arms and added, "Please, let's at least try, Chani. I'll come get you and bring you back. I should truly love to have you there with me. To hold you and dance the night away with you. 'Twould be a dream come true. I'll help you. We'll figure it out. I'll come back here on Thursday next to take you if you can go. Please say you'll at the least give it some thought."

She looked into his eyes and gave him her sweet, spirited smile and assured him, "I shall do everything in my power to attend the ball with you, Sir Peyton. 'Tis that you are right. We'll figure it out."

Peyton and Mordecai stayed more than two full days in the Rosskeene Manor district. The days Peyton spent in his peasant clothing discreetly checking with Rosskeene's farmers and tenants near the manor, and the heavenly evenings he spent with Chantaya. By the time he and Mordecai were preparing to leave in the dark of the third morning, he and Chantaya had fallen in love all over again. Both of them were devastated about telling each other goodbye, but Peyton felt he should return and report to the castle. Mordecai was much rested and felt ready to return home.

'Twas another of those times when she struggled not to have him see her sad as he left, only to crumble to tears as soon as he was out of sight. Still, that was better than making him feel guilty about leaving her when he needed to. The only good thing about Lord Rosskeene's homecoming that day and the household returning to being wary of the master was that it helped to keep her mind and heart from missing Peyton so desperately.

The issue of getting to the ball wasn't nearly so difficult as Chantaya had worried it would be. 'Twas actually Cook who suggested Chantaya take some time, in a way. They were working side by side in the kitchen when Lady Winifred came in.

She seldom came there and when she did, she was usually stewing about one thing or another, so 'twas a surprise to them when she actually came in acting remarkably happy and said, "His Lordship and I have been invited by the king himself to a royal ball this next week. 'Tis quite surprising. Usually these elegant gatherings are planned far in advance. At any rate, we'll be taking Master Damian, and my lady's maids and his Lordship's and master's valets, as well as two coachmen and leaving two days early in order to do some shopping in the city. I must have a suitable gown, of course. So you needn't plan on meals for all of us for those four days."

When she exited, Cook made Chantaya laugh as she rolled her eyes and mimicked, "I be taking m'lady's maids and 2 gardeners and a smithy and four weavers and seven valets, and I must have a suitable gown, of course. I pity the poor maids who must travel with them. Although, to the rest of us here, 'twill be as if we're all on holiday. Nothing to do but see to it that the beasts are fed and those of us as remain get a bite. At that, I 'magine most of us will fit in a visit to our families, we will."

Chantaya only dared to hope as she asked, "Would there be the possibility Mother and I could visit home as well? I know we haven't been here long."

Waving a hand airily, Cook said, "Take what time you will. As long as you leave after they do and return before they get back, mind you. There's harvesting to do, but we'll take a breath when we can get it, I say. Maybe 'twill be you can finally slip that touch of the weather. Your cough truly does linger. Of course you should go. In truth, the two of you shouldn't honestly have to be here anyway, should you?"

Shaking her head, Chantaya said, "No. We most definitely should not! 'Twas a crooked plot to harm my mother. Still, had we not come, I should never have gotten to know and love you, Cook. Nor Conrad, or any of the others.

So, while I wouldn't have chosen to associate with Lord Rosskeene or his family, I'll treasure the rest of you forever."

Cook smiled sweetly. "And we you, dear. Now run and tell your mother so the two of you can be making plans." She paused and added with a twinkle in her eye, "Or maybe 'twill be the three of you, with Conrad. He's gotten quite fond of his guardian responsibilities of your dear mother."

Happily, Chantaya replied, "Indeed, he has. And has been the most tender mercy blessing to us. 'Tis long my mother has been lonely. I was but three when my father was killed. Conrad has been a gift from the heavens."

Cook smiled placidly. "Seems to me that Isabella has been the heavenly gift. Be off with you now."

Chantaya fairly skipped out to the stable. Maybe she'd even have time to have her gown fitted properly.

Chapter 16

On Thursday, Chantaya spent a ridiculous amount of time looking out the windows of the manor, wondering when Peyton would come and if she'd even know he was there when he did finally arrive. She knew when he'd come before, he'd hidden in the trees just as Mordecai had, and all afternoon, as she worked, she watched toward the woods. Finally, as she was walking back toward the stable in the evening, she saw all the horses in the paddock looking that way and knew Peyton must be there somewhere.

She had mixed feelings about the king's ball. Part of her was so excited to be with Peyton and to be able to wear a lovely gown and dance the evening away with him. But another part of her was incredibly frightened at the prospect of trying to function in a society she had never been a part of, nor knew their ways. Granted, because she was more educated than a typical peasant, and even than most nobles, she had a better grasp than most of what society would expect. Still, the ball was in some ways quite a daunting undertaking. And that wasn't even taking into account that she would need to keep Lord and Lady Rosskeene from recognizing her. In truth, all told, she was quite terrified she wouldn't measure up, no matter what she was wearing.

When darkness finally fell, she drew on her cloak and was so excited to see what hid in the woods that her mother laughed at her as she all but raced out the door. She was so intent on reaching the woods undetected, that she almost screamed when Peyton materialized out of the shadows beside the paddock fence. Once she realized it was him, she flung herself into his arms, completely forgetting the soreness of the still healing wounds on her ribs and shoulder. It had only been a little over a week that they'd been apart this time, but still, she had missed him!

Standing in the shadows wrapped in his arms was more than bliss and she slipped her own arms around him, wondering once again if he hadn't grown even taller and broader in this short time away from her. He seemed so grown up now. 'Twas hard to believe this large and confident man was the same boy she'd grown up beside and had spent every day with just a few months ago. He felt years older and wiser. And much more mature than her sixteen years felt.

For several long moments Peyton simply held her and even the ache of the pesky wound at her ribs felt somehow less painful in his embrace. He affected her whole life that way. Anything he touched seemed brighter and more alive, just for his presence. With him near, her whole world moved in greater harmony and hope.

At length, Peyton finally stepped slightly back from her to look down into her face. For another long moment, he looked into her eyes and then he leaned and kissed her gently on the mouth and asked, "Are you feeling better than last I saw you, my love?"

She closed her eyes and nodded, feeling almost shy. Her cough lingered, but she felt immeasurably better than she had felt those first couple of days after her rain soaked ride. Physically, she was much improved and the nightmares of the ride and the swordfight that plagued her had finally begun to subside. Her spirit felt far lighter with peaceful rest. She felt so much improved she was almost embarrassed at how poorly she had felt when he'd been there. It had been heaven to cuddle into his arms when she'd been ill, but it couldn't have been terribly attractive.

He put a hand under her chin and lifted it in an effort to get her to look at him again and when she did, he was smiling his marvelously handsome smile as he whispered, "You look better. You look beautiful."

Still hesitant, she softly said, "Thank you, Sir Knight. I'm sorry I didn't look so last week."

Nuzzling the stray curl that hung about her ear, he murmured, "Oh, but Chani, you were most beautiful indeed last week. Fair too beautiful. You were near my undoing. All tousled and sleepy."

"Tousled and sleepy aren't usually words associated with beauty, Pey."

He kissed her below her ear and breathed, "Only because tousled and sleepy are usually spoken of between but the closest of lovers. Are you able to leave with me? Shall I go to the village and arrange for a carriage?"

When he kissed her neck again, she had to pause for a moment to remember what he was asking before she said, "I am able to go, but won't a carriage from the village be too obvious? People will remember you were checking here for the king. Won't they wonder why you need a carriage?"

"They might, Chani, but you're still ill. You're not up to riding, are you? And it will be much safer with you inside a coach where no one on the road will recognize what a rare beauty you are. You'll be safer hidden within. There might be highwaymen of a night."

Momentarily, Chantaya remembered the men who had waylaid her the last time she had traveled at night and she shuddered at the memory of that awful swordfight. That moment when she had had to kill the one came back to her as it had so many times in the past week and more. At the same moment, the wounds that were still in the process of healing on her shoulder and ribs seemed to ache afresh. Swallowing, she struggled to pull her mind away from the memories and to think wisely and said, "Must we travel at night? Would it not be wiser to leave early in the morning? Would we not be safer?"

"I've friends with me. Matthew, and my squire Shaun and two others. We shall be safe enough, but I worried you wouldn't have time to rest from the journey if we waited until morning. You can try to rest in the carriage. Either way is fine. Which do you prefer?"

"Twill be a tiring trip whether now or then, although you're right, tonight might be best. Yes, I could travel easier in a carriage, but we shouldn't rent one. Lord Rosskeene is bound to find out about you and me. I'd rather not go than risk that."

She paused again hesitantly and then finally asked, "Would your friends be completely horrified if I rode along instead? I wouldn't have to ride sidesaddle and advertise that I am female. I know it's not truly acceptable, but I can fair turn into a boy with some borrowed clothing and an old hat. I'll wear a long cloak, I swear it. And then you can rent a carriage in the city tomorrow. Maybe under the circumstances . . . If I look unmistakably feminine at the ball afterwards? Would I embarrass you too unduly? Do they already know I've ridden to warn you?"

"None save Mordecai know." Peyton narrowed his eyes in concern for a long moment and then asked, "Your mother would allow that?"

Raising her eyebrows, Chantaya said drily, "Oh, you'd be surprised how pliable my mother can be when there is the safety and the security of both her daughter and the kingdom at stake. And she would allow anything you would, Peyton. She trusts you with my life and more. She trusts you implicitly."

"But the only thing at stake here is a royal ball. 'Tis hardly a matter of the kingdom."

"Ah, but you don't realize how my mother would have loved a royal ball. 'Twould have been a fairytale dream to her. As long as you and those with you are the only ones who know."

Peyton smiled and then shrugged. "'Tis a wise plan. If you truly think it won't over tire you, we'll not worry about shocking my friends. They are to be trusted. And once they see you in a ball gown, they'll think nothing of the young lad who rode astride to Valais with us. Would you prefer to leave tonight? Or in the dark of early morning?"

Considering this, Chantaya finally said, "Let us away tonight. Surely we will be safe with five large men, one of whom is the bravest of all knights. I felt pure safe when Mordecai rode with me." She gave him a smile and continued, "Twill be a long night ride, but it'll be easier to carry off my disguise in the dark and that way I may be able to rest tomorrow."

Leaning to kiss her again, Peyton said, "Tonight it is. What shall I do to help you get ready?"

Laughing, Chantaya shook her head. "Just don't make the lecture overly long when you see me in boys' trousers, Sir Knight."

§§§§

'Twas a wise plan, but twenty minutes later, when Chantaya appeared in her boy's clothing, the figure they revealed was nearly scandalously female. Peyton was indeed about to change his mind and start in with a lecture until she pulled a long cloak over her tantalizing curves. She must have read some of the near panic in his thoughts because she was laughing at him as she tied a neckerchief about her throat, twisted her hair up into an old hat and went out to begin saddling her horse. Even Isabella seemed to be laughing at his expression as Chantaya strapped on a small sword and they said their goodbyes at their room door.

Just before they walked away, Isabella looked him in the eye and said, "I'm trusting you with my greatest treasure, Sir Peyton Wolfgar. Keep her safe. From those who would harm her. And from those who love her. Behave yourself, young man. I'm trusting you. Guard her life and virtue."

Wordlessly, Peyton nodded and swallowed. Never had he felt such responsibility. 'Twas a sacred trust more pressing even than safeguarding the kingdom. Still, he had accepted that responsibility, that honor, long before being spoken to by Isabella.

Walking beside Chantaya, he grimaced, but asked calmly, "What are you doing with a sword, Chani? I agreed to let you ride. Not to go armed."

"'Tis part of my disguise." She shrugged and added, "Mordecai gave it to me.", as if that was the end of it. Peyton let it go for the moment, but determined to speak to Mordecai and insist he take it back. That way, Mordecai would be the one in trouble and not him.

As she vaulted into her saddle, he marveled anew at how well she could ride and decided it was all going to be all right. At the very least, he was incredibly proud of just how truly capable she was. It may have been a trifle unorthodox, but he was the only man in the kingdom who had a true love who could help save it and then don a ball gown.

When she rode beside him to where he'd left his friends and he saw the confusion in their faces, he decided this might almost be an adventure. Who knew? Gathering the reins to his own charger, as he began to strap on the armor he'd taken off when he went in search of her, he said matter-of-factly, "There's been a change of plans. My lady friend is unable to attend the ball after all and won't be returning with us. In her stead, my young stable hand friend here will ride with us. He has a need to travel to Valais anyway."

Matthew, in his own armor, smiled and extended a hand to Chantaya as he joked to Peyton, "Poor Wolfgar. Thrown over for the ball. You don't appear unduly saddened." To Chantaya he said, "Welcome friend. Matthew Ansel." Chantaya only nodded her thanks as she shook his hand.

Shaun appeared more skeptical and said almost antagonistically, "We're taking a boy with us? On a night ride through the robber woods? He looks to be only a child. He hasn't even a hint of a beard, yet he sports a teeny tiny sword. What are you thinking, Sir Peyton? Leave him here." The others merely looked on to see Peyton's reaction without adding their opinions.

Chuckling at the indignation that fairly bristled off Chantaya, Peyton stepped into his own saddle, grinned at her and said, "There might be times when the lack of facial hair be a good thing. I'll bet he doesn't have to waste much time shaving, nor worrying about appearing overly scruffy." To Shaun he said, "You'd best watch yourself, my young squire. 'Tis that he's quite good with that sword. Pray don't rile him. I'd hate to have to defend you. He might make us all look amateur. Come. We've a long ride ahead of us. Let us away."

With that, Peyton spun his steed into the trail and he had to bite back a laugh when Chantaya's horse vaulted a downed tree to cut in front of Shaun's and turn in beside his own.

For the first hour and more, he kept the horses to steady a trot, hoping to get a good portion of the trip behind them before the moon went down behind the hills to the west. Chantaya seemed to be fine as she rode beside him, coughing only occasionally as they traveled through the brisk autumn air. He knew she'd spent a full day working at Rosskeene Manor, but she still kept on doggedly at his side.

When they were half way, he halted the horses at a brook and without even thinking, he stepped to her horse and helped her down, then realized what he'd done and glanced around at his friends. Shaun and the other two were still attending to their horses and hadn't even noticed, but Matthew was standing there with a look of confusion on his face that made Peyton smile. Matthew only shook his head and turned to watch Chantaya where she slipped into the trees at the edge of the roadway. He was still obviously confused as he turned back to Peyton, who only grinned and looked to his own horse and hers.

Matthew walked closer to Peyton, looking him in the face, questioning as Shaun said, "He's even fussy about privacy out here in the middle of naught but the rabbits to see a body. Look at 'im traipsing off into the wood. Why'd you let him come, Sir Peyton? ''Tisn't like you to let some little bugger tag along.'' He walked to the other side of the road and relieved himself, then stretched and added, "Me arse is killin' me. And this whole ride for nothin'. "

As Chantaya gracefully stepped back into the road and toward her horse, Matthew was watching. Peyton saw realization hit him and grinned again as Matthew said, "Pray, watch your mouth, Shaun."

Chantaya took her reins and vaulted back into her saddle and then sat waiting for Peyton to mount. He laughed quietly as Shaun and the others turned to look at Matthew like he'd grown horns and Shaun demanded, "What's the matter with my mouth?"

Shaking his head with a grin of his own, Matthew looked one more time from Peyton to Chantaya and back and said, "Aw, nothin'. Your mouth is fine. Get on your horse and quit whining. We've far to go."

Peyton caught Chantaya's eye and smiled at her as he led off once again, saying, "Indeed we do. Look lively lads. They call it the robber wood for reason. Keep your eyes open, Shaun. More open than they've been. We need your wits about you."

Hours later, Chantaya did finally begin to look like she was tiring as at long last the moon went down and they rode into an inky roadway before them. A breeze came up and Peyton halted the horses to put on his leather gloves and let Chantaya do the same. With their horses standing close together he asked quietly, "How are you, Chani?"

She nodded, "I'm well, thanks." He met her eyes and knew she understood he would have liked to comfort her and baby her more than he was. He reached across and squeezed her knee and then gave her another long look before he started on again.

They were not far from the outskirts of a town when Peyton realized there were some horsemen waiting at a crossroad up ahead in the dark. As they neared, he counted four of them and without his even having to say anything, Chantaya dropped back from where she rode beside him and Matthew came abreast of him. She drew her sword as she moved back, as did the others and Peyton cursed silently as he raised his shield to think he'd gotten Chantaya into such a situation. Four highwaymen. He'd been a fool to agree to let her ride without more riders. Still, there were only four of them.

As they pulled abreast of the waiting men, one stepped out, effectively stopping all their horses and Peyton threw his cloak back off of his shoulders so he could be free of any restraint. The pale starlight glinted off his armor and the man in front of him slowed as the other three murmured something, but then the man in front said, "Halt there!"

Suddenly feeling a slow burning anger start in his belly, Peyton ground out, "What do you want? We've no time for this."

The man only gave a humorless laugh as three other men walked their horses out of the shadows to the left of the roadway. Harshly, the man said, "You'll find the time. Give us your coin or we'll bleed you out here and now."

Truly angry now, Peyton knew there was no way to avoid a battle and snarled, "We'll give you nothing, thieves!" Without pause, he plunged his charger forward and in one great sweep, slashed at the man's throat and continued on toward the others as he saw his men leap their horses forward as well. Behind him, he heard Chantaya's horse rear and neigh and then he was into the thick of the fight, slashing right and left with his sword, silently willing Chantaya to keep out of it.

'Twas over in but a matter of moments, although it seemed longer because he'd been so involved. When the last man near him was down, he spun his horse to see where else there was an enemy waiting and in a single glance, he took in the fact that all were vanquished except the lone man who had gotten around him and his men and now stood toe to toe in front of Chantaya. She was off her horse and had thrown off her cloak and was locked in the intense, deadly dance of a swordfight. Shaun was just several strides from them and for an instant, the scene before Peyton appeared to slow to a surreal pace as Chantaya expertly parried the thief's blade once, twice, thrice.

At last, Shaun reached them and thrust his own blade. The last thief fell.

Chantaya lowered her weapon and for a long moment appeared utterly dejected, but then, as Peyton slid his horse to a stop in front of her and leaped to the ground, she turned and buried her face in his chest and began to cry. He had to ask if she had been hurt several times before she shook her head against him, and then he held her to him and stroked her back, assuring her over and over that they would be all right and that the danger was past.

After several moments, when she began to pull herself together, he looked up to see Matthew and the others watching the two of them, Matthew grinning, and Shaun with a look of profound confusion. At that moment, her hat brushed off and her silken, sable curls slid free of their twist. They tumbled down her back and Shaun actually recoiled in his surprise and near tripped over the body of the thief in front of them.

Peyton finally felt a hint of a smile break through the gut wrenching angst he'd been feeling, looked all around at the needless carnage and motioned to Matthew as he picked up her cloak and draped it round her shoulders. "Bring her horse. Let's get her out of here. I should have made her ride in a carriage."

Shaun was still in apparent shock as she twisted her hair back up and replaced her hat, and Peyton had to nearly snap at him, "Shaun! Mount up! We must away! She needs rest. She shouldn't have had to see that. Come."

Matthew brought her horse as Peyton gave her one last long embrace and then let her step into his hands to mount. When they were all aboard, Peyton lead off at a high gallop with her horse running close at his side. He glanced sideways at her, noticing how gracefully she rode and once again, berated himself for letting her ride with them through the night and not hiring more outriders. It had been a fool's decision. He should never have let her sweet smile influence him to give in. He looked all around them into the dark, wishing they were closer to Valais. At least in the city there would be patrols of other soldiers. They'd be safer there.

§§§§

This ride had been such a range of differing emotions that Chantaya had become more than a little exhausted long before their encounter with the band of highwaymen. After starting with the simple joy of being with Peyton again, she'd gone then to indignation at Peyton's upstart squire, to physically overdone, to remembering her fear of the last ride at the sight of that dark grouping of horsemen. Now she had graduated through relief, to plain and simple fatigue that threatened to overwhelm her as the memories of the last ride through the dark of night and thieves descended with a vengeance.

She was cold, and tired, and had felt the exact moment when the slice on her ribs from that last horrible swordfight tore through the old scab and stitches as she fought. Even now, she could feel the cool drip of her blood as it soaked through her borrowed shirt at the back, chilling her further still and only reinforcing the nightmarish memories of that freezing, awful ride.

The men could have this life. 'Twas far too harsh an existence for her to ever wish it upon herself. She shook her head and glanced to her side at Peyton to bring some of the reassurance his presence always brought her. His was an incredible gift. Even in the midst of this conflict, and outnumbered, she had known in her heart that all would be well with Peyton near. The only reason she'd succumbed to her tears was the sickening memory the fight brought on of having to kill the swordsman the week before.

By sheer force of will, she straightened her shoulders and tried to absorb some of the shock of her horse's gait with her knees to ease her tired back. She truly loved the freedom of riding occasionally, but some of her rather intimate parts got tender after hours and hours. The idea of that carriage was sounding more and more tempting.

At long length, when their horses clip clopped across a river bridge, bringing them at last into the outskirts of Valais, Peyton pulled up and gently insisted she get on his horse behind him. She had begun to cough again and her throat was aching. She got off of her own mount and onto his in mute gratitude. The thought of snuggling up to the warm strength of his back sounded fair heavenly. She was indeed tired.

Some miles inside the city, Peyton pulled the horses to a stop behind a dark and quiet house, and said, "This house belongs to the prince's distant cousin or some such, but he doesn't stay here much and the prince has kindly offered it to us for you." He helped her slide off and then dismounted himself and wrapped a strong arm round her waist to all but carry her inside as Shaun and the others took the horses. Matthew came inside with them and began to light the fires that had been laid and ready as she looked all around while Peyton dug into cupboards in the kitchen. He brought bread and cheese and mulled cider and handed it to her to warm over the fire.

As tired as she was, she said little as she watched and sipped the cider. After a few minutes, Peyton said, "I'll go retrieve your things from your saddle. Stay here with Matthew." He went out the door and she glanced up at his Matthew and caught him watching her with an easy smile. Peyton came straight back in with her bag and the other three with him saying, "They've brought your things." Peyton smiled. "Seems Shaun's far more patient with having you tagging along, now he's realized you're not truly a stable hand. Gentlemen, may I present to you, Miss Chantaya Kincraig."

Almost penitently, Shaun approached her and bowed. "Please. I beg your forgiveness, Miss Chantaya. I had no idea. Please accept my apologies. Both for being less than welcoming, and for questioning your fencing skills. I was a fool."

Chantaya gave him a wan smile and patted his arm. "You are quite forgiven, Sir. Please forgive me for my masquerade as well. We didn't intend to insult you. And thank you for saving me tonight. 'Tis certain I couldn't have held him off much longer."

Matthew smiled and interjected, "Oh, I don't know. You appeared to be doing quite well from where I was. We thought he was merely jesting when he said you were skilled. Pray, tell, where and when did you learn to fence and ride thus? You could best many of those in the king's military." He bowed before her as well and reached for her hand. "He told us you were a rare beauty. 'Tis that he doesn't tell an untruth. Please, m'lady, pray forgive us for ever putting you in such a compromising situation. 'Twill not happen again, I swear it." The others nodded in agreement.

She shook her head and said, "Kind sir, 'twas not your fault we were set upon by such men. You needn't apologize. Especially not when you've just ridden all night on my behalf. I thank you. I thank all of you. And I thank you for keeping Peyton all in one piece these months as well. I am in your debt."

Matthew smiled back and said drily, "'Tis no great feat. He typically has the foe beaten and contained before any of the rest of us even get a crack at them. He's a hard one to keep up with, he is. 'Tis a good thing he's so blasted friendly, or the rest of us would resent him terribly."

Peyton only rolled his eyes and said, "Don't listen to him, Chani. His is the silver tongue amongst us. May I take your cloak? Are you warming up yet?"

She nodded and then admitted hesitantly, "I'm warm, but . . . This apparel. 'Tis not truly modest. Even Conrad lectured me about being seen in trousers. I can only imagine the talking-to you'll spout at me, Peyton. I mean Sir Peyton."

Shaun waved a casual hand. "Ignore any lecturing, m'lady. One who can fence with such prowess, needn't worry about mere trousers." He slipped the cloak from her shoulders and turned aside to drape it over a nearby chair and assured, "Here, you're among friends. No worries."

Stretching her hands once more toward the fire, she sighed tiredly and then coughed. Looking around, she was wondering where she was to sleep when she saw Matthew nudge Peyton. They were looking at her back and she twisted to see what they were looking at and then winced with the movement. She sighed even more deeply as Peyton near shouted, "Chani! You're all bloody! Your back! You were wounded!"

As he strode toward her, she put out her hands and tried to calm him. "No. No, Peyton. I wasn't wounded. I'm fine. It's from before. It's old. It just broke open with the fencing. I'm well. I swear it."

He paused mid step in confusion. "What?" Glancing around at her back again, he said, "But Chani, that's a lot of blood. How? What?" His voice raised a notch. "Who did this to you? Was it Rosskeene? His son? They'll hang! I'll see them both hang! What do you mean, it's old?"

Chantaya looked at him and then at the others and back at him and sighed a third time. "Pey. Peyton, I . . . Peyton, could we discuss this in the morning? I'm fair exhausted this night. I'm truly not up to this."

"Up to what? What aren't you up to?"

Matthew cleared his throat and said, "I fear those horses need looking in on. I'll just head out to ensure they are secure for the even. Maybe you could help me check them, gentlemen. Could I trouble you?"

Nodding, Shaun said, "Of a surety, Matthew. I was just thinking I should look in on them one more time before turning in."

The others left the room and Peyton turned back to her grimly as he stepped closer and pulled the tail of her borrowed shirt free of the trousers and began to lift it. She yanked it back down and said, "Peyton! What are you doing?"

"It's me or one of them, Chani. Or we'll send for a physician. Someone needs to look at it. You choose. From the volume of blood, the physician is probably the correct choice. What happened? Was it Rosskeene?"

"No."

"Then who? His son?"

"No." He went to pull the shirt up again and she shook her head. Pausing with the shirt half lifted, he looked directly at her and said, "Then who? Tell me, Chani. The truth."

Finally, she simply decided to refuse. "No, Peyton. I'm not going to tell you, so you needn't ask."

He looked up in surprise. "What do you mean? Of course you'll tell me. You tell me everything. We have no secrets."

She shook her head. "We do now."

"Chani, we're to be married. We're closer than anyone I know. We've never kept secrets. Why are you doing this?"

"Because . . . Because . . . 'Tis better that I should. Just trust me, Peyton. Please. Trust me on this. I'll tell you someday. You have my word."

He looked at her hard for a long moment, then shook his head and picked back up the shirt tail. "Let me look at it,

Chani. We need to stop the bleedi . . . Great thundering Methuselah! Chani! Chantaya Isabella Kincraig! This is a huge slice! It's been stitched! What in . . . " He looked at her in horrified surprise as tears seeped into her eyes and he asked softly, "Is this what I think it is?"

She turned away and brushed sadly at the tears and said, "Don't ask me, Pey. Just don't ask. Just don't." She whispered almost inaudibly, "Please."

Taking her by both arms, he turned her back to face him and ever so gently wrapped his arms around her and pulled her to him. Tenderly, he said, "Oh, Chani. My love. 'Tis all right. 'Tis all right for us to love each other enough to share even the ugliest of this life. You can tell me. Never feel like you can't tell me. You needn't shoulder it alone. I'm strong enough even for this. I'm so sorry. So sorry."

He tenderly pressed a kiss to her forehead and she closed her eyes and let the tears come, but then she swallowed and said, "You are strong enough, Peyton. I'm not. Not yet. I will tell you. Later. Right now, I can't face it." She looked up at him, feeling the heartbreak of the situation they were in and repeated, "Later. Soon. As soon as we're together and this mess with Rosskeene is over."

He nodded and pulled her close again. "All right, love. All right. Soon. Don't worry about it tonight. Tonight, we'll just pull it closed again as best we can, and bandage it and try to get it healing. Let me go get some bandages out of my bags."

She shook her head. "In a moment, Pey. Can you just hold me for a time?"

Pulling her tighter still, he whispered, "For forever, Chantaya. Only for forever."

Chapter 17

When she awoke the next morning, the sun was high in the sky and someone had brought her a tub and filled it with steaming water. Whoever it was had even left her soap and a vial of scented oil behind the dressing screen there. Sitting up, she tried not to groan at how stiff she was from riding. She gingerly stretched to determine whether the wound on her ribs was sticking to her bed clothing again. Peyton had bandaged it, but it tended to break open whenever she changed. She was hoping to be able to make it through this ball without bleeding on the ball gown.

Arising, she stepped behind the screen and began to undress and then was surprised when there came a knock at the door and it opened a crack. Just as she was beginning to scramble back into her clothes, a feminine voice said, "May I come in, Miss? Sir Peyton asked me to bring ya these. 'E sent for some lovely new things for ya." She smiled across at Chantaya and then advanced into the room as she continued, "'E said he wanted you to feel like the princess herself, 'e did. I be Emma, miss. But you can call me Emmy. Everyone else does. I've been sent to assist ya."

She set a parcel down and began to unwrap it as she said, "'E didn't actually buy these things, mind you. Said 'e hadn't the slightest thought about what you'd need. Just tried to describe what size ya was. That was an adventure, I can tell ya. E asked Shaun's sister to help him, but 'twas 'is idea. 'Tis right sweet of 'im, I think. Don't you miss?"

Hesitantly, Chantaya nodded, "Yes, sweet indeed."

"Here be the under things and some slippers, and I'll be right back with the dress and hat. I'll just hang them on the screen there. Oh, and 'e said to tell you there would be a bite for ya to eat and then a carriage here to take ya to have your gown fitted at one o'clock, or there abouts, miss. That's about another hour. And will ya need help with doin' your hair? I often help with the ladies' hair here."

Suddenly worried about how she would wear her hair, Chantaya frowned and then said, "That would be very nice, thank you."

"Well, good then. I'll be back in 'alf the hour or so to help ya. If you need anything else, just let me know."

"Actually, if you wouldn't mind, Emmy. I could use some help here." Chantaya came out from behind the screen toward the diminutive maid. "My chemise is quite stuck here in this nasty scab where it has soaked through the bandage. I'm trying to keep it from opening and bleeding again. Could you loosen it, possibly? Would you mind? I know it's quite unpleasant. I'm so sorry."

Emmy bent to begin to free the fabric, gasped and said, "My laws, Miss. You've . . . You've got a . . . My gracious, but that's a large wound. I can't seem to loosen it. There, oh, I'm so sorry, Miss. The whole bandage has slipped rather than coming free of the blouse. We'll have to rewrap it. And it's begun to bleed again. My laws, however did ya acquire such a slice, Miss? If you don't mind my asking?"

Chantaya worked not to groan and said, "You don't want to know, Emmy. Trust me. Thank you so much for your help. I was having such a hard time by myself. Thank you. And would you mind finding Sir Peyton and asking for some clean bandaging?"

"Not at all, Miss. I'll go right away. You're sure you'll be all right by yourself?"

Chantaya nodded and the big eyed maid left. Chantaya hated to even let anyone see that, but she needed to be able to get her clothes off without ripping it wide open as well. She let out a breath as she slipped into the sweetly scented bath and decided to do just what she had been doing for ten days now. Try to ignore the wound and the reason for it and get on with the stuff of life without bothering about it. After all, tonight she was to go to a royal ball. Not one peasant in a thousand got a chance like that. And if she could contain her nerves, she was going to enjoy every moment of it.

Once bathed, she dried off, rewrapped herself with the bandaging Emmy had brought in, and then near basked in the clean, white underclothing that had been left her. Never in her life had she owned clothing so fine and soft. Even over the wound it felt as smooth as silk. Which was good, because the chemise was uncomfortably tight, and she let the lacing out as far as she could over the bandage.

The dress was easily the most elegant thing she'd ever had the privilege to wear as well. Indigo blue, it was made of a shiny, crisp fabric that had a subtle pattern to it that caught the light wherever it hugged the curves of her bosom and small waist and then fell into a graceful full skirt to the floor. 'Twas unspeakably lovely, and yet understated at the same time. The cut of it accentuated her superior height and set off her figure perfectly. As she attempted to do up the dozens of tiny, indigo buttons, she wondered how under heaven the princess had been able to find something that just fit her so well.

Emmy came back in and was indispensible in assisting her with the buttons and then exclaimed over Chantaya's curls as she helped her smoothly gather them up into an elegant cascade the small matching hat perched upon. Indeed, when Chantaya stood to stare into the looking glass before going out to meet Peyton, she wasn't sure who that exquisite, poised, genteel woman was who stood there, almost regally, looking back at her. It most definitely wasn't the tired and grubby stable hand who had dragged in, in the middle of the night last night. It would seem she was going to be able to play her part for this royal masquerade ball after all.

Moments later, as she walked out to meet Peyton, she was hard pressed not to laugh at the expressions of both Matthew and Shaun as Peyton approached her to give her a light hug and lead her to a laden table. They were apparently stunned speechless at her transformation and Peyton grinned at her as he said serenely, "Good morning, or rather, good day. It's just the four of us this morning. Did you get rested then? You look lovely."

He pulled out her chair to seat her as she replied, "I'm quite rested, thank you. And famished. This repast looks heavenly. How did you sleep?"

"Well."

She turned to Matthew and Shaun and asked, "And you gentlemen? Are you rested as well?" Shaun didn't even stop staring to answer. Matthew merely nodded and she went on,

"I need to thank you again for all you did to see me safely here last night. I am indeed grateful to the both of you. Thank you. Truly."

Matthew finally answered, "'Tis that you are most welcome, Miss Chantaya. 'Twas our pleasure." After a pause, he said more frankly, "I can hardly conceive you are the same soul who rode out to the woods to greet us last even. You look fair transformed. 'Tis sore scrambling my sensibilities."

Chantaya laughed lightly at this and said just as frankly, "Please. Let us keep my sensibility scrambling escapades of last even to ourselves. Poor Sir Peyton would be fair mortified if anyone but you, his closest friends, knew of my disgraceful behavior. Unfortunate man, he's forever trying to make me behave like a lady."

"Well, 'tis sure he's succeeding. You are every bit the lady today, Miss Chantaya. Wouldn't you agree, Sir Peyton?"

Peyton chuckled as the three of them sat down beside her, and said, "Looking the lady isn't the hard part for Chantaya. She's been this lovely since first I set eyes upon her when she was but three. 'Tis things like heights, and half wild horses that I have trouble containing with her."

Chantaya pursed her lips. "You poor man. You haven't gotten any gray hairs yet from me that I can detect. Shall we pray, Sir Knight? Your friends are undoubtedly starving. No more tattling on me now." She smiled and meekly bowed her head and Peyton chuckled once more before reaching for her hand under the table and saying a short prayer.

Several times during the meal, which was positively strange because it had been long since she had been served, instead of doing the serving, he again reached for her hand. Although he hadn't overreacted to how she looked, she knew he was proud of her here before his friends and it made her incredibly relieved. She'd been worried from the first time he mentioned the ball, and in truth, probably even before that, that he would be embarrassed by his young, unsophisticated girl from the country.

Shaun never did interject much conversation into that meal. Every time Chantaya chanced to look his way, he still seemed a trifle stunned for some reason. Matthew livened up and commenced to tease Peyton nigh unmercifully, and she was gratified to know Peyton had found good friends here to make up for having to leave the rest of his life behind in Navarre. That knowledge would ease her mind tomorrow when they went back to living far apart from each other again.

When they were finished, Peyton gently helped her up from the table and away from the others and asked, "Shall we be off to have your gown fitted, then?"

She looked up at him in concern. "Do you not think it fits well enough? I thought it a remarkably good fit for me never having tried it on before."

He only looked at her in momentary confusion and then smiled and put both hands on her shoulders to explain, "Chani, my love. This frock was from me. 'Tis only a lovely gift to ensure you are comfortable here among my friends and the nobles we will be around. This isn't your ball gown. Indeed, I've never yet set eyes on your dress for this evening, but this isn't it. The princess has arranged for your ball gown as a sort of gift of gratitude for our help in preserving the kingdom. Come. I'll take you to the dressmaker's shop to have it fitted, although it will have to be lovely indeed to be more beautiful than you look already this day. You are a rare vision."

Watching her eyes, he leaned and gently kissed her and then kissed her again, this time more thoroughly, before repeating, "An exquisitely rare vision. I was near struck speechless at your loveliness when you appeared this morning." He laughed softly. "Shaun was indeed struck dumb. 'Twas quite funny, actually. I've never seen the like with him. He's usually such a sharp witted fellow. Poor lout. Alas, it only proves you are beautiful."

A measure out of breath, she murmured, "Thank you." Then she smiled as she asked, "Pray, tell, how did you come to find a dress that so perfectly fit me?"

He grinned down at her. "I simply told the woman who helped me that you were about this tall." He put a hand to the top of her head. "About this big around." He wrapped his hands about her waist. "Had a heavenly figure. And fit perfectly inside my arms."

Chantaya laughed. "And she knew exactly how to gauge my size from that?"

"Exactly."

Chantaya rolled her eyes and laughed again as she shook her head. "I do wish I'd been there to see you say that. It seems to have worked. The dress fits well and is the loveliest I've ever dreamed of. Thank you."

"You are welcome, my sweet, intrepid Chantaya. Thank you for being willing to come here with me. I know it has been difficult for you. And I am so deeply sorry for what happened last night. But I'm so proud and happy to have you at my side. I've missed you so, Chani. And I've wished so to be able to share some of this life with you. Today is that rare chance. Thank you. Come. Let us away to that ball gown."

He settled her in the carriage, directed the coachman and then climbed in to try to fold his own large frame into the seat. He smiled across at her and it was fair strange. Back home, they had walked most everywhere for near the whole of their lives. Or ridden in the cart or even horse back. Never had she been in such a carriage as this and although it was exciting, in a way, it was troubling. For just a moment, she wondered if they would lose the sweet, carefree childhood friendship that had been so precious to them for so many years.

As if reading her thoughts, he turned and pulled her gently to him, leaned her head against his shoulder and said, "'Tis a shame Tristan can't be here with us today. Isn't it? He would have enjoyed this. A fairytale moment before returning to our real lives. An adventure of sorts. Although, I must admit, I'd truly rather tramp about the countryside with you and your herb basket than pretend to hobnob with the gentry."

He nuzzled her temple where her curls had been so painstakingly arranged. "Still, 'tis festive for a time. And this will all become a portion of our lives, now that I am a knight. Not a large portion, but necessary, all the same. I'm so proud that you are educated and astute enough to make the transition so gracefully."

She sighed and closed her eyes to enjoy his breath against her skin and admitted, "I do so hope I can indeed make the transition, Peyton. Truly, I'm quite frightened. But yes, what an adventure. I just pray I don't embarrass you."

"You won't. In truth, you look so stunning that I'm feeling nearly wicked, I'm so proud. Rather than worrying you'll embarrass me, I'm worried you'll over do. How are your ribs? And your cough? Last night I worried we'd set you completely back again."

Just the mention of her cough made her throat tickle and then she wondered if the bandage on her ribs showed through her elegant dress, but she only said, "I'm well, thank you. Perfectly well." She made a point of looking out the carriage window and added, "I've never been to a city. 'Tis almost a portion intimidating. I keep wondering if they all can immediately tell that I've hardly been outside of the village of Navarre. Valais feels huge by comparison. How far must we travel to the dressmakers?"

"You needn't worry. The only thing people can tell immediately is that you are uncommonly lovely. Surprisingly, most of these have never ventured further than their immediate part of the city. I would assume they would be just as intimidated by life in the countryside. The dressmaker we are to visit is but a short drive toward the castle you can see on the hill there. We're nearly there. 'Tis just up ahead. Are you ready then?"

She gave him a hesitant smile as the carriage slowed to a stop. "I must be. Please." She put a hand on his arm as he went to get out. "Please don't let me make too great a fool of either me or you."

Grinning, he reached to hand her out and said, "You truly needn't worry. 'Tis a masquerade ball. Even if we make utter fools of ourselves, none will have an idea of who we are. We have nothing to fear. Come, my love. Your ball gown awaits."

Stepping lightly from the smartly drawn carriage into the bustling street, she decided he was absolutely correct. She had nothing to fear in this night. 'Twas a fairytale dream and she was going to enjoy it.

Peyton took her inside, and once she was presented to the dressmaker there, he assured her he'd be back soon and left her there to have her gown fitted.

If Chantaya had considered the dress from Peyton elegant, the ball gown the seamstress helped her into was positively magnificent by comparison. A brilliant, cerulean blue that set off her eyes, it was of satin, with a full skirt, made even fuller by layers of individual gathers that were tucked one upon another from the slim fitting waist all the way to the floor. The close fitted bodice had swirls of tiny blue glass beads and a sculpted neckline that plunged just enough to be lovely without becoming immodest. Three quarter length sleeves narrowed to a point above her wrist.

The dress was again remarkably well fitting for those here never having seen her and the motherly seamstress needed only several minutes to mark where the necessary adjustments would need to be made. She helped her out of the dress again and then while she began the alterations, she sent Chantaya two doors down the busy, narrow street to the shoemaker there to select from matching shoes he had ready to accompany the exquisite gown.

Upon her return with the shoes, Chantaya was surprised to find two more people there waiting for her. One, a portly and amiable jeweler, who was apparently in the employ of the royal family, had a necklace that seemed to drip brilliant blue stones of the exact color of the gown, with dangling earrings and bracelet to match.

And Chantaya wasn't even quite sure what to call the other woman who stepped forward. Dressed in a bright, flowing robe of sheer, filmy layers, draped with multiple necklaces made of colorful stone beads, she was a striking beauty, with snapping green eyes, in spite of the wrinkles that testified she was no longer young. Her salt and pepper gray hair had been styled in a unique, twisting plait woven with ribbons and dried flowers that hung down her back and she wore ornate rings on nearly all of her fingers.

She smiled at Chantaya, then studied her face and hair for several long moments that made Chantaya wonder just what she was thinking inside that aging, but exquisite bone structure. She looked long enough that Chantaya had begun to get nervous, but then the woman nodded silently with apparent satisfaction.

Putting her hands into Chantaya's long tresses, she fingered them for another moment and mumbled, "Glorious. Simply glorious." She then proceeded to create an ornate, up swept hair arrangement that accented the silky, sable waves and curls. When it was sufficiently pinned to her liking, she wove in slim, iridescent peacock feathers and more of the same blue glass beads that adorned the bodice of the gown.

When Chantaya's hair was finished, the woman then produced a feathered and glittering masquerade mask in the same iridescent blues. It fitted against Chantaya's face above her nose and around her cheekbones and forehead, leaving a surprising large area around her eyes free.

At first, Chantaya was concerned with how little of her face the mask covered until the woman added a gossamer sheer wisp of veil with fine threads woven through it that caught the light. Draped like a harem girl, it almost imperceptibly concealed her lips and chin while acting as a frame to make her eyes appear a shocking blue. It allowed just enough sensuous shadows of her features to give her an ethereal mystique and yet hide her identity.

With that done, the woman then produced three small pots of paint and proceeded to paint the exposed area around

Chantaya's eyes in shades of cerulean blue, metallic sapphire and shining silver. Next she added a hint of inky smudge at the base of Chantaya's eye lashes and then painted the lashes themselves with some substance that made them longer and thicker than ever.

When she was finished, she stepped back to inspect her efforts, then nodded her head with a small smile of satisfaction and said, "Yes. I believe 'twill do. The princess wanted you to have a lovely disguise. You are lovely indeed." She handed Chantaya a handled looking glass. "Pray, what do you think? Will you be recognized?"

The effect was nothing short of masterful. The mask, veil, and paint accentuated, yet disguised her natural loveliness until Chantaya was truly taken aback. The design around her eyes turned them an azure that held the intensity of a bolt of lightning in the evening sky. It gave her an almost catlike look that was fascinating and all but seductive. She suddenly felt a bewitching enchantress, but there was also something faintly mystical and innocent about the allure. Something was reminiscent of a glittering, winged forest fairy nymph she'd seen pictures of in one of her mother's secreted books.

The whole of the image was strikingly beautiful, but there wasn't a chance anyone could recognize the scullery maid of Rosskeene Manor. In truth, Chantaya didn't even recognize herself. She could hardly believe the near wickedly, alluring woman who glittered back at her in the looking glass.

She turned in amazement back to the woman artisan who laughed at her expression and asked, "Do you like it?"

Nodding, Chantaya smiled in thrilled disbelief and asked, "Who is it? Surely that can't be me."

Packing up her materials, the woman smiled, "'Tis you. An uncommon beauty in any kingdom. The good Lord was generous when he gifted you. Whoever your suitor is tonight, 'tis sure he'll be enchanted. As will be the rest of the poor, defenseless louts at your royal gathering. 'Tis true that it almost makes me wish to be young and foolish again. Almost. Enjoy yourself. You look divine."

With that, the intriguing beauty hefted her bag of apparent magic, smiled one last time and went out the door to leave Chantaya slightly stunned in her wake. Slipping off the mask and the veil, she laid them aside and turned back to the demure seamstress who had been patiently stitching nearby, shook her head in wonder and asked, "Was she a mere mortal with a gift for miracles, or a sorceress? Is this going to be like the minstrel's story of Cinderella where the spell lasts only until midnight and then I turn plain again?"

The seamstress clucked her tongue, "As if you were plain. For shame. You'd best voice more gratitude for your extraordinary beauty than that, my dear, else the good Lord might think you ungracious. He might take it all away. 'Tisn't a spell. But you may be wishing it 'twas when it comes time to take that paint off. Nephritirie's potions can seem indelible at times. You look very nice, child. I pity the poor, mortal men there. They truly will be defenseless against such a one as you. Here. 'Tis that I'm finished. Help me wrap it up would you?"

Chantaya bent to help wrap her ball gown in a protective layer of light fabric and was securing it when the door opened. She turned at a sound and found Peyton standing just inside the door, nigh as speechless as Shaun had been earlier that morning. She straightened and walked up to him, wondering if the look on his face meant that he liked her hair and eyes, or if he thought she looked disreputable. When he didn't say anything, she finally prompted, "Well. Do you like it?"

He only nodded thoughtfully and she said, "Peyton, please. Is it suitable? Or shall I take it all back off? Is something wrong?"

He reached out to gently touch her cheekbone on a swirl of the color and smiled. "Nothing is wrong. You simply look like something out of a dream. A truly nice dream." He smiled and stepped back to take in her hair as well and added softly, "Possibly even a truly intimate dream."

"Peyton!" Her eyes widened and she felt her stomach do a somersault, but then he went on less suggestively, "I can only imagine what you'll look like with the gown on as well. I may have to go to the ball in my armor."

At that, she rolled her eyes and finally laughed. "Will I do then?"

He reached to carry the dress for her and replied, "You'll far more than do. I so feel for the other men who will be attending the ball. I shall be the only man there tonight with my own personal enchantress."

Chantaya laughed, "Why Peyton, you wax eloquent. I had no idea there was a touch of the rogue in you."

"But of course you did. I've had a touch of the rogue near your whole life. I was just too busy keeping you in line to get out myself. Or maybe it's my association with Matthew. At any rate, that look makes me feel the rogue; although I fear I may have to spend my time tonight defending my territory instead of the kingdom of Monciere. 'Tis sure even Matthew himself will try to woo you away from me. Are you finished here then?"

"Indeed." Chantaya thanked the dressmaker and put a friendly arm round her shoulder as Peyton offered to pay her. She simply waved his coin away, saying she had already been paid and the two of them went out the door to the waiting carriage. As Peyton handed Chantaya inside, she glanced around to see several people looking askance at her face painting and she laughed to herself, knowing all who saw her thus were probably wishing they would be attending the royal masquerade ball this even at the castle as well.

She settled into the carriage seat with a sigh and said to Peyton who watched her, smiling, "Thank you for not letting me talk us out of this, Pey. 'Twould have been such a shame to have missed it."

Two hours later, when she stepped from her room after dressing, she had to stifle a laugh as she walked into the kitchen. Both Matthew and Shaun were trying to help Peyton figure out how to keep his own mask from slipping as he put on a positively swashbuckling three corner hat that sported a most voluminous fluffy feather. The three of them worked at it for several moments without noticing she was there before Chantaya finally reached onto a shelf, dipped a dainty finger into the sweet syrup there and dabbed it upon his temples. 'Twas a trifle unconventional, but the mask stayed put instantly. Still laughing, she teasingly licked off her finger as all three of them turned to her.

Once again, their complete and utter silence as they stared at her made her wonder, just for a moment, if there was something wrong with her appearance. Finally, Matthew, ever the jester, let out a low whistle, walked all the way round her, then whistled again, and said, "I challenge you to a duel for her, Wolfgar. This very moment. This very day. He who wins gets to accompany her to the castle."

Peyton chuckled, "Oh for pity's sake, Ansel. No duel. You aren't even invited and you've never bested me in aught but telling tall tales. I'd only have to kill you and you would miss the ball anyway."

Matthew put a dramatic hand to his chest. "But at least then I wouldn't die of a wounded heart from watching such a heavenly vision of beauty walk away on another's arm."

At that Shaun chuckled and said, "You? The fair Romeo of the entirety of the kingdom? Die of a wounded heart? Please, spare me the jesting! In truth, he'd probably only wound you and leave you to die slowly anyway, rogue that he is. So give it a holiday, Matthew." Turning to Chantaya, Shaun said, "I however, have a much better chance of besting him with a blade for your favor, Miss Chantaya. Pray, I beg you, throw him over for me and 'tis that I shall waltz the night away with you in his stead. You deserve much the more virile and masculine suitor anyway."

Chantaya raised her eyebrows innocently and looked askance at Peyton, who fairly growled, "Best me with a blade? Surely you jest. And 'twould this be the virile and masculine suitor who called her a boy and a little bugger and pressed me to leave her home but less than one day ago?"

Shaun shook his head and laughed at himself, as he looked at Chantaya, saying, "How could I have ever been so blind and foolish, m'lady? Please, I beg of you, forgive me. 'Twas the ale. It had to have been. I was blinded by the ale. For never have I beheld such a vision of grace and loveliness."

Peyton bowed and doffed his feathered hat to Chantaya while saying to Shaun, "You hadn't imbibed yet a drop of ale.

'Tis simply that you've the brain of a turtle at times. Give it a rest, Squire Shaun. It shall be me, and only me, who will accompany said vision. And 'tis true that I would fight to the death for the honor." To Chantaya, he added mildly, "Although, 'tis also true, that I've spent the finest years of my life protecting you from any number of briar patches you've found yourself in, so in reality, I've truly earned this privilege. Have I not, my beauty?"

With a soft laugh, Chantaya admitted, "'Tis indeed that you have, Sir Knight. From the very day we met, I have ever been and shall ever be in your debt. You have earned all manner of privileges, the least of which is accompanying me to the castle this even. Are you ready then, Sir? Shall we away?"

"Now that my mask is properly pasted in place, indeed, we should away, before I am pressed to duel just to keep you. 'Twould be a short duel, to be sure." He looked pointedly at his two grinning friends. "But I'd hate to soil this fine feather with the blood of either a rake or a dimwit. Do let us be gone."

She dusted her hands together dramatically and then offered him the same dainty hand she had just licked. "As you wish, Sir Knight."

Jaclyn M. Hawkes

Chapter 18

They had only just been handed out of their carriage when people around them began to watch them and nod their greetings, although Peyton recognized only a handful under their masks. He'd simply been teasing Chantaya about having to defend his territory, but there was no doubt in his mind that he would, indeed have to parry the occasional flirtation from other men toward Chantaya. She simply looked too stunning tonight. There wasn't a man on the continent, let alone in the kingdom, who wouldn't want to at least speak to a woman as beautiful as she looked this even.

They walked up the cobblestone drive toward the big front door of the castle and Chantaya looked all around. She seemed to be drinking in all the sights and sounds of this life and place so far removed from what she was used to. Still, as they were admitted at the archway into the great hall, she smiled and walked confidently at his side as if she did this kind of thing every day.

Once inside, they joined a line of people waiting to greet the royal family who stood receiving their guests in front of a quartet of string musicians playing in the background. He knew she was nervous, but as she offered her lovely hand to the feeble dowager queen mother, she greeted the stately, older women with absolute grace and poise and soon the two of them were actually giggling like old friends.

Prince Laird was next in line and he grinned at Peyton with his usual mischief as he shook Peyton's hand and said, "Sir Peyton. She made it then. No wonder you wouldn't kiss the troll. I see what you mean by not seeming a sister. You were correct. There's absolutely no way."

Peyton glanced to where Chantaya was still conversing with the prince's ancient grandmother and agreed, "No. Truly not. You're not supposed to be able to tell who I am under this disguise."

The prince only laughed. "There are not two men with shoulders the likes of yours in the whole of the world, Sir Peyton. 'Tis not hard to tell." The prince was still all but staring at Chantaya and added, "The blue does suit her eyes. They're incredible."

With a smile that felt just a trifle tight, Peyton replied, "She's also incredibly taken, Your Highness. If I can say so respectably. You're not thinking about using your royal power to overthrow my kingdom, are you, Sire?"

Looking back to Peyton, with an honest smile, the prince assured him quietly, "Never, Wolfgar. I'm absolutely to be trusted. Well, unless I hear rumors that you've made her cry. Then, all bets would be called and you could know of a surety that I'd do my utmost to win her heart from you. Not only is she exquisite, but she can also get through the considerable cynicism of my grandmother. Look at the two of them. Your friend must be genuine. No one fools my grandmother."

Chantaya laughed just then. A happy, musical sound that made those around laugh with her and she leaned to touch the arm of the dowager queen affectionately, who grasped her hand to pat it. Peyton couldn't believe his eyes.

Never in his life would he have thought to visit so with the dowager queen and never would he have believed she would laugh like that in return.

He turned to glance at the prince, who only chuckled and raised his own eyebrows and then leaned in and said, "See what I mean? I almost hope you do make her cry. She's a lovely creature. You've got your work cut out for you here tonight. I see that Lord Baffin is considering eating her up, and that young, no-good Damian Rosskeene is considering worse than that. Look at him. At least he doesn't appear to recognize her. You'd best keep the wall securely up round your kingdom."

Glancing around, Peyton felt his gut tighten when he saw the way Damian Rosskeene was watching her and said, "Securely up, and well guarded. I may even call in reinforcements among the knights."

Still whispering closely, the prince shook his head. "I wouldn't do that, Sir Peyton. With a girl as lovely as that, even your brother knights are likely to want to overthrow."

The line moved on, although for Peyton, some of the glamour had worn off the evening as he watched the men watching Chantaya. Eventually, the guests were seated for an elegant dinner and it was almost with a sigh of relief that Peyton saw they were seated next to and across from either close friends, or elderly nobles who appeared to be somewhat trustworthy. Relaxing at last, as he helped Chantaya into her seat, he leaned in and whispered, "Now if only you had cooked the meal. The kitchen staff here could use a lesson in seasoning from you." After only one bite, Chantaya looked up into his eyes and gave him an understanding smile.

After the dinner, when the chamber musicians began to play the waltz, Peyton finally truly felt comfortable as he took

Chantaya into his arms to begin to dance. For the first time this night, he truly felt like he was just Peyton, and she was just Chani, the two childhood friends who had grown up inseparable. 'Twas infinitely comforting. Especially when she all but melted against him and he could smell the fragrance of her lovely hair and feel her body soft against his. Tonight, with its gentry and finery was fine, but what he really wanted—nay truly craved, was just soon to be her husband and be able to be with her as much and as closely as he'd dreamed.

They danced through several sets and the temperature in the room went up as the floor became more crowded. Finally, as they moved near one of the doors that had been opened into the courtyard for ventilation, Peyton deftly swung Chantaya to the side and they quietly stepped outside.

It felt cooler immediately and he felt her inhale a refreshing breath of air and sigh against his neck. He'd been thinking to slip off into one of the gardens, but she felt so good in his arms that he simply continued to dance with her to the music that floated through the open doorway into the darkness where they were.

Chantaya moved closer to him still and he smiled as she whispered, "'Tis far more romantic out here out of the lights and the crowd, is it not, Pey?"

He kissed her temple just above the mask that rested there beside her silken hair, gathered her close enough that he could feel the front of her thighs against the front of his and murmured, "It is. Far and away more."

In their swaying to the music, he pulled her behind a rose hedge that lined the path to the courtyard gardens and wrapped his arms all the way around her as she whispered dreamily, "When I was a little girl, I dreamed of someday dancing at a royal ball with a handsome knight. Did you know that, Peyton? Then, I never imagined it would come true. Have I ever told you?"

"Never." Their waltzing narrowed until they were almost standing in one place and Peyton whispered huskily against her hair, "When I was a lonely knight, I dreamed of someday holding you like this in the seclusion of an enchanted fragrant garden and kissing you until I drew you right into my soul. I hoped and prayed it would come true. Have I ever told you?"

"Mmm, never."

The music stopped then. At least Peyton thought it did, because he couldn't hear it over the beating of his heart as he bent his head to slip off her gossamer veil and kiss her sweet, warm mouth. Maybe tonight they weren't two young peasants who had been childhood playmates. But that was a good thing, because the emotions he was feeling weren't those of a boy and the glittering enchantress he held in his arms certainly didn't feel like a young girl.

He crushed her softness to him and kissed her until his heart pounded and his brain shut down, and he truly felt he was breathing her in. She moaned softly and he worried about hurting the great cut on her ribs. Backing off a portion, he released her mouth to look into her sparkling eyes and ask, "I'm sorry. Did I hurt you?"

She shook her head and he moved from her mouth to kiss her neck just below her ear where her earrings dangled and those exquisite, silken, sable curls caressed his lips. As he nuzzled her, she drew in a breath and it made him want her even closer still. Close enough that nothing could ever come between them. Gently, he bit the tender lobe of her ear and her body nearly seared his as she clung to him, her breathing almost intoxicating against his skin.

With a ragged breath, he broke from her in utter frustration and then took her hand to pull her further up the hedged path, away from the doors of the castle and deeper into the darkness of the garden. When the music was just faint melody, he backed her up against the stone wall behind them and breathed in deeply as he wrapped her back in his arms. He kissed her again, this time hungrily, almost desperately, with a passion he was hard put to keep gentle. Especially when Chantaya was so close to his body that he could tell she was feeling the exact same need.

He kissed her mouth, teasing it and tasting it and reveling in the power he wielded as he knew she felt that same, sweet, warm need. When he moved to her neck again, she sighed and it sounded like forever to him. How he loved this girl. How he needed her in his life and in his heart and eventually—soon, in his bed. He could never tell her that, but he admitted it to himself often lately. How could he not? She was the most exquisite, desirable woman he could ever imagine. He thought about that and knew immediately that it wasn't a good idea right at this moment. She was too close. Too sweet, and warm and innocently willing. She trusted him.

With a literal groan, he pulled himself back from wanting to swallow her in his passion. She trusted him. He cursed inwardly in frustration and kissed her mouth hard, one last, hungry, lingering time and then moved back to that sweet hollow on her neck below her ear that he was coming to know could turn her inside out.

He knew this girl as well as he knew himself. Still, he was only lately coming to know her in a physically intimate way, and while it was the sweetest, most tempting, most satisfying thing he'd ever known. 'Twas also the most frustrating and dangerous. She had far more power over him than any armored foe in battle. And generated a heat that could melt his usual iron willed self control if he allowed it. But he couldn't allow it. Not yet.

Stepping far enough away from her to break all contact between them, he sighed and ran a shaking hand through his hair as he watched her sparkling eyes look up at him in question. He blew out a breath and she self-consciously smiled up at him with utter, innocent trust in her eyes. Her complete faith in him made him feel almost guilty for the feelings that welled when he held her. They needed to get married. Maybe living so far from each other was a good thing as far as keeping him from her physically, but it was killing him, completely aside from the fact that she wasn't safe at Rosskeene Manor.

With another sigh, he leaned and gave her the most tender of kisses and then reached inside his dress tunic to grasp the medallion that hung round his neck. Pulling it off over his head, he stepped back again and reached for her hand. He turned it upward and dangled the medallion over it and then looked up into her beautiful, confused blue velvet eyes. After searching them for a moment, he whispered, "I love you, Chantaya Isabella Kincraig. Would you do me the honor of marrying me? Just as soon as we can possibly arrange it?"

She looked up at him in wonder and then teared up as she nodded and whispered back, "Yes." She gave a tremulous smile and he placed the medallion in her palm and gently closed her small hand around it.

"I know you can't wear a ring yet until you leave Rosskeene's, but wear this. Next to your heart. Wear it and know that even if we're still apart for a short while, I'm under this same moon somewhere. And that I love you, and I miss you and soon we'll be together. As man and wife. Forever and ever. It has my knight's crest on it. I pray it will bring you a measure of safety and peace." He gave her a grin and added, "Twill be more comfortable than a letter to keep there."

She smiled back, slipped the medallion over her head and down inside the bodice of her gown and snuggled against him once more. "The letters haven't been unduly uncomfortable. They warm my heart."

Closing his eyes, he wrapped his arms back around her gently and breathed in the sweet scent of her hair before leaning to kiss it. "As you warm mine, Chani. Ever you have warmed my heart."

They stood there like that for several moments and then she looked back up at him and he bent to kiss her again. Knowing even more surely than before that she was to soon be his wife made the passion rise in him stronger than ever and he swallowed a groan of frustration and slowly pulled away. He closed his eyes and shook his head and said, "We should go back inside. I uh, I, you . . . It's . . . You're . . . We should go back inside."

She gave him a sad smile, slipped her veil back on and took his hand to let him lead off toward the castle again and said quietly, "You're right. But sometimes I purely hate that."

Inside, they looked at each other for a long moment, and then wandered hand in hand toward a refreshment table. The thought of a cool draught of cider was welcome. 'Twas still warm inside, but not nearly so hot as those impassioned kisses had been.

As he reached for the cups of cider, he felt her stiffen beside him and glanced up to see Lord Rosskeene move up to stand nearby with a disgustingly confident smile for her. The warrior in Peyton reared up and it was all he could do not to step between them and literally threaten Rosskeene. Gently squeezing her hand, Peyton handed her the cider and then stiffened himself when Rosskeene spoke to her. "Your masquerade is quite complete, I can't for the life of me detect who you are, although you are somehow familiar. Pray, give a nobleman a hint as to the identity of the most stunning of all the beauties in attendance tonight. Do I know you, fair lady?"

Placing a hand at the small of her back, Peyton guided her aside as he said to Rosskeene, "'Tis the object to remain anonymous, yet I'm sure she would be unknown to someone of your generation anyway, m'lord."

The reference to the obvious difference in their ages only made Rosskeene narrow his eyes at Peyton as he replied, "Indeed she probably would, Wolfgar. You see, in noble circles, the world narrows remarkably. But then you wouldn't understand that, coming from your background, would you? Women, on the other hand tend to appreciate the finer things in life. They gravitate toward things like lands and power. But you wouldn't have any idea of those things either. I recommend you keep a wary guard up where she's concerned, boy."

Wishing he could slug him in his disgusting, noble mouth, Peyton felt Chantaya tighten her grip on his hand. He merely smiled at the older man and said, "I'm sure you're correct, m'lord. All women think only of wealth."

Chantaya gracefully, but obviously turned from Rosskeene and leaned close and whispered, "Moron *and* dimwit. Odious as well. Ignore him." Peyton's smile became genuine and then widened when he realized Prince Laird was moving through the guests not far from them, apparently intent on speaking to them. The prince was exactly what Peyton needed right now to restore both his good humor, and Rosskeene's perspective on class.

As the prince approached, and reached to shake Peyton's hand, Peyton noticed Princess Clarissa at his side, resplendent in flowing crimson velvet and jeweled tiara. Grinning at the prince, Peyton came right out and asked, "You're not going to get me in trouble with the princess again are you, Your Highness? It's ever I'm in trouble when you two are together. I'm fair becoming frightened of the two of you."

The prince only laughed and inclined his head to Chantaya as he replied to Peyton, "Nothing frightens him. Don't believe him." He grinned at his sister and added, "Although Clarissa truly can be scary at times, I'll admit. You should see her upon rising of a morning. Hair going every which way. It's pure terrifying."

The princess only daintily elbowed her brother and then approached Chantaya and said, "Please forgive my brother for being hopelessly indecorous. Father keeps trying to encourage him to behave more discreetly, but then here he is, telling the world I'm frightening of a morning." She reached a hand out to take Chantaya's. "So you are the girl who owns Sir Peyton's heart? I'm Clarissa. It's good to finally meet the woman behind the devotion. Sir Peyton is so faithful to you it near disheartens the rest of us girls of the kingdom."

Chantaya raised her eyebrows and looked at Peyton in surprise as the prince said airily, "'Tis true. He's pure smitten. But upon seeing you, Fair Chantaya The Unsisterly. 'Tis no surprise. Well, in truth, 'tis surprising that any woman could be so fantastically exquisite, but . . . Pray, would you be willing to dance with a mere prince instead of such a masculine knight?"

Looking half panicked and half amused, Chantaya glanced at Peyton for reassurance and he chuckled as he turned her hand over to the prince, saying, "Fear not, Chani. He's a monstrous tease, but he's given me his word not to try to win you away from me. And his word is good. Just don't let him step upon your toes. 'Tis rumored he's a pitiful dancer."

The prince gave a feigned look of outrage, "Pitiful! Why you . . . " To Chantaya he said, "I'll have you know I've endured countless months of practice. Nay, years of dance practice so as not to fall upon my face during a waltz." Lowering his voice a mere smidgen, he added, "I'll also have you know that I only gave Sir Peyton my word not to try to lure you away as long as he didn't ever make you cry. In which case, I should feel sufficiently vindicated in giving it my best effort. You will let me know if he ever breaks your heart, won't you?"

Peyton chuckled, "I've made her mad a few times, Highness, but I try never to make her cry. I believe you're sadly out of luck. But do enjoy your dance." He turned to the princess, "Princess Clarissa would you do me the honor?"

The prince grimaced teasingly and took Chantaya's hand to lead her to the floor beside Peyton and Chantaya, then said loud enough that Peyton and the princess could hear, "Blast him. It's ever been that he bests me at whatever he tries since he's been here. He's nigh immortal. Has he always been so?"

Falling easily into step with the prince who was a heavenly dancer, Chantaya smiled. "Always, Your Highness. I'm so sorry. I shall speak to him and remind him that it's frightfully disrespectful to best a prince at anything."

"On the contrary, my beauty. 'Tis that Sir Peyton is the only one who has the respect to truly challenge me. I'm certain 'tis why I enjoy him so. He hasn't a pandering bone in his body. It gives one the most comforting sense of certainty with him. Although, he has at times left great bruising on parts of my royal self."

At that, the princess laughed and said, "Only on your royal ego, brother. I fear you'll live." To Peyton she said, "Come, Sir Peyton. Let us dance this way a portion."

Chantaya watched Peyton twirl the princess away and wondered at the easy friendship he seemed to have with these two royals. How had this come to be? Especially in such a short time as Peyton had been here? In a way, she was thrilled, and in a way, she was intimidated beyond measure. These were the prince and princess!"

She glanced up to see the prince looking down at her and was grateful for all the times she and her mother and the boys had danced the evening away in front of the fires. She would have never been able to keep her composure dancing with the prince otherwise.

He gave her his grin again and then sobered and said, "'Twas more than my ego he bruised in all reality. A time or two 'twas all I could do to limp away from our encounters. But that was what made us certain he was capable of becoming one of the King's First Guard. He's a good man. We are grateful for him. And for you, fair Chantaya. All joking aside, I thank you for your service in bringing word of insurrection. It has been invaluable. You have our deepest gratitude. Thank you."

She could only nod and looked down humbly as he went on, smiling, "In truth, 'tis that I'm amazed a beauty such as you could also be capable of such as you've done. You don't look the least bit like a soldier."

"I pray not, Sire. Thank you."

The music ended and the prince offered her his arm to take her back to Peyton. As he handed her over, he said with his characteristic teasing grin, "If he ever does make you cry, I live in the big house with the flags and soldiers all around. You can't miss it."

At length, the musicians wound down and the king and queen finally took their places near the archway to bid farewell to their guests. Chantaya had had the time of her life, but her ribs were aching and even the smaller cut on the point of her shoulder had begun to throb from having to reach up to dance with Peyton.

They wended their way arm in arm toward the archway, and Chantaya was just thinking it had been one of the best nights of her life when she was bumped into from behind. Both she and Peyton turned to see what was happening and they found it was Damian Rosskeene in line directly behind them, positively drunken. Lord Rosskeene was attempting to steer him out the archway, but Damian had commenced to be rather happily gregarious as he made his exit.

Chantaya was surprised because the refreshments hadn't been of an alcoholic nature, then she was surprised again, when Damian once again bumped into her, looked up and said matter-of-factly, "Oh, so sorry, Chantaya. Good even to you."

With that, he waltzed on out the door, infinitely less frightening than he was at home in the manor house and Lord Rosskeene gave her and Peyton an embarrassed glance and said, "I'm sorry, Miss. He's but a boy. You know how it goes."

He went out in Damian's wake and Chantaya looked up at Peyton in concern and whispered, "No, I'm sure I don't know how it goes. And he's no more boy than I am. Just out of control. Did he know who I was, Pey?"

Peyton looked up in concern at the ruckus and said drily, "Remember you *were* a boy but yesterday. He seemed to know you, but don't worry. I doubt he'll know anything in the morning except that his head hurts."

He nudged her as they neared the outer doorway. "That's Mordecai. What the devil?" Peyton's face became grim and he tried to push ahead, but at that moment, Damian became ill and vomited on the cobblestone walk almost onto Mordecai's boots.

Lord Rosskeene rolled his eyes and cursed and Peyton led Chantaya to the side in disgust. Mordecai followed. After glancing at Rosskeene to ensure he was out of hearing, Peyton looked intensely at Mordecai and asked brusquely, "What is it? What's wrong?"

Mordecai shook his hand and then smiled as he took Chantaya's hand and said, "Nothing is wrong. Can't an old man come to see a lovely young woman in a ball gown? You are the picture of rare beauty, my girl. You look positively stunning."

Peyton let out a sigh of relief as Chantaya reached to hug Mordecai with both arms and said, "Thank you, Sir Mordecai.

You are kind. It's been a wonderful night. You didn't truly come all this way just to see my dress."

"The dress and the young lady in it. Indeed, I did. And worth the trip it is. I haven't seen such beauty since first I brought my wife Christiana to a royal ball."

Chantaya stepped back from him and smiled and said, "I'll bet she was far prettier than I. What was her dress like? Surely you remember."

Mordecai gave her a mellow smile as they continued on up the walk and mused, "A body couldn't forget that dress. 'Twas a pure fairy dress of pale yellow satin caught up with rows of lace and tiny ribbons. She was a vision."

Wrapping an arm round his waist, Chantaya prodded with a smile, "And did you kiss her in her ball gown, Sir Mordecai? Surely you didn't pass up the opportunity of a secluded fragrant garden to kiss your wife."

For a moment Mordecai was thoughtful and then he smiled again and hedged, "I'm sure I don't remember. Why? Should a girl be kissed in a secluded fragrant garden?"

Chantaya laughed and hugged him again. "You. Not remember? I'm sure I don't know either, Sir Knight. It just seemed like a romantic idea is all."

On the walkway behind the three, Lord Rosskeene looked up from where he and Lady Rosskeene were dragging their son back to meet their carriage to see the exchange in front of them. The striking dark haired beauty that had been with that impudent Wolfgar seemed to be surprisingly close to old Sir Mordecai. It made him wonder where she was from.

The unknown beauty had made him feel twenty-two again when first he'd glimpsed her there in the great hall of the castle. There was something about her that reminded him of Isabella when first he'd seen her those many long years ago. He'd felt an instant bolt of attraction upon first seeing Isabella and it had happened again tonight when he'd seen the way that gown had hugged Wolfgar's girl's stunning figure. A man should possess such a woman as that.

He glanced back over at his wife. She certainly wasn't seventeen anymore. She'd put on weight in their years together. They both had. And her perpetual grimace had settled into folds in her face that had begun to droop with perspiration and fatigue on this long, warm night. He looked again from her to the svelte and graceful beauty who was smiling up at Sir Mordecai on the cobblestones ahead of them and made a decision to find out what he could about the girl. He'd have to find out where old Sir Mordecai had gotten to and go from there. Once he was king, he would need a more suitable woman for his queen anyway.

§§§§

The royal seamstress had been right about the paint on Chantaya's face. 'Twas nigh indelible. By the time she had it scrubbed clean enough to keep the Rosskeenes from detecting it, her skin was fair tender. Peyton noticed the pinkness and kissed her brows tenderly when she appeared the next morning. He had a carriage waiting to take her home, with both of their saddle horses tied behind it and his friends and Sir Mordecai sitting their own horses nearby. He handed her into its luxury and she literally sighed as she leaned her sore ribs against the padded seat. This would be so much more restful for this long journey, although she fully intended to talk Peyton into sending it back long before they neared

Rosskeene Manor. She would ride the last way as a boy so as not to alert anyone to her tie to Peyton. If it was still light out, she even considered traveling alone to stay inconspicuous.

He did let her talk him into sending it back at the last inn they passed. But even though it was a sunny late afternoon, both he and Mordecai insisted they and the others ride along beside her in her stable boy clothing, with the duffle bag tied on behind carrying her dresses. When they passed the Rosskeene entourage not far beyond the inn, she was infinitely grateful for her boy's clothing and horse. Hopefully the Rosskeenes were all dozing inside their carriage and wouldn't even recognize Peyton.

When they arrived, Mordecai, Matthew, Shaun and the others waited in the wood behind the Rosskeene stables as Peyton went a little further with her before leaving her to ride the last bit in alone. Deep in the wood, they paused and got off to tell each other goodbye and it was difficult as usual to say farewell. They were officially betrothed now, and closer than ever and she could see the struggle in his eyes as he wrapped his arms around her one last time.

For a moment, he didn't say anything, and then finally, he said almost heatedly, "I'm never doing this again, Chani. Never! I don't care if Rosskeene is coming after the crown with gigantic flying ships and sea monsters. This is the last time. I'm going to go back to Valais and finish this whole mess, then come and get you once and for all. And we'll be married. We're not even going to say goodbye at the end of the day. We're going to say goodnight. I can't leave you here like this. It makes me feel less than a man. I feel I've failed you every single time even though you've helped the king."

Stepping back, she looked into his eyes for a long moment, wondering what to say and finally said simply, "As you wish, Sir Peyton." She reached inside her borrowed boy's shirt and fingered the medallion he'd given her and searched his eyes, seeing forever there. Once more, she whispered, "As you wish." She stood on her toes to kiss him and he pulled her to him almost roughly, whispering her name as he kissed her back hungrily.

Finally, he let go and gently helped her back aboard her horse, then stood beside her, his big hand upon her knee and still holding her captive with his liquid brown eyes. Knowing she was going to cry if she didn't leave, she leaned down and quickly kissed him, smiled and said, "I love you, Sir Peyton. God bless." Then she spurred her horse away so he wouldn't see her tears as she whispered the same words all the way back into the stable.

Chapter 19

After the ball, more rainy weather brought the first colored leaves of fall to Rosskeene Manor. With them came the heightened urgency to finish preparations for the coming winter, including the cutting of the huge stacks of firewood and peat bricks the manor would require. This was a gargantuan task for the men and it had Conrad, as well as the other young grooms out assisting, as they cut and hauled peat and whole trees into the yards to split and stack against the winter's cold.

At the same time, Chantaya and Isabella were also working near round the clock to gather in the herbs and mushrooms the manor would need when the snow was too deep to find them in the coming months.

For the first time since their arrival, the Kincraigs were left relatively unguarded by the servants. This brought a horrible feeling of vulnerability that was only slightly lessened by the marked focus Lord Rosskeene gave to the unsavory visitors to his study who Chantaya listened in to as she worked to keep the silver sparkling. There was something terribly important to Lord Rosskeene in the wind. She knew this was the biggest thing that had been planned thus far, but Chantaya hadn't as yet been able to pin down what it was that was so vital to him and his unsavory henchmen.

Even the visitors themselves made the women feel unsafe as the Kincraigs worked in and around the manor while the male servants were gone. Chantaya took to keeping the dagger Mordecai had given her in her boot all of the time.

All of it made that time in the evening when the day's work was done and Chantaya and Isabella could return to the safety of the stable and the reassurance of Conrad's presence that much more precious. Still, there was no word from the magistrate.

Conrad had become a surprisingly good reader in the weeks Isabella had been teaching him and it brought a sweet emotion when Chantaya saw the two of them with their heads together over one of Isabella's carefully hoarded books of an evening. That their friendship was deepening was clearly apparent and it brought a measure of peace to Chantaya that was almost puzzling. It lessened a sense of worry for her mother that, until now, she hadn't even realized she was feeling. 'Twould indeed be a wonderful thing if Isabella and Conrad could ease each other's loneliness in the old age that would come to them. Conrad had been a true and wonderful guardian to them these weeks they'd been here.

The extra time foraging had been an undue physical strain on Isabella and it was near every afternoon that Chantaya bade her lie down to rest as Chantaya went in to help Cook with making the manor's supper. On these days, without Conrad's care, Chantaya fairly ran between the stable and kitchen, and tried to make sure Cook was already in the kitchen when Chantaya arrived there. But it didn't always work out that way as they all had extra duties what with trying to store the fall's harvest as well.

One afternoon, when the low gray clouds threatened to bring more cold rain, Chantaya arrived at the kitchen door in a veritable burst of leaf laden wind to commence with the household's evening meal. She came in the door and then had to literally lean against it to get it to close against the buffeting gusts. Breathing a sigh of relief, she leaned against the door for a moment, enjoying the relative coziness of the kitchen before going to take her cloak off, but then looked up to see Damian standing in the doorway to the manor house with his disgusting meat-eating gaze.

Chantaya glanced around the kitchen in a moment of panic, hoping desperately that Cook or Conrad or even a housemaid would miraculously appear, but there was no one and nothing except Damian's wolfish smile as he almost lazily began to walk across the kitchen.

Strangely, he didn't say anything as he moved toward her, but even the near silence was incredibly frightening as he came closer. Without even realizing it, Chantaya backed up until she was halted by a set of shelves that held dishes and food stuffs against the wall. Still, Damian came on, raking his eyes over her in a manner that brought back the fear that had nearly choked her the very first day he had ever seen her. Without even thinking about it, she began to pray, and then glanced around almost feverishly for something she could defend herself with.

She could almost hear Mordecai speaking of anything being a weapon and then Peyton's voice seemed to come to her to use her head and think. She thought of the dagger in her boot and then discarded the idea the moment it came to her. Damian would just overpower her and use it on her. She grasped for anything on the shelves behind her and found nothing she could conceive of using to stop him.

Just as he reached for her, she tried to dart sideways away from him, but he only thrust out a hand and caught her by the sleeve to pull on it viciously. It tore away from the body of her dress, taking a portion of the collar and bodice and the last of the scab from the sword fight injury on her shoulder with it.

She almost lost her footing with the force of the jerk and she fell against him as he took in the bareness of her shoulder and chest, and the blood that began to drip from the scab. The look in his eyes brought terror as he seemed to catch his breath and become near entranced.

Reaching up, he pulled a pin from her hair, and then another as she watched him. She fought the panic that welled inside her and tried to listen for Peyton and Mordecai's voices as she looked around again for something to fight him with. Damian pulled yet another pin and her hair cascaded down from the twist it had been held in. His chest began to rise and fall in a rhythm that mimicked her own racing breath. Reaching again, he grasped the loose mass of dark curls that fell down her back and pulled her against him as she finally screamed for all she was worth.

Instinctively, she raised a knee, but he simply sidestepped it. She stomped down on his foot with her boot heel and heard him groan as he hauled brutally on her hair and brought her face to his, swearing against her mouth as he roughly went to kiss her.

Fighting him with one arm and still trying to scream, Chantaya reached behind her for anything to hit him with. All she succeeded in doing was knocking a crock of dried beans to the stone floor. It shattered on impact and beans flew in every direction, but it didn't cause Damian to stop his brutal attack on her mouth. In desperation, she bit him.

Raising his head, he snarled as he put a hand to his mouth where she'd drawn blood. Upon seeing it on his fingers, he backhanded her across the mouth viciously, the fury in his face, terrifying.

Suddenly, there was a scream, and then, almost simultaneously, the sound of metal clanging. Damian loosened his grip and took a step back, still snarling and Chantaya realized her mother was standing next to them with an iron skillet in her hand. The fury in Damian's face seemed to compound and he pulled even harder on Chantaya's hair. He raised a hand to hit her mother as well, but Chantaya caught at his arm in time to stop him just as her mother took another swing with the pan. The clang sounded again. This time, Damian went down in a heap into the glass and beans from the shattered crock, nearly taking Chantaya with him.

Chantaya caught herself and disentangled Damian's hand from her hair, then turned to her mother who was sobbing and hitting Damian over and over with the heavy pan. Chantaya reached to stop her, but she had to nearly tackle her mother with both arms to control her.

Just then the kitchen door flew open and Cook came in, followed by two of the housemaids. The three of them stood there staring and finally, Cook whispered, "Lord help us." She came inside, stepping gingerly over the spilled beans, glass and blood from a cut on Damian's head and came to Chantaya. She ineffectively pulled the remnants of the bodice of Chantaya's dress back up to try to cover her shoulder and bosom. Then wrapped an arm around Isabella, who was still fighting Chantaya and continuing to cry from fury and heart break with Chantaya fighting tears right along with her.

Cook patted Isabella's back and said resolutely, "I don't blame you, sweet Isabella, but 'tisn't you to want to maim. Calm yourself now. Calm. Calm yourself."

Over Isabella's shoulder, Cook said to one of the maids, "Go quickly to the men and fetch Conrad! Quickly! 'Twill be that we'll need his savin' strength for Isabella, and from the master, I expect. Run now! All the way!"

The maid scurried out and Cook asked the other one, "Is the young master still breathing then? Can you tell?" She continued to pat Isabella for a moment, and then turned and leaned herself next to the maid to feel for a heartbeat and breathing from the young lord. She gave a sigh that seemed an affirmative and then stood again just as the door opened and Lady Rosskeene stepped inside.

She gasped as she took in the situation and then began to scream even louder than Chantaya had screamed when she saw Damian lying there amidst the crockery shards and beans and blood with Isabella still wielding the pan.

Cook's eyes met Chantaya's for one exasperated second before she left Isabella and turned to Lady Rosskeene and began to reassure her that Damian would be fine and to calm herself, much as she had spoken to Isabella. Lady Rosskeene got only more shrill if anything, and it wasn't but a minute before the kitchen door came open again and Lord Rosskeene himself stepped in. His eyes widened as he took in the scene and then the door from the garden opened. Conrad and three of the men came inside the now crowded kitchen as well.

Upon seeing the men, Chantaya attempted again to pull her dress back together as Lord Rosskeene began to glower and then Lady Rosskeene, still screaming like the banshees were after her, threw herself against Lord Rosskeene. He rolled his eyes and shook his head behind her as the glower deepened. When yet another maid entered, Lord Rosskeene pushed his wife toward her and said, "Take her ladyship upstairs and bring her some tea. No, make it brandy. A good shot of it and then stay there with her. Go."

The two women went out the door and the resulting drop in nerve grating sound was a small relief until Lord Rosskeene looked around, taking in the mess, Chantaya's disheveled hair, swelling face and blackening eye, torn dress and blood, and that on Damian and the floor. Angrily, he demanded, "What on this earth goes on here? What has happened to Damian? Who has harmed him?" For a moment, the others didn't answer and he shouted more loudly, "Who did this? Is he dead? Who did this?"

Cook shook her head. "He's not dead, m'lord. Simply out cold, he is."

Isabella stepped forward, still clutching her iron pan and the heartbreak in her face eased as the fury there made her almost regal. "I did it! And if he's not dead yet, I'll do it again! And then I'll come after you, you dastardly beast! I may have had to take your abuse in a much younger, much more naïve time, but I'll die before I stand by and watch the spawn of a monster like you abuse my daughter!"

She raised the pan toward him and he actually took a step back from her before the anger rose in him to match hers. Chantaya could see the furious clash coming and she stepped out between them just as Conrad made the same move from near the outside door.

Lord Rosskeene raised his hand to strike Isabella but then there was a sound from Damian at their feet. As one, they all looked down and Lord Rosskeene bent to him. As Damian groaned and turned his head slightly, Cook leaned to move the broken crockery nearest him as Conrad whispered something to Isabella. He tried to ease the pan from her grip, but she refused to let him and instead, turned to Lord Rosskeene and spat, "Cook your own food and be damned, *Lord* Rosskeene! My daughter and I will go to prison and gladly, before being treated as she was treated here this even!"

Isabella cast him one last shriveling glance and then wrapped an arm round Chantaya's shoulders and pushed her toward the door. Chantaya, still unable to control her tears, was grateful not only to get away to where she could change out of the ruined dress, but also to where she could try to speak to her mother. Damian's behavior tonight had indeed been heinous and she had begun to shake as reaction set in, but she couldn't let this make her cave now. Too much was at stake. She knew it instinctively.

'Twas critical that she find out what Lord Rosskeene was planning. Time after time lately, as she listened, he had spoken of when he held the crown. Whatever it was, he truly believed it would be the end of King Dougal's reign and she couldn't leave today. Not until she understood what he intended. She couldn't! Not even at the risk of her very person. 'Twas too important to the kingdom and everyone in it! But how to explain that to her mother?

When they reached their little room in the stables as Isabella barred the small door, she broke down into tears again. The two of them hugged each other and cried and clung together. At length, Isabella whispered, "Oh, Chantaya, I'm so sorry. So sorry to have brought you into all of this."

Chantaya shook her head and said through her own tears, "Mother, you are not the one responsible for any of

Lord Rosskeene's behavior. Nor that of his son. Don't apologize, Mum. This is none of it your fault. None."

Still sobbing, Isabella said, "But I shouldn't have brought you here. I shouldn't have let you come. I should have left you with Rose and Willem."

Surprisingly, this was just the tact that Chantaya needed at this moment and she looked up into her mother's eyes and replied, "Maybe 'twasn't you at all who brought me here, Mother. Brought us both here. Maybe 'twas God himself who brought us here."

Isabella eyed her for a moment, reached out to gently touch the swollen spot on Chantaya's cheek and mouth and then collapsed into tears again with a shake of her head. "No. No, God would never work that way. He wouldn't put you in harm's way for his purposes. I don't believe that."

Chantaya hugged her and rubbed her back as she said, "Don't you suppose, Mum that at some point, before we came to this life, we agreed to the trials we would face here? God knew what would happen to us. He knows all. I'll bet we agreed with our earthly fates before we ever came down here. But God hasn't put us in harm's way. Rosskeene did that. And I'm fine, Mum. A bit sore, but, still mainly intact. 'Tis God who has kept us safe, in spite of what Rosskeene intended. And 'tis God who is using us to help King Dougal. It is. I know that it is. If you think about it, you know it as well."

Isabella only hugged her tighter and sniffled and Chantaya asked quietly, "Do you feel it as well, Mum?"

Her mother stilled for a moment, but then, "I'll admit that I feel it, daughter. 'Twas even a feeling that sent me into the kitchen tonight to see about you, but I can't do it anymore. Whether God wills it or not, I can't stand by and watch what happened tonight. I can't. Some may be able to sacrifice their child for the greater good. But not I. No more. We're leaving. In fact, we haven't a choice anymore. After what I said to him tonight, probably both of us will be in debtor's prison within a day's time. He has a furious temper. I know that from before. He'd never take what I said without making us pay."

Leaning back for a moment, Chantaya gave a small smile through the tears that still refused to abate, and said, "Where's your faith, Mother? 'Tis a plan the good Lord has. And yes, you can keep to the faith. 'Tis well enough I know it. After all, you're the one who taught me. Together, we can do whatever He will ask. And He will ask. Whatever is afoot here just now is huge. Rosskeene truly thinks he will be king within the week. We have to stay long enough to find what he's planning. Just that long." She gave her mother another small smile. "Then we'll go to debtor's prison together."

Her mother closed her eyes. Tears seeped out and down her cheeks and the proud and angry woman who had spoken so surely to Lord Rosskeene only moments earlier was completely gone. Sighing silently, Chantaya turned aside to find more hair pins and take out another dress.

Before she had even gotten the dress out, there came an angry knock at the door. Chantaya took a deep breath, pulled the torn dress back up over herself and squared her shoulders to open it. There was little doubt who stood on the other side from the demanding sound of that knock. When she opened it, she was surprised to see that not only was it Lord Rosskeene, but also Conrad and his three helpers and Cook herself stood there.

Before Chantaya could say anything, Isabella moved her aside, stepped out and asked Rosskeene brusquely, "What do you want?" Quietly, Conrad moved to come and stand near Isabella, casually leaning on a pitchfork he'd picked up on the way out, facing the nobleman.

Surprisingly, the other three young men came just as casually to side him, all of them carrying an implement as well, and Cook, on the other side said in a peace loving tone, "Now remember, m'lord. Remember the quality of your supper since Isabella's been here. Not a one of us truly wants her to be leaving us. We don't. Don't let your temper rule your belly. Forget all this rumpus and let's go see to the boy. Master Damian needs his father. And you have your business dealings to see to. No sense in bothering with this nonsense."

Isabella's pretty brow wrinkled in confusion as she looked about, wondering why all the others had come as well and Conrad gave her a calming, encouraging glance before turning back to Rosskeene. Lord Rosskeene himself glanced around in concern at the others before turning to Isabella and looking her up and down.

At his look, she stiffened and said almost as if she was the noble and he the servant, "Well?"

At that moment, another man, one of those of evil ilk who was involved in whatever it was that Rosskeene was planning walked into the stable and sauntered up. Slowly, as Rosskeene's evil face watched Isabella, the seething anger seemed to dissipate, to be replaced by impatience. He pulled his pocket watch to look at it and then growled at Isabella and Chantaya. "I haven't the time to waste with this foolishness. Pull yourselves together and get the supper made. I've company waiting."

Isabella shook her head and said staunchly, "No, Rosskeene. My daughter isn't going near your kitchen again.

Not so long as your son resides there, thinking she is his crumpet for the taking. We'll go to prison."

His eyes narrowed and he threatened, "You'll do as I say, woman. How dare you challenge my authority? I'll see to my son." Isabella only shook her head and he added, "I give you my word."

Again Isabella shook her head and said scathingly, "Your word. Your word is nothing!"

The anger flared again in his eyes, but then, surprisingly, he chuckled, glanced at Conrad and the others and turned his back. As he walked away, he said, "I always enjoyed that bit of fire you have to you, Isabella. Today, I've got more pressing issues than your ridiculous concerns. Damian may not even live. Bring Conrad to the kitchen with you for assurance. I've things to see to."

As he walked through the stable, the pigeons in the rafters warbled softly and he paused and looked up. The wooden crate sat among the other birds resting there. For a moment, he looked puzzled, and then thoughtful. He turned back around, glanced at the man with him and then back at the birds. Then, he studied each Conrad, Isabella, Chantaya and the young men in turn, looking more thoughtful with each one. Finally, still creasing his forehead in question, he silently turned with his associate and went out of the stable.

The servants stood looking at one another in open amazement and at length, Cook said, "Well. All righty then. Who'd have ever believed the master would just walk away like that?"

Conrad only shook his head, mumbling under his breath in disgust as he looked at both Isabella and Chantaya in pity and then herded his helpers away from where Chantaya's dress still exposed parts of her shoulder and bosom.

Cook made a comforting sound, then gently smoothed the dress again and pressed the two to step back into their room and said, "I wish I could stay here and help you, but I'd better get 'is supper while the sun still shines wi' 'im, I say. Stay here together and take comfort in each other. Chantaya, should I send the physician out here when 'e's done wi' the young master? How . . . How badly did he hurt you? Did 'e? Did 'e? Uhm . . . "

Chantaya shook her head and interrupted as her tears welled over again. "No. He didn't. He had just come in when Mum arrived. I'll be fine. No physician. Just let us know how badly injured Damian is, please."

Nodding, Cook said, "And some tea. I'll send Conrad wi' some tea. Take care now." Still making the sound of pity with her lips, Cook bustled out. Isabella shut the door with a huge sigh and turned to Chantaya again. The two of them looked at each other and then almost in unison, turned to go rummage for clean clothing for Chantaya. That was the first thing they both wanted to do. Get rid of the glaring evidence of just what Damian had intended to do to her.

Damian didn't come to for most of a day, but then the next afternoon, he awoke and became positively whiny about how his head hurt and his belly ached. Chantaya wasn't at all sure why his belly would hurt, but she was inexplicably relieved that he hadn't been killed by her mother, much as he deserved it. By late that night, Even Lord Rosskeene had resorted to a stiff restorative belt of brandy to deal with his offspring.

For some reason, Damian woke with a craving for his favorite dish and though Cook offered to try and make it if Chantaya would give her instructions, Chantaya used it as an excuse to get back into the kitchen and try to get things back to normal. She knew it indeed wouldn't take much to get her mother to pack up and leave and take debtor's prison over Rosskeene Manor, but Chantaya felt an urgency to try and find out just what Rosskeene and the others were up to.

The next morning, after breakfast, Cook sent Chantaya in search of the dishes and utensils the physician and the family had used the night before in trying to make Master Damian more comfortable. Damian was finally sleeping soundly from something Isabella had recommended for him and Lord Rosskeene was out of the house for the moment, so Chantaya felt relatively safe in her quest for the soiled dishes.

She went through the bed chambers and the parlor and was finally in the master's study and had collected a dishpan full of glassware and cutlery. As she reached for the last brandy glass on the master's desk, she was puzzled by a map that lay there. It had an obvious X placed upon it and Chantaya rested her dishpan on her hip as she leaned over to study it. She didn't know much about maps, but she could detect areas that appeared to be city, farmlands, wild lands and even rivers were labeled.

The X was in the city of Valais, near a river. Also nearby there was an area labeled with a cross. At first she wondered if it was another X, but then felt sure that it was indeed a perpendicular cross mark. At length, not really understanding what she was seeing, she took her load of dishes and went back into the kitchen and handed them over to Cook before starting on the evening's supper of roast chicken. It wasn't until the next afternoon that she understood the meaning of the cross.

Lord Rosskeene had taken two men and cloistered himself in his study and as was her habit, as soon as he did, Chantaya went in to polish the silver and listen to their planning. While she was listening, she heard them speaking of hiding in a ravine when the family went through the river, on the way to the church. The moment she heard the word church, she realized what the cross had meant. The cross was a church! Shaking her head, she actually felt a trifle silly that it hadn't occurred to her before.

Going back to listening, she tried to figure out what Lord Rosskeene was talking about. She didn't understand. She assumed the family meant the royal family, but it made no sense. Why would the king's family be crossing a river on the way to a church? And who was hiding in a ravine? Surely if Rosskeene knew of someone hiding then it wasn't someone the king and the knights would know of or want in the ravine. And why would the royals travel out of the castle proper to a church? The king's church was actually right inside the castle walls, well protected by his own guards.

A marriage maybe? But there had been no rumor of a royal wedding. Certainly, if there was to be a wedding celebration the royal family would attend it would be planned for some time. There were no new babies in the royal family who would need christening outside the regular church building. Things of that type would be done in the castle church anyway. She polished and listened and was thoroughly confused about what it was Rosskeene was planning and so passionate about.

When Conrad walked her back to the stable that night, she was still perplexed. And worried. What would make Lord Rosskeene believe he would shortly be made king that would involve the royal family and a church? A church they didn't normally attend?

She became even more worried later when Conrad said to her as he was telling her mother good night, "Watch yourself, Miss Chantaya. For some reason the master has some men watching us. Actually, I think he's got them watching me, or one of the boys. I'm not sure what they're watching for, but they're not to be trusted. Don't you be taking yourself off of a night on one of your wild rides. 'Twouldn't be safe. Not by any margin it wouldn't."

Nodding, Chantaya became thoughtful. None of this made sense. Why would Rosskeene have someone watching them? And why a church? It made no sense, but it made her and her mother feel all the more vulnerable.

When she couldn't sleep, and knew her mother was tossing and turning as well, she finally spoke out into the darkness to ask, "Mother, why would Lord Rosskeene expect the king's family to travel outside the castle on the way to a church? They go to church inside the castle. He's planning something to do with a river crossing near a church. Something soon. Whatever could it be?"

In a tired voice, her mother asked, "What are you talking about, Chantaya?"

"I heard Rosskeene and his friends talking about someone hiding in a ravine to do something to the royal family as they traveled to a church. And it was on the map on his desk in his study. It's a church inside the city, but outside the castle. But there's a church right inside the castle walls. I saw it just last week."

Her mother sat straight up in bed. "Chantaya, don't you dare try to make another trip to meet Mordecai like that last one! Don't you dare! Especially not when Conrad has just told you there are frightening men about! Leave this all to the knights. 'Tis what they're trained for."

Rolling her eyes in the dark where her mother couldn't see, she replied, "Mother, I'm not going anywhere but to sleep. If I can ever get my mind to shut down. I'm just trying to figure out what he's up to. But it's complete nonsense. At least to me."

Lying back down, her mother said, "Leave it to the knights, Chantaya. Leave it to Peyton. He's a wonderful soldier. Now go to sleep."

"Yes, Mother." Chantaya turned onto her side and tried not to be disgusted. How could her mother expect her to ignore both what she was hearing and the urgency in her very bones? Something was going on. Something big was going on. She couldn't ignore it. She stuffed her pillow into a more comfortable shape and sighed. She really, truly didn't want to have to make another frightening, lonely, cold, miserable night ride.

Turning onto her stomach, she opened her eyes to look out the little window at the moon. 'Twas Peyton's moon too. Her warrior's moon. How she wished Peyton was here. Or that she was there. He would know what it all meant and what to do. Why didn't the king just have the knights capture Lord Rosskeene and be done with it?

Jaclyn M. Hawkes

Chapter 20

The next morning, Conrad came into the kitchen with news that the dowager queen mother had passed away two days earlier and the funeral would be one day hence.

All the blood rushed to Chantaya's head! The dowager queen mother! She had been aged, but she had seemed so vital only last week. Suddenly Chantaya realized. It wasn't a church at all! The cross wasn't a church! It was a cemetery! They were going to try to kill the king on the way to the cemetery! That was it! 'Twas the only way to get the royal family outside the castle gates, because there wasn't room inside the courtyard for a cemetery.

She glanced around at Conrad and wondered if her mother would figure it out like she just did. Then she looked out the window, wondering where the men were who were watching them? Had Rosskeene figured out she was the one who had taken word to the knights? Or was he simply trying to ensure that no one could get word to the knights that he was about to do something? And how had Rosskeene known that the dowager queen mother would die? She turned back to Conrad and asked, "Pray, what did she die of?"

He shook his head. "'Tis a mystery to everyone. She took sick the other night after the ball and has gone down hill since then. The physicians have no idea, but they suspect she was somehow poisoned by something. That could just be a guess. She was nearly seventy. That's ancient for a queen. That's ancient for anybody."

Nodding, Chantaya considered what she knew of herbs and mushrooms. The dowager queen could easily have been poisoned the night of the ball. And then Rosskeene only need wait to hear when the funeral would be. If his attack was set up properly, he might indeed, kill the king and his family while they were grieving her loss.

She closed her eyes, remembering the sweet elderly royal she had laughed with the night of the ball. Rosskeene was a monster. A veritable monster. How in the world was she going to get past whoever Rosskeene had watching? How was she going to get past her own mother?

Chantaya tried to appear completely calm as she went about making the breakfast. Word had to get out to the castle, but it was more complicated this time. Not that the other two trips hadn't been difficult, but this time there were those watching and her mother. How could she get safely away?

She sifted through one idea in her head after another, only to discard them in the same fashion. She needed to wait for darkness, but that would be wasting precious time and the watching men would probably be far more attentive to someone leaving after dark. She could leave sooner, but anyone could see her go and she would be missed within a short time. And how would she get a horse out? In the dark or the light? Her mother would suspect instantly if she heard a horse moving.

The noon day meal was over and cleaned up before Chantaya finally came to the conclusion that she simply had to do something. She had to try. She couldn't not. There was too much at stake. Far too much. The kingdom would crumble under the rule of a monster such as Rosskeene.

With that thought in mind, she prayed for a solution the whole way from the manor house to the stable in the early afternoon. As she finished, just before she entered the big stable door, she looked up to realize there were horses in the far pasture along the bluff.

That was it! She'd have no saddle, but she'd tell her mother she was going after some spearmint for the night's dessert and she'd simply not come back. 'Twould give her enough time to at least get past the guards, if she could.

Her mother napped on their bed as she entered their room and Chantaya breathed in deeply as she pulled their biggest basket down. She filled it with the bread and cheese she had brought from the kitchen, and then knelt to retrieve her boy's clothing and Mordecai's wife's sword from under the very bed her mother slept on. For the time being, she'd have to conceal the sword down the back of her skirt as she wandered into the wood. Stuffing the clothing into the basket, she glanced at the sky out the window. At least it wasn't raining buckets this time. There was no way she was going anywhere this time without a heavy cloak.

Leaving a note for her mother that said simply, "Gone to the wood for spearmint. And some other things," she blew her mother a silent kiss, followed it with a silent prayer and ducked out the door of the stable. She dearly hoped Conrad had left the halters he had used to take those horses out on the gate post as he typically did.

§§§§

The short, blonde man with the ragged goatee had been watching for the girl to come back with her basket for better than an hour before he decided to get up from where he and his cousin Ned were sitting under the trees gambling. Several times, she had gone with her basket to the woods, and he truly didn't think for a moment that a girl, especially one that beautiful would be the person who had gotten word out to the soldiers of their activities, but Rosskeene had been adamant that no one was to leave the manor without his permission.

She hadn't truly left the manor anyway. Just taken her basket and gone into the wood there the way she always did. But she was not usually alone and she typically reappeared after an hour or two. This time, she had been gone for almost three and hadn't shown up yet.

He got up and began to meander that way. This was the easiest money he'd ever made. Sitting in the shade gambling and drinking. He won some too. Ned had never been an overly skilled gambler. Twenty minutes later, there was still no sign of the girl and he went back and kicked Ned where he lounged, sleeping off the ale they'd been sharing. "Get up. Come help me. That girl took off down here three hours ago and she haint come back. Somethin's wrong. Come look with me."

Grumbling sleepily, Ned got up. He scrubbed at his week's growth of beard, yawned widely, snapped his suspenders into place and followed into the woodland. His breath near caused the blonde man to gag. That brown ale tended to sour on you if you didn't eat something with it. What time was it anyway? It ought to be getting near to supper time.

They wandered through the trees and scrub brush on the lip of the stream bottom for another half hour and then walked back to the kitchen to pick up the food Rosskeene's cook had left for them. Going to their post, they ate it and then walked back into the woods again. Maybe the girl had come back another way or something. If they didn't find her in the next while, they'd go back and ask her mother where she was. She had to be around here somewhere.

§§§§

Cook emerged from the kitchen garden door and looked around the deserted yards of Rosskeene Manor in complete perplexion. What under heaven was going on around here this even? This morning the place had been fair bustling, but tonight, the whole manor was deserted. That had happened before, but never without the master or mistress planning well in advance for it.

The Lord and Lady and young master had packed up in a whirlwind and gone flying out with several of their staff with them. True, the death of the dowager queen wasn't something that could be planned for, but where in the world had even Isabella and Chantaya and Conrad gotten to? Never had Cook known them to not show up. Especially when, to her knowledge, they didn't know the Lord and Lady were going to be gone tonight.

She walked over to the stable, shaking her head. Empty. Isabella and Chantaya's door wasn't even shut securely. She peeked in and noticed a beautiful blue satin gown tossed across the bed and couldn't help herself entering and fingering the fine fabric as she wondered why it was there. 'Twas far too fancy a gown for a scullery maid to possess.

She stepped back out, closed the door firmly and looked out the big barn doors. Even the shady characters that Lord Rosskeene had had hanging around here making the rest of the staff nervous had taken off at a high gallop an hour or two ago. What under heaven was going on?

§§§§

Chantaya was well more than half way to Mordecai's when she heard the sound of galloping horses coming on the trail behind her. She would have been further, but the horse she'd taken from the pasture was being ornery and jumpy and she'd had to fight it to even make it that far. Without a saddle or spurs, she'd been hard put just to stay aboard at times. At the sound of riders, she turned off the trail into the woods beside it to ride far into the trees. It was unbelievably nicer to ride in the daylight, but it made concealment much harder.

She looked at the woods around her and the shapes of the surrounding hills and then veered left, deciding to simply try to make it to Mordecai's cross country. It would be much more rugged, but she hoped she could find her way without returning to the road again. By now, at least her mother and Conrad knew where she'd gone. Whether the men watching had found out was a guess, but the sounds of those running horses had to mean something.

She'd made it all the way to within a mile of Mordecai's when a nighthawk flew up in the gloom of dusk and spooked her horse out from under her. She felt herself falling and tried desperately to hang on to the reins, knowing she'd never be able to catch this half wild steed if it got away from her.

She kept the reins, but got a rope burn on her hands to show for it and grimaced in pain as she pulled the stupid thing over to a fallen log to get back on. So much for her believing she could ride anything with hair. This one trip on this mindless beast had near taken the adventure right out of horses for her. Not having a saddle made staying on ten times harder.

Finally, she topped the ridge above Mordecai's small stone house and breathed a huge breath of relief. She'd made it. She'd made it with no sword fights, rain storms, or inky black darkness and she couldn't even believe what a relief she felt.

Bartok neighed from his pen and just as Chantaya felt the horse under her take in air to neigh back, from somewhere behind Mordecai's cottage, another horse neighed. It made her pull her own horse up so shortly that it didn't neigh at all and she nearly went off a second time.

Something was wrong. Something was terribly wrong. There shouldn't have been a horse behind Mordecai's house. At the very least, the savvy old knight would have come out on to the porch to see who was approaching. 'Twas his way. Never had she come to his home that he hadn't come out to greet her. Something was wrong.

She pulled her horse into the thickest woods she could find and tied it securely. Then, in the gathering gloom of dusk, she slipped closer to Mordecai's house on foot. Maybe he just had a cold again. Maybe he had stepped out somewhere for a few moments. Maybe . . .

Her heart sank into her belly with a thud when she realized someone had started a fire in Mordecai's fireplace and smoke was beginning to rise from the chimney. Mordecai was home. Something was definitely wrong.

Sneaking closer, she found two horses behind the house and glimpsed a man through the window in the firelight and her heart sank further. 'Twas one of the men who hung around Lord Rosskeene. She backed up into the trees and knelt down, wondering how they had known to go straight to Mordecai's. She was heart sick to realize the help she had hoped to receive from the old knight had just wafted away into the night air like the smoke rising from his chimney. Looking around in the darkness, she tried to figure out what direction she needed to go to reach Valais. Panic threatened when she admitted to herself that she wasn't even sure exactly how to get there and that she wouldn't be able to go to Peyton's parents for directions. The men watching would no doubt be watching the village as well.

Tamping down the anxiousness, she squared her shoulders. She could do this. She mustn't allow any doubt. She had to make it to Valais and warn the king. 'Twas all there was to it. Doubt simply wasn't an option. She leaned over and rubbed at her temples and bowed her head to utter a short, silent prayer. Then she picked herself up and sneaked back into the trees toward her horse.

As she went to hop onto its back from a nearby stump, the skittish creature sidestepped and then spun away from her and Chantaya landed on her back in the understory hard enough to knock the wind out of her and make her wonder if she had started the cut on her ribs bleeding again. By the time she could breathe again, all that was left of her horse was the quickly receding sound of it running off through the woods in the direction she had ridden in.

Looking skyward, she wanted to rail at the series of events that seemed to keep piling up, but instead settled for another short silent prayer. It didn't matter what she was up against, she had to make it to Peyton. She had to. The kingdom was at stake here

She slowly sat up, put a hand to her ribs to find that she was indeed bleeding and then carefully stood up. Bartok would be far easier to ride anyway.

It took twenty minutes to sneak in, get the painted horse, and sneak back out again. She still didn't have a saddle, but at least Bartok was tame and used to her. As they picked their way through the trees back toward the roadway, she stretched her back and shoulders and rolled her neck, hoping her mother would eventually forgive her for being so blatantly disobedient. Pulling the heavy cloak closer about her, she sighed. This was looking like it was going to be a long, long night.

Far into the wee hours of the morning, she was beginning to wonder if she was hearing things because every other moment, she imagined she was being pursued. She finally decided she was truly hearing someone coming and she got back off the road just in time to avoid being seen by two men who went galloping by on lathered horses. Their horses' labored breathing, white necks and flanks, and the pounding of their hooves were the only impressions she got as they went by.

Tiredly, she rode Bartok back out onto the road once they'd gone, and wondered if they were the same men who had been at Mordecai's or if it was just another couple of highwaymen hoping to rob and murder a tired, lone traveler like herself on this dark and frightening road.

The sky was starting to lighten in the east, but she was still traveling and she began to fear she'd taken a completely wrong road altogether. She should have been there by now.

Shouldn't she? When she'd come to Valais with Peyton and his friends, it had been a several hour ride from Rosskeene Manor, but that time they had gone straight from the manor to Valais. Tonight, she had gone from the manor several hours across country to Navarre, thinking to give her message to Mordecai to deliver, and then from Navarre it was another four hours or so to Valais. At least that's what Peyton had told her once.

Still, even with all that distance, she definitely should have been there. Trying to see in this darkest hour before dawn, she looked around for a high spot. Maybe if she could get above the area around she could find something that looked familiar. She traveled on up the road a way and then climbed to the only higher ground she could see and looked all around. Nothing was familiar, but not far ahead there was a crossroad that would be labeled. Maybe from there she would be able to figure out where Valais was.

Sitting Bartok at the crossroad, she shook her head in disgust. She had indeed taken a wrong turn somewhere because the sign pointing to Valais was on an intersecting road. She sighed and stretched, wishing she had brought more food with her. She was starving. At least the sign said Valais was only seven more miles. There should still be time to make it before the funeral. And it was getting light now. Hopefully she could ride now without the suffocating fear that rode with her in the dark.

Resolutely, she pointed Bartok toward the city, wishing she had the energy to be more excited that she was going to be able to see Peyton. Only seven more miles. She wondered if she would be able to tell at all where to find him once she got there.

Slowly, as she rode in the gathering light, houses and farms began to appear more often. Finally, the castle appeared in the distance and she felt a surge of hope. She was almost there. By the time she had come to a relatively solid gathering of dwellings she could see clearly in the early morning gloom, although there was no one about yet. Except for that one small boy looking out the loft window above the shed there. She glanced up at him, wondering why he wasn't dressed warmer on this tooth chattering morning.

As she rode past, she looked curiously at the way the houses here seemed to be stacked one on top of each other. It was a strange way to live from her perspective of having had the whole woods around her house to play in.

Seeing movement, she glanced up to see that there were actually two more people about this early morning. Two men. Who were strangely familiar and just happened to be sitting their horses with crossbows pointed directly at her.

Slamming her heels into Bartok, she literally leaped him down a side road away from where the two men were and raced for the space of a couple of houses and then turned him up another lane. Behind her she could hear their horse's shoes clattering on the cobbles and she tried to evade them every time she thought it sounded like they'd changed directions. Without a saddle, Bartok's back was as slippery as a fish and she struggled to keep aboard him as they raced in and out of the tiny streets.

It would only be a matter of time until the two men split up and then they'd have her! No sooner had she had that thought, than they did split up and she ran Bartok even more frantically. Once, as she turned past the corner of a house, something hit her a mighty blow to the back that near unseated her and left her with a fiery, burning pain all the way through her upper body. She gasped in panic and kicked Bartok all the harder. She didn't have time to see what had just slammed into her, but a sickening suspicion that she had just been shot with an arrow made fear surge through her along with the searing pain.

People began to open shutters and look out and in desperation she raced back toward the main street and then ducked again into an alley and then into the open door of a barn there. Leaping from the horse, she ran through the barn and out the small door on the other side and then into the next barn over, trying to ignore the seething pain that was now radiating through the entirety of her chest.

She heard a sound behind her and whipped her head around to see if it was them as she began to search for some place, any place to hide, praying desperately all the while. At first, in the dimness of the interior of the barn, she couldn't tell what she was hearing and then a movement caught her eye. The small boy she had seen in the top of a shed earlier materialized into a sun beam that cut through the alley of the barn. He beckoned to her silently and she quickly followed him through another door and into a dark hallway that smelled of dust and cows and cobwebs.

He pulled the door to behind them and then they stood there, side by side in the near darkness, listening to the sound of her racing heart, the slam of doors and the clack of horseshoes outside in the cobbled lanes. The men were shouting back and forth and then a woman's voice shouted for them to get out as another voice called for someone to get help.

Chantaya leaned her head back against the wooden planks behind her and realized in horror that there was something terribly wrong with her breathing. She was coughing up something that tasted of blood. She could feel the moisture of more blood dripping from the front as well as back of her shirt and she knew that whatever was hurting her was still there, catching on the rough weave of the fabric. Both her head and her heart shrank from admitting what she suspected.

Putting a hesitant hand to her chest just above her breast and below her shoulder, she felt the bite of sharp steel poking through her shirt and got an instant urge to vomit. Not only had she been shot, but the arrow was still there, lodged in her and impaling all the way through her body. She gasped in fear, remembering the way animals she had seen shot struggled for breath and then slowly, piteously died. She would die! She knew it. Animals shot through the lungs always died. They bled to death. She would never see Peyton again. Or her mother. She would never get to be married. Or hold her own child.

A deep sense of sadness permeated her soul as she admitted to herself that worse than any of that, she had failed the king. Failed. Rosskeene would win. After all she had done. How hard she had tried. She had failed.

A small sob escaped her lips and the child who stood so still beside her put a finger to his lips to quiet her. As he did, his eyes got wide as they heard the sound of the barn door opening and the unmistakable sound of the two men entering. The men walked through the barn opening gates and doors and crashing the items that got in their way viciously aside, and Chantaya realized she was praying silently again.

As they neared the door Chantaya and the boy hid behind, there was a sudden movement and a gasp and then the sound of a rat squeaking. One of the men began to curse as the other one let out a raucous laugh and the first one swore even more bitterly. There was the sound of blows and they both cursed together. Then more pummeling as they continued on toward where Chantaya and the boy waited.

Directly outside Chantaya's hiding place, the two men began to shout at each other and then there was another blow and a groan. Slowly the groan sank to the floor and the other man continued on up through the barn, while the groaner mumbled more hoarse curses.

It felt like hours that they waited, mouthing her fervent prayer, her breathing becoming more difficult and more painful while the man paused on the other side of the door. The boy silently reached for her hand and held it desperately tight. Finally, they heard the man move.

They held their breath as they heard him grasp the handle to the door. The latch squeaked and there was a grating sound and then the latch apparently came apart in his hand as a sliver of light escaped through where the latch had been and the man began to nearly rage in disgust.

Chantaya could hear him ranting about Lord Rosskeene and somebody named Ned, and then there was a crash across the way where he'd apparently thrown the offending handle. With a final curse, the man stomped off down the way and out the door and Chantaya finally attempted to draw a deep breath. It hurt like all the fires of hell and made a gurgling sound that she could hear from outside her bosom. The fear she'd been fighting surged. She was dying. She'd seen it too many times with animals to believe otherwise.

When the sounds of the men were long gone, the boy beside her finally reached and began to fiddle with the door handle in front of them. The fact that they were apparently locked in this dark hallway hardly even registered as she slowly sank to the barn floor and closed her eyes. Fatigue nearly overwhelmed her. She wanted to take a deep breath. Desperately needed to take a deep breath, but all that happened when she did was pain and that sickening sound.

After several moments, the boy somehow got the latch to work. He hesitantly pushed it open a tiny crack and peered out and then pushed it another few inches before looking back in at her. When the sliver of sunlight hit the part of her shirt that was visible under her cloak, the boy sucked in a breath and dropped to his knees to open the cloak further. It only exposed the arrow tip through a tear in the shirt and more blood and he looked up at her with wide, frightened eyes and said, "You've been shot!"

"Yes." She whispered, wishing she had more energy. Then the boy, who appeared to be about seven or eight, did a strange thing. He took a deep breath, nodded almost as if he was saying something to himself and seemed to take charge. He looked around, then looked around outside the space they were sitting in, came back to her and said, "Come. Let's get you next door where you can stretch out and I can fair see." She grimaced and he leaned down and repeated, "Come. I'll help you."

He was young, and small, but his sense of self gave Chantaya just the last bit of energy she needed to let him help her to the stall next door and make a decision herself. She may not be going to make it to tell Peyton herself, but she wasn't going to fail the king. This small, but very capable child was going to succeed for her.

As she sank down into the straw of the stall, she asked the boy, "Pray, tell me, what is your name my little rescuer?"

"I am Daniel." He bent to begin working at her cloak, but she pushed him away.

She tried to smile at him and said haltingly, "Well, Daniel, my small friend. You're about to become a hero as well as a rescuer. I need you to do something which is more important than life itself. Far more. I need you to take a message to one of the knights. Can you do that, Daniel?"

"Yes." He nodded positively and then answered more tentatively, "Sir."

She could see him hesitate as he looked her over. Obviously wondering if she was male or female and it made her smile again as she said tiredly, "I need you to find Sir Peyton. He's a knight in the knight encampment near the castle. He's tall, with blonde hair and kind brown eyes and big shoulders."

Almost eagerly, he said, "Yes, I know who Sir Peyton is. 'Tis that he's my favorite knight to watch in the competitions. He wins at everything! He's the best!"

His enthusiasm warmed her heart, as she said softly, "Yes, he truly is the best. Truly. You *must* find him. Tell him Lord Rosskeene is going to attack the king on the way to the cemetery as they cross the river near a ravine. Tell him exactly that. It's very important. Can you repeat it back to me?"

The boy repeated it word for word and Chantaya sighed in relief and then groaned from the pain of it. She squeezed the boy's hand. "Good. Good boy, Daniel. That's perfect. Now go. You must find Peyton. Tell him. No matter what. Tell him." Her chest gurgled and there was bloody foam coming out of her lips as she paused to catch her breath and then added, "Take my horse if you can find him. And tell Peyton, Daniel. Please. Don't let them . . ." She had to rest a moment before she could finish, "Don't let them kill the king. Go."

She closed her eyes and whispered, "Godspeed Daniel."

The boy hesitated for a moment, then got up and began to run out of the barn, but Chantaya called his name. He came back to stand in the stall door and she added wearily, "Please. Tell him. Tell Sir Peyton . . . that I love him."

He nodded soberly and then said, "As you wish. Sir."

With that, he turned and rushed away and Chantaya closed her eyes wearily. Her world had narrowed down to a haze of pale pain and utter weariness. He would find Peyton. Daniel would find him and Peyton would save the king. She could die in peace. She hadn't failed after all.

Jaclyn M. Hawkes

Chapter 21

Peyton was in front of the garrison stable buckling on the last of his horse's armor in preparation for the funeral of the dowager queen that would begin in two hours thence when he saw the ragged boy. He was riding bareback on a piebald horse that looked remarkably like Bartok. It had a splash of white across its chest and shoulder, and a face that was an uncanny match for the old knight's charger.

Peyton watched the boy slowly push his way down the crowded street, frequently looking toward the garrison, and as he came, Peyton got the strangest prickling up the back of his neck. He knew that horse. That was Bartok. Something was wrong. Peyton got on his horse and began to move toward the boy.

The crowd became ever more congested the closer the boy got and finally, the boy got off the horse, tied it to a post and continued toward Peyton, pushing through the throng as fast as his size would allow. The boy's focus never left Peyton in spite of the crowds around him grumbling at his pushing.

Finally, as he neared, Peyton got down off his horse and bent to the little boy. The child had to pause to catch his breath before leaning into Peyton's ear and whispering, "Lord

Rosskeene is going to attack the king on the way to the cemetery as they cross the river near a ravine."

Stunned, Peyton narrowed his eyes and looked hard at the ragged, but absolutely stoic little boy and asked urgently, "What? What did you say? Who told you that?" The child nodded soberly. "A boy, well, an older boy. Some men were chasing him. They shot him with a crossbow, but I helped him get away. He told me to take this horse and come find you. He said 'twas more important than her life. I mean his life."

Utter fear gripped Peyton's heart as he put a hand on the child's shoulder and asked, "'Twasn't an old man? On the horse? 'Twas an older boy?"

The child nodded again, but then hesitated as he said, "He was wearing boy's things, but he didn't sound like a boy. And his chest, where the arrow was sticking out." He shook his head and looked down and then back up. "It didn't look like a boy's chest." He looked up into Peyton's face and added, "She said to tell you she loved you."

Peyton closed his eyes and tried to inhale, but his entire soul had become stone. An arrow in her chest. Chantaya. Pain slammed into him like a hammer. Chantaya.

The child in front of him made a sound and Peyton opened his eyes and realized he was squeezing his shoulder. Releasing it, he numbly patted it and apologized clumsily as he tried to right his toppled world and focus on the message the boy had brought him. The king. Rosskeene was after the king again. She'd been shot trying to help the king.

He turned and stepped onto his charger and then reached to pull the boy up behind him and woodenly questioned the boy about which direction he had come. His mind was still reeling from what the child had said. She'd been shot in the chest. He railed at the image in his head. The ride through the city streets seemed interminable although it was probably only minutes and Peyton kept looking at the sun in the sky, trying to gauge the time and wondering if she was even alive.

At a rundown barn on the outskirts of the city the boy jumped off and Peyton hurriedly looped his reins around the hitch post there and followed the boy into the dim interior. Chantaya lay in a stall filled with old straw, her face so pallid that at first Peyton thought she truly was dead until he heard a gurgling noise as she tried to breathe and he saw the bubbles at her lips.

Kneeling beside her, whispering her name, his relief that she was alive didn't last as he carefully pushed her cloak away to reveal the blood soaked shirt. It was torn around the pointed end of a short crossbow arrow that still protruded from her chest below her shoulder. The sight of it was more frightening than anything in his life had been and sickening as he closed his eyes against it. Shaking his head, he uttered a quick silent prayer and then opened them again.

Pulling his knife from his boot, he carefully cut the shirt away around the arrow and swallowed the bile that welled. Placing a hand gently under her shoulder, he lifted her ever so carefully to see where the arrow had gone in and groaned aloud to see the other half of it still impaled her upper back. Her cloak and the straw below her were soaked with a huge amount of blood and he was truly surprised that she was still breathing at all. It looked a wound that should have killed her.

It would soon. There was no doubt of it. There was simply too much blood. His heart contracted in utter pain at the sure knowledge. She was dying.

As he gently let her back down, surprisingly, her eyes slowly opened and he noticed one was bruised. At first, she seemed confused and then she gave him the smallest of smiles. She struggled to speak, but it seemed to take her an eternity to get her lips to move. Finally, in the faintest of whispers, she said, "You came." She gave the small boy beside him a weak smile and then to Peyton said, "I'm sorry, Pey. Please. Forgive me."

He shook his head in abject heartache. "Don't Chantaya. There's nothing to forgive. You do your best. Always. I know that."

Her blue eyes teared up and she struggled to whisper, "But, I am sorry. Truly. I wanted to marry you and live happily ever after."

Swallowing a huge lump in his throat, he couldn't face telling her she was dying and instead he whispered back, "Me too, Chani. And we will. We still will. It just might take awhile to get you feeling well enough to marry." He took her hand and bent and kissed it. "Just be strong, love. Be strong and I'll get you out of here and to a physician. Be strong as you always are."

Turning to the boy who stood beside him, he asked, "When did this happen? When was she shot?"

The boy shrugged. "Just after it started getting light. I think they were watching for her. They started to chase her as soon as she came up the road."

"Where did they go? How did you get away?"

He suddenly looked concerned, "I don't know where they went. They looked through here, but they missed us. Then they left. I don't know where to."

Facing Chantaya again, Peyton asked, "Did you know them?"

She barely shook her head, "They've been watching us at the manor. That's all I know." She suddenly became anxious and strained to look out the door as she said, "The king! Peyton, you have to go! They're going to kill the king! On the way to the funeral! You need to tell them!"

"I'm taking you to a physician first. We have to get you . . ."

She interrupted him and tried to sit up, wholly distressed. "No! You have to go! They'll kill them! Peyton, go save them! Think what would happen to the whole kingdom if they're all killed!"

He tried gently pushing her back down as she was trying to sit up. She started to cough up blood and then to cry almost uncontrollably. He stopped pushing at her and leaned right down to touch her face tenderly and pleaded, "Don't cry, Chani. Please don't cry. That will only make it worse."

She shook her head, sobbing brokenly and struggled to speak, "Peyton, I've tried so hard. I did my best. Truly, I did. I've ridden all day and night. I've been hurt. I've put up with Lord Rosskeene. And Damian's violence. I've been so cold." She closed her eyes and sobbed, "I had to kill a person."

Her utter misery at that admission was heart rending as she went on hoarsely, "And now I'm giving my life. Don't make it be in vain. Please. Please." Her voice faded to the merest sound and she repeated, "Please don't make me die for nothing. Go to the king. And his family. Stop Rosskeene. 'Tis so much more important than watching me die. Daniel will stay with me. Go. Please go."

She began to choke again. The tears flowed out of her eyes and dripped down into her hair and Peyton's heart ripped in half and began to bleed just like she was. How could he leave her like this? How could she expect him to care if the entire earth, moon and stars blew apart? Nothing mattered without her! How could she expect him to walk away from her right now? He couldn't!

He gently stroked her hair and felt his own tears while she quietly sobbed as she lay there in the bloody straw. He heard a sound and turned his head to find the boy crying as well. The boy scrubbed stubbornly at his dusty cheeks and said, "Sir Peyton, why are you not doing what she's asking? She's begging you. You're hurting her. And she's tried so hard. Can't you at least give her her dying wish? Can't you save the king? He's the world's greatest king. He loves us all. Even the orphans. She's begging you, Sir Peyton." The tears coursed down his face as he ended softly, "She's begging. Can't you let her die happy?"

Peyton closed his eyes and struggled to channel the pain. When he opened them again, Chantaya was looking at him with the most tragic expression and he gulped back a sob and touched her face tenderly. "All right. All right. I'll never be able to forgive myself if I go, but I'll never forgive myself if I fail you either. I love you, Chani. No matter what happens, know that. I've loved you from the moment I first saw you. Be strong, Chani. And please forgive me for leaving you."

He turned to the boy. "Watch over her. Do the best you can. Remind her that I love her, and watch over her, since I can't. I'll come back." He put a big hand on the boy's shoulder. "God bless you, son."

With that, he got up and almost violently slammed out the door, climbed onto his horse and galloped up the cobblestone road toward the castle, praying as if her life depended on it and hating himself with a passion for leaving.

§§§§

At the castle he wanted to kill the guard at the gate who hesitated for a moment to let him through, and he even wanted to strangle the priest at the castle chapel door who intimated that it was inappropriate for a fully armored night to interrupt the prince as he tried to comfort his father at such a time.

When the prince noticed the commotion at the chapel door, he came over and must have known instantly that something was terribly wrong because he literally shooed the priest out and shut the door behind him before turning back to Peyton with absolute intensity. When Peyton told of the imminent attack, the prince spun on his heel and went to his father and had a moment's whispered conversation before returning to Peyton and asking, "What do you think we should do, Sir Peyton?"

Squaring his shoulders, Peyton said, "Forgive me for seeming cold hearted, Your Highness. But if it were up to me, I'd recommend that instead of your family getting in the carriage that will take you up to the cemetery, they be concealed here in the leper's squint, and in your place, we load the royal carriage with warriors and precede it and follow it with more. Then, when they make their attempt, we deal with it militarily. Then return here to pick up your family to go bury your grandmother after all has calmed down. Forgive my lack of sympathy at this time, Sire."

The prince nodded thoughtfully. "An excellent plan, Sir Peyton. Please, step outside and find Sir Kendall and pick which knights you believe should be in the carriage. Have Kendall arrange it all. And leave us a number to discreetly guard the family here as well, in case Rosskeene suspects. I'll have the carriage be drawn so closely to the door that our duplicity won't be detected and I'll let my father know. Thank you for your devotion, friend. With your help, we'll all live to see the end of this dreadful day."

At that, the prince strode off toward his father and Peyton turned to go back out of the church to find Sir Kendall, feeling as if his heart had been hacked out of his very chest. If only Chantaya could have survived this dreadful, dreadful day.

§§§§

Lord and Lady Rosskeene, dressed in full impressive noble attire, stood respectfully at the front of the crowd that had been ushered from the castle church to allow the royal family a few moments before the final closing of the casket of their grandmother. Lord Rosskeene wore a suitably solemn face, but his eyes were as busy as his thoughts as he waited. These were the final moments before his dream of becoming monarch in the wake of the loss of the entire royal family came true. 'Twas all he could do to maintain a measure of stoicism in the face of his inevitable success. He'd been waiting for this for years and could hardly contain his sense of victory.

At last, the casket was carried out and loaded into the carriage and then a second carriage with windows shrouded in sheer black was drawn to the church door to carry the family. Rosskeene near gloated as he watched it too pull away into the solemn procession that would travel in a slow and stately manner to the cemetery more than a mile away from the castle gate. The cemetery that just happened to be beyond the ravine where his companies of men waited.

His demeanor nearly cracked as the procession disappeared and the crowds began to disperse. How he loved being a military genius. What great things he was going to be able to do when he took the reins to the entire kingdom. Turning to survey all he now considered his, he suddenly frowned. That was Sir Mordecai standing near the walkway between the buildings. Rosskeene wasn't sure why he would find Sir Mordecai's presence troubling, but he did.

Glancing further, his frown deepened. Sir Kendall stood not far from Mordecai, as did a number of the most highly esteemed knights. That was strange. Why would the bravest and best have been left at home to guard an empty castle, when the entire royal family was traveling elsewhere with those not so highly respected?

Something smelled of a rat here. That didn't make sense.

Trying to appear nonchalant, Lord Rosskeene tucked his wife's hand over his arm and began to stroll toward one of the castle rose gardens. The roses were mostly dead at this time of the year, but he didn't need the roses, he needed a moment to think.

Jaclyn M. Hawkes

Chapter 22

The funeral carriages were long gone, and the tension was rising in the leper's squint behind the stained glass window of the royal chapel. The king and both of his children stood absolutely motionless, appearing to almost listen for the sounds of the battle that they suspected was being fought at that very moment a mile or so away.

Positioned directly in front of the door to the tiny room that had long ago allowed lepers to partake of services even though they weren't allowed to mingle with the congregation, Sir Peyton Wolfgar stood at attention. He was trying with every bit of mental and emotional control he had to keep his head on protecting these people instead of bowing into his shaking hands over the loss of his beloved sweet, beautiful Chantaya. He was trying. But his heart and mind were slowly breaking into a hundred thousand pieces. He couldn't control the image in his head of her exquisite body lying there with a bloody arrow protruding from it. 'Twas the most ghastly of nightmares.

A sound from outside the door brought his head up. The chapel there had been empty and silent, and it still was. Mostly. Someone had quietly opened a door and entered and was now, ever so slowly and stealthily, walking up the aisle toward the pulpit. The sounds were nearly undetectable, but Peyton had been trained by Mordecai. He could almost read those sounds like a book. Someone was slipping through the chapel toward the leper's squint.

Peyton silently placed his hand upon his sword. It may only be a lone mourner, come back to pay their last solitary respects, but the hair on the back of Peyton's neck told him otherwise.

The royal family was watching him and when another sound came from outside the door, the prince stepped in front of his father and sister and touched his own sword. The tension in the room became suffocating.

Almost silently, the door of the squint moved ever so slightly and began to swing in. When it finally did emit a slow, coarse grating, it sounded unnaturally loud in the thickness of the angst.

The revelation of who was opening the door, when it came, was almost anticlimactic. Lord Rosskeene himself stood there, his own sword drawn. Quietly, almost conversationally, he said, "Sir Peyton, how good to see you, here in the defense of your crown. How quaint and thoughtful. And foolish. Did they truly leave only one of you here to protect them all?"

He clicked his tongue in disapproval as he calmly stepped inside the door and to the side, taking a stance in front of Peyton as if they were engaging in a polite fencing contest at a village fair. Peyton moved to contain him, staying always between him and the others and wondering who else had made it past the knights stationed outside the church. Peyton was to be the final layer of protection for the king, but Rosskeene didn't appear to have engaged in any prior battles. He was too calm. Too sure. Too relaxed. Except for the beaded perspiration on his upper lip, Peyton wouldn't have thought him tense at all.

Rosskeene continued his seeming stroll and Peyton drew a mental line on the floor. He determined at exactly what moment he was going to attack and slay this monster.

A sound from out in the chapel brought Rosskeene up. Another had stealthily entered the church and was headed their way. From the hesitation in Rosskeene's stance, Peyton deducted that it wasn't someone Rosskeene had arranged to be here.

Rosskeene took another step toward the line in Peyton's head and whoever was outside the door took another step toward the leper's squint.

Pausing, Rosskeene chuckled. It was an abrasive and absolutely belligerent sound that nearly broke Peyton's fragile control. This man had taken the only thing that mattered to Peyton in the whole of the universe and destroyed her. And now he was laughing.

He was sick. Sick and monstrous and as Rosskeene lifted his foot to take another step he crossed the line.

Feeling the enormity of his loss, Peyton loosed all the latent anger and pain and heart break in one raging roar as he pulled his sword and fair exploded into Lord Rosskeene.

To his credit, the nobleman thrust and parried most admirably in the face of the onslaught. But in only several seconds Peyton had drawn blood any number of times and had backed him right up to the doorway in a fury fueled by the unsurvivable pain of Chantaya's loss. As Peyton pushed him to the entrance, Mordecai appeared in the doorway behind Rosskeene.

Inexplicably, his presence both helped Peyton to become inwardly strangely still, and yet caused the pain of his loss to swell until it threatened to consume Peyton's very core. Mordecai too would be devastated by Chantaya's death.

Not realizing that Mordecai was standing right behind him, when Peyton paused for the sparest moment, Rosskeene actually smiled and foolishly began to verbally spar with Peyton as well. In a tone that was insanely confident under the circumstances, Rosskeene prodded, "You have no business being here, Wolfgar. You're nothing but an oversized peasant boy, trying to dabble with men."

He smiled and wiped a bloody sleeve across his forehead that left him gory. It only amplified Peyton's bitter, churning fury. Feinting, Rosskeene went on, "After today, when the others learn what a pitiful farce you've been, even your parents won't mourn the embarrassing loss of such a son. Oh, and in case you haven't heard, I raised your parents' rents forty percent after the ball last week. You shouldn't have acted so smug with your beautiful friend here the other night. It irritated me. And one shouldn't irritate someone as powerful as I."

Mention of Chantaya made the blood rush to Peyton's heart and he tried to focus on Mordecai's presence to quell the mad desire to maim Rosskeene before taking his sadistic life. This blood letting leech on society wasn't worth Peyton losing his higher sense of humanity. Peyton knew that, but the natural man in him wanted to annihilate Rosskeene anyway.

Then Rosskeene went much too far, when he said, "Once I'm king, I'm going to take your friend to wife, you know. I decided it the moment I saw her the other day."

Something inside Peyton broke and he gave in to the ancient warrior's berserk. In a mere moment, he'd sliced both of Rosskeene's arms beyond use, flipped the older man's sword up and shattered it into pieces, and had him up against the wall with his blade at his throat.

In a voice awash in rage, Peyton snarled, "She's dead! You killed her! You hounded her mother heinously! You allowed your beast of a son to attack her! And then you set your blood dogs on her with crossbows! You killed her!"

Rosskeene seemed confused, even as he was obviously fearful as Peyton raged on, "The sweetest, purest, most precious girl in this world! She's dead! All so you could be king!" Peyton leaned in close and roared in complete disgust, "King!" Then he lowered his voice to an ominous quiet and said scathingly, "You're no king. You're nothing but an animal."

With that, he spun and with a mighty slash, all but severed Rosskeene's leg at the thigh. The nobleman went down in a gasping, bloody pile and Peyton lowered his sword, turned to King Dougal and with infinite sadness asked quietly, "Shall I kill him here, Sire? Or would you prefer to hang him publicly?"

Appearing deeply shaken, the king shook his head. "Leave him, Sir Peyton. He deserves hanging. And if his son assaulted your betrothed, I'll hang him as well. Leave him."

Suddenly tired beyond belief, Peyton nodded, "Thank you, Sire. I'm sorry he got in. Please, stay here for a moment and I'll go see if there are any more of his men out there."

As he went to go out the door, two of the other knights appeared, wondering what the ruckus had been and were shocked to realize that Lord Rosskeene himself had made it past them and into the leper's squint. Peyton looked on woodenly, staying only because word hadn't come back yet about what had happened to the carriages on the way to the cemetery.

Mordecai came to him, looked him solemnly in the face and asked gently, "Is it true? She's truly dead?"

Peyton considered the amount of blood she'd lost before he'd left her and knew she would be gone by now. He nodded and closed his eyes. His pain so great that he didn't even want his dear friend and mentor to see it. Mordecai, better than any other, understood how this felt, but it was still too painful to handle. With or without understanding.

Peyton went to stand at a window, looking out into the exact rose garden he and Chantaya had danced in but a week ago. He'd asked her to marry him, thinking that they had forever. But they'd only had that next day.

He wondered, had he known, what he would have done differently? Would he still have taken her back to let her try to figure out how to save the crown and the kingdom? After all, it appeared they'd succeeded. That night long ago, they'd spoken of risking his very life to protect the kingdom, but he'd never dreamed it would cost hers. Risking his life seemed reasonable. Losing hers felt infinitely, hopelessly wrong.

He took one last, long look at the rose garden and turned away. She was gone, and he hadn't even stayed with her to the end. She'd been right. He had needed to be here to save the king, but he loathed himself for leaving her anyway.

Hours later, at least it seemed that, word came that there had indeed been a vicious attack near the river on the way to the cemetery. One hundred and forty six of Rosskeene's men had either been killed or imprisoned and seventeen of their own had been killed. The soldiers with the carriages had seen no sign of Lord Rosskeene, although this time there were scores who were aware that Rosskeene was behind it all. His son and wife had been picked up on the way back to the castle.

Once Peyton was sure the king and his family were safe, he quietly slipped out the door to leave. He needed to go and get Chantaya's body to take home to her mother for burial. Peyton hadn't even dared wonder how he was going to break the news to Isabella. Rosskeene had now taken her husband and both of her daughters from her, and Peyton wondered how a person could ever survive devastation like that. He'd only lost one and felt it would literally kill him.

He climbed back on his horse, and as he turned to go, Mordecai showed up riding Bartok, with the prince at his side. Peyton looked at them, then shook his head and said flatly to the prince, "No, Your Highness. We've just been battling to keep you safe. You're not going across town without an entourage, and honestly, I'm not up to taking an entourage. Stay near the castle where your safety can be assured."

For once, the prince didn't smile. He simply said, "I shall be in the company of two of the greatest knights to ever grace the kingdom of Monciere. And I shall be paying homage to the most loyal, and patriotic woman ever known. While I respect your request, Sir Peyton, I shall respectfully ignore it. Accompanying you is the least I can do to show my gratitude to Chantaya."

Peyton only nodded and then galloped ahead of them. Though they were indeed his dearest friends, he couldn't handle their friendship just now. He honestly wasn't sure he could handle anything.

At the barn on the outskirts of town, he slid his horse to a stop and got down, feeling like an old, old man. Without even waiting for the others, he walked into the barn and through to the stall, then paused before opening it. The wound in his heart at what he knew he would find making it hard to breathe.

He pushed open the stall door and was brought up short when all there was in front of him was her cloak and the blood soaked crushed straw. Backing out again, he nearly bumped into Mordecai and the prince as he looked around warily. *Who had taken her?* The thought that he had left her only to have her body be taken made him loathe himself all the more. Not only had he left her to die, but had he left her to be further victimized?

Moving silently down the alley way of the barn, he looked all around, wondering what had happened here in the two hours he'd been gone. Seeing a door ajar, he carefully looked through the opening to see the body of a man sprawled with the handle of a knife sticking conspicuously out of his chest.

As Peyton went to step through the door, a rustle warned him. Another man moved out of the shadows to come at him with a drawn sword. Peyton parried his blow, and then Mordecai thrust his own sword into the man. He slumped almost soundlessly to the floor nearly on top of the other man and the prince quietly came through the door with his sword drawn as well.

The three of them stood there, every muscle tensed, looking for Chantaya, and wondering how many more armed men they'd encounter before figuring out where they'd taken her body. Suddenly, there was another rustle above them and then the sound of a child saying angrily, "Leave her alone or I'll kill you as well, I swear it!"

Peyton looked up just as Daniel appeared in the loft above them with a pitchfork poised in his hand. Even as his arm began to move forward in a thrusting motion, his eyes widened and he stopped himself. The boy's face held fear and then surprise. Finally, his shoulders slumped visibly. He let out a huge breath and said, "Sir Peyton. It's you. Oh, thank God it's you. They've still been trying to harm her! We need to get her away quickly!"

His eyes moved from Peyton to the others and he gasped and took a step back as he almost stammered, "Prince Laird. Your . . . Your Highness . . . "

Peyton didn't even notice the boy's surprise at finding himself face to face with the prince. He was still processing what the child had said about harming Chantaya. It didn't make sense. Shaking his head in confusion, he asked, "Where is her body, Daniel? It's not in the stall. Were they trying to take her body away?"

The child let the tines of the pitch fork come to rest on the loft floor at his feet as he shook his head. "No, Sir Knight. She is here. Up here, with me. They've taken her nowhere. You told me to watch over her. When I heard them coming, I struggled to help her up here. We thought it would be easier to hide above them."

Peyton took the loft ladder two rungs at a time and fair leaped into the dim, cramped space, hardly daring to even hope the child was intimating that Chantaya hadn't died.

When his eyes adjusted to the low light, he saw her there, lying motionless in the scattered hay, her face so pale it terrified him and he haltingly asked, "How did you lift her?

Is she . . . Is she . . . Is she not gone then? Did she not die in my absence?"

Daniel shook his head solemnly. "Not yet, Sir Peyton. With me mostly lifting her, she was strong enough to make it here, although it was terribly difficult for her. But I think it took near all her strength, for she hasn't opened her eyes for awhile now. I fear it won't be long. I'm sorry, Sir. I tried. I truly tried. I'm sorry, I didn't know how to help her better."

Peyton finally saw her chest rise ever so slightly and nearly exploded in relief. He dropped to his knees beside her and wrapped an arm round the boy's shoulder and murmured, "You did a hero's work, today, Daniel. You've done pure excellence. You need not feel sorrow." Almost to himself, Peyton whispered, "She's alive. She's truly still alive. God bless you, Daniel. Thank you. Thank you, Lord."

He laid a single finger on her cheek almost reverently and closed his eyes in overwhelming gratitude. She was alive. Barely. But that was so much more than he'd dared to hope. She was alive.

Turning back to Mordecai and the prince who had come up the ladder behind him, he looked at the old knight and saw the same, tender emotion on his face as Peyton was nearly drowning in. He gave his dear friend a sad smile and wiped at his eye with the back of his hand. He turned back to Daniel, "Are there more here after her? How many men were there? Beyond the two below?"

Daniel shook his head and then shuddered as he said, "Just the two that I saw, Sir Knight. If there were more, they didn't come inside."

Nodding, Peyton turned back to Mordecai, "Will you go down and ask around for the use of a cart? Surely someone here will help us move her."

The prince shook his head and said, "Keep Mordecai to help you check her. I'll find a cart."

Peyton grimaced, "No, Your Highness. You mustn't. 'Tis not secure. Take Mordecai. We can't risk your safety."

The prince looked around and then said, "Sir Mordecai has great experience with wounds. He can help her. Maybe even save her life. But we do need the cart. And I'm sure there are several knights coming in our wake, somewhere, knowing my father." He gave an encouraging smile to Daniel. "Perhaps young Sir Daniel would be willing to guard me in the quest for a cart for his mistress, Chantaya? Would you mind, Daniel?"

Daniel looked down at himself and then up at the prince's smiling face and swallowed loudly as Peyton looked to Mordecai who nodded and then knelt beside Chantaya as well. Hearing a commotion outside, Peyton stood up and strode to the door at the end of the loft that looked down over the yard below. He cracked it and peered out and then returned saying, "Twenty knights and your father himself. Daniel, know you any who would lend a cart?"

Near rushing to the loft ladder, Daniel scampered down. "I know just a one, Sir Peyton. 'Tis certain that he would lend it."

Peyton nodded, "Guard the prince then as he helps you procure it, if you would." The boy and prince left and Peyton knelt beside Mordecai and Chantaya again, pushing the others out of his thoughts as he looked to the older man to help him know how best to help her. With her coat off, the arrow tip was wholly more visible and Peyton asked, "How do we remove it?"

Mordecai shook his head as he examined her and gently lifted her to look at her back where the arrow had entered, much as Peyton had. Shaking his head, Mordecai carefully laid her back and tucked her shirt back. "We don't. Not until we have her safely to a physician who is prepared. If she's lived this long, 'tis because the bleeding has subsided. Trying to remove it will start it up again. It can't be chanced."

Grimacing in near horror, Peyton asked, "You want to leave it?"

Mordecai nodded and smoothed her hair back gently, "We need to leave it Peyton. Trust me."

At Mordecai's touch, Chantaya's breathing caught ever so slightly and Peyton leaned to her and whispered, "Chani, we're here. Mordecai and I. We're going to help you. We're going to take you to a physician." She never opened her eyes, but for some reason, Peyton still felt like she knew he was there and that she was safe.

§§§§

It had been two days, and Chantaya was still hanging on. She hadn't died, but she hadn't ever become conscious again either. Peyton sat beside her bed, listening to her struggle to breathe, softly stroking her hand and praying, much as he had been for the last forty something hours now.

The king had insisted Chantaya be taken back to the castle, and though Peyton was strangely uncomfortable with that, in truth, he hardly noticed where they were. His concern was only for Chantaya and whether she would survive being shot and the subsequent trauma of being moved and having that horrible arrow removed.

His own short span of experience with such mortal wounds was enough to make his prayers near constant. Isabella had come and seemed to be confident that between what the physician had been doing, and some herbs she had been applying, Chantaya would survive. Still, Peyton intended to do anything he could to help, which included his constant prayers and his touch. Chantaya had always claimed his touch strengthened her.

The concern he felt for Chantaya overrode anything else. He didn't bother with things like eating or sleeping or even noticing who came and went, checking on her. He was grateful that Isabella had largely taken over caring for the grief stricken Daniel as well, because Peyton was doing a frightfully poor job of it, even after Daniel's wonderful care for her. In truth, Peyton hardly even noted when the king himself came in. Or Princess Clarissa, much as he should be repentant of that fact. But, the princess understood and respected his near state of oblivion.

Sometimes the prince came and sat with him. He rarely said much, just seemed to be worrying about her, as Peyton was. So, Peyton was surprised when he came in, looked long at Chantaya's pale, still face and then asked, "So, what do you think of a knight's life after all of this, Sir Peyton?"

Peyton looked up at him, wondering whether he dared say what he was truly thinking, or if he should be more discreet. At length, Peyton decided to be honest and said, "Today probably isn't the best moment to ask such a question, Your Highness. Please forgive me."

For the first time since that awful day of the dowager queen's funeral, the prince gave Peyton a grin and said, "Actually, Father and I were hoping you'd say that."

§§§§

Deep in the night of the third day, Peyton was standing beside the window near her bed, looking at their rose garden and watching the full moon tease in and out of wisps of cloud when he heard her breathing change ever so slightly. The gurgle that was so troubling had largely subsided, but she still seemed to struggle for every bit of air that she took in. This time, for once, she took a deep breath.

He turned back to her in the dimness of a single tallow candle and almost couldn't believe it when he saw her eyelids flutter and then slowly blink. In sudden near euphoria, he whispered her name and came to kneel beside her bed as she finally truly opened her beautiful eyes and breathed in again.

For a moment, she seemed disoriented, then recognized him and gave him the smallest, sweetest smile. After a couple of tries, she asked in a whisper, "Have I died and gone to heaven then?"

He leaned and softly kissed her temple and said, "Surely you don't believe heaven is as painful as your chest must be." She gave him the merest hint of a smile and closed her eyes again.

§§§§

Nearly a full twenty-four hours later, she opened her dear eyes again to find him sitting beside her still holding her hand. For a moment, all she did was return his long look, then asked, "Is the king well?"

He knelt beside her again and in a voice husky with emotion, he answered, "The king, and the kingdom. And Rosskeene vanquished, thanks to you, my brave, strong love."

She gingerly tried to barely shake her head and struggled to whisper, "No. No more brave, strong loves. I'll leave bravery and strength to you and the other knights. I've decided that if I live, I'm staying in Valais for the rest of my life."

Her answer, as sure as it sounded, puzzled him and he narrowed his eyes. "Why Valais?"

With great effort, she said, "Because you're here. I fully intend to stay within walking distance of you forevermore." Again she tried to shake her head and went on, "I know we're under the same moon. But . . . I'll wait here for you in Valais when you're gone with the knights."

Taking her hand, he wove his fingers through her smaller ones and said, "I'm no longer going to be traveling with the knights."

She looked hard at him for a moment as if trying to figure out what he was inferring and then tears welled into her eyes as she softly said, "You are a knight, Sir Peyton. A warrior. Please don't quit because of me. Please. Don't stop doing what you love."

Reaching, he smoothed the tears from her cheek with a gentle hand and put his chin right on her bed as he said, "I'm not quitting. And not because of you. Well, in a way, it may be because of you." He tenderly kissed a tear that slid down her cheek and continued, "The king has asked me to step in to take over a portion of Rosskeene's holdings. Mordecai and me. And you."

She was completely shocked and took a moment to finally ask, "Truly? Are you saying you'll be a nobleman? Can they do that?"

He nodded. "He is king, Chani. He can do whatever he deems is best. They want us to try to work to make those lands and tenants productive and happy again. They felt that with your willingness to sacrifice everything to protect the kingdom, and my insight of both growing up there a peasant, and fighting for them, that we would be fair and honorable stewards."

"And with your wisdom, Pey. Don't forget your wisdom, and patience, and your marvelous selflessness." She smiled tiredly at him. "You will make a good and true noble. People will move into your lands instead of moving out."

He put his chin down upon her bed again to look into her eyes and said, "I pray it is so, Chani. Will you still be by my side if I am a landowner, instead of a knight?"

"I will be by your side even if you are a jester." Her breath caught and she coughed and winced. Then looked at him solemnly and added in a whisper, "The only thing that would keep me from you would be death, Sir Peyton."

Raising a hand to caress her cheek, he looked at her deeply and said, "Then don't die on me, Chantaya."

She turned her head slightly to kiss his hand and said quietly, "I'm trying not to."

"I know, Love. And I thank God for your life. For you love. For your sweet, intrepid willingness to do whatever it takes. You have indeed earned your lands the hard way."

Nodding almost imperceptibly, she said, "I have. But it wasn't land I wanted, Sir Knight. 'Twas to be preserved a strong kingdom, and to be protected from tyranny that I wanted. And you, Pey. I wanted you. Forever. 'Tis a pity that peace comes only at the cost of the soldier."

Smoothing her hair, he assured, "Soldiers understand the cost, Chantaya, because they understand what is at stake." He gave her a sad, half smile. "The kingdom is strong now with Rosskeene gone, but the truth is, there will eventually come a time when another wicked soul will try to take control for his gain. It has always been that way. Surely, it always will."

For a long moment, she considered this, and then asked, "Will you have to go with the knights again when that happens?"

He shook head, "Probably not. But, honestly, I'll also probably hate being left behind. I have the need to protect what I treasure."

Lifting a weak hand to touch his hair, she said, "You have the heart of a warrior. A mighty one. You always will. But there are sometimes even greater ways to fight for right than battle. Helping your tenants to provide for their families is a worthy work. Ensuring secure homes is as vital as ensuring a secure nation. Yet, if you need go, I will wait. And you will come. After all, you are *my* warrior."

He leaned to kiss her with infinite gentleness for a long, long moment, then pulled back and said, "I am truly *your* warrior."

She smiled tiredly. "I think I shall love being simply a wife. We'll both still be under that same, beautiful warrior's moon, together."

Smoothing a finger across her cheekbone ever so gently, he looked into her eyes and whispered, "Yes. Under the moon together. Forever."

The End

About the author

Jaclyn M. Hawkes grew up in Utah with 6 sisters, 4 brothers and any number of pets. (It was never boring!) She got a bachelor's degree, had a career and traveled extensively before settling down to her life's work of being the mother of four magnificent and sometimes challenging children. She loves shellfish, the out of doors, the youth and hearing her children laugh. She and her fine husband, their family, and their sometimes very large pets, now live in a mountain valley in northern Utah, where it smells like heaven and kids still move sprinkler pipe.

To learn more about Jaclyn, visit www.jaclynmhawkes.com.

Author's Note

I am a patriot to the bone. I love my country and hope I would be like Chantaya and Peyton in putting the strength of my country over my own personal desires.

Sadly, it has taken time to make me understand the importance of patriotism. If I had known as a younger, single woman what I know now, I would probably have ended up in the military. As it is, I am now content to write occasionally and be the mother who tries to instill a sense of patriotism and gratitude for the blessings of this great nation into my children and those around me.

I also try to teach gratitude for those who defend our freedoms and blessings. I've come to more fully realize the sacrifices our men and women in uniform make to protect us. I'm sure I don't have a clue to the real extent of their service, but I am infinitely grateful. God bless them. God bless us all,

Jaclyn

www.ingramcontent.com/pod-product-compliance
Lightning Source LLC
Chambersburg PA
CBHW060155260626
47160CB00001B/281